# The Ghost of

# Blackwood Lane

by

Greg Enslen

*GYPSY PUBLICATIONS*

Published in 2012, by Gypsy Publications
Troy, OH 45373, U.S.A.
www.GypsyPublications.com

Enslen, Greg
The Ghost of Blackwood Lane/ by Greg Enslen
ISBN 978-1938768-01-9 (paperback)

Library of Congress Control Number
2012942601

Edited by Jon Williams
Book Design by Tim Rowe
Cover by Pamela Schwartz

For more information, please visit the author's
website at www.GregEnslen.com

PRINTED IN THE UNITED STATES OF AMERICA

# Dedication

This book would not be possible without the tireless involvement of my parents, Albert and Delores Enslen. I actually wrote this book back in 1997, but I set it aside to work on what turned out to be my first book, *Black Bird*.

While I always liked this story, I thought it needed a complete reworking to be good enough to publish. But before locking it away in the vaults, I gave my folks a chance to read it.

Ten years later, after marriage and three kids and more changes than I can enumerate, I decided to start resurrecting my writing. My folks strongly suggested that I revisit this piece, one of their favorites. On my reentry into the world of Gary and Judy and the Luciano brothers, it dawned on me that they were right—this book didn't need major revisions, only a good edit and the thoughtful feedback of a few trusted readers.

What you hold in your hands is as much my parents' work as mine. I wrote the words, but they spent hundreds of hours shining and polishing this rough stone into something that I can be proud of.

Mom and Dad, thank you for your dedication, your hours scribbling on manuscripts and updating timelines, and most of all, your patience. Here it is, finally!

Thanks also to my wife Samantha, who edited the book, making it infinitely better. I have a tendency to be verbose, and she helped me rein it in with her red pen of doom. She's probably tired of hearing about this story and the scores of other goofy tales that patter around inside my mind. But she always listens—or at least does a good job of pretending to listen.

A final thanks to my sister, Pam Schwartz, for creating the beautiful cover—it's just the right amount of creepy.

# Prologue

It all started out very simply.

There was a set of books, filled with pages of financial information. And in those pages, there were columns and rows of numbers that added across and down, meaning little to a non-accountant.

But a single row of numbers in one of those books started it all. That row of numbers and two vastly differing opinions about what those numbers represented.

One man felt that the numbers were perfectly normal—they portrayed a reality that he and his family had always considered "good enough." The numbers were numbers, and it didn't matter how they had come into being—they just were.

But another man felt that the numbers spoke of a deeper problem. John O'Toole saw the numbers for what they really were, because that's what he was paid to do. And once he had seen the undercurrent beneath the sea of digits, and the illegality they represented, he couldn't "un-see" them. No matter how much he tried.

After a few tentative discussions with his employer, he began to feel that others should know about the problems in the ledger. John needed to find other people who could do something about it. He felt the reasons piling up behind him, pushing him like an unceasing tide, to do the right thing. Even if it meant risking his life and the lives of his family and friends.

But the numbers in the thick accounting ledger? They were perfectly innocent.

# Chapter 1

Agent Sims wasn't comfortable with this procedure.

He didn't like being in town at all, so this outing was already a bad idea. They were exposed just by being out in public.

The windows worried him the most. They extended from floor to ceiling and overlooked O'Fallon's quaint downtown. Across the street sat several other small buildings that looked right into the room. FBI agents had immediately closed the blinds upon entering the doctor's office, but Sims was still worried. He hoped this procedure wouldn't take long. It sounded like science fiction, anyway.

Besides, the O'Tooles should be locked away, not trotting about in town where people might see them.

But the decision wasn't Sims' to make—his higher-ups were eager to see the prosecution finished, and they'd ordered this procedure to move things along.

The doctor's office was large and nicely decorated. A desk and chair sat to one side of the room, a couch and coffee table were grouped in the center, and bookshelves lined the walls. To Sims, it looked more like someone's living room than a psychiatrist's office.

He glanced at a wall calendar of Rorschach drawings. To him, the splotches of paint for this month—July 1987—looked like braying hounds.

Sims saw Hanson, another agent, standing by one of the windows, his hand resting on the butt of the gun peeking out from beneath his suit coat. The other two agents moved restlessly around the room.

Gloria, the primary witness's wife, had been killed by a car bomb less than twenty-four hours ago. Her son had been walking to the car when it exploded outside the FBI safe house. The bomb had been meant for his father, John O'Toole.

But if they couldn't get the kid under control quickly, the whole case might get blown.

Witness relocation was always a tricky business. The team really couldn't afford this wasted time, especially here in town, but the boy's father had insisted. In the last few hours, the man had made his testimony contingent on this early morning visit to the doctor's office.

Sims glanced at his watch again. They'd already been here almost ten minutes, and John O'Toole, his son, and the doctor were just sitting on the couches, talking. It didn't even look like they had started yet.

Sims and the other agents knew Gino Luciano owned this town—it had always been that way here in O'Fallon, Illinois, with the Lucianos and their money, for as long as anyone could remember. The Bureau had known about the family for a long time, known about their activities and their influences, and had been trying to make a case against them for almost as long.

John O'Toole was the most important witness they had found so far. And instead of holing him up safely somewhere on the other side of St. Louis, far away from this little town, they were here, right in the lion's den, wasting time talking.

And Agent Sims felt like a sitting duck.

The boy had dropped his baseball cap and gone back to pick it up. If it hadn't been for that, the boy would've been in the car, too, when it exploded.

The FBI already had a location picked out for them, but the boy didn't want to leave O'Fallon. No one, not even his father, could convince him how necessary it was. After the car bomb had gone off, the boy had confessed that he'd called his girlfriend the day before—her line must have been tapped. It was the only explanation for how they knew the location of the safe house. But even the death of his mother hadn't convinced the kid to leave town, so now John O'Toole was taking drastic steps to ensure that the boy would go with him to Sacramento.

The doctor, the boy's uncle, was a respected psychiatrist and seemed to be dealing with the grief of losing his sister. But still, Sims didn't think this would work—the whole plan sounded like hocus-pocus to him. But the boy would have to say good-bye to his girlfriend once and for all. If this was the only way to do it, then so be it.

It came down to the fact that the boy was only 17, and his father was still making the decisions in his life, even the drastic ones.

Sims had never seen anyone hypnotized before. He'd always had a nonprofessional's interest in psychology—you had to if you were going to be a good cop or federal agent. He wondered if anyone really understood what happened when someone was hypnotized.

------

"Is he under?" the father asked anxiously, his attention turning from his son's face to Dr. Martin.

Dr. Frank Martin nodded, his eyes on the boy. There was the gradual fluttering of the eyelids and a general relaxed posture that indicated a very shallow relaxation pattern, the first stage of any hypnosis. The boy had been fighting it all along, and now the doctor would need to deepen the relaxation.

"Yes, he is relaxing, finally. But you see how long it took to get him to this stage, so he's obviously resisting it, consciously or subconsciously." Frank shook his head again. "I still don't like this, John—hypnosis isn't a carnival act. It's a serious, clinical tool, and must be carefully used. This ludicrous request of yours—it can only lead to failure."

John O'Toole looked at his brother-in-law, and Frank could tell he was collecting his thoughts. "Look, Frank. I know you blame me for Gloria's death, but there was nothing I could do about it. The men I used to work for are bad men, very bad, but I didn't think they would ever go after Gloria or Chris. Even the Bureau didn't think it would get this bad this quick."

Frank saw the tears coming.

"I was in the living room when the car blew up, Frank," John said quietly. "The explosion was huge—it blew in the front windows of the house. And I thought for a moment that this couldn't be happening. It all happened in slow motion," he said, looking down at his hands. "Now Gloria is gone, and I almost lost Chris...."

Frank saw his brother-in-law look around the room slowly before continuing. "Frank, Chris and I have to go away—I have to testify, and then Chris and I have to get away or this will all be for nothing. But Chris...he just won't listen to me. He doesn't understand what's at stake. He's in love."

Dr. Martin glanced at the framed picture of Gloria and himself on one of his shelves—he had just graduated from medical school, and Gloria had come down to Carbondale to watch the ceremony. She had been his little sister, so full of life. Now she was gone.

He glanced away and his eyes came to rest this time on his diploma and medical license. Was this ethical, what he was about to do? Or was he saving this patient's life by blocking out some of his memories, allowing him to start a new life somewhere else, out of harm's way? If you looked at it that way, then **not** performing the memory suppression could actually kill his patient.

But was it right?

He didn't know. But time was growing short, and the FBI agents were clearly nervous.

That was what finally convinced Frank. The agents were glancing out the windows, and the lead agent, Sims, looked like he thought this was a bad idea. Obviously, it was a last resort.

This was a dangerous situation, and it was his responsibility as a doctor to do whatever he could to see that his nephew got out of this situation safely. And after all this settled down, after the trial and after the boy was out of danger, Dr. Martin would remove the block and let the boy get back to a relatively normal life.

The lead agent was looking at the doctor.

"Sir, if this is going to be a problem, let me know now," Agent Sims said. "We are risking exposure being here, and if necessary, we can take the boy here to a different doctor. But Mr. O'Toole has requested that you carry out this procedure."

Frank shook his head, glancing at the boy.

"It's okay. I just wanted to explain to John again how dangerous this could be, and allow him to reconsider."

Frank glanced at John, who nodded at him, and then Frank realized that this was out of his hands anyway. If he didn't do the procedure, John O'Toole was desperate enough to find another doctor. And Frank wouldn't have that.

He turned back to his nephew.

"Chris, can you hear me?"

The boy answered sluggishly, as though he were half-asleep. "Yes, Uncle Frank, I can hear you."

Sessions like this, with a reluctant or openly combative patient, were usually carried out in a different fashion. Patients who came into his office with preconceived notions about hypnosis, usually gleaned from TV or the movies, had to be slowly drawn into the hypnotic state. Usually, this was done with the progressive and laborious "transferral of power" process, whereby a patient slowly gives up conscious control over his or her situation and allows the doctor to gradually deepen a relaxed, suggestive state into a more formal hypnotic state.

For those patients that were the most difficult to hypnotize, creative methods had to be employed that allowed the patients to be hypnotized while still hanging onto some semblance of control. Often, those patients were put under using the "choice" progression technique—that is, giving the patient various choices of how the therapy session would proceed. All of the choices offered the patient would eventually lead to a suggestive state, but by giving the patient choices, the most stubborn conscious mind could concede power and yet still stay in control. The patient wasn't choosing to be hypnotized—but was being hypnotized, nonetheless. Either way, it would usually take three or four two-hour sessions to even reach a hypnotic state in the most resistant patients.

And once the doctor was comfortable with the deepness of the state, a post-hypnotic suggestion could be implanted that would make subsequent inducement of hypnotic states much easier and much quicker.

But Frank didn't have time to do that here—Chris needed to be under for a very short amount of time.

"Chris, remember, you are relaxing comfortably. You are safe and happy, and nothing can harm you here. Do you understand?"

"Yes," Chris said.

"Good," Frank continued. "Now, I would like you to imagine that you see a long staircase, with you standing on the top step, and the stairs leading down away from you. Can you see it?"

The boy nodded.

"Okay, Chris, I need you to answer me out loud when I ask you a question. Can you see the staircase in front of you?"

"Yes."

"Good. Now, as you take a step down onto the top stair, you'll notice that you feel a little more relaxed. I want you to imagine walking slowly down these steps, and with each step, you're descending into a more relaxed state, a state where you feel more at ease."

The boy was silent, but as Frank watched closely, he could pick out the signs. The body posture was becoming more relaxed, and the hands that had been fists on the boy's chest relaxed, drifting down to rest on the couch on either side of him.

"Okay, Chris, you continue to descend, feeling more and more relaxed, until you reach the bottom step. There's a landing there, and a large door. This door doesn't frighten you or make you anxious. Instead, you feel calm and relaxed as you open the door and step into a large, beautiful room. Do you see the room?"

"Yes."

"Tell me about the room, Chris."

"There's a lot of nice furniture, and a big window with light coming in. Very bright light, like summertime, when it's really warm outside. It looks like a nice place, maybe like a mansion, and it looks like they're getting ready to have a party or something. There are trays of food and drinks on the tables."

Frank always marveled at what the mind constructed when posed with an imaginary image. For some people, a beautiful room would look like a palace, or a sunroom filled with plants, or even a brothel with a score of scantily clad women. The "comfortable room" technique was Frank's favorite, allowing the patient to construct his or her own mental image of a completely comfortable place. Residing even temporarily in this relaxing environment would free the conscious mind.

"That's good, Chris. It sounds like a beautiful room."

"Yes, Uncle Frank. Mom would love it."

Frank glanced up, and John was just reacting to the boy's words. The father stood suddenly and walked to the other side of the office, pulling a cigarette from his jacket and lighting up, taking a few quick puffs.

"Good, Chris. Can you see your mom?"

"No, Doctor. She's dead. She died in the car and I was walking to it and dropped my hat. I flew through the air like Superman and landed on my head. She isn't in the room because she's dead...and I could be...dead too, but I'd dropped my hat and went back to get it and I wasn't in the car when...."

Too much anxiety.

"Chris, that's okay. Remember, this room is calm and soothing and relaxing. You're feeling very relaxed and not upset at all."

The boy seemed to calm almost instantly.

John leaned in and whispered into Frank's ear. "Do it, Frank. Hurry. And say something about his mother, too, so he won't be upset."

Frank looked up suddenly at his brother-in-law, angry, and he stood, walking John over to the wall, pushing him up against it. Out of the corner of his eye Frank saw an agent step toward them, but the lead agent held him back.

Frank had been concentrating on the boy so much that he hadn't even heard John walk over, trailing a hazy layer of smoke. Frank's eyes caught John's and held them.

"This isn't a game, John," Frank said, his voice tense. "I can try to suppress the boy's memory of his girlfriend, but even that makes me very uncomfortable, and it's unlikely to last long. I will not suppress his grief of Gloria—grief is healthy and something we all need to deal with. And I will not rob him of any memories of his mother, no matter how painful they are. They're all that he has left of her. I won't take them away."

John was looking at him, the cigarette forgotten. Blue smoke drifted up between them. After a moment, John turned to look at his son, and Frank grabbed John's jaw, meeting his eyes. "He has to grieve over her—she deserves nothing less. Agreed?"

John nodded slowly, and Frank let go of his jaw, straightening his jacket before sitting back down in front of the boy. He noticed that the boy's eyes were open now. Chris was staring at a patch of reflected light on the ceiling, a patch of bright whiteness crisscrossed with thick, black bars.

The eyes coming open on their own like that—Frank was sure that the boy's eyes had been closed before he stood up to confront John O'Toole. It was a sure sign that the hypnotic state was weakening.

Frank needed to get this finished and get out, and quickly.

"Chris, you might want to close your eyes and relax and think about the room." At this point, suggestions would probably be more effective than outright commands.

"Yes," the boy said, and just as Frank was about to continue, he spoke again. "Yes, I can see the room. There are bright bands of dark and light on the ceiling. And I smell smoke, cigarette smoke."

The boy was incorporating reality into his dream-room; it was another sign that the hypnotic state wasn't as deep as Frank would have liked.

"Okay, Chris. Now, we need to talk about something else. You're relaxing in this room, noticing the calming and soothing things around you, and you're completely comfortable talking about Judy, Judy Nelson. Do you want to talk about her?"

"Yes. She is very nice, and very pretty, and I want to marry her. I like to talk about her."

Frank glanced at John, but John was looking out the window.

"She's a great person, Chris. Wonderful, in fact. But she's in danger, isn't she?"

Chris nodded, seeming to grow restless. "Yes. She knows me, and people who know my family are in danger. The Lucianos want to kill us."

"That's right, Chris. And you don't want that to happen to Judy, do you?" This was dangerous—Frank was treading a very thin line. If the boy got too upset, he could suddenly emerge from the hypnotic state.

"No. I don't want anything to happen to her. I love her, even if my father doesn't want me to be with her. I just wish I hadn't called her—it caused a lot of trouble."

Frank shook his head. There was too much of a connection here, too much to gloss over. He had gone into this planning to suppress the boy's attachment to Judy, but that wouldn't work. If he saw the girl, his memories would come back as soon as she confronted him.

No, it would have to be all or nothing.

He had to make the boy forget all about Judy Nelson. Every feeling, every memory, everything about her down to the smallest remembrance of her smell and her voice. For her sake, and for the sake of Chris and John.

"Chris, is there a closet or a chest in the room?"

"Yes. There's a large cabinet against one wall. It's decorated with lots of gold and frilly stuff, and there are big mirrors on the doors. I can see myself in the doors."

Frank wasn't sure what that was supposed to mean—usually, the patients saw mirrors of some sort in their dream rooms. Frank didn't have time to explore the meaning.

"Good, Chris. I want you to go to that cabinet and open it." He waited for a few moments. "Is there a lot of room inside?"

"Yes. It's very big. There are shelves, some made of glass."

"Good. Now, you know that Judy's in danger, and you'd do anything to protect her, isn't that right?"

"Yes." His response was immediate.

"Okay, to protect her, you need to conjure up all of your memories of her. Every thought, every action or scrap of emotion you have about her. Can you collect every single memory?"

It took a few long moments, and in that time the boy's hands rose up off the soft leather of the couch and crossed on his chest again, and the muscles in his neck and arms stood out strongly. His feet moved on their own.

"Okay, Chris, now I want you to take all of your memories and all of your emotions about Judy and put them into the cabinet. They'll all fit, and if there are shelves inside the cabinet, you can set some of those memories on them. She's in danger, and putting your memories of her inside the cabinet will protect her. Do you understand?"

"Yes." Frank could see the boy's hands moving around slightly, twitching as if he were arranging delicate items. After a moment, the boy seemed to relax, and his feet stopped shaking.

"Okay. Are all of your memories of Judy in the cabinet? Everything you've thought about her, every dream you've told her about, all the memories you've shared?"

"Yes," the boy said, his voice low and quiet. Frank didn't know what that meant, other than the boy's conscious mind might be fighting the suppression of memories. He'd never heard of anyone trying to suppress all the memories of a person, and he had no idea if it would work. Selected memories could be suppressed or at least isolated in protective layers, but trying to completely forget someone, someone you were close to—was it possible?

"Okay, Chris. To protect Judy, you must forget her. All of your memories of her are inside the cabinet, and if you close the doors, you'll no longer remember her. You must close the door and lock it. We'll make a key, so that later, when she's no longer in danger, you'll be able to open that cabinet and remember everything about her. Do you understand?"

A long moment passed, and the boy didn't answer.

"Chris, do you understand?"

The room was silent. The father, sitting on one of the couches, leaned forward.

Finally, Chris nodded slowly. "Yes, Uncle. But I don't want to forget her. I love her."

God, this was going to be trouble. Even unconsciously, he was fighting the exclusion process. There would be trouble down the line when the wall started to weaken. What would happen if he saw the girl? He'd have no memory of her, but she, of course, would remember him. Best to make sure they never met.

"Chris, I know this is difficult for you, but you have to forget her. And after the danger is passed, we'll meet again and release those memories. Do you want to think up a few words that will be the key?"

"Yes. I want the key to be '*the pearl is in the river.*'"

Clever, Frank thought.

"Why did you choose that particular phrase, Chris?"

"I saw it in a movie last night," Chris answered.

That wouldn't do at all—God forbid the kid saw that movie next week on late-night TV and all his memories came flooding back at once. It could cause a mental break.

"That's a good phrase, Chris, but let me come up with one for you, okay?"

Dr. Martin glanced around the room, his eyes finding one of his favorite paintings, an ocean scene with a lighthouse and a boat in the distance. He'd always wondered how those folks in the boat felt, seeing the lighthouse and knowing they'd soon be rescued.

"Okay, Chris—I've got a phrase for you. The key should be, '*the faded lighthouse caused a wonderful fire.*' Okay?" Frank couldn't imagine any conversation in which that particular phrase might come up.

"Now, I need you to close the doors of the cabinet, and in so do-ing, forget everything you know about Judy. Can you do that?"

The boy was quiet for a long moment.

"Chris, have you closed the cabinet?"

"Yes," the boy answered, his eyes open again and staring at the ceiling. And in the bright reflection of the dark and light pattern painted on the ceiling of his office, Frank saw a single tear form in the corner of one of the boy's eyes and fall down his cheek.

Frank heard a loud sigh behind him. He turned and saw that John O'Toole was smiling and lighting another cigarette, but the cool look Frank gave him removed the smile.

"Okay, Chris. Do you have any memories of a person named Judy?"

"Yes."

"Tell me about her," Frank said.

"Judy is the lady at the Fairview Heights Library, near the mall," Chris said. "She is an old lady, and sometimes she smells like freshly baked bread."

Good. "Do you remember anyone else named Judy in your life, like a friend or schoolmate?"

"No."

Frank glanced at John one more time, giving him a final chance to back out, but John wouldn't even make eye contact.

Frank nodded and then started with the second thing they needed to accomplish before bringing the boy out of the hypnotic state. They had agreed to try this only if the first part had gone well. It involved finding a second cabinet in the imaginary room, a larger one this time, that could be unlocked using the same mental key.

"Okay, now let's move on. Your name is Chris, right? Chris O'Toole?"

"Yes," the boy answered quietly.

"Okay, let's look in the room for another cabinet, a different one altogether. And let's gather up your memories and thoughts about your name...."

This second task didn't take as long, surprisingly. Dr. Martin thought it would be easier to erase memories of a particular indi-vidual from a person's mind than to change their identity, but that didn't prove to be the case. The procedure was over faster than he had thought possible.

"Okay, you're still in your comfortable room, but it's time to leave and start back up the stairs. As you pass from the room, you remember it clearly, and you'll be much more open to the suggestion of returning to it in the future. Do you see the stairs?"

"Yes," the boy answered quietly.

"Begin climbing the stairs, and with each step you take, you'll climb toward wakefulness. And with each step, you'll repeat your name by saying, 'my name is Gary, Gary Foreman.' Each step brings you closer to wakefulness, and at the top step, you'll awaken, feeling refreshed and happy and not remembering anything that we've talked about."

The boy was quiet for a couple of moments, and then he began speaking.

"My name is...Gary Foreman."

He repeated the name several more times, and then his eyes fluttered and he was awake, aware of himself and his surroundings. The boy sat up and looked around the room, seeing his father and smiling at him. "Wow. Did I fall asleep or something?" he asked good-naturedly.

His father spoke up. "Yeah, Chr...Gary. You fell asleep while your uncle and I were talking. Are you feeling okay?"

Gary nodded. "Yeah, I feel great."

Agent Sims stepped over and helped the boy to his feet. The other agents moved to the door, stepping out into the hallway, guns drawn.

Frank stepped over to John O'Toole and began speaking rapidly in low tones.

"Look, John," Frank said, serious. "I don't know how long it will hold. He might never remember her, or he might see a picture of a girl on TV tomorrow that reminds him of her, and the memories will all come back at once. If that happens, he could have a psychotic break. Seriously, he could have permanent psychological damage."

John nodded, and Frank continued. "After you testify and the heat is off, you **must** come back here and let me release those memories, or it could damage him for life. And, needless to say, he and the girl can have no contact until I release those memories. Got it?"

John nodded, obviously anxious to leave. "Yeah, Frank. As soon as the heat is off, I'll bring him back. And that phrase about the lighthouse, I'll make sure not to say it," he said, smiling.

"This isn't a game, John," Frank said, scowling. "Those are his memories, and he has a right to them. Suppressing them isn't fair to him or the girl. As soon as it's safe, those memories need to come out. And write down that phrase, just in case. But keep it in a safe place, somewhere where he won't find it."

The boy's father nodded again, shook John's hand, and turned and left, followed by the boy and Agent Sims.

After they were gone, Frank sat at his desk, thinking about what had happened. If this weren't a police case, it would make a fascinating paper on exclusionary hypnotherapy. It would be interesting to see how long the mental block lasted—of course, it would need to be removed as soon as possible, but it was still interesting from a clinical perspective. Impulsively, Dr. Frank Martin asked his secretary to cancel his patient load for the rest of the day and left his office to go home and relax.

And he felt like he should write everything down, everything that had just happened, just in case.

# Chapter 2

The prosecuting attorney spoke to the witness.

"And how did you feel about this?"

John O'Toole looked up from the wooden box next to the judge and eyed the prosecuting attorney. It all came down to this. If Gloria had died for anything, this was it.

John cleared his throat and tried not to look at his son.

"Well, I knew that these monies had come from an illegal source, and I felt for the first time that I had absolute proof of Mr. Luciano's illegal activities."

There was a murmur in the courtroom. As usual, the defense attorney objected, and the lawyers and judge carried out a short sidebar. John tried to avoid looking at anyone.

The jurors quieted. The prosecutor's office had been building up to John's three days on the stand, and several times he had been mentioned as their "star witness."

Ginovese Luciano, John's former boss and the man on trial, stared at him, his eyes blazing and fingers tapping. He sat with two of his lawyers—the third was at the judge's bench, arguing again over the inclusion of testimony from Luciano's former accountant.

Chris O'Toole— his new name being Gary, though nobody else knew it—sat behind the prosecutor's table with his uncle, Dr. Martin. John looked at them and thought how strange it was to not see Gloria sitting there with them. The police had said she'd died almost instantly, but knowing that didn't really help. And strangely, the attempt to get him to pull his testimony had actually strengthened his resolve to bring the Lucianos down. If he backed out now, her death would mean nothing.

Judy Nelson was in the courtroom too, and that was bad. Frank would need to keep her away from Chris—that is, Gary—at least for a while. He'd noticed an engagement ring on her finger, too—that certainly complicated things. Chris—Gary—hadn't said anything about that.

But this was too important to jeopardize. She would get over Chris, someday. And Chris—Gary—would not remember her at all, at least in the short term. If this all blew over, in a year or two they could be reunited, if things worked out. Or maybe just a clean break—

The sidebar ended, and Judge Tackett gave the jury a short set of instructions, reminding them that the witness was an employee of the defendant's and would be privy to intimate knowledge of the man's business dealings. Any questions about the veracity of his testimony would be addressed in the cross-examination.

The prosecutor continued. "And what did you do then, Mr. O'Toole?"

John glanced at the jurors, making eye contact with a few of them as the prosecutors had coached him to do. "I checked back through some of the books and began to discover other discrepancies. And when I could no longer explain them all away as simple accounting errors by other people in Mr. Luciano's employ, I went to him and asked him about the 'irregularities.'"

"And what was his answer?"

One of Luciano's lawyers stood quickly. "I object, your honor. This is all hearsay."

The judge shook his head. "Mr. Jones, you should know that a witness's testimony cannot be hearsay unless he heard it from someone else and is repeating facts he cannot verify."

"Yes, your honor—but he is repeating something someone else said."

"Mr. Jones, he is repeating what the defendant told him. Objection overruled, and don't interrupt again unless your objections can be reasonably argued or I'll hold you in contempt."

The lawyer sat down, glancing at Luciano. Even from the little John knew about courtroom procedure, the objection seemed flimsy. Maybe the guy was trying to impress Luciano by making as many objections as possible. Maybe Luciano had told his lawyers they'd be taking a dirt nap if he were convicted.

"Continue," the judge said to the prosecutor, who nodded and turned to John.

"Mr. O'Toole, what did Mr. Luciano say?"

"I explained the problem, which totaled almost six hundred thousand dollars in income that could not be accounted for by his normal business practices. I had suspicions about illegal activities, so I expected—"

"Objection, your honor," the lead defense attorney, Jones, said again, standing. "Obviously, the witness is giving his opinion based on hearsay from other people."

The prosecutor stepped over to address the judge. "Your honor, the witness says he had suspicions about his employer—he did not say where those suspicions were based. It is not hearsay unless he recounted suspicious knowledge related to him by others."

The judge pondered for a moment and then addressed the witness. "Mr. O'Toole, just stick to your actions and conversations—your suspicions may have driven your actions, but they can't be defended until you have proof of any alleged activities."

John nodded, continuing. "I asked my employer about the money, and he laughed at me."

The prosecutor seemed surprised, his eyes wide as he played to the jury. "Mr. Luciano laughed at you?"

"Yes. He laughed and said 'I wondered how long it would take you.' Well, I wasn't sure what he was talking about," John said, glancing at the judge. "I told him that there was a lot of money in several of his accounts that I couldn't trace to a legitimate source of income, and then he asked me to sit in one of the chairs in his office. Mr. Luciano came around the desk and sat on one corner of it and lit up a cigar."

"Then he said 'John, you are very good at what you do, and I want to reward you. I think you deserve a raise, and maybe a little vacation with that nice family of yours.' I answered him, saying that I did the best job I could, but I was concerned about those extra funds. And I asked him if he was involved in any illegal activities, because if he was, I wouldn't be able to work for him anymore."

The courtroom was quiet for a long moment. "And what did he say when you asked him about these activities?" the prosecutor asked.

John shifted a little in his seat. The prosecutor had told him to stay calm, but that a little nervous apprehension would make his testimony seem more believable to the jury. At this moment, however, John wasn't faking anything.

"Well, he said that those funds came from other areas of his business, areas that I was not privy to. He assured me that the income was perfectly legal."

"And you believed him?"

John nodded. "Yes, because I knew very little about some of his operations, especially those in other states. I really only did his books for the businesses in St. Louis and southern Illinois, so it was very possible that the money came from somewhere else and that he was investing it in different accounts."

The prosecutor nodded. "Okay, so—did you get a raise or a vacation?"

O'Toole smiled. "Yes, actually. I got a nice raise, and Mr. Luciano sent my family and me to Disney World. That was in the spring."

"Okay. What happened after that?"

"Well, when I got back, Mr. Luciano called me into his office and we had a discussion. Evidently, one of the other accountants had left his employment, and Mr. Luciano asked me to take his place, mentioning his appreciation of my skills. There was another raise involved, and my son was in his junior year of high school, and I felt that the additional money would help fund his college. That wasn't the only reason I took the job—I have to say that I was very curious."

The prosecutor leaned in. "Curious about what?"

"Well, I still felt that some of Mr. Luciano's activities might be illegal, and I didn't like the way he treated some of his people. His family and his associates made me very uncomfortable, and there were just too many suspicious things going on in O'Fallon. On the surface, he seemed like a successful businessman, but I wasn't sure."

One of the lawyers started to stand and object, but the judge shook his head and pointed the lawyer back down into his chair.

"So you took the job?"

"Yes. I was to oversee all of the business accounting, and after only a week or two, I found several accounts that he seemed to be funneling money into, money that seemed to come from nowhere. Money simply appeared in the other business accounts with no paper trail, with entries like 'Petty Cash,' but for amounts like twenty or thirty thousand dollars."

"And did you ask him about these monies?"

"No. I started moving the money into another account."

There was a quiet murmur though the courtroom.

"Mr. O'Toole, why did you do that?"

John shrugged, looking at the floor of the courtroom. "Well, looking back on it, I know that it was stupid. I thought I could siphon some of this money off and either use it myself or hide it and force Luciano to tell me what was going on. It started out not as a conscious decision to confront him or steal from him—I only wanted to know what was going on, what I was getting myself into. After a while, the money in this 'secret' account I had created started to pile up, and no one noticed or asked me about it. I started to entertain ideas of taking the money and disappearing with my family. In less than seven months, the balance in 'my' account was up over $830,000."

The prosecutor let that sink in, not speaking for a long moment.

"You say you managed to hide that much money without anyone noticing. How much money did Mr. Luciano have moving through his accounts over that seven-month period?"

The jumpy defense lawyer again objected. "Mr. Luciano's financial standing in the community is not on trial—we are willing to concede that Mr. Luciano is financially solvent and owns several successful and legal businesses that turn a healthy profit."

"Your honor," the prosecutor countered, "I am simply trying to compare the amount of money in this additional account—the figure of $830,000 is pointless unless we have something to compare it with, such as Mr. Luciano's overall assets. And Mr. O'Toole can easily speak to that question."

The judge nodded. "I'll allow it, but the jury should remember that amounts of money made by legitimate means should not be considered unless they are used to hide illegal activities."

The prosecutor nodded to O'Toole, who continued. "Well, in those first seven months, at least forty million dollars moved through the hundred and twenty-six accounts I was overseeing. Most of that money came from businesses that I knew to be legitimate, but other money was shuffled around so quickly from one account to another that it was very difficult to track where it came from originally. Or where it ended up."

"Did Mr. Luciano have any offshore accounts?"

"Not that I knew of," John said, "but I was not privy to all of his information."

The prosecutor glanced at the jury. "Okay, what happened next?"

"Well, I went to Mr. Luciano. I'd decided that taking the money could put my family and me in considerable danger. I thought at the time that if I told him about what I'd been doing, he would understand that I was simply trying to teach him a lesson about being more careful about where his money came from."

The prosecutor moved to the table and pulled up a large color picture mounted on a piece of white cardboard. The front of the picture was labeled "State Exhibit 22-A." He set it on an easel near the court reporter, angling it so that it could easily be seen by everyone else in the room.

"Okay, so you went to Mr. Luciano and told him what you had been doing. Weren't you concerned about possible illegal activities, or facing the moral dilemma of working for someone who might be involved in activities that you could not condone?"

John shook his head. "Actually, no. I'd spent several months thinking about it, and I'd begun to rationalize the activities, if there were any, as simply business. Mr. Luciano was a very good business-man, and anything he was involved in, illegal or not, made money. A lot of money. I guess, after a while, I became more flexible, morally speaking. And seeing all that money in my secret account may have swayed my thinking, too."

"So what happened when you told him about the money you had skimmed?"

"Well, I didn't get a chance to tell him. We sat down and I expressed to him my concerns about the hundreds of thousands of dollars going through his accounts from unknown sources, and he started to get angry. He said that we had already had this conversation and that he would not have it again with me. He also said that where his money came from or went to was none of my business—I was only to take care of it while it was in my accounts, and not concern myself with other details. I began to get upset too, saying that I had worked for him for a long time and deserved to know where the money came from, or if any of it came from illegal activities. That was when I let it slip about how easy it would be for someone to make some of that money disappear."

John O'Toole glanced at the jury and the prosecutor, trying to avoid the eyes of the man he was talking about, sitting ten feet away at the defense table.

"Evidently he had known about the secret account all along," John said. "As soon as I said that, he came around the desk and grabbed my arm, hard, and demanded to know where the money was. I told him, but he didn't let go of my arm. He just kept squeezing and squeezing, and that's where I got the bruise," he said, nodding at the picture of his bruised arm that the prosecutor had set up on the easel.

The prosecutor pointed at the picture. "Is this the bruise?" he asked, pointing at a large black and blue and yellow, vaguely hand-shaped form.

"Yes. That's the bruise. My wife took that picture." He was quiet for a moment, thinking about Gloria and the concern she'd had for him when she'd seen his injuries.

The prosecutor nodded.

"Well, the man was very upset. He wanted to know exactly how much money was gone, and he didn't let go of my arm until I swore that all the money I had moved was in that one account. He told me he was very disappointed with me. He walked back around his desk and sat down, and didn't say anything for a long time. I wasn't sure what he was thinking, but I started to worry about my safety, and that of my family. I had no idea what this man was capable of."

John paused for a moment and sipped from a glass of water before continuing.

"After a few minutes, he picked up the phone and called in a couple of men who worked for him. He thanked me for telling him about the money, and assured me that I needn't concern myself with where it came from, only do with it what he asked. And that was when the men came in, and Mr. Luciano said that I needed to be taught a lesson about loyalty. The men led me out of the room, and that's when I started to get really scared. They took me into another room in the back of the building and beat me up pretty badly."

At this, the prosecutor replaced the color picture with another one, which caused a series of gasps in the courtroom.

"Your honor, I would like to mark this as State Exhibit 22-B. Mr. O'Toole, can you tell me what this is?"

John nodded. "Yes, that's a picture of me after they beat me up."

The picture clearly showed John O'Toole, looking like he had been worked over pretty good. Bruises blackened his face and upper chest, and one eye was a bloody red. There was blood on his chin and around his eyes and nose.

The prosecutor replaced it with another group of pictures, all mounted on one backing. "Your honor, I would like to mark this as State Exhibit 22-C. Mr. O'Toole, do you recognize these pictures?"

He nodded again. "Yes. The first is a close-up of my hands— both of my thumbs were broken, and most of the other scratches and cuts I got when I was trying to defend myself. The next three are of my back and chest, showing the bruises. The last one is my left leg, which was broken. The doctors said it was broken in three places and that I will probably always walk with a limp."

The courtroom was utterly silent—this was easily the most riveting testimony so far in the three-week trial. Big color pictures of a bloodied victim always quieted a jury.

After a few long moments of silence, the prosecutor started up again. "What happened after that?"

"Well, the account I had opened was closed out, and the money disappeared back into Mr. Luciano's general accounts. Mr. Luciano restricted severely the accounts I was allowed to work on, and that was when I was contacted by the FBI. They met with me, saying they had been monitoring associates of Mr. Luciano and had read the hospital reports of my injuries. They shared their concerns over illegal activities by Mr. Luciano and asked me to cooperate with them, and I agreed. Over the next three months, I did what I could to gather damaging or incriminating information. Between me and Mr. Sanders, another individual they had managed to place inside Mr. Luciano's organization, they gathered enough information to begin a prosecution."

"And the information you gathered proved that Mr. Luciano was involved in illegal activities?"

"Yes."

"Good. Ladies and gentlemen of the jury, we will delve deeper into the accounting paperwork secured by Mr. O'Toole and Mr. Sanders at a later time. No further questions."

The judge nodded and called for a recess until the next morning.

The cross-examination wasn't as bad as O'Toole had expected, but it was still pretty bad. His personal life was laid open and examined like a cadaver. Jones, the lead defense attorney, brought up John's drinking days back in college, and all of his family relationships were scrutinized for the slightest imperfections. The defense attorney's tactic was simple—besmirch this witness by any means necessary. The whole case hinged on the testimony of this man and Mr. Sanders.

They finished with O'Toole in two days, and John quickly and happily left the stand. The other star witness was called, and that was when the court learned that he would not be testifying.

Mr. Sanders was dead—evidently the victim of an "accidental" fall down the stairs of his own home.

------

Less than a week later, the federal prosecutor offered Luciano a reduced sentence of eight years in prison in exchange for a guilty plea on tax evasion and money laundering. Under advice of his counsel, Luciano took the lesser plea in return for admitting to various money schemes, and the federal case in which John O'Toole was an essential witness was dropped.

Of course, the dismissal and plea bargain did not remove the danger to the O'Tooles—they had crossed the Luciano family, and they would have to be protected.

The Federal Bureau of Investigation arranged for the move of the two-member family to a small town north of Sacramento, California, called North Highlands. There was an Air Force base nearby, so the people in North Highlands were used to seeing new faces as airmen were transferred in and out. The O'Tooles blended in easily.

John O'Toole—now known as John Foreman—never arranged for any further treatment for his son. The memory blockage worked well, and the boy seemed to be getting along fine. John listened carefully, but Judy never seemed to resurface in the boy's mind, and Gary expressed no interest in returning to St. Louis. The boy was healthy and happy, except for missing his mother.

John Foreman was wary about telling his son the code words or taking him to see a psychiatrist—if the boy learned about his past, he might head back to St. Louis, and Judy. That would be dangerous for all of them. It came down to the fact that there was no way to tell the boy the truth and guarantee his safety, so John Foreman hid the truth away.

The elder Luciano began serving his time at Waynesboro prison, a minimum-security facility, in August 1987, but the family business continued unimpeded, a juggernaut of legal and illegal activities that couldn't be stopped, even by the FBI and a couple of inside men. Tony and Vincent, the two sons of Ginovese Luciano, took over the family businesses, running it for their father until he would be released.

Two days after the testimony of John O'Toole, a contract was put out on the life of the man who had provided such damning testimony. The sons needed to avenge their father's incarceration.

And late on a Monday afternoon a few weeks after the plea bargain, someone knocked on Dr. Frank Martin's door and was admitted. The police had no information on what happened after that, except that the doctor had evidently been asked some difficult questions for which he did not have the appropriate answers.

After some time, the doctor was killed for his trouble.

Only three people had heard the key phrase that passed between Dr. Frank Martin and his patient. The first, Dr. Martin himself, was now dead. The second, Agent Sims, had heard the words but had forgotten them almost immediately.

The third, John O'Toole, locked the words away like a dangerous treasure. And after a few years, he forgot them completely.

# Chapter 3

He sat up suddenly in his bed, wide awake.

His heart was pounding and his face and body were covered in a thin layer of sweat. An ocean breeze blew through his partially open apartment window, but it didn't cool him or calm his sleep.

The dream left his mind slowly, reluctantly. It was the same one, every time. At this point, he prayed for a change—any change. But it never altered in any way, relentless in its repetition.

Gary Foreman kicked free of the sheets twisted around his legs and sat up, climbing out of bed. He crossed to the window and looked out, feeling the salty air on his face. Sometimes it helped calm his racing mind.

Rosa knew that he liked his room cold at night—it helped him sleep, so she had tolerated it. But she wasn't here anymore. Somewhere along the line, she'd stopped worrying about him, about the dream, about where they were headed as a couple.

The breeze breathed in as he slid the window open further, realizing that it was almost 2 a.m. on that May evening in 1997. The cold must have helped—usually he woke several times each night as the dream replayed over and over. Tonight he'd woken only once.

*It never really gets dark in Los Angeles at night*, Gary thought to himself. Gary couldn't see any stars—even at two in the morning, all he could see was the orange haze of a million streetlights smoldering. It looked like the dull glow of a perpetual dawn.

Los Angeles. Moving here had been a mistake. His job was going well, but his social life was rocky. He couldn't seem to find anyone special—none of his relationships had lasted more than five or six months. And since the dream had started up, it had only gotten worse. Rosa's complaints about it and how it disrupted their relationship were only an excuse—they had been falling apart for weeks.

Her offers to leave him alone at night had slowly grown into leaving him alone during the day too—and then all the time. The dream had presented a perfect opportunity to end things between them.

But Gary's loneliness affected him more than he let on to his friends—one friend, actually. Gary thought of himself as one of those hopeful romantics—he liked the idea of being in a relationship more than the actual being in a relationship. He loved the flirting and the getting-to-know-someone part, but things never seemed to last after that.

Rosa was just the last in a long, sad parade of botched relationships.

Of course, he could never have let her very far in anyway, and that hadn't helped either.

A shriek of tires came up from below his window, and Gary leaned to look down. A car was trying to take the intersection in front of his apartment building way too fast, and as he watched, the car skidded sideways loudly, throwing up smoke from the tires as they tried to hold the pavement. The driver seemed to almost lose control, the path of the car wavering. The car slid all the way through the empty intersection and almost crashed into a brick storefront before the car righted itself and raced up Emerald.

The guy was probably drunk. If Gary had been in a better mood, he might've felt sorry for the person. But tonight, he felt nothing.

Gary shook his head. He saw his cigarettes sitting on his side table, right next to his tarot deck, but he resisted the urge to light one.

He didn't understand these people, or this Southern California lifestyle. Everything in it, everyone in it, revolved around appearances and facades. Big cars, fancy name plates on walls, servants and chauffeurs and gardeners. Business cards with shiny metallic printing, distributed by the dozens to impress others. Corner offices and limos and private, trendy little restaurants where the food was lousy and lauded.

Lies, big and small, dictated the pace of life in Los Angeles. They were the fuel that powered the endless parties and the neon lights and the lives of these people.

Everyone strived recklessly to prove their own personal worth to others but never to themselves. Nobody here went out in the morning until they looked perfect, and no one went home at night until they were sure that their friends had seen them and taken notice of their new clothes, new car, new girlfriend, or new whatever.

Superficial didn't quite begin to capture the sheer level of audacious preening and posturing that happened all day long in L.A. And no one around here seemed to care that in the long run, none of it would matter. Gary shook his head and crossed back to his bed, climbing in.

He had grown up in the Midwest, in a small town east of St. Louis, and he'd learned shortly after arriving here that the middle of the nation was a region of the country disdained by the residents of L.A. Everything between California and New York was considered "a flyover state."

But Gary had been raised in the Midwest with a set of morals that didn't apply out here in Los Angeles. The instincts ingrained in him from birth marked him as an outsider. Here, who he was on the inside was much less important that what he had, what he made, or who he was seen with.

Gary hated Los Angeles.

He'd moved down here two years ago after graduating from California State University–Fresno, just south of Sacramento, accepting one of the offers he had received after obtaining a master's degree in architecture.

He'd thought it would be good to get away from his father and his new wife, to get away from his life in Sacramento. But now he knew that the characteristics that made him so much of a loner in Sacramento were actually worse here in L.A.

He had a nice apartment, a great career, and a bright future ahead of him. And he'd never felt so alone in his whole life.

He wanted a drink so badly he could taste it.

Gary turned over and ignored the impulse, distracting himself by staring at the hospital plans hanging on his bedroom wall, architectural renderings of a project he was working on. The urges came and went, but they were the worst at night. Two months and ten days since his last drink. But the drive to visit his old friend was getting stronger and stronger every day. Lack of sleep, probably, and the dream.

------

Judy sat on the hard wooden floor next to her bed, sobbing.

She cried silently, only to herself. A few bars of yellowish moonlight penetrated the closed blinds, falling diagonally into the room and across her bruised and bloodied face.

She stared straight ahead of her, her face blank, hopeless. A patch of blackness was growing around her eyes, and a thin trickle of warm blood traced a thin line down her delicate chin.

She glanced at the back of the bedroom door. He was gone now, but he would be back.

One hand reached up and slowly curled around the handset of the telephone on the nightstand next to her. She pulled the receiver off its perch and raised it to her ear, but her other hand made no move. The phone hummed softly, then after a minute a recorded voice told her to hang up.

The sound of another person's voice, a voice other than his, seemed to stir something in her vacant eyes. She seemed to notice the grating recording, and her eyes turned from the back of the bedroom door to look at the thing in her hand, staring at it as if she'd never seen a phone before.

She was in their house, in their bedroom, sitting on the floor. Her bed was behind her, and she'd been sleeping when he'd come in....

She stood suddenly, unsteady, and hurried to the bathroom, making it to the toilet in time to throw up. The tile of the bathroom floor was cold on her legs, but after a moment she finished and stood teetering, leaning on the counter. She glanced into the mirror and gasped at what she saw.

An unrecognizable face, contorted by bruises, stared out at her. A long line of blood ran from cheek to chin, and she absently brushed at it. *His ring must have cut me*, she thought. She remembered that part. The bruises and black eyes all ran together in her memory, but the sharp sting of his ring cutting her skin—that she remembered.

She started the water, watching it run for a long moment. It swirled around the expensive porcelain and gurgled down the sink, and she found herself wishing that she were that water, escaping. Her joints, swollen and painful, cried out, and her arms and legs felt sluggish, heavy as metal. She could see in the mirror a series of bruises on her arms and chest—some were fading, but many were new. After a moment, she switched off the water in the sink and started the shower.

Vincent had never been a gentle man, not when they had been dating and certainly not since they had been married. It had attracted her to him at first—his "bad boy" side. Not anymore. And that side had been getting steadily worse over the past year. And over these last few weeks it had gotten really bad.

She was in her own personal version of hell, and no one could help her. She was in a prison she had made for herself, serving eight years so far in a term with no definitive end date.

And her jailer was her distant, angry husband.

Tonight she'd been sleeping when he'd come home. He'd come into the bedroom with his usual mixture of cursing and kicking, and Judy had known immediately that things would go one of two ways: he'd fall asleep, or he'd make her pay for today's incident.

He made her pay.

At one point, Judy Luciano had looked up at her husband as he stood over her, and she had seen nothing in his eyes that even approximated compassion or love or caring. All she saw was anger. It hadn't always been that way. But that's the way it was now.

And then she knew why he was beating her—it was because of that boy at the grocery.

Earlier that day, she had gone into town to pick up some groceries at Kroger. She usually went alone and preferred it that way—sometimes she drove past Wood Bakery, remembering when she and Chris had met there, so long ago.

For some reason, Vincent had decided to invite himself along.

She had been shopping quietly, looking over the produce, and that's when she'd noticed the young man stocking apples and bananas. He was looking at her—why, she wasn't sure. She'd been pretty once, she knew, but the years with Vincent had changed her.

The young man couldn't have been more than sixteen or seventeen. When she'd noticed him looking at her, she'd tried to make eye contact, to somehow tell him to stop looking, but those kinds of words were impossible to convey silently—or at least she hadn't figured out how.

Then Vincent saw the boy, and instead of ignoring him or moving on, he had done what he always did in those situations.

"What are you looking at?" Vincent had shouted across the vegetables.

The boy's expression had gone from quiet, distant admiration to one of shock. He'd opened his mouth to say something, probably to apologize or deny the undeniable, but nothing came out.

"You looking at my wife?" Vincent shouted again. His face contorted with sudden anger, and he swung. He punched the boy right in the mouth, knocking him down.

Judy knew what would come next.

Vincent had stood over the boy, shouting at him for several minutes, and when he straightened up and looked around, she knew what was coming. Vincent kicked the boy hard in the ribs. Judy noticed that the produce section of the grocery had miraculously cleared.

People avoided Vincent in this town, and not just because of his reputation for beating his wife's admirers. Judy watched as he kicked the boy once more for good measure, grunting as he did it, and then walked back over to her.

"I saw you looking at him, you stupid bitch. We'll talk about this later," he said.

He'd brushed past her, his eyes hard. The words hurt her, like he knew they would, and she knew that it was only the beginning.

And forcing her to lie helpless on the bed while he shouted at her, accusing her of all kinds of horrible things—that had been the payback.

"You still think you're beautiful, don't you?" he'd asked her, his voice low and husky with excitement as he'd pinned her to the bed. "When are you going to figure out that you're mine? All mine. And no one else is going to have you, not ever."

On some level she understood that it was his jealousy that drove him to do the things he did, but that didn't make it better. She had come to dread going into town, dreading the accidental glances and looks that he saw or thought he saw, looks that always seemed to drive him into fits of rage. It still amazed her that she even warranted any looks of admiration. And surely word must have gotten around about what happened when people looked at her, especially if Vincent were around to see it.

Judy had lain there on the bed, helpless, defenseless against his anger.

"No, honey," she'd said, trying to calm him, hoping that he wouldn't hurt her. "I know I'm not pretty, not to anybody except you." She repeated the mantra again and again, words that had once calmed him. In the past few months, these and other words of self-deprecation didn't seem to chill the fire in his blood. But maybe this time they would work, maybe he would calm down and....

Vincent had swung, punching her hard in the belly. The wind was knocked from her—he was a strong man, and there was really nothing she could do but take it. Take the beating, try not to think about it, pray for it to be over.

He slapped her hard across the face and she felt the blood well up in her mouth. It was a feeling she was getting used to. The feel of the warmth of her own blood flowing freely no longer surprised her. He would beat her until he felt better about himself.

He'd been looking at her, waiting, and she'd known what he'd wanted. He was waiting for her to cry out, make some kind of response. But something defiant bubbled up inside her from someplace she was only vaguely aware of. She knew that this time, she would not give him the satisfaction of crying.

It was a crazy, rebellious thought. On some level she knew it was stupid, a gamble that would just prolong the pain, but suddenly she was tired of it all—tired of the helplessness.

He wanted to hear her beg him to stop. Usually she would—but not tonight. She would endure silently until he tired of hitting her and left.

She knew that Vincent loved her. But he loved her the way you love a car or a beautiful watch—like a possession, not a person. And he jealously guarded his possession from the rest of the world.

It used to be different, back when they started dating. Chris had proposed to her and then disappeared. She'd been devastated, and Vincent had been there—even though she'd known the history between the two of them, she still needed someone. She'd been so lonely....

Judy looked at herself in the mirror again. Thinking about Chris wouldn't help, not now. Or thinking about his ring.

Her shoulder screamed as she started the shower then reached up and pulled open the door to the medicine cabinet. She pulled out a half-empty bottle of Advil, taking four at once with a handful of water from the sink. The Advil would help with the swelling and especially the black eyes to come.

After a few minutes, she felt slightly better. She stripped off her clothes and stepped into the shower. The water ran hot over her. She soaped and rinsed three times, scrubbing her entire body, going easy on her shoulder and ribs—she could already see the bruises forming. Taking long, hot showers and scrubbing with soap had become her new ritual, cleansing her mentally as well as physically.

She stepped from the shower and dried off, dressed in clean clothes. Weekend nights were her favorites, usually. Vincent went out with money in his pocket from his regular Friday paycheck, and he stayed out late. Often he would come home drunk and force himself on her, but sometimes he was too drunk to even do that.

Any night he went out drinking with his buddies, she prayed that he would drink too much and wreck his car on the way home. There were sharp, twisty corners on Blackwood Lane. And Vincent always drove too fast.

Blackwood Lane was supposed to be haunted—maybe one night, the woman's ghost who was said to haunt the lane would rise up out of the road and scare him. Maybe he'd swerve his car into a tree and crash and die. It was a terrible thing to think about, to pray for, but she couldn't help it.

Her stomach rumbled, and she remembered that she'd been planning to eat after her nap, the nap that he had interrupted. She cleaned up the bedroom and went into the kitchen. She wasn't that hungry, but she forced herself to eat—she'd lost twelve pounds in the past nine weeks, since the beatings and humiliation had escalated, and she knew that the smaller she got, the more trouble she'd have standing up to his abuse. Nothing in the refrigerator looked good, so she pulled down a pot from above the stove to make some instant soup.

As she waited for the water to boil, she went into the living room and turned on the TV. *Baywatch* was on, a show Judy watched every chance she could get. She knew it was stupid and the acting was horrible, but the men and women were beautiful, and exciting things happened to them every week.

And the show took place in California. Chris was out there somewhere, probably living a good life, enjoying the sun and the beach, far from her pain.

She knew Chris was in California because Vincent had gone looking for him and his father there. That had been back in October of 1989, just after she and Vincent had gotten married.

But the trip had been a failure—Judy had surmised that much from Vincent's return from Sacramento and his subsequent dismissal from the *familia.*

He'd been a changed man after that. He was disgraced.

That's when he'd really turned violent.

After that trip, Vincent had been forced to fend for himself—he'd started his own crew, and Tony, the new head of the Luciano family, had looked the other way.

It was times like this when she couldn't help but wonder what might've happened if Chris hadn't gone away.

She wouldn't have sunk into a fit of depression that lasted over a year, and she would never have been out at that restaurant by the highway, "The Hole," that night when Vincent Luciano had asked her out. She wouldn't have dated him out of some desperate need to break out of her funk. She would never have fallen for his silly lines. Or slept with him with some crazy notion of making herself feel better.

She would never have married Vincent, or gotten pregnant, or lost the baby as a result of his first beating just months after their marriage.

None of it would've happened. Or maybe it would've. Maybe she just wasn't supposed to be happy.

Tears welled up in her eyes, tears of regret and longing for happier times—times that existed only in her dreams, the kind of dreams she imagined prisoners had, looking out barred windows at a glowing crescent moon hanging over their prison.

But prisons came in all shapes and sizes.

The soup was done and it smelled good. It was the first pleasant sensation she could remember feeling all day. She poured some into a bowl, carried it into the dark, wood-paneled living room, and sat down cross-legged on the floor in front of the TV. She sat on the floor because the chair was his, his favorite place to park himself when he was home, and she didn't want to sit in it, whether he was here or not. Sitting on the floor was her own pitiful version of rebellion, but it was rebellion just the same. These little rebellions and her paintings were about all that kept her on this side of sanity—those things and that short, horrible letter she'd gotten from San Antonio, Texas, four years ago.

But it was her little rebellions that felt the most constructive. Something still lived inside of her, something that still allowed her to dream of other times, other places. She still fought against Vincent in her own small ways, and as the punishment and abuse grew more frequent, so did her dreams of freedom, of release.

Sometimes she fantasized about killing Vincent.

Sometimes she thought about smothering him as he lay in bed next to her sleeping, a smile on his face after satisfying himself with her. She wondered if she could do it and get away with it, and wondered if it would be worth it to kill him even if she *couldn't* get away with it. Prison would be bad, but could it be worse than this? At least the pain would stop, and the beatings.

But she didn't think she could do it. He was a powerful guy, and he could easily kill her if he really wanted to. If she tried and didn't succeed, he could snap her neck in a second. And with the friends around here that he had, he could probably explain his way out of it. His family was too powerful to be messed with, especially by someone like her, with no power.

Anyway, if she did manage to kill him, Vincent's family would find her no matter how far she ran—even if she ran all the way to California.

No, if she was going to kill him, she would have to find a foolproof way to do it. And sometimes it was just those sorts of thoughts that got her through her days and nights.

Judy finished up her soup and switched off the TV.

The thought of running away slipped through her mind as it did almost daily, but she had no money that she could easily get to—San Antonio was a long way off, and California was even further away. She doubted she could even get the twenty miles west to St. Louis before being spotted and returned to her fuming husband like a wayward pet. He had told her once that if she tried to leave he would break both of her legs, slowly.

No, she wasn't going anywhere soon. She was just a dog tied to her husband by an invisible leash. She shook her head as she washed up her dishes and headed to bed, wondering how drunk he would be when he got home.

------

Gary tried to sleep, but nothing happened. He lay in bed for a long time, staring at the plans and trying to work out the layout for the water pipes and ductwork in his head. Sometimes when he visualized the interiors of his work projects, his mind could let go of the dream and move on. It was the reason he had ten or twelve large architectural renderings hanging on the walls of his room. If the window was fully open, the corners and edges of them sometimes moved in the light breeze.

He wondered about the car he'd seen earlier, the one that he had assumed to be driven by a drunk. Maybe the guy had cracked up his car and needed help. Maybe someone would get him off the road before he killed himself, or someone else.

Any responsible bartender wouldn't have let the guy leave if he was that plastered, would they? Maybe he'd come from a party. Drinking was so easy—just relax, sit back, and let it take over.

He tried not to think about the dream or the memories of bourbon and gin that taunted him. He turned over, flipping on the radio next to his bed. Quiet music drifted over him—maybe it would help him sleep.

He grabbed his tarot pack and flipped idly through the cards, looking at the pictures more than anything else. He didn't have the energy to lay out a spread and do a reading. The Moon card came up and Gary glanced out the window, where the true moon hung low near the horizon, a thin crescent, pointed on each end as if sharpened by God himself. It glowed a dingy shade of smog gray, hanging motionless just above the horizon.

------

She awoke several hours later as he came home, and she carefully stayed out of his way until he went upstairs to collapse on the bed. She slipped quietly out through the front door—the air outside was cool, and the early May breeze smelled of rain. Judy sat in one of the chairs on the front porch and flipped on the small, cheap clock radio that sat rusting on the metal table between the two old metal chairs, dialing it from Vincent's all-sports channel to an '80s station.

Sometimes it seemed like her only real connections to the outside world were this radio and the TV inside, but she didn't enjoy new music—it seemed too loud and vibrant, too full of life. Or maybe it just reminded her that she couldn't be out there, experiencing it all for herself. She preferred older music, songs from her high school days, back when she was with Chris, back when she had hopes for a future she cared about.

She felt the light wind play across her face and enjoyed the cool sensation. The stars sparkled brightly over her head, sharp diamonds in the darkness. She had always been interested in the night sky, and one of the few books she owned was an atlas of the stars. She knew all of the constellations, both by their normal and Latin names, and she regularly followed the looping arcs of the planets as they traced their way across the darkness. Venus, Jupiter, Saturn; she had spent hours staring at each through a battered pair of binoculars, wondering what it would be like to be there, far away from Centerville and O'Fallon. And Vincent.

Judy stood and walked out into the short grass of the yard, her arms crossed across her chest, looking up at the sky. Tonight, Venus sat low on the southern horizon, hanging in the sky just above the patchwork of dim lights that was O'Fallon, Illinois. Population 7,000, fifteen miles east of St. Louis, Missouri. Beyond O'Fallon, she could just make out the runway lights of Scott Air Force Base, just southeast of town, and sometimes she imagined stowing away on one of the big planes that sometimes flew over her house. Flying away, east to New York or, even better, west to California, flying out there to look for Chris.

Chris was in Sacramento, but that was all she knew—somewhere in that huge city, he was living and working. For some reason, he had forgotten all about her, about them.

Music flowed quietly from the radio behind her, Elton John and Billy Joel. The old songs from before.

The moon hung in the sky above her, a sharp crescent that in a few days would grow full and bright. She knew the phases of the moon like the back of her hand. He was like an old friend.

As she stood there in the scraggly grass of her lawn, looking up at the thin sliver of the moon hanging in the sky over her, part of her mind wondered idly how many more full moons she would look up at. How many more full moons before something happened?

------

In a quiet radio station south of St. Louis, Burt Lancer watched, bored, as the large console played each song in turn, selecting each from the large CD jukebox sitting in one corner of the broadcast studio. The unit had been programmed earlier by the PD, the program director, who chose what songs would be played at which times. Burt got a kick out of this place—the station was so antiquated that the manager was only now pondering going full digital. They still used CDs, and on occasion, albums. Most of the rest of the country had been digital for years, and the PD picked the songs from a massive hard drive before broadcasting them. Another station he'd worked at in Knoxville had the advertising spots on digital, too, so all he'd had to do was an occasional weather and time check.

But here at WGDE, Burt babysat the commercials and the CD jukebox, making sure that everything bumped up against each other right and that there was never any dead air. He had to change the commercial cartridges that played every thirty-three minutes, pulling out the small black tape cartridges, or carts, with one set of prerecorded commercials and replacing them with the next. It was a boring, thankless job, but Burt got a lot of reading done on his textbooks and it was easy money, pulling out one tape and popping in the next. A monkey could do it, and sometimes that's exactly what he felt like.

WGDE was a best-of-the-'70s-and-'80s station, so the rotation was full of old songs, tunes by Elton John and Billy Joel and an occasional Paula Abdul. It wasn't a popular station in the St. Louis market, but it did satisfy a particular demographic, the one jam-packed with 34–to–52-year-olds who owned Volvos and were well-settled in their careers and enjoyed listening to the old stuff they had grown up on. Jimmy, the PD, snuck in an occasional newer song by the likes of Mariah Carey or Hootie and the Blowfish, but it was the old hits that never went away. "Sussudio," by Phil Collins, was something of a station classic, remaining in the PD's rotation continuously since the song had been released.

Burt kept the sound down most of the time, not caring for the music. He'd heard all the songs a dozen times before, and he preferred to listen to newer music, songs more in tune with his age and background. He used some of the equipment in the studio to listen to the CDs he brought in, CDs that were out of place here: Metallica, Live, Gin Blossoms, Collective Soul, Better than Ezra, whatever. He was careful to never get the music crossed—there was probably no quicker way for him to get canned than for the PD to wake up in the middle of the night and hear WGDE, "the best sounds of the '70s and '80s," pumping out "Welcome to Paradise" by Green Day. Burt didn't love working here, but at least it was a paycheck.

He set his book down and turned to the computer monitor on top of the CD jukebox. The green screen displayed a list of the next two hours of music, taking the station up to seven o'clock, when the station would kick over to a nationally syndicated morning show. Sometimes he felt as if really worked in some kind of big spaceship that cruised through the night on autopilot, totally devoid of life. The tunes were played, broken up by an occasional commercial, filling time playing quiet music for those out there driving the dark streets or those who couldn't sleep.

John Cougar Mellencamp was just finishing up "Jack and Diane," and that was soon to be followed by Billy Joel with "Uptown Girl." Burt glanced down the log, the list of upcoming music and breaks, not seeing anything that sounded good. Hootie and the Glowfish, as he liked to call them, were coming up in a few songs, one of the few tracks on the list from the '90s.

Nothing on the list matched his mood, but then the chances of that song coming up were pretty slim. He didn't even know if they had the song he was looking for in their library.

He had been listening to *Dookie*, the latest Green Day CD, but he had been thinking about Becky, his girlfriend. She wasn't in town this week—she'd gone to visit her cousin in Thomasville, Georgia, and Burt missed her.

And a song had been rattling around in his head all night, not the sort of song he usually wanted to hear, but it was driving him crazy. He pulled up to the jukebox and began typing on the keyboard.

First he did a search to see if the song was in the hundred-CD jukebox, but it wasn't. The chances had been pretty slim, but it hadn't hurt to try.

Burt stood and walked out of the broadcast studio, glancing at the big red neon clock over the desk. It read 3:18, so he had fourteen minutes before the next station break and commercial set. The cart was already in, so he had nothing to worry about, but after the set he would have to take it out and put in the tape marked "4:05" for the next set of commercials.

He walked down the dark hallway and turned into the PD's office, flipping on the light. There were stacks of unopened CDs on top of the cabinets, and long lists taped to the walls all around the office. There were opened copies of *Variety* and *Billboard* on the desk, along with magazines that catered to the easy-listening radio stations around the country, filled with lists of articles related to the industry. Sometimes he flipped through them just for kicks, reading serious articles with titles like "How much '70s is too much?" and "New Artists—How long to wait before including them in your rotation?" The articles were great, seemingly all written by old men concerned with the encroachment of all of this "new music," a loose term that seemed to include anything produced or recorded after 1980.

Burt glanced at the bookshelves, some weighed down with CDs, and he found what he was looking for: the 1997 *Schwann's Guide*. The thick book, an industry standard, listed every song ever recorded, including what year the song was recorded, the artist, the backup singers, and the record producer. It also broke out each song by category, a valuable tool for PDs when trying to decide if a song was appropriate for their station's format. Of course, the good PDs didn't need a book to tell them what songs went in which category—they had heard all the songs a hundred times before.

He opened the book to the "G"s and flipped through the titles until he reached "Georgia (On My Mind)." Ever since she'd left for Georgia the song had been running through his head, and he figured it was so late at night, no one would notice the slight change in format.

The song had been recorded in 1953 by Ray Charles, and as he read the *Schwann's* entry he realized that he probably could've figured that out on his own—the man had a unique voice. The *Schwann's Guide* also listed the title of the album: *All Around the World*.

He put the book back on the shelf and picked up a spiral-bound printout of all of the albums and CDs the station owned. The list was constantly changing and therefore reprinted on a regular basis, each title and song inventoried and tracked by interns at the station. He flipped though and found the album title listed, meaning the station did have a copy available.

Burt put the spiral-bound book back on Jimmy's desk and walked around the corner to the library. This small room, really no bigger than a large closet, had walls covered with shelves, and the shelves in turn were covered with rows and rows of old albums and CDs. Knowing the title and artist helped Burt find the CD in a matter of moments, and he pulled it down from the shelf and headed back into the studio.

The cut was listed as the fifth on the CD, clocking in at 3 minutes and 42 seconds. Burt sat back down at the computer console for the jukebox and scrolled through the listing of songs. Paula Abdul's "Forever Your Girl" was about halfway through, and it would be followed by "Take It Easy" by the Eagles. Three songs down the list he saw "Centerfold" by the J. Geils Band. A good song, but what really caught his attention was the length: 3 minutes and 51 seconds.

Almost perfect.

A few more seconds of tapping on the keyboard, and the J. Geils CD moved around inside the jukebox and was ejected from the unit through a slot on the top. He slid the Ray Charles CD into the slot and tapped a couple more keys, and the unit accepted the CD, inserting the song into the rotation. He would have to remember to make up the extra nine seconds of dead air space by pausing the tape cartridge between commercials on the next break.

Burt sat back and relaxed for a few minutes, waiting for the song to begin.

------

In the basement of the largest radio station in Los Angeles, adult contemporary station WMES clicked on through its rotation, playing each song in order. The DJ was away from her desk, recording bumpers and ad spots for the next week's "All '70s Show," a popular addition to the station's nightly lineup. She sat in the production studio, earphones covering her ears, reading from the copy that had been prepared for her earlier in the day by the station's advertising staff.

The digital hard drives clicked in as the music was played digitally and broadcast—the station was literally on autopilot, programmed with music and commercials and needing almost no attention. On the computer screen in the main broadcast studio, the log of songs ticked slowly through, playing each cut in turn and interspersing the songs with commercials or digital traffic updates.

One song title drifted toward the top of the stack, and when it reached the top, the song began as the track on the other CD player faded out, mixing the two songs together seamlessly as only expert DJs and very expensive audio equipment can do. The song began, its low melody drifting out over the airwaves.

------

Judy stood, looking up at the moon and quietly listening to the music from the old radio when their song came on. One minute she was just standing there, relaxing, looking up at the crescent moon, wishing to be anywhere else in the world, and then suddenly there it was: their song.

"Georgia," the song that they had loved to listen to together, the song that she used to sing for him as he played it on the piano in his parents' living room. The song that they had always played when they sat together in his car, parked out on Pine Drive, a hill north of Centerville and O'Fallon that looked out over the sparse lights of the small towns. Pine Drive, where she and Chris O'Toole had spent so many warm summer nights in each other's arms.

She hadn't thought about Pine Drive in a long time, and now, as the familiar words of the song washed over her, she found that she remembered them perfectly. She remembered Pine Drive too, a little road not five miles from the porch where she now stood, a porch where she would never have expected to end up.

The moon hung bright in the sky over her head as she crossed her arms and started to cry. Judy hugged her arms a little tighter around her and quietly sang the words of their song to herself, glancing up at a bleary crescent moon.

------

Beside his bed on the nightstand, the clock radio purred with quiet music, and as the next song came on, he reached over and turned it up. The song was "Georgia," by Ray Charles. He loved it. But every time he heard it, it made him sad, for reasons he didn't know. The song was mournful, yet the melody and lyrics were beautiful.

Gary Foreman lay in bed, looking out at the smog-tinged moon, and quietly sang the words of the song to himself. It made him think of loss, of smoky rooms and lost memories and missed opportunities.

The song ended, and as Gary drifted off to sleep, as he slowly crossed the hazy line between wakefulness and sleep, a random thought crossed his mind.

*It had been their song.*

# Chapter 4

"The way I feel right now, I couldn't care less if another woman talks to me ever," Mike said, playing with his food and talking more to himself than to Gary.

Gary was trying to listen to his friend's latest tale of romantic woe, but he was rubbing his forehead and wondering when his days would begin to look brighter. Sleep had been difficult last night, as it had been for months now. His mind just didn't work right if he didn't get enough rest. He wanted to pay attention to his friend, but he had an almost-permanent headache, a tight band of pain across his scalp.

Gary wanted a drink badly, even though it was early in the day. Any kind of drink, anything to get his mind off of what he had dreamed about the night before.

Mike Sampson put down his chicken sandwich and offered Gary some fries.

"Now, I know what you're going to say. Probably something like 'It's only Tuesday, Mike, and too far from the weekend to start getting so depressed already.' Something like that, right?"

Gary looked up at his friend. Mike had just broken up with his girlfriend, and he and Mike should've been comparing wounds and consoling each other over the failed relationships. Rosa had left Gary about a week ago, and Denise had broken up with Mike three nights ago. But Gary couldn't equate the two—Rosa had gotten sick of the endless nights of tossing and turning and waking to screams. And Mike never had trouble finding women—he was the prototypical southern California male, skinny and tanned and fit.

Mike continued. "It's just that I know there are other women out there, plenty of them, just waiting for some hunk of a man to come along and sweep them off their feet. And then, when those hunks dump them, you and I will be there to comfort them. Right?"

"Huh? Oh, yeah. Sorry, Mike. I'm sorry to hear about you and Denise."

Mike shook his head. "Is that all you've got to say? I've been sitting here complaining about it for a half-hour and you've said maybe two words the whole time." He ate another fry. "You still upset about Rosa?"

"Yeah, I'm depressed," Gary said as he took a drink of his soda, wishing for something else in the glass. "And hearing you talk about Denise is reminding me about her."

Mike continued, nodding. That seemed to be the answer he was looking for, although Gary didn't really care much.

"Just remember: move on," Mike said. "That's what I keep telling myself—you've just got to keep looking 'til you find the right one. That's the whole point of dating all these women, didn't you know that? You date and date and date some more—it's like trying on clothes at a store. Everything looks good in the window, but you have to try it on before you see if it fits, right? Denise was a nice girl, but there'll be a dozen more where she came from."

Gary was only half-listening, and when Mike said that about a dozen more, he looked up at him as if he'd been speaking in Swahili. This was a perfect example of the difference between him and Mike, between the way he thought and the way people from Los Angeles thought. People were a commodity here, especially women—there was always another attractive girl arriving on a bus from some hick town, trying to make her way in the "big city."

After a second, he remembered what Mike had said and nodded, agreeing. "Yeah, yeah. I know all that. I've told you the same exact thing a dozen times, same words and everything," he said, pointing a French fry at the sandwich in Mike's hands. "You wouldn't eat at all for a while after you broke up with that one girl last year, remember?"

Mike nodded, smiling. "Yeah, there was a good month in there when I was only wearing sweats and watching Springer."

They ate in silence for a few minutes, each wrapped in their own thoughts. Gary was sure Mike was thinking about a woman—and in a way, Gary was too. But he was thinking about the voice of the woman in his dream. It sounded familiar.

"Mike," Gary said, tentatively. "Have you ever thought about… well, finding, you know...*the one*?"

Mike's eyes widened. "The one? The one what? You mean marriage, Gary?" Mike smiled, in on the joke. "Settling down with a woman and having kids and a mortgage on a house in Thousand Oaks? Come on, Gary, that's not going to happen to you or me, not here in L.A. This town is about meeting people, but nothing serious is ever going to come out of these relationships. You know that. The women out here, they're just too...." Mike said, struggling for words.

Gary knew his friend's problem: it was hard to qualify the difficulty with socializing in Los Angeles.

Mike started falsely a couple of times but then seemed to find inspiration. "It's like the women here in L.A., they're just out shopping. It's like they're all out at the mall or down on Wilshire, but they've forgotten their purses. They shop around and pick up things and study them for a while, but they always put them back down and move on. Nothing serious, no commitments. No need to buy anything when you can rent whatever you want, right? Or just borrow it." He smiled, and Gary could see that he was happy that he'd been able to come up with such a clever analogy.

Gary looked at him, shaking his head, and ate another bite of his sandwich. "Yeah, I know what you're saying. It's just that I'd like something more...stable. I'd like to wake up every morning and know that there was someone there with me, someone to share my life with. Is that wrong?"

Mike was looking at him strangely, like he'd asked to borrow his spleen.

"What are you looking at?" Gary asked him, catching him staring. "Trying to figure out my problems?"

"Yeah, something like that," Mike said, looking down at his food. "That might've been the longest speech I've ever heard you make." Then he was quiet. They ate, Mike working on his chicken salad sandwich and Gary nibbling around the edges of a large pita concoction. The food here was good, but he wasn't that hungry.

"Gary, have you been having that dream again?"

Gary looked up. Mike was one of the few people he'd told about his dreams. But he wasn't in the mood to talk about it today. Last night's dream had been...too much.

"No. No dreams," he said, and he knew from the look on Mike's face that he wasn't buying it.

"Really? Because from the way you look, it's getting worse. You look like crap. How have you been sleeping?" He stared at Gary.

"Okay, I guess. I'm a little tired, that's all."

Mike shook his head. Gary smiled. He was grateful to have such a close friend—he'd had very few in his life. But Mike was like a bulldog, always rooting in the dirt until he found the truth. "Am I right? Is that where all this talk is coming from, about wives and settling down—this dream is scaring you, isn't it?"

Gary was uncomfortable talking too much about himself—he was so used to keeping things inside. "I don't know. Seriously, I can't remember every time I have it. Sometimes I just wake up tired, like I didn't get any sleep. And then other times I can remember the whole thing, and it sticks with me through the whole day...."

Mike just looked at him, the lunch between them forgotten.

Gary was quiet for a moment, then looked up and saw his friend looking at him expectantly. He wanted to hear, and Gary wanted to tell. He wanted—needed—to tell someone.

Slowly, reluctantly, he began. "But this morning, I woke up feeling angry, like I could beat the crap out of someone. The dream was so vivid that I could remember it for hours, everything about it."

Mike looked at him as if trying to come up with something positive to say. "I'm sorry, friend. I don't know what to tell you—it sounded pretty scary to me the last time you told me about it."

Gary shook his head. "It's like total fear, coming at you in complete darkness." There was also a feeling of having no control over the situation, of being powerless to change it. He always felt trapped, like a wounded animal.

Gary would always be in a darkened room, a bedroom, but one he didn't recognize. The source of his fear, unseen, approached from outside the room and began pounding on the closed door, the sound deep and echoing like someone pounding on a coffin. The door would shimmer and slowly buckle and then, finally, burst inwards, spraying bits of wood all over the room. Gary had told Mike that this was when he would wake up, never having seen the thing that had come for him, the source of his bottomless feelings of dread.

"What were you angry about?" Mike asked. "Do you remember?"

Gary sighed. "Yeah, the dream's gotten a lot worse since the last time I told you about it. This is really starting to scare me. This morning, I woke up screaming."

Mike looked at him with a mixture of concern and fear. "Screaming? Seriously?"

"Yeah," Gary nodded. "Remember that I would always wake up just as the man broke down the door? Well, last night, he got all the way into the room and over to the bed and was holding something behind his back, something I couldn't see. Some part of me, the part that knew I was just sleeping and that it was all just a dream, that part told me that it wasn't going to be pretty. Just then, his hand moved, incredibly fast, and I saw the glint of light off a metal blade and I knew it was a knife, a big one. The man was grinning at me, and I could tell he was enjoying himself, like he was living off my fear, stoking it up like a fire. He held the knife over me and stared at me for a few long seconds, a horrible smile on his face, and then he brought the knife down, fast, right at my chest."

Gary was quiet for a moment, reliving the dream. He wasn't used to talking about it, but it felt good to get it out. Was this the way it was for normal people, just talking about themselves to someone else and getting feedback? It felt strange and good, but it also made him feel exposed, vulnerable. For so long, his father had reminded him about secrecy, about the need to be careful. To never share.

"I think I'd scream too," Mike said, interrupting Gary's thoughts.

Gary nodded and ate a couple of fries.

"Okay," Mike said. "Well, first of all, this is the first time that you could see the person in your dream was a man. And not just a man, but a Man, like with a capital letter. When did that happen?"

"Well, the past couple of nights I've seen him coming at me after he breaks the door down, but it wasn't until last night or this morning that I saw the knife."

Mike nodded, continuing. "Okay, does this guy look familiar to you? Maybe he's someone from your past, or maybe your mind is using his face to symbolize something else. Do you know him?"

Gary shook his head. "Yeah, sort of. Like I recognize him, but I don't. Maybe I knew him when I was younger?"

"Or maybe your mind is just using a face from your past or someone you saw in a movie or on TV. Could he be someone from St. Louis? Maybe you could look through your old yearbooks or something. Do you still have any of that stuff?"

"No, he's not from St. Louis."

"You're sure? You don't talk about it much, so maybe...."

Gary interrupted him brusquely. "No, he's not from there. And I don't have anything from back then."

Mike looked at him oddly. It was the look of someone wanting to know more about his past than he was willing to tell. Gary was used to that look.

"Okay. Sorry, didn't mean to pry. Now, you said the room was completely dark?"

"Right."

"Okay, and you also said that when he lifted the knife, you saw the glint of steel. Where did that light come from?"

Gary relaxed a little, thinking about it for a moment. "I don't know. I don't remember any light in the room, but when he crashed through the door, there was light all around him. I guess there was light coming from the other room. And I remember the knife very clearly, because it scared the hell out of me. My heart was pounding when I woke up."

Mike nodded. "Well, that doesn't surprise me. Dreams can be very stressful, and they can seem very real. And a lot of times they're just your mind or subconscious trying to tell you something through symbols."

"Yeah, I can understand that. The realism, that's what scares me—it felt too damn real to just be a dream. It was like it was all really happening, like I was really there. This guy was busting down that door, and I was lying in that bed, unable to move. It's the first time I can ever remember having a dream where I knew I was dreaming the whole time."

Mike looked away and then picked up his sandwich and finished the last two bites. This had started off as such a quiet lunch, no big deal. Now the rest of Gary's sandwich sat on the tray in front of him, unfinished. "Yeah, well, it had to be a dream. Oh, I was going to ask you: was there any sound, any at all, during the whole thing?"

Gary felt a chill pass over him. "Yeah, now that you mention it, he did say something to me. I can remember it as clear as day."

"Well, what did he say?" Mike said impatiently.

Gary stared at Mike. "He looked down at me for a long moment, the knife held over me, and just before he brought it down, he called me something...and he was so angry when he said it." He didn't want to think about the dream anymore, but it was impossible not to.

"And? What did he call you? You gonna make me wait all day?"

Gary shook his head. "Sorry, I was just trying to figure it all out. Anyway, he called me a 'whore.'"

------

Gary leaned over his drafting table, trying to concentrate on his work, but he couldn't. His lunch with Mike had stirred up memories, things he hadn't remembered about the dream, and now they ran riot in his mind.

The dream was getting worse every time he had it, like a cancer growing in his mind. What did it mean? Who was the guy? At first, he'd thought the dream might just be a memory of a story he'd once heard, or maybe a scene from a forgotten movie, but now he didn't know.

Mike was his best friend and a good listener, but talking to him wasn't helping. Gary felt like if this went on much longer, he would have to break down and talk to a professional.

He looked up at the other drafters around him, each of them bent

over their slanted desks, surrounded by plans and proposals and el-
evations for a dozen different projects. He worked in a large, high-
ceilinged room with good ventilation and great lighting (necessary
for the draftsmen), but he still felt cramped, like he was suffocating.
His shirt suddenly felt too tight and he stood, weaving between the
other desks and out into the hallway, heading for the restroom.

Gary went in and splashed cold water on his face. He rolled up
the sleeves on his starched white dress shirt, ignoring the office's un-
spoken but formal dress code. He ran cold water along his arms and
wrists, letting it drip off his elbows like a doctor preparing for surgery. It felt good. After a couple of minutes, he shut off the water and
dried his face and arms, rolling his sleeves back down. He felt better,
much better. And then he caught a glimpse of himself in the mirror.

There was something different about him, something he couldn't
define. His hair, his face, his clothes, they all looked normal. His eyes
were dark and bloodshot—it looked like he was coming off a long
night of drinking.

If only that were the case.

The door to the bathroom swung open and one of the other draftsmen came in, greeting Gary warmly and making his way over to one
of the urinals. Gary said his good-bye and left, leaving the man to his
privacy.

Gary started back toward the "pit," as the drafting room was
known, but took a quick detour to the kitchen, a small room off to
one side of the pit that held a refrigerator, microwave, and a couple of
tables with chairs. Draftsmen and other employees sat at the tables,
sipping old coffee and chatting. Gary greeted a couple of people he
knew, bought a soda, and headed back to his desk.

He was working on the plans for a new hospital to be built in
San Francisco. Gary had been put in charge of the ventilation and air
circulation plans, something he had very little experience in. But it
was a semi-promotion, being put in charge of a specific aspect of an
ongoing project, and he had eagerly accepted the challenge.

There were a few other draftsmen in the room working on other aspects of the hospital plans: structural, lighting and electrical,
plumbing and utilities, elevation, and seismologic plans were all
underway or already completed. One of the facade planners, those
who designed the outside of the building, had already constructed a
large-scale model of the hospital exterior and placed it on one of the
high display tables at the front of the large room. Sometimes, when
Gary would glance up from his work and look around at some of the
others involved in the design of St. Jude's, he would see them staring

at the model with glazed-over eyes, and he knew exactly what they were doing: looking at the model and seeing the completed building in their heads, filling in all of the details and laying them out on the plans before them. It was good to have a model to look at. It gave them something tangible to hang their dreams on.

Other draftsmen in the pit were working on various plans: a detailed plan for the new International Airport in Austin, Texas; a bank in Tokyo; and an extension campus for the University of Iowa. Some of the projects were only proposals, ideas submitted to the coordination teams for each project in hopes that MacMillan Architecture would receive the bid and be allowed to design the final structure.

They had received the St. Jude's Hospital contract only after several months of preliminary designs and submissions had been FedEx'ed to the contractor's office in San Francisco, and Gary counted himself lucky that he was working on an actual project rather than just on proposed structures—it made him feel like his work was actually useful.

MacMillan Architecture was one of the premier design firms in Los Angeles, and Gary had been lucky to hire on with them. He had started out doing erasures and cleanups on others' work, but after several months, he'd been asked to work on the underground parking structure design for a hotel being built in Queens, New York. He had warmed to the task and come in with his drawing early and spotless, earning him a reputation for producing good work quickly. In his three years with Macmillan, he'd progressed slowly, and now, he felt like things in his professional life were finally firing on all cylinders. Amazing, considering how much of his past was a fabrication. Even the social security number that showed up on his paychecks was not the real thing.

But he was used to that kind of life, and his days here at the firm were good ones, filled with hard work and good pay, and he felt like he was finally getting out from under the shadow of what had happened in St. Louis and Sacramento.

It was his nights that he worried about.

Gary bent back over his work, trying to find a place for ventilation ducts in the emergency room, referring constantly to the appropriate state and federal regulations for their placement. Next to his drafting table was a side table covered with notes and books and photocopies—the government strictly regulated airflow and circulation in hospitals, especially in areas such as surgery, maternity rooms, and emergency wards. Gary had to find a way to make that type of airflow happen while at the same time locating the air shafts and vents along central avenues convenient to the air circulation system. And he had to use the minimum amount of piping and venting to keep costs down.

He lost himself in the hospital. In his mind, he navigated the halls and rooms, feeling a breath of cool air on his face as he walked past the imaginary vents. It was the only way he could plan a space: imagine it all in his head and then step into his mind, the ultimate in virtual reality.

The afternoon passed quickly as he worked out the details, and by five o'clock, the plans were nearing completion. The airshafts and ducting systems were in place, and he felt sure that by Friday, his deadline, he would have something that he could be proud of to submit to Simmons, his supervisor.

Mike, coat and briefcase in hand, came over to Gary's desk and glanced at the plans. He was a drafter also, seated three desks away, and Gary knew he'd spent the day working on the Austin Airport proposal. He studied the plans for a long moment, taking the structure in, before saying anything.

"Looks good, Gary. Good flow of air through the waiting areas without mixing air in from the ER or surgery. Hospitals are tough." Mike had worked on the plans for a hospital on his last assignment, and he had given Gary a couple of suggestions. Mike was the same age as Gary, but he'd been in the field a little longer—he'd skipped college and gone straight to work for an architectural design firm with his uncle. He'd moved on after a couple of years, but his experience in the field had made him a valuable member of the MacMillan staff—Gary wouldn't be surprised to hear him be put in charge of the whole Airport project, assuming the Austin folks signed off on the MacMillan plans.

Gary stretched and grabbed his coat. "Yeah, the flows can't mix, but they both need to be recirc'd back to the blowers though those huge banks of carbon filters in the basement. I think I've got it, though."

Mike nodded. "Yeah, looks good. Going down to Slade's?"

Slade's was the bar on the corner across from the MacMillan offices, and going there was a nightly ritual for some of the employees. Gary usually only went on Fridays or when there was some type of event planned—he wasn't a social drinker, or any kind of drinker anymore, and he always felt awkward with his coffee or soda while the other architects pounded their beers. But the idea of a gin and tonic sounded so good right now....

"No, think I'll pick up some stuff at the store and head home."

Mike nodded. "Okay, but if you need anything, call me. Anytime, day or night." Gary knew what he meant and patted him on the back, thanking him. Mike had been just about the only person he'd talked to about his dreams, and Gary was glad he was there.

"I'll do that," Gary said as they walked out together. He waved at Mike as he left to meet up with some of the others. Going to Slade's was fun once in a while, but when he'd started here at MacMillan's, he'd gone every night for months on end. Going back in there anytime soon would be a very bad idea.

# Chapter 5

Gary's apartment was small and within walking distance of his work, but the neighborhood left something to be desired, especially at night. Usually when he got home he just locked up and made himself something to eat, watched a little TV or read, and then hit the sack. It wasn't the kind of neighborhood where you hung out at night on your front porch, chatting with the neighbors—nothing like living in the Midwest, where friendly neighbors were the norm. And besides, he didn't have a porch—he lived on the fifth floor with a great view of an intersection.

He changed clothes and put some water on to boil, pulling a box of macaroni and cheese from the cabinet. Not fancy cuisine, but he consoled himself by remembering how much money he was putting into savings every month. Someday soon, combined with the money from his father, he'd be able to drop completely off the map—forever.

Gary's place was a mess, with dozens of uncompleted projects vying for space. Two different puzzles sat on his small dining room table, and a half-completed model of a lighthouse took up half of his kitchen counter. There was a chair in one corner of the apartment that needed to be stripped and repainted, and four huge stacks of magazines and newspapers waiting to be read.

He dialed the number as he waited for the water to boil.

As much as Gary had called it lately, he should've put it into the speed dial, but he just couldn't bring himself to do it. It would have felt like an admission of defeat.

The clicks ended and the phone picked up immediately. They never made you wait—no chances to back out. A recorded voice came on, the female voice sounding European and a little mysterious. He'd heard the message many times before but had never figured out a way to skip it.

"Hello, and welcome to the Psychic Counselors Hotline. We can help you for just $3.99 a minute. Why go through life wondering what the world has in store for you, when our psychic counselors can help you with all of your needs? We've got dozens of proven counselors just waiting to talk to you, so hold on. You'll be billed $3.99 a minute. If you are under 18, you must have your parents' permission to call this number. For entertainment purposes only. Now hold on, as we connect you to your own personal psychic...."

He waited, glancing at the water on the stove. There was a whirring sound and then a voice came on the line. "Would you like a particular psychic or the next available?"

"Meredith, please," he said, feeling silly.

A long pause, and he killed the time by opening the macaroni package and premeasuring the milk, setting it on the counter next to the stove.

"Hi, caller, this is Meredith," the woman answered cheerfully. "Have I spoken to you before?"

"Yes," he said. "It's Gary from Los Angeles."

"Oh." The voice grew more serious. There was a long pause. "You're the one having the dreams, right?"

"Yes. Actually just the one dream. I don't know what it means, but it's getting worse."

He explained all that had happened in the dream since the last time he'd talked to her, about two days ago. It took about ten minutes, but it was money well spent. The conversation was private and anonymous. He could tell this lady just about anything, more than he could ever tell Mike. "And I don't know what to do about it."

Meredith was quiet for a moment. "This dream sounds like a portent of things to come. Do not interpret it too literally—often the mind is just using representations." Gary heard rustling in the background. "I just threw some bones for you. I think you are about to understand what the dreams mean, and when you do, it will change you greatly. Do you want me to read your tarot?"

"Yes, please." Holding the phone in the crook of his neck, he stirred in the shells. He knew they were getting to the end of the call and he tried not to think about what would come after, the dream that would come when he tried to sleep.

He could hear the low sound of the shuffling of cards. The sound had grown familiar. Somewhere along the line, he'd bought his own deck and tried reading his own fortune, but it was better from someone else.

"You are in a very difficult place in your life, I know. I'm putting down the cards and...let's see here.

"I see happiness on the horizon for you," Meredith said quietly.

"I know you are glad to hear that, right?"

"Yes, that's good."

"The Wheel of Fortune is your third card, and that means that your destiny and fortune are culminating. You are approaching the end of your problem, but that advancement toward the outcome could be good or bad. But it looks like you're moving toward completion. Your fifth card is...the six of swords, the man in the longboat. That usually means travel or a voyage—are you going somewhere?"

"Not that I know of." Maybe MacMillan would win the St. Jude's contract and the firm would send him to San Francisco as a reward.

"Hmm, that's strange. Well, maybe you'll be taking a trip soon. Or it can also mean success after anxiety, a journey through difficulty that results in happiness. The next cards all seem to be working along those lines, about overcoming your problems. You are definitely moving toward some type of resolution. Now your last card is...oh, my." The line was silent for a long moment.

"You didn't pull the Death card for me, did you?" He tried to sound jovial and uninterested.

"No, my son. The tenth card is the Sun Card. Usually that is a very good card, representing happiness and light, but your card is reversed."

"What does that mean?" He thought he already knew, but her interpretation of the arrangement of the cards was as important as knowing the meaning of an individual card.

"Unhappiness and loneliness. Fire and death, hell, the opposite of the life-giving sunlight when the card is right-side up. It can also mean a broken engagement of some sort, or maybe a triumph delayed, though not necessarily lost."

He thought about that for a few moments, and then thanked her and got off the phone. The cards supposedly held some kind of power, but even if it was all just a big pile of hocus-pocus, it made him feel better to talk to someone about his problems. And every phone call helped him delay the inevitable moment when he would have to sleep.

Gary turned on the TV and sat down to eat his dinner, putting the pack of his own tarot cards nearby. He flipped through the channels, looking for anything to watch, but his mind was still on the tarot reading and on the delay of triumph.

# Chapter 6

Judy stirred the pot, bringing the soup to a boil. Lately, all she made was soup—it was easy and required minimal attention.

Life for her had recently morphed into a day-to-day struggle. Her shoulder ached as she moved the wooden spoon around the large pot, and her mind wandered.

It would be a late dinner tonight because Vincent was working late at The Hole. Tuesdays were usually slow and, as the head bartender, Vincent's tips would be less than stellar. Fridays and Saturdays were better, with lots of tips and money skimmed from the till when Armand and the bouncers weren't looking. And even if they caught him, they probably couldn't have done anything about it.

Her husband was a drunk and a thief.

For the past few years, Vincent had tended bar at The Hole. It was part of a hotel and restaurant that catered to highway travelers heading west to St. Louis or east into southern Illinois and Indiana.

Usually he made pretty good money. It had snowed a lot earlier in the year and that had helped—travelers tended to stop at a hotel/restaurant combination so they wouldn't have to go out again. There had been several nights over the past winter where he'd brought home big wads of ones and fives, showing them off to his wife. Judy had looked hungrily at the wads of money, but Vincent had always locked them away in his little metal safe before going to bed. And every morning they would disappear.

She figured he was plowing back into his criminal schemes. And every time he told her about the money, she felt like a silent partner.

He also bragged about his ability to steal from his boss. On busier nights, when business was good, he would charge for the watered-down drinks he made and tuck the money underneath the cash register, collecting it at night after Armand or whoever was in charge would leave. Sometimes he could scrape together a hundred or a hundred-fifty; adding this to his tips, he could clear two hundred in a good night on top of his miniscule hourly wage.

Of course, Vincent wasn't as concerned about the money lately—it used to be that the money he made at The Hole was all they had to live on—that and the money that came from his "friends." But lately, he'd seemed less worried.

Judy had only a vague idea of what he and his friends did—but she knew it was illegal. Sometimes boxes of alcohol or cigarettes or unlabeled crates would rest in the living room for a day or two before disappearing. Sometimes there were mysterious trips up to Chicago, or down to Mexico.

And then there was Vincent's family. The Lucianos were famous in southern Illinois. For five decades, until Ginovese Luciano had gone to jail, they had been the most notorious crime family in the Midwest. But now the family was split.

Tony, frightened by what had befallen his father, wanted the family to go legitimate. Most of the *capos* and higher members of the family agreed, so they had slowly started to divest or subvert the family's criminal activities, focusing for the first time on the family's legitimate businesses.

Vincent, disgraced after his failed attempt to find the O'Tooles in Sacramento, had retreated into what he knew: a life of crime. Tony had allowed him to take any members of the organization with him that he wanted. It really hadn't been a peace offering—Tony had known that Vincent would recruit from within the family, and that Vincent would take with him the most violent and criminal elements of the family structure.

That would make it much easier for Tony to take the family legit.

Judy had pieced all of this together over the years, just as most of the people in O'Fallon who kept their ears open could have. Some of the story had come from Vincent, but most of it was common knowledge. So over the past nine years, the brothers had each come to control a different aspect of O'Fallon—Tony worked within the law, using his money and influence to try and gain even more money and power. And Vincent, Judy was convinced, ran a small and completely illegal operation of his own.

But lately Tony's legitimate side of the family wasn't doing that well. Judy had heard that his money was running out.

Vincent wasn't doing badly—this house was not something a bartender could afford. It wasn't a mansion by any stretch, but it was a nice two-story house and it sat on almost two acres, fronted by Blackwood Lane.

Over the past few months, things between Vincent and his brother had changed, and Judy had noticed that it seemed to coincide with Vincent's growing appetite for violence. Vincent had been seeing a lot of his brother, spending time with him at the complex of offices his brother had bought in Belleville as part of the move to take the family legit almost ten years ago. She wondered if Vincent might get back into the business again, helping his brother. That would be good for Vincent—he'd make more money from more legitimate means, and maybe if that happened they might move to a bigger house. And he might start taking better care of her. Surely if he became a powerful businessman, someone would talk to him about pounding his wife's face in, right?

If there was one thing that man loved in this world, it was money. He'd spent his life chasing it. He'd left his family convinced that he could make more money by retaining his family's discarded illegal activities, and that had failed to bring him the level of wealth he felt he required.

But it had proved him right in one way—the Luciano family's income had fallen steadily as Tony had tried to right the ship and make his crime family into a real business.

She stirred the soup and wondered when Vincent would be home, and if he would be good to her.

As strange as it sounded, she knew that sometimes he was. Sometimes his spirits would lift, and something in his heart or in his head would loosen temporarily. Sometimes he would walk happily through the door carrying a new dress that he had impulsively purchased for her, and it reminded her of when they had first started going out. For those few moments, she would question her own memories of the things he had inflicted upon her—how could that be the same man that would smile and hand her a small bouquet of wildflowers?

This morning, before he had left for work, he had come at her with a knife and almost killed her. And he'd never said why.

She no longer even tried to understand what was going on inside her husband's mind. Days would pass where nothing happened, and now, two incidents in less than a day.

She tried not to cry. The soup was done enough for her to leave it alone for a few minutes, so she set the lid on it, leaving it tilted a little to let the steam out, and wandered out onto the porch to watch the sun set.

On a good day she could watch the sun paint the clouds a hundred shades of red in the western sky. On a really clear day she could see the very top of the glittering Gateway Arch in the distance, standing over St. Louis fifteen miles to the west, its arcing shape a dark rounded streak on the horizon near the setting sun.

Vincent hadn't always been this way—he had been nice to her, sweet, at the beginning. During the trial, when Chris's father had testified against Vincent's father, the famous Luciano boy had begun taking an interest in her, and she'd assumed it was just something related to the trial. It made sense, too, on some level—everyone knew that Chris and Judy were dating, had been for quite a while, and she had figured that the Lucianos were looking for any kind of advantage.

Of course, no one had thought that the trial would turn as violent as it had, with Chris's mother getting killed and the other witness falling to his death. Ginovese Luciano had been convicted after Chris's father had completed his testimony despite the fact that he had just lost his wife.

The attention from Vincent had been flattering and more than a little strange at the beginning. Vincent had traveled around her like a planet circling a sun, watching her. After the trial, Chris had simply disappeared. Vincent's attention didn't wane, and the occasional visits and dinners together became more frequent.

After Chris left, it had been what she had needed. The months after he left had been horrible. The loss was baffling. And Vincent had been there, listening to her frustrations. She began to rely on that attention. He'd denied knowing anything about the death of Chris's mother Gloria, and at first she had not believed him, but after a while he'd convinced her that it had been other elements in the *familia*.

She hadn't known at the time his level of involvement in his family, or the power struggle that was playing out. She'd only known that he managed to fill some small part of the emptiness inside her.

All of her senior year she had spent with Vincent, slowly growing to love him in some way. Nothing like what she had felt for Chris, but something, nonetheless. He'd helped her when she'd needed it, and his concern for her was obvious. He was good to her, and sometimes that's all a person really needs.

When he'd asked her to marry him as they danced in stiff clothes at the senior prom at the Marriott in downtown St. Louis, she had only hesitated for a long, silent moment before she'd smiled and whispered "yes" into his ear.

That pause had been filled with her memories of Chris, memories of a love that was gone. And in that moment before she'd whispered her response, in that moment as her neck pressed against her fragrant corsage, she'd asked for forgiveness from Chris, wherever he might be. She couldn't wait any longer for him—she was ready to make a new life, accept Vincent as her husband.

Unfortunately, she didn't meet her real husband until their wedding night.

She had insisted on keeping her virginity until then. She thought of it as a gift that she would give to him, the most precious gift she could give anyone, and she spent many heated nights trying to explain this, trying to defend against his advances like the queen of an embattled castle. She even compared him to Chris, who had never pressured her for sex, and that had angered Vincent. Looking back on it, she had seen some of his fire even before they had wed.

And it had been an unfortunate set of circumstances that had led up to that particular evening. The wedding had been fine, a glittering affair marred only by the protestations of her parents and their pointedly obvious absence from the ceremony. But Vincent's brother had chosen their wedding reception to break the news to his younger brother that he would have to leave the family organization and strike out on his own.

It had been a blow to Vincent, Judy knew, and hearing it at the reception had meant that he had been unable to react how he would have preferred. His smile had been forced the rest of the evening.

She found out what had happened when they got into the limousine.

All her life, she'd looked forward to this evening. But instead of a wedding night for a happy couple, they were mired in a heated discussion about Vincent and his family. She didn't feel like talking about it, but Vincent was upset, so she'd tried to understand.

Tony had made it very clear: the Luciano family was going legit and Vincent was out on his ear. He'd talked to some of the guys at the wedding reception after he'd gotten the news, and they'd agreed to join him in setting up a smaller organization.

His eyes had darted angrily as he'd told her these things, and she'd listened, but inside all she wanted was for him to put this family business aside for the evening and enjoy their new life together.

On their wedding night, she didn't have the opportunity to give him the gift that she had so carefully preserved for so long. He simply took it, like a pillaging conqueror.

He was rough and angry and distracted by the events of the evening. His immediate pleasure was all that mattered. She glimpsed in his dark eyes as he moved roughly over her the beginnings of her new life. He seemed to hardly notice her weeping.

And after it was all over, as he lay next to her, sleeping contentedly, she pulled the sheets tight around her, feeling violated and humiliated, crying softly to herself.

*Rape.* That was the only word she could think of to describe what had just happened to her.

Lying there in that spacious bed in the honeymoon suite at the Adams Mark hotel, with its breathtaking view of the Mississippi River and downtown St. Louis, Judy Luciano began to wonder, for the first time, if she had made a terrible mistake.

She'd started to sob. The tears came and there was nothing she could do to stop them. Moments later he stirred, and the words he said to her were like a slap in the face, almost as brutal as what he had done before.

"Shut up, bitch," he'd said.

*I should've gotten up and run out right then*, Judy thought as she stood on her porch and watched the sun sink below the horizon. The Gateway Arch was visible just to the left of the setting sun, its graceful curve now dark in the shadow of the red sun.

Judy went back inside and took the soup off the stove, checking to make sure it had thickened up before putting the lid on snugly. She would have some now and put the rest in the fridge, and when he got home she'd warm some up for him. It was her favorite, chicken and dumplings.

She poured herself a bowl of the soup and some of the peas she'd boiled and carried a tray back out onto the porch. The sky was ablaze with colors as the sun slipped out of the sky, and wide orange streaks painted the sky and the clouds above her with the palate of the gods.

Her parents had told her not to get married so early, especially to someone like Vincent, but she hadn't listened. So they had refused to come to the wedding, and her attempts to contact them over the years had been rudely rebuffed.

Then she'd gotten the letter from San Antonio, Texas, and her last avenue of escape had been ripped away. The letter from her parents' attorney, dated four years ago, stated coldly that her parents had been killed in a car accident, and that a sizeable amount of money was hers to be claimed. At the bottom of the letter was the name and address of the lawyer that she needed to contact.

They hadn't approved of her wedding and had refused to listen to her complain about the marriage, but it seemed that after they had moved away they changed their minds and decided to look out for her in their own way. If only they had come to her and offered their help.

Now she was on her own. Chris was gone, her parents were dead, and no one in this town dared to help her.

# Chapter 7

It seemed like Gary was asleep for only a minute before the dream was upon him again.

The darkness of the room, the feeling of dread, they all returned, but this time the dream felt deeper, more real. He noticed more, saw more, felt more.

Gary was in the strange bed as always, the sheets pulled up around his strangely skinny body. Again, the pounding began on the heavy wooden door—incessant, echoing, the wood sounding like it would give at any moment. With each pound of the man's fist, the door threatened to break. The wood wasn't thick enough to keep him out. After moments the wood buckled and shattered inward, pieces of the door flying past him as he cowered in the bed, waiting.

The man came into the room slowly, dragging one leg painfully. He was outlined in the hazy light from the room beyond, and then, for the first time he could recall, Gary heard himself speaking. The words came high and fast—and they were spoken by a woman.

"Please. Please, don't hurt me again, please? I'm sorry about the accident! It wasn't supposed to be like that. No...."

The words sounded odd coming from his lips. And the voice sounded familiar—or did it?

He wished he could say something else—he would have yelled at the man, or jumped out of bed and tried to run away.

Anything but just stay there, begging. And waiting for the knife to come at him, sharp and angry.

But the woman was in charge, and all she did was scream. Gary wished he could somehow *turn* to her inside the mind they seemed to share to warn her about what was coming.

And then the man spoke, his mouth bleeding, his eyes red, his anger palpable. "Shut up, you whore. You could have killed me with that stunt. I'll make you shut up...."

Gary could tell the guy wasn't listening to her pleas. And somehow, inside the dream, he knew that this was the clearest look he'd gotten of the man—even asleep, Gary realized that every other time he'd had the dream, he had awakened before this point.

The knife whispered into view as the man's arm came around. His left arm and hand were wrapped in something. One of his legs looked pretty messed up, but the man didn't seem to notice it—he was powered by anger and adrenaline. The man looked down at her and Gary, cowering in the bed, and smiled.

The knife danced in the man's crazed hand.

"And now, bitch, you die," he croaked, the words full of menace.

Gary tried to put his hands up, but they wouldn't move. The knife curved toward his face, and just before the knife was to strike, he heard something shouted inside his mind.

Gary knew immediately that the woman had not yelled it—he had heard what the woman was thinking in her final moment. "Their" lips had not moved, but the words were clear in his mind. They were the last thing he heard before the dream ended as abruptly as a car wreck on a dark country road.

"Oh, God, Chris, help me!"

Gary sat up, fully awake.

The headache was on him like an angry surf, crashing over him, pulling him down. He got up and went to the open window, leaning his head down against the sill like he'd just run a marathon.

This time it had been different—he had realized that he was somehow inside the body of someone else, some woman, and the man was talking to her, not Gary. The man with the knife had called the woman a whore before, and tonight he had called her a bitch. But the knife was the same, sharp and shiny with reflected light from the doorway behind him.

And that last word before the dream had ended—the woman had called out a name in her mind. That hadn't happened before.

And then the man's face clicked in his mind.

It lasted just a second, the sudden recognition. The face, the hard line of the man's jaw, the way the hair had receded back from the forehead in a way that made the man's eyebrows look ominous and scary. There was something he'd glimpsed in those bloodied features that reminded Gary of someone, some face he'd seen before.

Gary sat back down on his bed, the windows open, and thought back.

They say that the brain works in crazy ways. And the dreams we have use images and people from our past—could this guy be someone he knew?

And then something clicked into place—he could almost hear it. The man *was* someone from his past.

The headache surged, cresting like a wave on the ocean. He sat down hard on the bed, reaching for the bottle of Advil on his side table. He popped some in his mouth, neglecting to count them. He'd stopped counting them a while ago—now he just went by the size of the pile in his palm. He swallowed them dry and tried to sleep.

# Chapter 8

Vincent could see that his brother, Tony Luciano, wasn't having a very good Wednesday.

Vincent sat in one of the comfortable chairs at the massive wooden conference room table, watching his brother run the meeting. Vincent was trying to not shake his head in disappointment. His brother just didn't have a backbone—no wonder his "business" was going into the toilet.

This meeting and the one that had come just before it hadn't been good, and Vincent could sense the storm of problems that had been born. Tony would have to deal with all of those issues before Vincent and he could even get started on all the other things they needed to get done today. But it was still a very big day for their family—it felt like things were finally coming to a head, after weeks and weeks of talking. This meeting would resolve at least some of their problems.

One way or another.

"And lastly, we have those truckers up in Champaign–Urbana that aren't working with our union. Those men will have to be dealt with, because if we don't, the other trucking companies in the area will be able to undercut our prices and service levels. Someone needs to talk to them about things," Jack Fremonti said, sitting back from the conference table. "That's all I've got."

There was a smattering of polite laughter from the other men arrayed around the polished oak table—Jack Fremonti, the director of operations, had been speaking for over twenty minutes straight.

Vincent figured it was always like this—Jack looked like the kind of guy that once he got started talking, it would be exceedingly hard to shut up.

And Tony had never cut him off.

What was wrong with him?

All these stupid men quibbling about their little problems, talking and talking about how they were going to solve them.

Vincent knew that none of the people at this table, least of all his brother, knew the first thing about really solving problems. If there was anyone at this table that could fix problems, and fix them for good, it was Vincent.

While these people had been playing around for the past ten years, he'd really been *out* there, running an organization, making money, getting things done.

Sure, he'd run into trouble here and there, especially with the East St. Louis gang called the "Red Dogs," but he had dealt with them as best as he could.

Vincent thought this meeting was a huge waste of time. Tony's methods clashed horridly with Vincent's gut impression—he understood that Tony had tried to take the family legit, but it hadn't worked, and now he had to sit here and listen to these men drone on and on about nothing.

Things had changed so much in the thirty years since he and Tony had sat and listened to their grandmother talk about the old days in New York City. Had all her words been lost on his older brother?

Tony Luciano nodded at Jack Fremonti. "Okay. The St. Louis Beverage Company problem is being looked into. Louisville is fine—I just talked to them this morning, and they're informed of my concerns. Louisville will be an important market for us, and we need to grow them right, from the start, if they're going to make the kind of money I think they're capable of. And it might be a good idea for some of us to go down there next month and make an appearance, just to show them how it's done."

Some of the other men glanced at each other curiously. Vincent looked up at his brother, interested for the first time during the entire meeting.

Tony looked around at the six other men around the table, his eyes stopping on Vincent for a moment, as if drawing strength and resolve from him.

Vincent glanced around the table and saw the six other men dressed exactly as his brother was, all decked out in expensive, conservative business suits, each wearing a muted tie that drew no attention to itself. None of them was wearing jewelry; none was dressed in a way that set them apart from ordinary businessmen—none of them even smoked. Smoking was illegal in the entire office building where they had their offices, for Christ's sake! No stogies, no guns, no lackeys or women to run and get them drinks or take notes, nothing but legitimate business.

His father wouldn't have recognized this meeting for what it was supposed to be—even if he were still alive to stroll in here and observe.

And right now, there was nothing Vincent needed more than a smoky room filled with fighters and scrappers, working hard in whatever way they could to grow their business. He had never seen that kind of fight in his brother, so it made sense that no one in his organization would either. But somewhere along the line, Tony had realized that he'd taken the family down the wrong road.

He'd tried to save the family from itself after his father went to jail—at least, that's what he'd told Vincent not too many weeks ago. Tony also said he'd almost destroyed it in the process.

No, this wasn't a meeting of powerful men—this was like an undertakers' convention or some corporate meeting in downtown St. Louis. There was no way that any of these men could project the kind of respect they deserved. This family was dying out, victim of a hostile corporate takeover from a bunch of suits and a bunch of ideas that would have served the Disney corporation well. A powerful organization, turned into a boring and toothless corporation.

Vincent Luciano hated it.

He hated even sitting at a table with these men. But after many, many months of talks with his brother, it sounded like things were about to change.

Tony continued, still looking at his brother and avoiding the eyes of everyone else in the room. "As for the St. Louis Beverage Company, their trucks and transportation equipment are privately owned and operated out of garage in Lynwood, Missouri. It's time to play hardball with them. A couple of truck fires, or maybe a fire at the garage itself, and they'll come around."

Silence around the table.

It was as if Tony had stood up and said that he had recently engaged in sexual congress with all of these men's wives at the same time during an amazing weekend in Cancun.

The silence was so thick that Vincent almost laughed. He'd expected some type of reaction to his brother's words, but this was what he had feared the most. There were no shouts, no anger, no one raising their voices or arguing with Tony.

These men had done business in such a civilized manner for so long, they couldn't even imagine infighting. Vincent's grandmother had warned them about betrayals and double-crosses; she'd cautioned the young boys about the inherent problems that came with any familial, patriarchal organization. Always keep one eye on the men around them, she'd said.

On the "good" side, there was not enough fire in the bellies of any of these men to challenge Tony for leadership of the organization—but Vincent would have to keep an eye on that, if things changed the way he wanted them to. If something happened to Tony, control of the family would fall to him.

It had been decided a long time ago, not long after his father had gone to jail, that there would be no more strong-arm tactics and no more of the behavior that had, for so long, typified the way his family had done business. Tony had led the change, taking the family in a new direction. Vincent had argued against it, too loudly and for too long, and it had gotten him kicked out.

Many years had passed without any words between the two brothers, and so the recent spate of invitations to lunches and dinners from his older brother had surprised Vincent. At first it had been about getting to know each other again, but inevitably the talk had turned to the family business. Vincent had fibbed, but only a little, saying things were going well, and that was when Tony first spoke about the problems he was having with the organization.

For all intents and purposes, the American Mafia was dead, as far as anyone could tell. Gotti had finally fallen in 1992, and with him the inestimable power of the East Coast and New York Mafia. It had been coming for years. The FBI and the New York City prosecutor's office, especially Rudy Giuliani, had swept in with too much money and too many sweetheart immunity deals. Too many "made" guys and people with damaging information had rolled over and testified and then disappeared to Idaho or somewhere else in the Witness Protection Program. The Mob's connections inside the New York City government and the federal government evaporated, and with them, the wealth of information the various families had used for decades to stay ahead of the authorities. Now, the golden years were gone. The current thinking was that the New York Mob was dead, or at least lying very low for a few years, watching and waiting.

But that didn't mean the entire Mob was dead. There were splinter groups and cells of activity all across the country, and sometime in the late '80s and early '90s, most of those groups had done exactly what the Luciano family had done here in St. Louis—gone legit. Now, all or most of their activities were completely legal, and even those that were illegal were so carefully concealed that only a few people inside each organization knew about them.

But Vincent knew there were still old-fashioned mob guys out there—he only had to look at the sudden and extremely profitable resurgence of legalized gambling across the nation to realize that they were out there, working behind the scenes, "lobbying" lawmakers to bend the rules and legalize activities that used to be contained in Atlantic City and Las Vegas. Those bastions of mob rule were still clicking along and turning a healthier profit every year, but now groups in Louisiana and Arizona and Florida had managed to convince their local officials to let them have a little taste of that pie.

And Vincent respected those groups for it. He thought his brother was on to something with his latest idea.

Tony owned two gambling riverboats permanently docked in East St. Louis, Illinois, just across the Mississippi from St. Louis proper. Actually, Tony owned one and a half—one was turning a good profit, but the other was months away from opening and months behind schedule. Tony had staked all the money he could get his hands on to build the spectacular new riverboat from the keel up, but it had cost more than he'd expected. Now it was delayed, and the business was in real financial stress.

Tony was planning on buying two more riverboats in St. Charles, just ten miles west of St. Louis, but that was down the road—he needed to get the second riverboat open and running first. He had people looking into floating one of the East St. Louis boats down to Louisville on a twice-monthly basis, where gambling was still illegal but riverboat gambling was judiciously overlooked. If his boat could get down there, it would be all the money they could scoop up and bring home.

But these were all "legit" businesses—at least, they were operating inside the law.

Jack Fremonti finally broke the long, painful silence. "Well, Tony, I don't know if that's the way we should approach this situation. They want out of our contract with their drivers and deliverymen, and I'm sure there's some way we can negotiate with them and come to a peaceful solution that's still in our favor. To burn them out," he said, glancing at the others around the table, "well, that seems a little harsh, don't you think?"

The other suits were nodding along with him.

Vincent Luciano frowned and wondered what his brother would say. He'd coached Tony for weeks leading up to this meeting, but Vincent still didn't know if his brother would have the stones to move forward. He was sure that if his grandmother was still alive and sitting in on this meeting, she'd be laughing at them.

"Mama Leo"—Leonita Luciano—had been the real thing. Only two generations back from her was the one name that had been most responsible for establishing the New York Mob's power base.

Her grandfather had been Lucky Luciano. She'd learned much from her grandfather and visited him many times while he was in prison at Dannemora and later at the minimum-security prison at Great Meadow.

The man had started the organization of competing Italian and Sicilian families into cooperating ventures instead of competing businesses. It had been Lucky that had instituted the *"Padrino,"* or godfather, concept, where the oldest man in each family had the last and final word on the policies and businesses of each *'familia.'* He had established the cooperative spirit and divided up the city of New York into areas for each family to oversee, organizing them and at the same time reducing the likelihood of violent confrontations by clearly defining each's area of responsibility.

Leonita's father had been the head of the Luciano family during the sixties, but he'd gone down in the 1967 wave of police actions and arrests following the establishment of the now-defunct Italian Defense League. The League, established by an ex-*capo* by the name of Joey Paloma, had been borne out of the need for Italian Americans to feel better about the public's opinion of them. In effect, it had been a civil rights movement for Italian Americans. It had ended up also being a very public embarrassment to the Mob.

The police backlash had jailed her father and three other *capos.* Senior men in each organization had stepped in and kept the businesses going, and each of the jailed *capos* had been out of prison within a couple of months, but for Leonita's father, it had signaled the beginning of the end. He had felt that the organizations would never be breached, but his informants in the police force and mayor's offices had evaporated, and no word had come to any of his men that there was a move planned against the Lucianos by the cops. He'd been taken completely by surprise and arrested right out on 53rd Street, handcuffed and taken off in a police car like a little kid stealing apples off a fruit cart.

That, more than anything, had angered and saddened the elder Luciano. He was the head of the Luciano family and one of the most powerful men in the city. The public embarrassment had sickened him. The lack of respect that his organization and his money should have earned made him angrier than even his own arrest, because they were harbingers of things—and times—to come.

Leonita was his eldest child, a daughter, and she had been smart and ruthless. And she'd learned well from her father and made good use of her knowledge and connections. And those connections had been important: because of her name, she enjoyed a free ride in the business for a few years. And instead of sitting back on her laurels and just taking, as many of the younger generation had done, she'd worked her connections and established herself as a powerful leader of her own small group on the Lower East Side.

But "Mama Leo" had also seen the writing on the wall—she had always been very good at picking up on little details. She was a sponge for knowledge. She'd had success in building her organization, and when her father had come to her on the last day in August of 1968 and told her to leave town, she hadn't taken it personally. In fact, she'd already considered the idea herself, rejecting it out of respect for her family.

He'd come to her, given her a sizeable sum of money and a warning—bad times were coming and she should leave town for her own protection. When she'd asked him where, he'd said, "I don't know. Just someplace away from here, someplace where you'll be safe. Your mother and I will visit as soon as we can."

With a heavy heart, Leonita Luciano had come west, bringing her smarts and her money and some of her organization with her. Her parents and friends had been sad, but anyone in the family with a sense of what was to come saw the move as an intelligent one—for the family to survive and grow, it would have to branch out.

She made it to the Mississippi before she found what she was looking for—virgin territory. A place where they had never known her type of criminal. Of course, the mob had been and was still very powerful two hundred miles north, in Chicago, but St. Louis and the areas around it were open for the taking, and that was where she settled down and started her own "business."

"Mama Leo" Luciano and her soldiers arrived in St. Louis in 1946 and settled in a small bedroom community east of town named O'Fallon, Illinois. The town was just starting to grow, and there was some talk that "Mama Leo" used her growing influence in the local and state governments to get the new Scott Air Force Base located near O'Fallon, overnight doubling the family's lucrative real estate investments.

It had all started out as a typical mob operation, with "Mama Leo" setting herself up as the boss and making four or five of her top soldiers into *capos* and allowing them to recruit soldiers from the local population. There was already a small Italian population in the St. Louis area, and they recruited from these men, growing the organization up to almost a hundred members, fifteen or twenty of them "made" men. They got into real estate, money laundering, and loan sharking and began influencing the local unions, especially those involved in the booming downtown construction business. "Mama Leo" began the idea of hijacking shipments of cargo at Lambert Field, the big airport north of St. Louis, an idea that was adopted back in New York City by the Gambino family at John F. Kennedy Airport in Queens.

By 1971, when "Mama Leo" officially retired and her son Ginovese took over, the business had grown to rival that of the Chicago mob. There had even been official negotiations between the St. Louis and Chicago mobs as to the agreed-upon extent of their influences.

She would be laughing at them right now, if she were here. Laughing at Tony and his bunch of suits. They looked like city council members, not a group of men to be feared or respected.

"No, I don't want to do it the normal way," Tony began, tentatively. "If other 'clients' see us negotiating with the St. Louis Beverage Company, they might feel encouraged to do the same."

The others sat, listening. They hung on his words, wondering where Tony was going. To Vincent, it looked like they were scared.

"I know we've been a lot more civilized in the past few years," Tony continued, "but maybe we've gotten too civilized. The '90s have not been kind to us or our business. We're barely hanging in there. And we need cash to finish the *Princess Margaret*. None of these other enterprises," he paused and glanced at Vincent. "None of these other things will earn us enough money to finish the casino boat, and without that, we're finished. I'm tired of waiting for this organization—this *familia*—to be successful."

There was no response from the others. No reaction to the use of the old name for their now-defunct organization, except for a few quick glances at Jack Fremonti. He was the most senior of them, and they were following his lead. If anyone was going to argue this point, it would be him.

Vincent liked the use of the Italian term for family—it added a Sicilian tone, something that had been sorely lacking for years. But they were too entrenched in the way things had been done for so long—they would never see the direction Tony needed to go, much less go along with it.

Such auspicious beginnings, Vincent thought. Such honored roots. Didn't these men understand what flowed through his and his brother's veins? Didn't they want to remember what it felt like to have control and power and to wield it to some end?

The Mafia in the United States had grown from desperate roots to such power because they had wanted it more than anyone else. They had taken all the opportunities, and made a few of their own.

They had started out protecting their own, and it had grown naturally, organically, from a mutual aid society to an organization that wielded real, tangible power.

And never, not once in the entire proud history of the Mafia that Vincent had spent the past few years carefully studying, had a group of men sat around a table like this in fancy suits and tried to 'negotiate' with someone who wouldn't give them the respect they deserved.

It didn't work that way.

The old ways had been better, when a neighborhood respected its leader, when the *padrino* would set up his office in the local tavern every few weeks and the citizens of the community would line up to ask for his advice or his assistance in their welfare. The *padrino* would quietly sip his drink and listen as each man or woman was led in to tell their stories, each asking for assistance. Sometimes it was for a loan, or a job for their oldest boy. Sometimes it was for a little protection from toughs, or maybe it was for a kind word in the right ear that would allow their youngest daughter to attend the school of her choice. Or maybe it was a plea for help because the police could or would not intervene.

Each a favor, asked with grace and humility, and granted or denied by the *padrino* with a simple nod or shake of his head. Assistants would take notes and take each person away to get pertinent details. After a moment, the next story would begin.

But it wasn't just a chance for them to speak to the most powerful man in their neighborhood—it also served to remind the citizens that the *padrino* was their godfather. He ran the neighborhood and everything in it, and if you needed something straightened out or you needed someone spoken to, he was the man you came to. First. You didn't go to the cops—how could they care as much about you as your *padrino* did? There was no need to involve 'outsiders'—your *padrino* was all you needed to rely on, and it would only take a humble, honorable request for assistance to solve the problem.

Of course, that meant that if your *padrino* ever needed something of you, hesitation or reluctance would not be tolerated. And in most cases, the citizens would not flinch to help.

Such is how neighborhoods were supposed to run. And cities, and towns, for that matter. What people needed was a strong, caring family to watch over them. It had worked for a long time back in the old country, and it had worked even better in the United States until the government had stepped in and tried to stop the families from caring for their neighbors.

These men had long ago forgotten the traditions of his family and its proud history—more importantly, they would fight his brother every step of the way.

Every night on television, it seemed Vincent saw another story about another senseless killing somewhere: some kid walks into his junior high school with a rifle and blows three or four classmates away, or some nut-case kills his family and tries to blame it on mysterious intruders burglarizing his house, miraculously leaving him with only minor scratches while the rest of the family is mercilessly killed.

Or that story he'd seen on the news not too recently about the mass murderer guy the police had finally caught after he had spent years wandering the nation in his dirty white van, killing people indiscriminately and even taking small parts of them with him. And they'd only caught that guy on some kind of fluke, from what he remembered. What was going on with these people? What kind of country was this, anyway? Was no one in control? Someone needed to step up, to take charge.

Jack finally spoke. "No, Tony," he said. "There is no way that I can sign off on this—the organization cannot proceed in this manner. Your heavy-handed tactics won't work, just as they didn't work for your father. He was a great man, but the days of that type of practice are long dead." Fremonti shook his head. The other men around the table nodded in agreement.

Vincent watched his brother closely.

Tony nodded slowly, formulating his answer.

"I'm sorry that's the way you feel, Jack. But I've spent a long time thinking about it, and I've decided to scale back on our legal activities and take this family back to its proud roots. If that means 'heavy-handed tactics,' so be it. Can you get on board with that?"

Jack Fremonti glanced down at Vincent, then around at the others. After a long moment, he finally shook his head.

"I know you've been talking to your brother—I don't know what he's been filling your head with," Fremonti said, "but taking the family back into criminal activities will only bring the cops down on us. It'll bring us back to the 1950s. And I doubt even that could save your casino, Tony."

Tony glanced at Vincent. Vincent knew what was going through his mind, but there was nothing he could do to help him. And he wouldn't have helped him, even if he could. His brother had to do this on his own, had to get his fire back.

"My brother and I have been talking, that is true," Tony said, leaning back in his chair. "We've decided that the riverboat is the future of our family here in St. Louis—if we play our cards right, we could control all legalized gambling up and down the Mississippi from here. But with the gambling comes a whole host of less-than-legal activities, and we need to control those too, from the start. And we need an infusion of cash to finish the *Margaret*."

His brother, Vincent thought, though finally showing some back-bone, was defending his position. He needed to remember he was the *padrino*—he didn't need to explain anything to anyone.

Vincent moved his hands slowly under the table. He watched, but none of them reacted. Too bad—anyone from his crew would have known better.

"Well, Tony," Fremonti said, "if that's your course of action, I must insist on leaving and staying out of it. I'm not going to be a party to that kind of thing. Pressure applied correctly, yes. But nothing violent, and nothing illegal."

Tony nodded carefully. "Are you sure, my friend?"

Jack nodded and stood.

"I'm afraid so. Gentlemen, please excuse me."

Tony glanced at Vincent, nodding.

Vincent pulled the Beretta automatic out of his snakeskin boot and raised the gun from beneath the table, pointing it at Fremonti.

There were looks, gasps.

"Will you reconsider, my friend?" Tony said quietly.

All the eyes in the room were on the gun, but Fremonti's eyes moved from the gun to look at Tony, his eyes narrowing. After a moment, he shook his head and strode quickly for the door.

Vincent pulled the trigger twice in rapid succession, practiced, calm. Fremonti slumped to the floor.

Silence in the room.

Vincent stood and walked around the table and he shot Jack once more, just to be sure.

A cloud of gunpowder hung in the air, and one of the men coughed awkwardly. It broke the silence and, as Vincent sat back down, placing the gun on the table in front of him, the other men all started talking at the same time, suggesting ways to turn the family around, ways to make money and complete the riverboat.

Vincent picked the gun up again after a moment and the table went quiet again. He pulled the slide free and checked the gun, then looked at Tony.

"Anyone else unhappy with the situation?" Tony said to the men at the table, his voice low but clear.

Their eyes met Tony's, inevitably glancing at the body on the floor, blocking the exit. They shook their heads.

"Good," Tony said. "Let's make a new start of it then."

Vincent stood, walking to door in the conference room that led into Tony's office.

"Meeting adjourned," Tony said. "Please leave through my office."

The others stood and fled, let out the second door by Vincent. As each filed past, they looked at him like frightened sheep, leaving Tony and Vincent alone.

Vincent smiled at his brother. "So, we're really going to do this, then?"

Tony nodded, staring at the body on the floor. To Vincent, he looked a little sick to his stomach.

"Yeah, we are. When is the buy?"

"Tomorrow night."

"Can you get this cleaned up quickly?"

Vincent nodded. "Yeah. I've got it covered. It's a clear shot out through the hallway out to the van, and I know a place for him," he said, nodding at the body.

"Cleaning the carpet will be the hardest part," Tony said.

Vincent handed Tony a card, which read A-1 Carpets and Floors. "They're coming tonight to rip up the carpet and replace it with a darker color. I told them we had a party and some grape juice got spilled. We only have to make the stains a little less obvious—one of my guys will do that," he said, nodding toward the other room.

Tony smiled and Vincent knew what he was thinking—Tony had always been the thinker of the family, and Vincent had been the doer. It was nice to see that they could work together so well after so much animosity, after so much time apart.

And as Vincent looked at the body on the carpet, he saw the clear evidence. They were on their way.

# Chapter 9

She was sitting on the porch when the song came on once more, mocking her. She'd been crying, hoping they would play "Georgia" like they had a few nights before, hoping it would remind her of Chris and their good times. Instead, they played the song that made her think of crazy things, of freedom, of revenge.

It was "Independence Day" by Martina McBride, a song about an abused woman who kills her husband by burning down their home around them. It was a sad song, told from the point of view of their young daughter as she watches the home burn, but it was also joyful—the woman was free, finally, from the man who was slowly killing her. And the mother had saved her daughter from a similar fate.

The song had been on the radio a lot lately, and every time it came on, it made Judy feel strangely empowered. Maybe she didn't have the courage to do what the woman in the song did, but maybe she could escape, at least. Could she be clever enough to get away forever? There had to be a way out of this endless cycle of hell in which she found herself trapped.

He was upstairs, in their bed. She couldn't be near him right now—she wanted to be as far away from him as possible.

Trying to do anything to him was pointless—his family was too powerful. Maybe a year ago, but now he and his brother were getting along, working together, and if something happened to Vincent, Tony would surely be able to find her no matter how far she ran.

No, if she were going to get out of this, she'd have to do it on her own. She would have to get away from him once and for all. That meant that she had to make him think that she was dead.

She could lose herself in her paintings, but that only worked for as long as he wasn't around—she shuddered at the thought of Vincent finding out.

But if things kept going the way they were, she wouldn't have to pretend.

Tonight, he'd cut her hair off.

There had been no warning about what was coming. He'd come into the house in a huff, the alcohol so evident on his breath that it was like a hazy cloud around his face. His dinner was warm and ready. The house was clean, and she had a cold beer sitting out waiting for him, but none of that mattered.

He had come straight at her, angry about something out in the yard that she couldn't even understand, muttering about the plants looking dead and screaming at her for not keeping up a nice yard so that when people drove by they didn't laugh at him. She had no idea what he was talking about—he was the one who usually took care of the yard—and was about to say so when he punched her hard in the face.

Usually his beatings started with slaps or squeezed arms or pulled hair—the punching and kicking came later, if at all. Sometimes he just got tired and went away. A fight that started with a full-on punch told her that he was really spun up about something, and as the punch leveled her, she made an instantaneous decision as she crumbled to the floor. She fell and lay perfectly still.

He'd bent over her in the kitchen, yelling, but without someone fighting back or fending him off, he quickly lost interest. She could feel his eyes on her. Judy just lay there, perfectly still, and then out of the corner of her eye she saw blood on the floor under her head.

When he stood again and kicked her in the ribs, she really did pass out.

There was no way to know how much time had passed before she woke up, but the lights in the kitchen had been flicked off. She could hear the sound of the TV coming from the living room, and as she sat up, she noticed that some of the food was missing from the kitchen table.

She put her hands on the floor to push herself up, and that was when she noticed the hair on the kitchen floor. It was all around her, patches and clumps and straggly pieces, and some of it was on her clothes.

Her hands drifted up to her head.

He hadn't shaved her clean, but the hair had been roughly cut, sharply angled. It had been one of the few things of hers left, one of the small things she could be proud of. Now it was scattered around her. She hadn't been to a beauty salon in a long time, but this is what the floors of those places looked like—covered with hunks of hair. Her hands told her that her hair was now short as a boy's on all sides.

She'd looked at her reflection in the toaster and saw that she looked like a doll some mean little girl had tortured.

Judy didn't know anything else to do but cry.

After a while, her tears faded, and she got up and cleaned up his mess. She could hear him upstairs snoring, so she busied herself in the kitchen, cleaning up the dishes and the floor. The hair was hard to throw away, but she scooped it all up onto a folded newspaper and carried it carefully to the trashcan. It wasn't until the third trip to the trash that Judy actually looked at the paper she was carrying.

Man Dies in Car Accident, the headline read.

She didn't notice the clumps of hair that slid off the paper and fell to the floor around her feet.

The story was about a man from a town one county over who had been driving through O'Fallon. He'd cracked up his car on Blackwood Lane, crashing against a tree on a lonely stretch of the road that ran north of the town. The man had evidently been drinking and speeding—not the greatest combination.

And Blackwood Lane was a bad place to try your luck—the long winding road had few lights but plenty of notoriously sharp turns, blind corners, and narrow shoulders. Wrecks happened every year, and so many people had died in accidents on the road over the years that a mystique had built up around the area.

Blackwood Lane was supposedly haunted.

The author of the newspaper article had pointed out ominously that there had been twelve fatalities on a short stretch of Blackwood over the past twenty years, including an accident involving a carload of teenagers that killed two teens and left two others paralyzed. One of the teens killed in the wreck was a young woman, and in subsequent years, it was said that her spirit haunted that stretch of road, causing even more accidents. The guy writing the newspaper article sounded like he was swaying in the direction of believing the tale.

Judy couldn't tear herself away from the description of the car wreck. She'd dreamed a thousand times that Vincent would have an accident on the way home, and here was the story of some other poor sap who'd done that very thing.

Why couldn't it have been Vincent?

Vincent had come home drunk tonight, driving his Mustang with gusto and gunning the engine as he'd come up the long dirt driveway.

Why couldn't it have been him?

Suddenly, she knew she couldn't wait anymore for something to happen to him. If she were going to escape, she'd have to do it herself.

She had to run away—or disappear in a way that made Vincent think she was dead.

I have to drown, or do something else where there would be no body for them to find, she thought to herself.

Lake O'Fallon was just two miles from the house. She could walk there, leave her clothes and shoes on the shore, and swim to freedom. Or at least to somewhere she could climb out without leaving any footprints.

It would be hard to leave her paintings, hard to leave the few mementos she had collected over the years. But she could do it.

This latest incident, his cutting off her hair, had pushed her over some mental line she had long ago drawn for herself. Judy felt like she had just spent the past four years floundering on the "good" side of that line.

Now she was over it, and there was no looking back.

She sat on the porch and wondered, and for the first time in more years than she could remember, she didn't feel afraid.

But she knew the feeling would last only until her next beating. If she were to ever be free, she would have to start planning—planning for real. No cathartic dreams of freedom, no hopeful and helpless fantasies of a real life.

No. It had to be real for it to matter at all.

# Chapter 10

He couldn't sleep. Gary got up and headed to the kitchen, looking for a drink. He got the glass of Pepsi poured and was looking for the bottle of Jack before he realized what he was doing. All the alcohol was long gone from his apartment, but the habit was hard to break. He could taste the bitterness of the whisky as it mixed with the sweetness of the cola.

He downed the cola, then drank two more. He didn't care about the caffeine at three in the morning—he wasn't planning on sleeping anytime soon. It was already Thursday, and he had to be at work in four hours. Gary grabbed the two-liter bottle and sat down in front of the TV, flipping it on and mindlessly surfing the channels. He grabbed his cigarettes and smoked two in a row, enjoying the scent of the smoke. For some reason, the smell of cigarette smoke always calmed him down, more so than the cigarettes themselves.

It didn't make any sense. He'd felt better, finally understanding that the dream wasn't about him—it was about some woman. And the crazy guy in the dream seemed familiar, but he'd not yet figured out who it was. He'd hoped the dream would go away, but it still came, night after night, over and over. And every time it was just as scary and ended just the same, with the name shouted in his mind and the intense headache upon waking.

He poured another drink and downed it, finding an old movie on the TV. It was some B movie, people running around being chased by dinosaurs. That wasn't the way it was in real life—when people were chasing you, bad things tended to happen. And you almost never escaped.

When his mother had died, it had only been dumb luck that he had survived. They'd been leaving to go somewhere unimportant. He'd dropped his baseball cap and gone back for it, and his mother had climbed into the car across the street and turned the ignition. Gary had picked up his hat and was hurrying toward the car. She was looking at him, smiling at him when she turned the key and the engine exploded and the car was engulfed in a fireball that knocked him off his feet, roiling over him like an angry animal made of fire and shrapnel.

Gary didn't remember much about the rest of that day. The federal agents had whisked him and his father away from the "safe house" where they had been hidden, moving them to a hotel for their safety. He remembered looking out the back window of the van as the agents drove them away—his mom's car still smoldering, the street full of firemen and policemen blocking off the area.

There had been an ambulance too, but Gary could see that the lights were off and he'd seen the two EMTs leaning casually against the vehicle. At that moment it had hit him—his mother was dead.

The movie on TV was boring—dinosaurs loose in some town, killing everything, and the Army trying to figure out how to stop them. Gary lit another cigarette, drawing deeply. He thought of stripes, white against dark, and smoke drifting through them. His mind drifted like the smoke around his head.

After a moment he shook his head, returning to reality. He grabbed the remote, flipping again through the channels, looking for anything to watch. Anything to get his mind off the dream.

# Chapter 11

Without much in the way of advance planning, Judy decided to move forward with her plan. She was being stupid, she knew it. Stupid and impulsive.

But at least running away would give her a fighting chance.

So on Saturday morning, just after the sounds of his new car faded into the distance, she found herself climbing up off the couch and going upstairs to pack.

Judy carefully picked through her small closet, getting out a set of clothes to wear—they had to be clothes he would not notice were missing. She dressed in a pair of jeans and a shirt she hadn't worn in years. She gathered a few things together in a roomy backpack from the attic: some makeup, some pictures, and all the money she had. Last, she picked out a skirt and top he would remember and put them in the backpack, too.

The top drawer of her dresser always stuck. She pulled on it and finally wiggled it free, setting it on top of the dresser and reaching around the back.

Taped to the wood was a resealable plastic bag containing the two things in life that she cherished the most: the letter from San Antonio and the engagement ring from Chris. She stuffed it into her pack.

On top of the dresser, she left the note in a place where he was sure to find it.

She'd worked on it all day yesterday and hidden it—her brain couldn't fathom what he would do if he'd found it before she left.

Judy looked around their bedroom and saw nothing else she cared about. It was sad how little of her there really was in this house. Even when she and Vincent had been getting along better, this place had never really felt like a home.

Judy set her bag at the top of the stairs, then reached up and pulled down the attic stairs, climbing back up into the stuffy attic.

The low ceiling of the room was studded with nails, poking in from the roof. The small room was filled with boxes, a few pieces of old furniture, Christmas decorations, and a tree leaning up against one wall. She wiggled around behind several large cardboard boxes and pulled out her paintings—she wanted to look at them one more time. There were quite a few—she had been painting off and on for years. They were all here: her friends, her sanity. She knew it was a stupid thing, but the paintings had brought her so much joy, especially in the past few months.

It would have been great to be free to display them—sometimes she dreamed of having her own place, with every wall decorated with her paintings. But she knew that would never happen here with Vincent, and there was no way she could take them with her.

Every painting was of the sea. Several were of waves crashing into rocky coastlines, throwing up a foam of white and blue. Some were of boats at sea, lashed by heaving waves as they tried to right their keels and save themselves. Others were of whales or seagulls or empty beaches, lonely and quiet.

Her favorite painting was in the back—she pulled it out slowly, dusting it off, admiring it. The painting was of a lighthouse perched on a tall cliff at night, the huge yellow beacon of light piercing the dark clouds, reflecting off the peaks of the waves as they came in from sea. Near the base of the lighthouse was a small parking lot with several cars, and nearby was a high cliff. Below, breakers crashed into a rocky shore. It was a detailed piece, with every element seeming to leap from the canvas. It was a beautiful work, and the one that Judy most wished she could take with her.

But where she was going, she didn't need these paintings. She would be free to buy all the canvas and acrylic she wanted and paint however often she wished. She wouldn't have to race to hide her things in the attic when she heard him roar up the driveway.

Judy Luciano climbed downstairs and left the house, locking the door behind her. She sighed, looking at the front of his house, then turned and left. Judy had with her everything she would ever need.

------

They were having dinner soon, and she had the kids ready for their father. He'd be home any moment from work—he worked for one of the most prestigious architecture firms in Sacramento. He was successful, and Judy was happier than she had ever believed she could be.

Chris came in, looking great, as always. Taller than when they had dated in high school, and happier. He only had time to throw his keys onto the little table by the front door before the kids rushed him, smothering him with hugs. Judy stood to the side and watched—this was her favorite part of the day, when Chris came home.

Her husband spent a minute with Tina and her younger brother Joshua, asking them about their day and smiling at their stories—he was a good father to their children. He was always patient and never raised a hand to either of them.

Chris was a good man.

When he was finished, Chris gave each child a good-natured swat on the fanny and told them to get ready for dinner. They scooted off, giggling, as he walked over to her and put his arms around her.

Perfect.

Judy stumbled on a rough patch of the field she was crossing, falling out of her daydream. She looked down at the ring she was wearing—she almost never wore his engagement ring, but walking to the lake, it had seemed perfect.

The trail led from the field through a small stand of trees, and she could see the lake just past them, heat shimmering off the surface and distorting the far shore. Someday she'd find him—she'd find him and they'd make a life together. Or she would die trying. She was tired of prison.

This edge of the lake was deserted—she'd planned on coming out here, on the opposite side from the boat docks and the merry-go-round, the quiet side of the lake. It was Saturday, and already there were several boaters on the other side of the lake.

Setting down the backpack, she opened it up. Inside the backpack was everything she was taking with her—two changes of clothes, her money, a couple of trinkets Vincent would never miss, and the letter from San Antonio; she slipped off the ring and put it into the envelope with the letter.

Judy would go there first and see if she could get her inheritance from her parents' estate. She hoped that the intervening years would not have had any effect on her ability to claim the money.

From among the contents of the backpack she took out a large plastic bag that she'd removed from a sleeping bag in their attic, the kind you could seal along the top. She also took out a roll of fishing line. Opening the plastic bag, she stuffed the backpack down inside, sealing up the bag tight with as much air inside as she could manage, then tied a long length of heavy fishing line around it.

She stripped down to the bathing suit she had on under her

clothes, dropping the clothes she had been wearing in a small pile on the muddy beach. She walked out into the water, leaving obvious footprints, and threw the plastic bag as far as she could into the water, smiling when it floated to the top.

The water was intensely cold and smelled brackish. She walked out to the pack and fished the line out of the water, tying it around her waist, and then swam off, moving parallel to the lake shore.

After a minute, her body warmed to the exertion and she swam harder, feeling like an escaping fugitive.

She glanced up at the distant boaters—it was important for no one to see her. The note she had left at home would bring Vincent to the lake and make clear what she had done. She hoped they'd drag the lake and eventually give up on finding her body.

Judy swam for another fifteen minutes and then began scouting the shore, looking for someplace where she could climb up and out of the water without leaving any footprints. Finally, she saw a large rock under some overhanging tree limbs.

Judy swam toward the stone, suddenly growing tired, as if her body knew the swim was almost over. The rock was large and difficult to climb, but she finally managed to pull herself up and out of the water. That was when her weakened body betrayed her.

The swim had been more exertion than she had known in weeks, and the effort required to pull herself out of the water and onto the large rock was too much. Her legs buckled and she began to slip off the rock, now wet from her body. She scrambled, reaching for the top of the rock and a low branch, getting a tenuous grip on the rough tree limb. Judy curled the other hand around the limb and started to pull herself up, but there just wasn't any strength left in her arms or her shoulders. She scrabbled her legs against the slick rock and finally managed to get her feet up onto the top, and she let go, collapsing.

Judy lay there for a long moment, shaking, her hands scraped and bloodied from the bark of the tree. The sun beat down on her, drying her and the rock. It felt warm and glorious.

Finally, Judy sat up. Her left thigh was scraped and cut, seeping blood onto the boulder. It was amazing that she hadn't noticed it.

She looked around but saw no one else.

Judy tugged on the fishing line gingerly and saw the plastic bag come around the boulder, bobbing in the greenish water. She pulled it out. It was heavier—some water must've gotten inside.

Using the wet bag, she sprinkled lake water onto the bloodstain she had left atop the rock, trying to wash as much evidence of her presence as possible back into the water.

When she was happy with the way the boulder looked, Judy reached inside her swimsuit and pulled out the flip flops, putting them on her feet. Sliding over the top of the boulder, she turned around, hung her legs off the side facing away from the lake, climbed down off the rock, and started for the woods.

The boulder sat astride the shore of the lake, and behind it was a line of trees and a small path leading back into the woods. She tried to step on large rocks and tree branches to leave as few tracks as possible.

She followed the path for five or six minutes, winding into the forest, and in a clearing sat down to do something about her bleeding leg. She went through the bag—some of her clothes were wet, and there was water at the bottom. All the money was stuck together. She took her clothes out of the backpack and, glancing around, slipped out of her swimsuit. She pulled the clothes on, hating their wetness against her skin.

She wrapped the swimsuit around her thigh and tied it off—the bleeding had slowed, but she didn't have anything else to bandage with the cut. And she didn't have the time. The key now was distance—she needed lots of it, and the money would help.

It wasn't far to the highway. She could get a ride with someone there going south.

# Chapter 12

Gary's headache pounded like a drum, breaking his concentration. He swore he could feel the bones in his head pulsating with each heartbeat.

He'd taken twelve Advil so far today and still couldn't work—the light was too bright, streaming down from the skylights of the pit. It felt like a hangover, but not the good kind.

Fridays were usually busy at MacMillan, and today was no exception. Gary wasn't on a deadline, but he wasn't getting anything done, either.

The dream would not leave him alone.

Five more times last night, it had come. The accompanying headaches had come in waves.

Gary had started thinking about going to Sacramento to talk to his dad. He was hoping to describe the man in the dreams—maybe his dad would remember him, or help Gary place him.

It was a stupid idea, the mother of all stupid ideas—he hadn't been back to see his dad for a while. In fact, he planned on never returning. It didn't make sense; but then, neither did having these dreams.

He reached for the phone on his desk.

"Hey, man," Mike said into his phone—Gary could see him two rows away. "You look like crap today."

Gary smiled weakly. "Thanks, man—love you too. I gotta pass on tonight—I'm just gonna head home. Cool?"

Mike was quiet for a moment. "You have that dream again?"

Gary felt a chill run up his arm. It was not good, letting anyone know this much about him. "Uh, yeah. Not sleeping a lot. I'm going to relax and try to get some rest." He didn't think he sounded very convincing.

"Okay," Mike answered, sounding skeptical. "Call me if you need anything."

"Sure thing," Gary said, hesitating for a long moment and not hanging up. Mike waited on the other end, not breaking the silence. Finally, Gary spoke up.

"I need to go to Sacramento."

Mike glanced over at him, then put the phone down and came over to Gary's desk, motioning him into the hallway.

Gary joined him, sipping from the water fountain. Mike leaned on the wall next to him. After Gary finished drinking, he put his hands under the water and splashed some on his face.

Gary stood and dried his face as best he could. "I need to leave. I need to go up and see my father in Sacramento."

"Why?" Mike asked. "Do you think this dream is connected to your folks?"

Gary shook his head. "My mother died back in Illinois, and my father remarried a few years ago. And I don't know about any connection, but I know that...the dream is so real," he said, trailing off. "It has to be a memory. I need to talk to my father and see if he knows who the guy is."

Mike shook his head. "These are just dreams, Gary. They might be related to something in your past, but you would remember the guy if you had ever met him, don't you think? The guy can't be somebody from your past, can he?"

"I don't know, Mike. I really don't know," Gary said, shrugging. "All I know is that these dreams are ruining my life. And I don't remember this guy, but maybe my dad will. He doesn't sound like anyone I know or met out here in California, but maybe it was some guy back in Illinois. There's something in his voice that reminds me of the Midwest."

Gary looked at his only friend.

"Mike, I don't want to talk about this stuff. About my past."

Mike nodded, looking around. "Why?"

Gary was quiet. "I can't really get into it. But I need to go, and I'm worried about—well, this morning I blacked out."

It was so hard to ask for help.

"I'm worried about driving," Gary said finally. "Would you come with me?"

After a long moment, Mike nodded.

# Chapter 13

Vincent was standing on his front porch, reading the note.

It was a suicide note from his wife. She had gone to the lake, gone to kill herself.

He couldn't believe it. This was crazy. Things were finally starting to come together for him, and now this had to happen. He'd come home early to change clothes—tonight was the big meet, and he'd wanted to look halfway respectable. He'd pulled up around three o'clock, but he hadn't found his wife waiting for him. Vincent had gone upstairs to their bedroom, calling out her name. As he'd picked out some clothes to wear, he'd seen the note leaning up against the lamp on the dresser. Vincent guessed he was supposed to find the note tonight.

Maybe he'd have time to get her before she did anything stupid. God knew she wasn't bright enough to take care of herself. He was always trying to talk to her, to get her to listen, but she was just too thick-headed to see that he was trying to help her be a better person. She was always flirting with people in town, always trying to embarrass him.

He'd reminded her over and over about how important he was, about how many people in this town looked up to him, respected him, feared him. And things were only looking up, with the new deal he'd set up with his brother. Things were finally working out.

He shook his head—he didn't have time to deal with this. He walked back inside and picked up the phone, dialing Marcus.

"Hello?"

"Marcus? Vincent. I've got a problem I need you to help me with—my wife's gone missing. Can you meet me at Lake O'Fallon? The east side, by the boat docks."

The immediate and unquestioning affirmative response, followed by a couple of quick and insightful questions, reassured Vincent that Marcus was the man for this job. If anyone could track her down and find her, it was Marcus.

After Vincent ended the call, he grabbed his things and locked the house behind him. He threw the bundle of clean clothes and a nice pair of shoes into his new Mustang—he'd have to change after he finished at the lake. He didn't want to get his good clothes dirty.

Vincent gunned the engine, cursing his wife under his breath. She was going to have to learn to obey him, learn to be a proper wife if they were ever going to get along again. Tonight was too important for him to miss because of a rebellious wife—if anyone else heard about this, he'd be a laughingstock.

Taking Blackwood Lane, Vincent headed for the lake. Hopefully he could take care of this quickly and get on with the important events of the day. And when all this was over and he could concentrate, he and Judy would need to discuss this. Discuss it at length.

------

Judy wasn't making very good progress.

It was almost four hours later, and she was only a mile closer to San Antonio, or a mile further from her prison. She'd tried to concentrate on imagining how she would feel when she was finally away from this place, but the brambles and thorns kept pulling her back into reality.

It had taken her longer than she had guessed to get to the highway—for a while she had thought she'd gotten lost, but finally the din of traffic had cut through the trees. By then her leg had been throbbing, and she had to stop every few minutes. How could she make it to Texas when she couldn't even get out of the parklands that surrounded Lake O'Fallon?

Finally, the highway was before her, several lanes wide in each direction. She knew where she was. Staying in the trees, she started along the highway, heading south.

The truck stop was not far. Her plan was to walk there and get a ride from one of the truckers who'd stopped off there for lunch, but now it was almost three o'clock, and lunch was over. Now, she wasn't sure what to do.

Judy walked on, favoring her injured leg. The blood had slowed but not stopped—even with the ridiculous-looking tourniquet she'd fashioned, she knew she was losing blood and would have to stop soon and rest. She was tired and frightened, but the constant roar of the highway off to her side assured her that she was on the right path.

------

It took Vincent only a few minutes to get to the boat docks at the lake. He loved his new Mustang—it was fast and took the corners of Blackwood Lane like a champ. He used just a tiny tap of the brakes to slow the car going into the curves. And accelerating out of the tight turns was a blast.

He hated taking time out of his day to deal with stupid people, but he never minded getting there.

Judy had gone on foot to the lake—that was no surprise, since he didn't let her have a car. After he'd called Marcus, he'd searched the house but wasn't certain what, if anything, she had taken with her. He didn't know for sure what her intentions were.

He'd finished renting a small boat and was checking out the rope and anchor when Marcus arrived.

"Any idea where's she's gone?"

Vincent shook his head. "We'll check the other side of the lake—she was walking and would've come out over there," he said, pointing with his elbow as he coiled the long rope. "We'll start there and then move around, looking for her. The note said she was going to kill herself, but I don't believe it. I think she's trying to leave."

Marcus nodded and said nothing. He pushed the boat away from the dock and jumped in as Vincent pulled the engine to life.

Twenty minutes later, they found the clothes. Marcus stayed in the boat while Vincent waded to shore. He poked at the pile of clothes with a stick and then picked them up, digging through them. Just some clothes.

Was she thinking about getting away from him? Had she really killed herself?

He unfolded the note from his pocket and read it again. It said how she was supposedly tired of it all and needed to escape. Escape from what? He provided her with everything she needed. Sometimes he could get a little physical with her, but that was only when she angered him. The rest of her life was a breeze—she could sit around and do nothing all day long!

"What did you find?" Marcus shouted from the boat.

He waved the clothes in the air. "Some of her clothes. But I don't buy it—I think she's smarter than this."

Something in her eyes over the past week had changed. He'd seen flashes of defiance, moments when she'd fought back. Was she really trying to leave him?

A small part of his mind suggested letting her go. If they let her go and followed her, she might lead them to Chris and John O'Toole and all that beautiful missing money.

But Vincent didn't want to let her go, or admit that he had been unable to hang on to her. He had to find her.

Vincent waded out into the brackish water and muscled himself back into the small boat. "She's here somewhere. I know it." He pointed south. "And if she's running, she'll go for the highway. Go that way, but stay close in to shore. She couldn't have swum far."

Marcus pointed the boat in the direction of Vincent's outstretched hand. Vincent moved to the front of the boat and began scouting the trees and rocks that bordered the murky water.

------

There was supposed to be a road south from where she'd come out of the woods, but she hadn't found it yet. Crossing over the highway would've put her on the right side of the road to find the truck stop, and from there she'd be able to find a ride south to Texas. There were always truckers. Maybe one of them would find her attractive and feel sorry for her—Vincent had done everything he could to erase her beauty, but maybe some of it was still left.

Her foot caught on an exposed root and she tumbled to the ground, scraping one of her hands. Instead of getting up, she lay on the ground for a long time. The swim had been more exhausting than she'd guessed. And the hike afterwards even worse.

The ground was soft and wet, and for a moment she thought about just lying there on the cool ground until she died.

The truck stop was what got her moving again—that and thinking about Chris. She knew that if Vincent found her now, she was as good as dead. He'd beat her senseless and take her back to the prison he'd constructed for her. And somewhere along the line, he'd hit her too hard or push her down the stairs and kill her.

No, she needed to get away, to find Chris and start her life over. Her life in O'Fallon was on a downward spiral that could only end badly. Leaving would be the only way she would be able to salvage anything of her former self.

The blaring horn of a truck stirred her, and she climbed to her feet. She should've found the crossover by now, and as she continued for a few more minutes, she finally saw the bridge over the highway through the dense trees.

------

"Hold up, Marcus!" Vincent shouted, pointing.

There was a stain of red painting the top of a large rock that jutted out into the lake.

Marcus steered the boat over and Vincent jumped out, wading up to the rock. It was a large one, and on the side facing the lake, a long, dry runner of red snaked down into the water. On top of the rock was a flat area that looked as though it had been washed clean.

And on the side of the rock facing the shore, Vincent saw tracks in the muddy soil.

"This has to be it," Marcus said as he came ashore and tied the long rope off to a tree stump. "Looks like she hurt herself somehow."

Vincent nodded. There were no footprints but plenty of shoe prints, and all very fresh. They led off into the woods.

He walked over to the large rock and dabbed at it with his finger. It was blood. "She's hurt," Vincent said. "She won't be making very good time."

Marcus nodded, following the footprints with his eyes as they disappeared into the woods.

"Marcus," Vincent said quietly, his voice low. "I don't have time to deal with this right now. I want you to follow her, find her, and take her home, okay? She probably hasn't even made it to the highway. Just follow the tracks and don't come back 'til you find her, okay?"

Marcus nodded. "Sure, boss. Anything else you want me to do to her in particular?"

Vincent knew what he was talking about and shook his head, even though out here in the woods would be the perfect place to do it. "No, just take her home. If she fights back, you can smack her around a little, but don't kill her. Just take her home for me and make sure she stays there until I get back."

"Okay. You'll take the boat back?"

"Yeah," Vincent nodded. "When you find her, call one of the boys and have them pick you guys up. Keep it low-profile, okay? Just get her home and stay there."

Marcus nodded and headed into the woods, following the trail and the occasional prints that Vincent could see, even at this distance. She hadn't been careful in hiding her tracks.

He took a long last look around after Marcus disappeared into the trees. The clearing was small and would've been hard to find without the bloody stain on the rock. He'd gotten lucky, and that only made him more angry.

Vincent Luciano waded out to the small boat and climbed in. With a long glance back, he powered up the engine and headed for the pier on the far end of the lake.

------

The truck stop was a bustling place. She'd stopped at the rarely used ladies' room first to clean herself up. She'd torn her swimsuit into strips and bandaged her leg, and she'd pulled her jeans on over her bloodied shorts.

It had taken her longer than it should have to get here, but at least she was here. All she had to do now was find someone who could help.

A huge lot full of semis and large trucks encircled a low complex of buildings. She thought about the just climbing aboard one of the trucks and hiding until it was far away from this place, but she thought better of it and headed for the restaurant building, next to the gas station. She didn't want to waste time going in the wrong direction, now that she'd managed to get away.

Vincent would come home tonight and read the note and be furious. She wondered when he would go to the lake to look for her. Would he go tonight, when he found the note? She didn't think so. It gave her a perverse thrill to dream about him upset, out of control and madder than he'd been in a long time. He'd probably get some of his buddies and come out to the lake in the morning, and then, with any luck, he'd find the pile of clothes.

And he would think she was dead. Finally, she would be free.

Judy entered the restaurant and looked around, wondering what to do next. She wondered if she should start asking around for someone going to Texas, or maybe get a quick bite to eat first. Part of her realized that she was famished and needed food and water badly, but the rest of her wanted to just climb onto the first truck going south.

Finally, after a moment of standing in the entryway to the diner, her fear of Vincent won out over everything else. If he found her now, after what she'd done, he would probably kill her. She'd have time to eat later. Now she needed to get away.

"Excuse me!" she said loudly, screwing up her courage. "Is anyone going to Texas? Anybody I can catch a ride with? I'll pay."

There were low murmurs around the tables as people looked up at her and then went back to their sandwiches and newspapers.

Nobody was going? What were the chances of that?

"Is there anyone who can give me a ride south, maybe to Louisville, or Atlanta?"

A long silent moment with no responses from anyone, and she

was starting to think that she was going out of her mind when a voice spoke up from behind her.

"I can take you wherever you want to go, lady," the voice said.

She turned and was about to begin thanking the man when she realized who it was. Marcus Wright, one of Vincent's men.

Her stomach dropped as she saw two other guys with him—all of them were friends of Vincent's, and all worked for him.

"So," Marcus smiled, "where do you want to go today?" The smile was not a friendly one.

Judy realized that they had come in before she had. How? How had they found her so quickly?

This was going to be very bad.

She lowered her head and started to cry.

The three men surrounded her and led her outside. One of their cars was waiting, running. The tears came then from her eyes, strong and helpless, as they bundled her inside the car and drove off.

# Chapter 14

Vincent's wife was safe and sound and tucked away, waiting for him to come home. Marcus had done a good job, tracking her down and getting to the truck stop out on 64 before she'd even arrived.

But Vincent had other things to think about now. He wasn't worried about tonight's meeting, but his brother was—in fact, he was a twitching, nervous wreck.

It was almost 7 p.m. on Friday, and the sky was starting to darken as the sun dipped below the buildings of downtown St. Louis. The Luciano boys waited in Vincent's Mustang, parked on the top level of the Arch parking garage. The tall ribbon of steel and concrete arced across the sky above them, dominating the skyline and casting a long, parabolic shadow over the Mississippi River and East St. Louis beyond. Tourists were returning from the landmark, climbing into their station wagons and minivans and heading elsewhere. Vincent had parked the Mustang so that they would have a great view, but they weren't looking at the sights—they were watching for D.W., their contact, or for Shotgun or any of his men. Alphonse "Shotgun" Pope was the head of the East Dogs, the main gang in East St. Louis. There was always a chance that his group of thugs had somehow heard about this first meet and shown up to make things interesting.

Vincent glanced at Tony—the man was counting the money again, probably for the fifth time. Vincent knew he was worried.

The buy was set up to happen in about twenty minutes, and they had gotten here early. Ten grand took a few minutes to count. In the movies, money was always bundled in pretty stacks with wrappers on them—who had time to do that? It was all dirty money, anyway, so why clean it up? Besides, anyone who handled a lot of money knew that those little paper straps broke too easily—rubber bands worked better.

"Tony, it's all there," Vincent said, his eyes on the ramp that led to the top level. "You don't need to count it again."

Tony nodded, and Vincent could tell that he wasn't listening. This was their first buy together, so they were taking care of it themselves—nobody built up a relationship with major suppliers by farming it out to assistants. Or at least not until much later in the relationship. Vincent knew the dealer, having made many smaller buys from him over the past three years, but Vincent was preparing to move up to a whole new level of distribution. That meant a lot more of the raw material. And that meant much more contact with men like D.W.

Most of the narcotics for the region came in through the docks in East St. Louis, Illinois, which was a notorious place—all the freeways through the dirty, broken-down town were elevated so that people traveling through (or over) the town wouldn't have to see or experience it in any way. There were rumors about carloads of tourists accidentally taking the wrong exit, getting off in East St. Louis, and getting mugged or killed. The town had a reputation as a place to avoid.

The city government barely existed above the poverty level; sometimes residents' trash would go months before getting picked up. The town was the perfect example of inner city urban decay, and the Lucianos had big plans for it.

Tony and Vincent's new alliance, and Tony's realization that he would never be able to see his dreams come true by staying in the safe but unprofitable world of legitimacy, had produced a new plan for the dingy town.

Things had changed in the last couple of years, after Tony Luciano had based his gambling riverboat in East St. Louis, building a huge, secure pier and docking complex with expansive and well-lit parking lots. Hundreds of customers a day now braved the "wilds" of East St. Louis to visit the floating casino known as the *Princess Anne*. The *Princess Anne* was a conversion job, an old barge that had been converted into a casino and towed up from New Orleans. The renovation had almost bankrupted him, but now the casino was finally turning handsome profit.

Very little of the money that Luciano and his casino earned went to the city of East St. Louis—he had negotiated the agreement long before the mayor and city council had realized the extent of the cash flow from the legalized gambling.

Now Tony's organization had to make only a small monthly contribution to the city's coffers to retain the lease on the dock and pier area.

Although the *Princess Anne* was doing well, Tony had decided ten months ago that to truly make a killing he'd have to design and build a real casino riverboat from the keel up. After months of planning, they had started construction in the slip next to the *Anne*. The *Princess Margaret* would be a beautiful ship, unlike anything else along the Mississippi.

Vincent glanced over at the casino boats—they were upriver from the Arch, on the opposite side of the wide Mississippi River. The *Margaret* and the *Anne* leaned up against the casino dock complex, the larger boat towering over her smaller sister. Gambling had to occur on the river to be legal, so the buildings on the dock were support buildings and warehouses that fronted the huge parking lot. Vincent could see people working on the larger boat—one of the tiny workers was walking up the gangplank carrying what looked like a large piece of drywall. The *Margaret* would be a beautiful ship, capable of holding four times as many gamblers as the *Anne,* if they could ever get it done. But the project was almost out of money. That was part of the reason Tony had turned to his brother for advice and eventually agreed to partner with him.

Vincent, for what it was worth, thought the new casino would be a success. He and Tony had walked these docks not long ago, talking. Vincent had been impressed by the construction and genuinely saddened to hear about the organization's financial problems. He could've predicted them—and had. But he'd kept his "I told you so's" to himself. They had talked during the whole tour of the half-completed ship, and somewhere along their meandering walk among the decks of the *Princess Anne*, they had decided to get back into business together.

They had also decided to take a huge gamble of their own and try to revolutionize the narcotics industry in the St. Louis area. They would make it efficient, and it would be run by professionals, not by a bunch of thugs. And, most importantly, the business would turn a massive profit. Lastly, they had agreed that if they were going to move into this business, they were going in with both feet. Vincent would pocket his portion of the profits and grow his new portion of their shared venture. And Tony would finally have the funds to finish his floating beauty.

"It's a beautiful boat, huh?"

Vincent turned to look at his brother and smiled.

"I was just thinking that."

Tony had finally finished his latest count of the money.

"You're gonna need a lot more than that, though," Vincent said, nodding at the bag of cash in his brother's lap.

"I know," Tony said. Vincent knew the man was obsessed with

money, but sometimes, obsession was a good thing. It was a strong motivator.

"You nervous?" Tony asked.

Vincent shook his head, trying to look bored. "Nope. These guys are good. I've worked with them before, bought a lot of stuff from them. Their organization is clean—we'll have no problem."

Tony nodded, and Vincent knew what he was thinking: he didn't want to worry about trouble, like a police sting, while they were just getting started. It pleased Vincent that his brother was joining him down here in the gutter—it would make him a better man, and a much wealthier one. Of course, the cash in the bag was Tony's seed money—Vincent wouldn't have been able to front that kind of cash on so short a notice. Even though Tony said his organization was going broke, he still had deeper pockets than Vincent's fledgling criminal organization had ever known.

A couple of minutes later, a shiny black Volvo appeared on the ramp of the parking garage. It made two large, lazy circles around the empty concrete crisscrossed with white lines, and then slowed to a stop a few yards from the Mustang. Two large black men climbed from the car and leaned against it; a third man remained in the back.

The Lucianos got out and walked over to the Volvo. Vincent could sense Tony's nervousness as their shoes clicked against the concrete on their way to the meet. His brother would have to learn to control his apprehension.

Each was patted down by the waiting men, and then one of them nodded at the man in the car. He climbed out and walked up to Tony and Vincent.

"So, you're the older brother I've heard about," D.W. said, smiling in a way that Vincent hadn't seen before in their various meets. "Vincent has spoken of you often. I'm Dwayne Williams. Most folks just call me D.W."

He put out his hand and Tony took it. Then he stepped back and nodded at the other two men, who wandered off to form a perimeter around the group of men.

Tony glanced at him, and Vincent nodded. The older brother stepped forward and handed D.W. the large duffel bag. He took it and smiled, opening it on the hood of the car. He flipped through a couple of the bundles, probably more out of habit than out of a lack of trust, and closed the bag back up.

"Very nice. Now, am I correct in understanding that this is simply an opening step in our venture?" D.W. asked, his eyes on the Luciano brothers.

Tony and Vincent nodded in unison. Tony started to say something, but Vincent touched his elbow and shook his head to quiet him.

D.W. looked at them for a moment longer and then seemed to decide. He picked up the bag and walked around to the trunk of the Volvo, motioning for them to follow. In the open trunk was a metal suitcase. D.W. pulled it from the trunk and kneeled to open it, showing the contents to the Lucianos. Inside were dozens and dozens of tightly packed, carefully wrapped packages that looked like white bricks.

"Now, please listen to me carefully," D.W. began. "This is a sign of my good will. Normally, for ten grand in cash, I would sell you ten grand worth of the finished product. That would have a street value of around 40 grand. For you, it will be different. This is 10 grand worth before it's cut—you'll have to do that, but it will effectively double the size of this shipment. You're looking at close to 70 grand."

D.W. studied their eyes for a long moment.

"I think you understand why I'm doing this—I want to do business with you for a while. If I understand you correctly, you'll be able to buy and distribute more coke than this town has ever known, and that's good for my business," he said, closing the case and handing it to Vincent. "When this is gone, let me know. And don't let it get out where it came from. I also sell to Shotgun Pope and his crew, but they've maxed out what they can handle. He won't be happy when you move in." D.W. nodded at the suitcase in Vincent's hand. "But what you've got there, that should get you started."

They shook hands again—a gentlemanly gesture to conclude a dirty agreement—and then D.W. and his men got into their Volvo and drove away.

Vincent looked at his brother. Tony was smiling and staring at the case in his hands, but Vincent's expression wiped the smile off of his face.

"This is going to be ugly," Vincent said, his voice low and serious. "You know that, right? He was talking about the East Dogs and Pope. Those guys are not stupid—they have a distribution network in place already. I've come up against them before, several times. The East Dogs are not to be messed with, unless we take them out all at once, and that is messy. Do we take over their network or start our own?"

Tony was looking at the empty ramp where the Volvo had left their sight.

"I think we use them for a while and then start our own on the side," Tony said. "Of course it will be ugly, but first, we offer this stuff to the gang lords and let them send it out through their channels. That will tell us who they are and where they are. Then, we get rid of the higher elements and take over."

Vincent shook his head. "No, that will never work. The soldiers in Shotgun's set are too loyal—they'll never leave, and we won't be able to buy them off. They're all Bloods. They have a code, and they're serious about it. It's not something a group of white boys can just step in and run—they only hire from within, so to speak."

Vincent could see his brother thinking it through as they walked to the car and climbed in. "Then we need to start our own organization of dealers. We can hire away a few of his less loyal dealers by giving them better cuts. Distribution will be faster and more efficient with our own people. The final product will be better, and we'll own the market," Tony said.

Vincent was pleased. He knew Tony was good at organizing—that's why Tony had ended up running the family business while he worked at that dump of a restaurant and scratched by on whatever jobs he could drum up with his crew.

Tony could see the big picture—that's what made this partnership so great. Vincent had the killer instinct, which his brother sorely lacked, but his brother knew how to pull things together.

Vincent looked over at his brother as they drove off, and smiled. "This is going to be ugly. But after it's done, we'll run this town."

# Chapter 15

Judy gingerly climbed up from the couch and made her way into the kitchen for more Advil. Vincent had beaten her so badly when he got home that it felt like every part of her was throbbing. After a while, he'd gotten tired of yelling at her, saying over and over again how she'd almost messed up something big for him, and he'd gone to bed. She'd stayed near the scene of the beating, lying on the couch and watching TV with the volume on low.

It had been a beating to end all beatings, too much to even think about. On some level, she felt completely dead.

But somewhere deeper, she felt strangely overjoyed. She had done it, almost—she had come up with a plan, carried it out, and almost gotten away. If she had just climbed into the bed of one of those trucks, she would be halfway to somewhere else by now. The failure should have defeated her, but for some reason, even after the beating, she felt giddy, energized, and alive at taking control.

But running wasn't the answer. During the beatings, she usually tried to visualize something happy to distract her; this time, all she could think about was Vincent, dead.

Over and over, she watched him die.

Watched herself killing him.

It wasn't that she was a violent person. The idea of taking someone's life made her sick to her stomach. But this man, her husband, was going to kill her soon. She had come to accept this. And in response, some part of her had become more animalistic, more desperate to survive. They say that a cornered animal fights the fiercest, and that's how she felt—trapped, cornered, with only her nails and her attitude keeping her alive.

Sometime during tonight's beating, as the punches and slaps had come over and over, along with the yelling and the shouting and the insults and the threats, she had realized that, in the end, it would have to be him or her. And she really didn't care which—just as long as this all ended.

Judy paced around her house, pinching her lip with her fingers. She was too deep in thought to notice that, for the first time in a long time, she was standing a little taller.

Okay, so, she had to die. Or he did.

Just thinking the words made her feel better.

How...that was the only question.

Well, everyone knew that Vincent was flighty. If given the chance to make a really good score, he probably wouldn't hesitate to skip town.

But she knew that Vincent was getting involved with the family business again, so it made a lot less sense now for him to score a huge paycheck and disappear. Plus, Tony might start nosing around if he went missing—and any play of hers to "make him disappear" might not stand up to scrutiny.

She strolled around the house, looking for inspiration.

The kitchen reminded her that she could leave something on the stove and burn the house down. Could she do that on one of those nights when he came home drunk and passed out on the couch? How drunk would someone have to be to not notice a house on fire?

In the kitchen, she glanced under the sink—there was enough rat poison under there to kill an army. But she knew that that kind of stuff could be easily discovered by the doctors who would inevitably examine Vincent after...after he was dead.

Some part of her mind wondered at the fact that she was seriously contemplating killing Vincent, but another part of her mind kept thinking.

One night he could be coming home drunk, driving too fast on those twists and sharp turns on Blackwood Lane—

Drunk driving.

Something turned in her stomach. Maybe that was it. She'd dreamed about it, begged God to let it happen a million times, begged Him to make the car swerve and crash. Maybe she could do it herself. They always said that God helps those who help themselves.

How she would arrange it, she didn't know. But at least she had a ghost of a plan. And that made her smile.

# Chapter 16

Without much in the way of advance planning, Gary and Mike left for Sacramento on Saturday morning.

They drove in Gary's Saturn, heading north on the I-5. It would be about a seven-hour drive, plus whatever time they needed for lunch, so they left Mike's place in the Valley before 5 a.m. It was strange, cruising along the stretches of asphalt while just across the median, there was already a parking lot of headlights trying to get into the city, even on a Saturday. Where did all these people need to be?

The traffic on the southbound Golden State Freeway was notoriously bad in the early morning, as trucks coming into the city from the north clogged up the roads trying to make their early morning deliveries.

Gary drove and Mike slept. That was fine with Gary—he needed time to think. Thoughts of the dream were there all the time now, never leaving his conscious mind, and as he cruised along, doing 70 up the long, slow grade known as the Grapevine, he pondered his dream and ignored the lights falling away behind him.

The dream—he didn't understand it, couldn't even begin to explain it, only knew that it disturbed him down to his core. There were no words to describe the terror he felt each time he realized he was again in its grip.

In his years in L.A., he had explored a few different areas of the occult, starting with getting his palm read one windy autumn night on the Santa Monica Pier and expanding into a pursuit of tarot cards and numerology and crystology, searching for answers. He went to psychics to get his aura read and his tea leaves read and his palms read, and every time he came away with nothing but a lot of mysterious and exceedingly unspecific notions about his future and his past. Funny how they could never pick up on even the simplest things.

Once, he'd visited a psychic called Redinato at a shabby establishment in Redondo Beach. Gary had sat in front of her, a hokey prop-like crystal ball on the round table between them, and watched as she peered deep into the reflected light of the candles around them. After a few minutes, his impatience got the better of him.

"See anything in there?" he'd asked, already regretting the visit.

She continued to rub the milky glass of the orb, peering deep in it. "You...you've come from a long way away, haven't you, boy?"

He nodded—they always started out like that. Gary wondered if there could be a more generic prediction. Anyone coming from anywhere further than San Pedro could consider that distance far—London or Long Beach, didn't matter.

Gary had read up on psychics—he'd been searching for the real thing for so long, but was understandably wary of the charlatans and fakes that the industry produced in great numbers. He knew what common sense told him: the more generic the prediction, the more easily applied to anyone's circumstances. It was just like the horoscopes in the newspapers—anything specific in them would immediately invalidate them for a vast portion of the populace.

She continued to peer into the ball. Gary wondered how much of her show was for his amusement and how much of it was just habit.

She glanced up at him and made a face, then went back to looking. "You've had a troubling past, my friend. Lost faces, lost people. There are many things that you have lost along the way. Is that right?"

Gary Foreman nodded, but hadn't everyone "lost" people in their lives? Gary had lost his mother a long time ago, and he'd been forced to move away from the town he'd loved. Now he was an outcast in a place he despised, but that didn't make her insight real.

"Yes, I lost my mother a long time ago."

She nodded, still staring. She adjusted her arms to hold the crystal ball tighter.

"Yes, I see fire and death, my son. But not in the way you think. And there is much more to this, things that you will learn in time. The name you call yourself now—what is it, boy?"

He was confused—what did he call himself? She'd seen fire—could that be the death of his mother?

"My name is Gary, Gary Foreman. Why would I call myself something else?"

Driving in the car north to Sacramento, Gary remembered the next part as if it had happened yesterday.

The old gypsy woman had stood suddenly, her robe flowing around her. She'd come around the table, her eyes suddenly wild as she grabbed his arm.

"You must leave now, boy. There are things that you must see to, events that will only transpire if you start down that path, and quickly."

He'd tried to ask her another question, but she had pulled him up from the ratty chair he'd been sitting in with surprising strength. She'd shushed him, shaking her head, and walked him to the door.

Gary remembered that he'd tried to pay, her but she had refused, shoving his hand away.

They had gotten to the door and she'd pulled it open for him. He'd started to leave, but she'd grabbed his elbow and stopped him abruptly, her hand gripping his arm so tightly it hurt.

"Listen, boy," she'd said. "You must follow your dreams above all. You must follow wherever they lead, and you must not shirk from them. They will be your relief, and your future. Promise me that, boy."

She stared into his eyes, and her eyes seemed to shift and change colors subtly. The sight made him queasy.

He'd nodded and muttered something about promising, and then she'd backed up and slammed the door in his face.

That had been last summer. And the old woman's reaction still scared him. Could she have known that these nightmares were coming? He'd driven down to Redondo a few weeks ago to try and ask her, but she was gone.

There had also been a tarot card reader in Mission Vallejo that had reacted strangely to him.

Gary had attended one of those Renaissance Festivals out at Irvine Meadows. The festival had featured jousting tournaments and folks walking around in medieval outfits, chomping on enormous turkey legs.

The sign on one small tent promised tarot readings, so Gary had entered and paid his money, and the woman had laid out his cards. She'd used a T-Cross field instead of the more traditional circular field. The books he'd read had said that the T-Cross method of laying out the cards was more impressive to paying customers, and although it was generally regarded as less accurate, it was preferred over the circular method. She had set out his cards, slowly turning each over and telling him what they meant. Supposedly the cards were able to tap into each person's energy field, and the influence of that field would help the cards come out in a way that allowed the reader to ascertain something about the customer's fortune. It sounded like crap to him, but when you were looking for answers, sometimes you had to go down a few dark alleys.

The woman was good, reading something important and positive into even the more pessimistic cards.

She started out lying to him from the very beginning, giving him positive feedback. He knew that the inverted five of Cups, with its picture of a court jester, meant the exact opposite of the regular five of Cups, which represented happiness, but she'd whitewashed it for him.

But as she continued to slowly turn the cards from her well-worn deck, she grew less and less jovial.

The Death card came up seventh, and after that, she'd stopped and looked at him intensely, then glanced at the air next to him, as if looking for some invisible companion.

"What is your name, son?"

He told her, and she nodded slowly, looking back down at the arrangement of cards on the table before her.

"I must confess," she began. "I have not been entirely truthful with you. Reading the cards as often as I do, it is rare that something appears in them that actually requires my attention. Forgive me."

Curious, he nodded. "I've had several readings, and I've studied the meanings of some of the cards. I know that the inverted five of Cups does not signal happiness."

She nodded, looking at him.

After a long, uncomfortable silence, he shifted in his chair. "So, what do they say?"

She held his gaze for a long moment, long enough for him to notice the distant sounds of tourists laughing outside the tent. She looked down at the cards and, in a sudden motion, swept up the cards, shuffled, and started over.

Remarkably, several of the same cards appeared again, and in the same place in the formation. She flipped them slowly from the deck, speaking the name of each card now and explaining it, as if she could sense his awareness of her craft. She gave him the unvarnished truth as each faded card appeared before her.

The last card revealed was the Angel. She sat back, studying them. The woman was young, but in thought, her face appeared much older, concentration creasing her forehead.

After a minute, she looked back up at him.

"You are but a shadow of yourself."

He didn't know what to say, but he hadn't been expecting that.

"What do you mean?" he asked.

She looked at the cards again. "You will need to discover yourself before you can be free. I see your face, and then I see another face behind yours, someone lost to you, a brother or sibling. But your eyes tell me that you are an only child."

He nodded, unsure if he should say anything.

The woman sat back and looked down at the cards. He watched as her hands moved over them slowly.

"You have been searching in the wrong places," the woman said, finally, smiling. "Start over, my son. Start at the start."

After the reading he had gotten up, his knees shaking. He had left, thanking her, but had no idea what any of it meant.

For some reason, the psychics and the Tarot readings and the palm readings made him feel better. He had always felt a strange, deep restlessness that was hard to explain, as far back as he could remember.

The sun was peeking over the eastern mountains of the southern San Joaquin Valley, and Gary smiled. He was making great time, and they might make it to his father's as early as 1 p.m. Of course, they might hit some traffic in Sacramento, but it would be nothing like the parking lots of Los Angeles.

This was a good first step, Gary thought. Talking to his father about the dream would help—maybe his father could identify the man's bloody, shadowed face. Or help explain why everything in the dream seemed so familiar.

Gary Foreman drove on, heading north.

------

"Gary!"

His stepmother came down the steps of the house and ran up to the car, barely giving him time to get out before she swept him up into her arms. She was a big woman, and she loved to hug. He didn't remember anything like this about his real mother—and even though he loved his stepmother, he longed for more knowledge, for any one sensation that could remind him of his mother.

He enjoyed the hug for a long moment and then disentangled himself, introducing Mike to his stepmother. Mike also received an enormous bear hug, albeit not of the same intensity as his own.

She finally pulled away and put her arms around both of them, treating them like returning conquerors. "You boys hungry?"

Mike nodded vigorously—he'd been complaining for almost an hour before Gary had pulled the Saturn to a stop in front of the small ranch house in North Highlands, a suburb north of Sacramento. Gary told them to head inside and offered to get the bags.

His stepmother and Mike went inside. Gary heard introductions being exchanged before his dad came out onto the porch and slowly made his way down the steps toward the car. He still had the limp from back in O'Fallon, and it made stairs difficult for him. His leg had been broken in three places, Gary remembered sadly. He remembered the trial, and his dad on the stand—

"Hi, son. Need some help?" John Foreman offered.

Gary smiled, hugging his father. "I think I've got it, Dad. The leg getting worse? You're moving slower than the last time I saw you."

John Foreman looked down at his leg and shook his head. "Not well, son. The doctors said that the hips have gotten bad—they think it's all my fault. And the years of awkward walking. I don't use the cane as much as they would like, so now they're talking hip replacement. They've got me on seven different pills, I think."

Gary nodded, concerned, and pulled the other suitcase out, closing the trunk behind him. "You're having surgery?" he asked as they slowly headed for the house. He was carrying both suitcases, and his father was still having trouble keeping up.

"Well, they don't know. They want to do one hip and see how it goes before they operate on the other one. I hope it's soon, though."

Gary saw his father grimace as he used the porch rail to pull himself up the steps. Gary stepped up and set the suitcases down before going back and helping his father.

How many times had his father helped him walk, or helped him along after he'd hurt himself? Gary remembered a particularly bad bike crash that had resulted in a nasty skinned knee. His father had comforted him, cleaning the bleeding wound and bandaging it in the middle of the gravel road where Gary had crashed. Gary still had a scar on his left knee. His mother had been there too, taking care of him, but he couldn't remember her face. He remembered how his father had doted over him, saying his name over and over to calm him—

A tight, viselike headache washed over him suddenly, and he let go of his father, now safely on the porch, and grabbed the railing to steady himself.

"Are you okay, son?" his father asked, eyes tightening.

Gary brushed it off. "Yeah, I've just...I've been getting these horrible headaches lately, especially in the last couple of months. Maybe it's the lack of alcohol," he said wryly, and saw the disapproving look on his father's face. His problems with alcohol had been a sore spot between them for years, and his father had actively encouraged him to get control of his drinking.

As they headed inside, his father leaned closer. "I know it's difficult, son, but you're doing the right thing. You can't let alcohol control your life, or you'll never be happy."

As he followed his father inside, Gary wondered if he would ever make it to happy. At this point, he'd settle for a good night's sleep.

------

The dinner was a pleasant one, filled with questions from Gary's parents about life in Los Angeles and from Gary's stepmother, Denise, about Mike's many girlfriends. Mike couldn't help but notice how quiet Gary was. Mike wondered how long it would be before things started coming out—he figured Gary would want to talk privately to his father about the dream he'd been having, but that wasn't the way things worked out.

This family was interesting but strange. It almost seemed like there was an undercurrent beneath everything that Gary and his father said, almost as if they were speaking their own coded language. Everything was accompanied with a long pause, or a glance, or a strange phrase.

Mike kept noticing the way Gary glanced at his dad—there was a lot going on here that Mike wasn't privy to. He'd known Gary for almost two years and always found him to be exceedingly private. Now, Mike knew where he got it.

They were busy eating, and Mike was explaining to Denise about his latest architectural project when Gary interrupted and asked his father the question for which he'd driven 500 miles.

"Dad, do you remember a guy from St. Louis that looked like a gangster, with dark eyes and a strong chin? He had dark hair and looked very mean."

The sudden silence around the table was palpable.

It was obvious to Mike that they must never talk about these kinds of things. Gary's father had been caught so completely by surprise that his forkful of pot roast hovered between the plate and his half-opened mouth. It was all Mike could do to keep from laughing out loud, and he stifled his chuckle with a sudden cough into his napkin.

John slowly set his fork down and sipped from his water before answering.

"Gary, what is this about? Why do you care about someone from back there?" Mike noticed that John had said the words "back there" like they tasted bad.

Gary shook his head, though Mike didn't know why. "Dad,

I've...I'm trying to remember some stuff from back there, from back in St. Louis. Do you remember anyone who looked like that?"

"No," the father answered immediately, glancing at Denise before going back to eating. Mike wondered if he was telling the truth.

Denise spoke up next, obviously curious.

"Why do you ask, Gary? Is something wrong—is this why you're visiting?"

Gary didn't answer for a long minute, and John Foreman was the only one eating. Denise looked concerned. Mike was very curious to see what, if anything, Gary would say.

It took a few minutes to come out, but Gary began slowly describing the dream, starting with how it had begun a couple of months ago and ending with last night, describing how the dream had repeated over and over, ending only because the alarm had gone off to wake him for the early drive.

Gary described the bloodied man in the dream so clearly that Mike could almost see him, walking into the darkened dream-room and standing over Gary with that big knife. Mike had heard the story before, but only in bits and pieces. To hear it all again, all from the start and all at once, made Mike realize just how much stress his friend had been under the past few weeks.

His parents' reaction was interesting, to say the least.

When Gary was finished, Denise sat quietly and seemed to be pondering what she should do.

Gary's father got up and walked out of the room.

Mike watched Gary's eyes as they followed his father out of the room. Then Gary rose and left the dining room in the opposite direction, heading out the front door.

After a long, awkward silence, Denise finally took a drink of wine and nodded at Mike.

"Sorry about this, dear," she said by way of apology to Mike. "They don't talk about this kind of stuff very often. When it comes up, it takes awhile for them to get together. I just wish...wish it was easier for them to talk."

Mike nodded. "Well, all I know is that Gary's freaked out about this whole thing—he's been talking to me about it for weeks. The other night, he saw something in his dream that he couldn't place, and he just suddenly decided that he had to come up and ask you two about it. In person."

Denise nodded.

"It seemed sudden to me," Mike continued. "But now I guess I understand why. His father doesn't seem like the chatting kind, and trying to talk to him on the phone about something like this would be pointless, I'm guessing."

Mike stared at the empty chair where Gary's dad had been sitting. "Do you know much about their time in Illinois?"

She shook her head and looked away. "No, not really. I met John a year after they moved out here. We married while Gary was in college."

Denise stood and started picking up dishes. "John doesn't talk about his life back in Illinois at all, and we've never been back to visit. He doesn't even get any mail from anyone back there, so I guess we've really got nobody and no reason to visit." She leaned in a little closer. "His first wife died in a car accident, so the memories are very painful for him. For them both."

Yeah, Mike thought, but that didn't help Gary unless the old man would open up and talk about it. Gary seemed convinced that the face in the dream was someone from his past, someone that he could almost remember. And his father was the only link he had to the past, his only link to his life back in St. Louis.

------

Gary walked through the quiet streets of North Highlands, a small suburb of Sacramento. Walking always helped him clear his head.

He smoked a cigarette, his third since leaving his parents' house. They always calmed him—the relaxing and familiar habit of removing the cigarette from the pack, tapping it on the back of his hand, lighting it, and taking that first deep breath.

The scene at the dinner table was typical of his dad—if there was something that needed to be discussed or some problem that needed to be solved, his father would more than likely avoid the topic. If pressed, John Foreman would get up and leave the room to avoid answering a question.

It had always been that way with his father, back as far as Gary could remember.

Gary could remember some things about St. Louis very clearly, but others were fuzzy. Of course he could remember his mother and his house and the friends he had had, but it always seemed to give him a throbbing headache when he tried to remember too much. It was as if his mind was protecting him from the horrible memories of seeing his mother killed.

Gary remembered the car blowing up, and he remembered flying through the air and landing painfully on one leg, rolling away from the fireball as it consumed his father's car. Afterward, the FBI had moved them to a hotel, and it had been some time during their stay when their home had been ransacked and burned, destroying many of his things, including his high school yearbooks and all of the other memorabilia from his childhood. He didn't have anything from before the time of the trial—no childhood baseball trophies or old report cards or pictures that he had drawn as a child.

Gary's dad wouldn't even let him visit the burned-out wreckage of their home—John had described it clearly to Gary, but had told him that going to the house or even seeing it would be too traumatic. But some of their things had been recovered and had been sent along with them to Sacramento when the FBI had placed them in the Witness Protection Program. When he got back from his walk, he planned to dig through some of it to try and see if any of it would spark a memory.

More out of habit than anything else, his hand reached into his pocket and pulled out his tarot deck, shuffling it mindlessly as he walked, the cigarette dangling from his lips. He pulled out a few cards and looked at them, but his heart wasn't into trying to ascertain their meaning.

His father—there was just no good way to talk to the man. If it was about school or work, he could listen and would contribute to the conversation, and that was when he and his father had their best discussions. But if the conversation ever turned to their past in St. Louis, his father would clam up, or worse, just walk away.

The topic of girls was even worse—whenever he tried to ask his father for advice, the man would get the strangest look on his face and then change the subject. Once when he had been complaining to his father, saying that he didn't think he would ever find a woman to spend the rest of his life with, his father had actually teared up and left the room—and his father never cried!

Gary had gotten used to not having a father to talk to about certain topics. But now he needed his father's help. It was either that or fly back to St. Louis and—

Fly back and do what? Would anyone back there recognize him? The FBI had told both Gary and his father that they were never to return to St. Louis or O'Fallon. Even though the man Gary's father had worked for had long ago died in prison, there were still plenty of people who wanted John Foreman dead and, by proxy, his son.

So what could Gary do? Fly back to St. Louis and drive around O'Fallon in dark sunglasses until he saw the mysterious yet familiar guy from his dream?

Gary didn't know. He pulled out his cigarettes and lit another, enjoying the smell. He didn't feel like he knew anything—and the lack of sleep wasn't helping. He needed rest, and he knew it, but the Dream made him want to stay awake as long as possible. The caffeine and cigarettes were keeping him going, but he didn't like the feeling of his heart racing all the time.

It wasn't the fear or the crazy dark-haired guy with the knife in the dream that really frightened him. It was the unanswered questions about why he was having the dream that scared Gary to his very core.

He continued walking, trying to dredge up answers from the murky depths of his mind. He walked and walked, but nothing came.

# Chapter 17

Tony Luciano's East St. Louis operations were centered at Pier 32: the docks for the gambling riverboats, the warehouses, and an expansive and guarded parking structure used alternately by customers and the reenergized Luciano crime family. The docks were located right on the water, with the shining buildings of the St. Louis downtown standing just across the wide expanse of the Mississippi River.

The Lucianos' first boat, the *Princess Anne*, had been in operation for almost two years. Customers poured across the river and joyously parted company with their money in the glitzy surroundings of the rebuilt barge.

The *Princess Margaret* was docked about ten yards downriver from the *Princess Anne* and was not yet open to the public. There were roulette wheels to be installed and carpet to put down, but everything was on schedule for the opening date. The second boat was twice the size of the *Princess Anne*, almost 200 feet long. Tony Luciano was betting the future of his fledgling gambling empire on this expensive and impressive showplace, and its gala opening with all the trimmings was scheduled in less than three weeks.

Next to the parking structure that had been built especially for customers of the new boat, two large warehouses stood, guarding their contents with blank, glazed-over windows.

Warehouse One contained the offices and construction staging areas for the *Margaret*. This building also contained the main complex of offices for the riverboat operations.

Warehouse Two contained a different type of staging area, and it was abuzz on this Saturday evening. An entire complement of men was hard at work in various areas of the large building, moving boxes of items onto trucks or offloading pallets of goods with forklifts and handcarts. There were crates and crates of liquor and cigarettes and electronics and microwave ovens and frozen fish and a dozen other commodities. They'd all been stolen or purchased illegally and were being loaded onto trucks bound for Chicago or Tennessee or wherever they could be sold at an inflated price. As soon as Tony Luciano had decided to take the family back to its roots, these old methods of doing business had become exceedingly profitable—in the ten days since the fateful decision had been made, they had managed to ramp up to a full organization that trafficked exclusively in stolen goods.

In one corner of the warehouse, a completely different sort of commerce was taking place.

Inside a large, guarded room, around a series of long tables, trusted men carried out the laborious task of cutting down the original shipment of cocaine that the Luciano brothers had procured only the day before.

First, the individual coke packages had to be opened carefully. This was done with a very sharp knife over a normal cookie sheet that had been polished almost silver, so that any coke dropped from the opening plastic bag could be easily recovered. The contents were poured into shiny stainless steel bowls, which were then weighed on a large, expensive electronic scale to calculate the exact weight and volume of the cocaine in each brick.

Next, the cocaine was tested. A small dot of the substance was taken from a random location on the rounded mound of cocaine in the bowl and mixed in a beaker with some chemicals. The color of the resulting concoction was compared to a test strip to determine the purity and quality of the cocaine. After testing the first couple of batches, the word had gotten around quickly that this stuff was very pure and of extremely high quality, words that had pleased Vincent as he watched the men work.

Next, a man carefully measured out a portion of a different white powder, in this case common household flour, and added the flour to the mound of cocaine in the metal mixing bowl. A highly polished metal spoon was used to mix or "cut" the cocaine down to a lower level of purity, but not enough to reduce a user's potential reaction.

Next, the powder was carefully measured into small plastic baggies, each holding only about an ounce. About two-thirds of the shipment would go out at this dilution level of about half cocaine and half flour.

At a second table, a higher concentration mix of cocaine and flour was being produced. These bags were cut with a two-to-one ratio of coke to flour, and these would be distributed to the dealers and more important clients. Hopefully the dealers would test the goods and find them to be of high quality, prompting more sales in the future.

At another table, a more specialized concoction was being created—crack cocaine. Several large kettles were being used to boil a liquefied solution of the cocaine down to a hard, crystalline form that could be easily transported and sold. Two of the men wore goggles and carefully stirred each of the boiling kettles, checking the temperature frequently and methodically draining off the liquid mixture to reveal small nuggets of hardened, crystallized cocaine at the bottom of the tubs. The men fished these out of the tubs using metal tongs and placed them on a cookie sheet to dry before putting them into small plastic vials. This form of cocaine was more popular in urban areas and could be sold at a much higher margin of profit—the mixture required less cocaine to produce, but the boiling process concentrated the power of the substance, making for a much more powerful high. And that meant a much higher selling price per ounce.

Vincent watched the entire operation with jealous eyes—this was the kind of operation he and his men had attempted numerous times but had never been able to make work. Purity control, or security issues, or internal theft had always prevented Vincent from making this type of operation really profitable, and now he knew why—all of these men could be trusted, something he was unable to honestly say about the men in his own small organization. These men knew exactly what they were doing and were doing a great job. And using this private room in a secured and guarded warehouse in East St. Louis was perfect.

And the money—it would start coming through in only a few days. Selling cocaine was like printing money, and if he could convince his brother to let him handle this side of the business, he would be a very rich man in a short amount of time.

He walked to the end of the first table, the one with the most diluted mixture of coke and flour that would make up the bulk of the shipment. There were several large piles of the small plastic bags, each weighing less than an ounce, and he picked one up to test the weight. He watched the powder slide from side to side as he held it up and moved the bag back and forth, and the mixture looked good—no clumping or sticking to the inside of the bag, something that could indicate humidity in the room.

He glanced over at the air purifiers and dehumidifiers that had been set up in one corner and smiled. That was what he admired in his brother. He was always looking out for the details, making sure nothing slipped through the cracks.

# Chapter 18

It wasn't very long before Denise said something—John Foreman could tell she'd been waiting until the boys had gone to bed. Gary was in his old room and Mike in the rarely used guest room. Gary had finally come home after hours of walking the streets of North Highlands alone.

"You know you have to say something to him," Denise said quietly. "Don't you?"

The house was quiet. John Foreman was lying in bed next to his wife of eight years, staring up at the ceiling and trying to decide what to do. His son had been gone for hours. Gary had done a lot of walking like that when they'd first moved to Sacramento—it seemed to be his way of dealing with things.

"I can't say anything to him," John said quietly. "You know that, and you know why." In the darkness of their bedroom, his words sounded pathetic, like he was trying to convince himself. "Things were bad back then. Very bad. I did what I had to do to get us out of there in one piece."

He couldn't see her nodding in the dark next to him, but he could feel the movement of her head. "Yes, you did the right thing then, but maybe it's time to tell him the truth. She's probably married and happy by now. There would be no reason to think that they would get back together."

John sat up on one elbow and looked at the dark figure in the bed next to him. "That's not what I'm worried about, honey. The Lucianos were a dangerous bunch and still are. They killed my wife to shut me up. After the trial, they killed her brother trying to force him to reveal our location."

They were quiet for a moment, and John could smell cigarette smoke coming from somewhere—probably Gary.

"From what I've heard," John continued, "the Lucianos are still powerful. If Gary goes back there, they could find him. And hurt him, or kill him—I don't know if the contract on us ever expired. It's just too dangerous. They could figure out where we've been hiding all these years and come after us, too."

His wife was quiet for a few minutes. He was starting to think she'd fallen asleep when she asked another question.

"Do you know that boy in Gary's dream?"

John wasn't sure. "I don't know. It sounds like it could be Luciano's younger boy, Vincent. He was at the trial. He was always the crazy one, the one Gino worried about."

"So, why do you think he's having these dreams?"

"I don't know. Dr. Martin said that the block might eventually break down on its own, even without the phrase."

John was quiet for a moment, knowing the next question without her even asking. She'd asked enough times over the course of their marriage for him to know when it would come up, and this was the perfect time.

"And no, I still can't remember the phrase."

He heard her sigh loudly. "That's really something you should've written down, you know. If it comes out on its own, it could really mess him up, couldn't it?"

"Yes, yes. It was just...things were crazy then, and I thought it would be a bad idea to write it down—what if he'd found it? And I thought I could remember it, but I guess I just had too many other things going on in my mind."

Denise sighed again. "Then maybe you should tell him what you do know and let him find out the rest for himself."

John shook his head.

"I can't do that. It's just too dangerous. He would be in danger, and he would try to find her and see her, and who knows what the Lucianos would do to him if they got him."

"But he'll never be happy," she said. "You know he can't find a girlfriend—maybe some part of him won't allow him to be happy. Maybe the wall is breaking down, and that's where the dreams are coming from. Either way, he's a terribly sad boy, and you have it in your power to fix that, even if it's dangerous. He'll never be happy the way he is," she said, summing up her eight years of arguing about this topic in one concise sentence.

He had told her the truth about what had happened only a year or so after they were married, and she'd been working on him ever since to tell Gary the truth. But he couldn't.

After a while, John finally spoke up.

"No, I can't do it. I hate to see him sad and confused, but at least he's alive to be sad and confused. I can't do anything to put him in jeopardy, even if he's suffering. The secret has to stay a secret. Or we could all end up dead."

She offered no further argument, and he drifted off to sleep. If she had other thoughts on the topic, this time she kept them to herself.

------

"Here, take this."

Mike was drying the breakfast dishes with Denise when she turned and handed Mike a small envelope. He took it—it was taped shut, with Gary's name written on it.

Mike looked at her strangely.

"Don't worry," Denise said hurriedly. "This will answer some of Gary's questions—that's all I can say."

Mike looked back down at the envelope, this time with much more curiosity.

Denise grabbed his arm. "Now, you have to promise me something. What is inside this envelope will take him to St. Louis in search of...well, it should make him search for answers. Will you please go with him, keep an eye on him? It could be dangerous. There are bad people back there...not to mention the fact that the answers he's seeking could be very traumatic for him. He'll need a friend."

Mike had no idea what to think.

She glanced back over his shoulder. "They're coming back—hide it." He pulled up his shirt and stuffed the envelope into his belt as she continued, her voice low.

"Don't show him that until you get back to L.A.—and he'll need you around when he looks at it."

Gary's stepmother plunged her hands back into the warm dishwater just as Gary and his father came back into the kitchen, each carrying more dishes from the breakfast table.

"So, thanks again for the breakfast, Mom. It was great," Gary said, setting his dishes on the counter and kissing her.

"No problem, honey," Denise said. "Now you boys hit the road—it'll be late before you get back, and you have to work tomorrow." With one long glance at Mike, Denise scooted them out of the room.

# Chapter 19

O'Fallon Township High School was located on the eastern edge of the small town, or at least what used to be the eastern edge until the building boom of the late eighties spurred the construction of a dozen new housing communities and property values on the eastern side of town increased by fifty percent.

The housing market in O'Fallon was always in flux, but in 1986, Scott Air Force Base, the lifeblood of the small town, received word that the U.S. military was establishing a new Joint Command Headquarters of the U.S. Transportation Command to be located at Scott. With an estimated one thousand new families moving into the area, real estate developers in O'Fallon and northern Belleville and Fairview Heights began salivating.

Building began in earnest as soon as the new personnel started arriving, and the past ten years had seen O'Fallon almost double in size. A new theater complex by the Interstate 64 interchange, two dozen new restaurants, and a number of big box stores had opened in the past few years, further increasing property values.

But O'Fallon Township still had only one high school, and it had managed to grow along with its student base by adding new buildings and temporary structures. There were plans in the works to build a new high school on the western side of town, but the city council and mayor were still bickering about funding. The groundbreaking ceremony had been pushed back four times and finally put on hold until the budget could be ironed out.

The high school now included a large complex of buildings grouped around a long central corridor. The gymnasium sat off the southern end of the school, with tennis courts and baseball fields right outside. The football stadium stood on the land south of the school and was the center of the town's attention during the months of September through November. The O'Fallon Panthers were considered one of the best high school football teams in southern Illinois, regularly defeating rival teams from cities all over the state.

On this quiet Sunday evening, there were no planned activities on the high school campus. The parking lots and the streets surrounding the school were dark and quiet, save for a patrolling security guard.

South of the fenced-in football field was Highway 50, the main road through O'Fallon. To the east, it ran toward McKendree College and Carlyle Lake. To the west, it ran through the O'Fallon proper and intersected with Interstate 64 before continuing west to Fairview Heights.

The 1997 O'Fallon Mayfest, the town's most anticipated annual carnival, was less than a week away, and preparations had already started in O'Fallon Park, a large park and baseball field complex in the heart of the town about a mile to the west of the high school. The main pavilion had been decorated, and the first of the carnival rides had started arriving.

But the high school grounds were not completely devoid of life.

Tim, a young black man in a Dallas Cowboys jacket, was hanging out by the varsity baseball diamond stands, looking for the high school's security guards or cops. And he was watching for customers.

It didn't take long—ten minutes after he'd shown up, a white boy in a scraggly flannel shirt appeared from behind the bushes separating the bleachers from the school and wandered nervously over to him.

"You got anything?"

Tim smiled and nodded. "Yeah. Not a problem. How much you need, man?"

The boy looked around nervously, and Tim knew exactly what the kid was thinking—if the cops showed up, it would be very bad. Tim knew that all of his best customers in O'Fallon were kids from the high school and local colleges. They always looked like rabbits, about to bolt.

"Let me get a hundred worth," the kid said, flashing a short wad of twenties.

Tim opened his large, dark jacket and pulled out four small packets of cocaine. Glancing around, he handed them to the kid and took his money in one practiced motion, counting the cash as the kid gingerly tested the weight of the small plastic bags in his hand. The money was all there, and as soon as Tim said so, the kid thanked him and took off.

Another half hour passed, and Tim was starting to think he should move to his next location—he had two dozen regular spots where his customers could look for him—when a car appeared and slowed to a stop a hundred yards away. Smiley Road ran north and south along the western edge of the high school campus, and Tim watched as the car stopped and two men climbed out, heading toward him.

They didn't look like cops. The car wasn't a typical police make and model—in fact, the car was too small to even carry suspects in the back seat. But it still wasn't a good sign, and Tim started to move around the bleachers and head in the other direction when a third man, dressed the same way, stepped around the bushes and blocked his exit.

"Hold up, son," the man said, smiling.

Tim already knew what this was about, and he didn't see a good way out of it.

The other two men joined them, but the one in front continued doing the talking.

"You run for Shotgun, right?"

It didn't really matter, Tim thought. This could end one of two ways—one of which would hurt a lot and the other would hurt for only a moment before nothing ever hurt again.

He nodded. "Yeah, I'm with the Baker Crew."

Somebody grabbed his arms roughly from behind and another set of hands frisked him, pausing on the coke but not finding a weapon. He never carried—it was too easy to lose control of your piece and have it end up pointed at you. The hands came off of him and he straightened his jacket, staring back at the man in front of him.

The man stepped out of the darkness and even Tim recognized him. Everyone in this town knew him.

Vincent Luciano smiled. "You make good money for them?"

"I do okay." He nodded uncomfortably.

Vincent reached up and pulled open Tim's jacket, drawing out a small vial of crack cocaine. He held it up to the light of the moon, hanging low in the sky, and shook the vial. The coke looked brittle and powdery, a sign of low quality.

Vincent handed it back to Tim and then reached inside his own jacket and pulled out a similar vial.

"This stuff is much better. See how the rock isn't starting to powder? Much higher concentration."

Tim looked at it.

"Okay, I'm not going to waste your time," Vincent explained. "I'll give you twice the amount of product you have on you now. You sell all of that and keep the money. After that, you push for us only and keep 30% of the cash for whatever you sell. I know you get 10% now from the East Dogs and Shotgun. This is a good deal for you.

What do you think?"

Tim was surprised and apprehensive. The deal was a great one, much better than he would've ever dreamed of getting with the Dogs or by striking out on his own. He'd expected to get the crap kicked out of him, not a job offer.

"Your stuff any good? Is it regular?"

Vincent Luciano nodded. "We buy from the same supplier, my friend. And we cut our powder one-to-one, not two-to-one or three-to-one like your guys. And we've already lined up the next shipment. Whatever you can sell, we'll have more. And if you're interested, we can even take some of that money you'll be making and invest it for you—of course the money is still yours, but we'll invest it for you and guarantee a higher return."

Tim nodded, interested. This was a great offer, but he hated leaving the Dogs—Shotgun was a good guy, and a brother. It made sense to stay loyal to his boys. But this new deal was good....

"Can I think on it?" he asked.

Vincent smiled. "Sure. Call me when you decide, either way. We've talked to eight of Shotgun's boys so far tonight, and three are already on board. The rest are like you—cautious. I would be too. But we're going to make this a great business, and we want you in on it," he said, handing Tim a card before turning around and walking away.

The other two men turned and drifted back toward their car. Tim looked alternately at them and at the card he'd been handed—it contained only a hand-written telephone number that would surely only be in existence for a day or two. That much had been implied by the conversation—this was a limited time offer.

Tim had been told there was a war coming, and it looked like it was going to be bad. He'd have to pick the right team.

He liked that part about investing the money for him. If the deal was good, he'd start out with a nice bundle to sell and keep the cash for himself.

Tim pocketed the card and walked away, heading for O'Fallon Park. He scouted for cops in unmarked cars and sold to an occasional nervous buyer, but his thoughts were elsewhere. His hand nervously toyed with one corner of the card in his pocket, fraying the paper.

# Chapter 20

The drive back Sunday night was long and uneventful. Mike and Gary chatted off and on, talking about the visit and Gary's parents, and some about what Gary could remember about living in St. Louis, but the trip had been ultimately frustrating for Gary. He wasn't any closer to learning anything about the identity of the man in his Dream.

Mike seemed distracted all the way home, more quiet than usual. Gary left it alone—he had enough on his mind without trying to draw out of Mike whatever was bothering him. If Mike wanted to share, Gary knew he would, in time.

He stopped the car in front of Mike's apartment just past 11 p.m. Mike had one more opportunity to say what was on his mind, but he seemed to decide not to share and hurriedly climbed out of the car, tugging his suitcase inside.

Gary started for home—he'd insisted on driving both ways, and he was tired—but decided to avoid his apartment for a little longer. Any delay in going to bed was a good delay. He was suddenly inspired to go on one of his favorite drives, alone, with time to do some thinking. He popped a cigarette in his mouth, lit it, and dragged slowly on it, enjoying the wind in his hair and the complete lack of traffic on the streets.

He headed south toward Redondo Beach and the southern coastal towns. Manhattan Beach, Hermosa Beach, and Redondo stretched around the coastal arm from Venice Beach down to the Palos Verdes Peninsula. Gary planned to take the road down and around the Peninsula before heading back—it was a long trip, but the scenery was gorgeous, and the moon would look good reflecting on the water. And, most of all, he needed to think.

The traffic was light on the Harbor Freeway. He got off at the exit for Torrance, heading east on the Pacific Coast Highway. He headed past his favorite Chinese restaurant, then west through Torrance and part of Redondo Beach until he met up with Palos Verdes

Drive, a two-lane highway that ran along the water. The road circled the rounded peninsula that jutted so dramatically into the channel that separated Los Angeles from the distant and mysterious Santa Catalina Island.

The car purred along as Gary thought about his trip north to Sacramento. The trip hadn't been completely unproductive—it had been awhile since he'd seen his parents. But the question he had driven all the way up there to ask remained maddeningly unanswered.

Who were these people in his dream? Did he know any of them, or were they constructions of his mind? Did they have anything to do with him? Was the story something he remembered from his past, a story he had overheard, or just some scene from a half-remembered movie? And why did the dream repeat, over and over?

The road curled south as Malibu and Redondo disappeared behind him. He loved to drive this road, even when it was fogged over and a little dangerous. The roar of the ocean off to his right was loud, helping to clear his mind. Both sides of the small highway were decorated with huge, expensive homes with breathtaking views.

He passed through Camino Del Rey and the large ornate fountain that stood in the middle of an intersection—he remembered a nearby Italian restaurant there just a few hundred feet off the water with the most astonishing view of the ocean he had ever seen. He remembered sitting there with a date, looking out at the ocean, wondering at the support structures that held the restaurant precariously above the surf far below—no matter how he tried, he couldn't help wondering how things worked, how the pieces of a building fit together. As long as he could remember, he'd been fascinated with stairs, rooms, interior spaces.

Gary's thoughts wandered back to Sacramento—why was his father always so reluctant to talk about St. Louis? Gary knew a lot about the situation, and he still couldn't figure it out. With the loss of Gary's mother in that car bomb, it was a wonder that his father had even been able to go through with his testimony. The FBI had arranged for their move and had set them up in Sacramento with new lives and new last names, changing O'Toole to Foreman.

It was still strange that his father never talked about it. The words would not come, no matter how many questions Gary asked.

The Point Vincenté Lighthouse appeared from around an outcropping of rock, painting the cliffs and water with a cone of yellow light. On an impulse, Gary decided to stop the car. There was a large parking lot at the base of the lighthouse with a visitor's center and tables for picnicking.

The beam of light spun lazily from the tall, striped lighthouse as he turned into the parking lot, easing the car to a stop. The sound of the roaring waves hitting the rocks two hundred feet below was much louder with his engine turned off. There were no other cars in the parking lot.

He got out, closing the car door behind him, and stretched. It felt good to stand after so many hours in the car. Gary strolled down to a wooden fence that overlooked the ocean far below—there were gravel trails that ran along the cliffs on both sides of the lighthouse, and a long wooden fence along the cliff to keep those appreciating the ocean surf from experiencing it too intimately.

The light spun slowly, searching the distant water. Gary watched as it picked out and highlighted the gray crests of the far-off waves. He loved the ocean, loved the sounds it made as the water crashed against the rocks, slid up the sand, and retreated, hissing its way back into the ocean. He'd loved the ocean since he'd seen it the first time, shortly after he and his father had arrived from St. Louis.

Gary needed a smoke—it was cold tonight. He'd tried giving it up many times, but couldn't. It was his crutch. He'd given up drinking, and defeating one life-altering vice at a time was enough for anyone.

He pulled a cigarette from his pocket but couldn't find his lighter. He turned and walked back to the car, opening the passenger door.

Reaching for the cigarette lighter and pushing it in, his knee brushed against something crinkly in the area between the passenger seat and the open doorway.

Gary stepped back and saw a small white envelope that had fallen down beside the seat. It had to be Mike's—Gary didn't recognize it. He picked it up and felt it—there was something inside.

On the outside of the envelope was Gary's name.

That was strange.

Why would Mike have an envelope with Gary's name on it? Why wouldn't Mike have given it to him, and where did Mike get it?

The beam of the lighthouse brushed over him, picking out his name again, and he recognized his stepmother's backhanded scrawl.

A breeze picked up, bringing the salty scent of the ocean in off the water, bending one corner of the envelope back in his hand.

He turned the envelope over and pulled up the glued-down flap, reaching inside.

It was a photograph of a group of people, young kids in high school.

Gary recognized himself in the middle, and he was smiling with that mouthful of crooked teeth he had always wanted to get fixed.

The Gary in the photo was wearing a pointed hat, one of those plastic ones they make you wear on your birthday when you go out to eat at a restaurant.

There was a girl sitting on his lap that he didn't recognize, but she had one arm around him, smiling and leaning over to give him a kiss while still managing to look at the camera. There were three other people in the picture, arrayed around a table at a restaurant.

There was a large cake in the middle of the table.

The sharp cone of light from the lighthouse swung around again and lit up the picture clearly for the first time, and he saw the writing on the cake.

It said, "Happy 17th Birthday, Chris."

The pain came without warning, stabbing him in the head like a hot icicle through his temple. He put a hand to one eye and gripped the picture, squinting at it. Obviously, it was a birthday celebration for him, but he couldn't remember it. Gary's hand suddenly began shaking as the intense migraine squeezed his head, pounding, pulsating. He put his hands to his temples, feeling like he was holding his brains in. Gary stumbled against the side of his car, sliding down to the ground and passing out.

The picture fluttered and dropped to the parking lot along with the envelope. The light breeze scooted the picture along the dark pavement, blowing it toward the tall cliffs and the sea below.

------

A bright light washed over him.

For a long moment after Gary sat up, he had absolutely no idea where he was.

It came back in a flash of recognition as the lighthouse beam passed over him again, and for a moment he caught the strong scent of cigarette smoke. He pinched the bridge of his nose hard between his thumb and forefinger, squeezing right between his eyes, and the pain in his head seemed to back off a fraction.

Gary had been looking at a picture of a scene he could not remember and the pain had come suddenly. He guessed he'd passed out, something that had never happened to him.

Gary turned and looked around for the picture, but didn't see it. The moon had gone under a cloud, and it was dark except for the regular spinning of the beam of light.

He stood up slowly, holding onto the car for support, and then began walking around, looking. It wasn't windy, but he had no idea how long he had been out—the picture could have gone out to sea, or blown along the coast all the way down to the old abandoned Marineland Park, for all he knew.

Gary angled toward the wooden fencing that kept people from falling the hundred or so feet into the jagged rocks and roaring surf of the water below. There were rocks and small brush along the base of the fencing, and he spotted the photograph near the edge, one corner of it stuck under a rock.

He picked it up, dusting it off without looking at it, and headed back to his car, the passenger door still standing open.

Waiting for the next pass of the light, he looked more closely at the picture and picked out the name again.

No, he was not mistaken—it said "Chris," not "Gary."

Another wave of pain crushed his skull, but he resisted it, staring at the picture. The cake was obviously for him—the others in the picture, other faces he did not recognize, were all looking at him and smiling.

The girl on his lap was getting ready to kiss him. She had one arm draped around him in a familiar way.

The cake was right in front of him.

Had it been some kind of joke? Had someone been playing a prank on him, calling him the wrong name? The version of him in the picture looked about seventeen years old—surely he should be able to remember this occasion.

As far back as Sacramento, he had had trouble remembering people and events from back in St. Louis. He'd chalked it up to his mind preferring not to remember all those horrible times, like the trial, or watching his mother take her last breath.

But this picture didn't look that bad—he was smiling and happy. He looked happier in the picture than he could ever remember.

The cigarette lighter in his car popped out, but he didn't hear it—he was looking at the girl.

She was perfect. She looked like the kind of woman he would describe if someone were to ask him about his ideal companion. She had long, curly brown hair that seemed to shine with subtle red highlights—it looked like it was moving, even in the picture. She had big beautiful eyes and a tomboyish figure. The way she was draped over him, one arm casually around his neck, looked like she belonged there on his lap. They looked like they made a good couple....

Pain, like a wave, crashed over him. He stumbled and leaned against his car for support, for strength, as if he could somehow borrow some of the car's solidity.

He felt like he was losing his mind.

Gary forced himself to look at the picture again. The smile on her face, her lips pursed as she prepared to kiss him, told Gary that she was happy to be sitting there on his lap.

Who was she?

This was frustrating—he squeezed the bridge of his nose again, trying to relax and think clearly. His head throbbed from the pain. A cigarette sounded good right now, and a couple shots of tequila sounded even better. Or maybe just some wine, or a simple bottle of American beer.

He didn't care anymore—distraction was what he needed, not a thousand questions ricocheting around inside his mind.

The girl looked like she knew how to relax and have fun. She looked like she would be as comfortable at a formal dinner in a little black cocktail dress as she would be lounging on the couch in her sweats, watching a ballgame.

Why didn't he remember her? He could remember every woman he had ever known, could remember the names and faces of every woman he had ever dated. He should be able to remember this one.

The pain grew, a wave moving over him, threatening to wash him away.

He forced himself to look into the girl's eyes.

Her eyes.

There was something strange there, something that reminded him of....

The moon wasn't giving off enough light. He angled the picture up, and when the cone of illumination from the lighthouse spun around again, he stared at the picture.

Her eyes were the same.

Somewhere along the line, he'd dreamed different bits and pieces of the whole "drama" of the dream, experiencing different portions of it at different times. Sometimes he just dreamt of the horror and the pain. Other times he would dream of just being there in the bed, and knowing what was coming in the dream had made the waiting even more dreadful.

At one point he had started the dream even earlier in the narrative. The woman was sitting in bed, brushing her short-cropped hair. Gary could feel the hairbrush against his scalp, but as always, he was a passive observer, unable to warn the woman about the man about to come through the door, the man with that horrible smile and sharp knife. The woman continued brushing her hair, and then stopped, setting the brush down on a bedside table and picking up a small mirror.

Gary had gotten a glimpse of her face, just a quick one, as the mirror showed a reflection of her eyes. The woman gingerly touched her black-and-blue left eye—the bruise looked several days old—before turning the mirror up to look at her oddly cut, close-cropped hair.

But the eyes were the same as the girl in the birthday picture.

The same eyes.

What the hell did that mean? He was dreaming about this woman, a girl he'd supposedly met but couldn't remember.

Gary slowly put the picture back into the envelope and walked around the car, the ocean and his cigarette forgotten. He climbed in, wondering what, if anything, to do next.

He headed north, toward Redondo and the city. In the other direction was the rest of the loop around the Peninsula—the road ran past the abandoned Marineland Amusement Park, whose empty pools were so popular with skateboarders, finally leading to San Pedro and Long Beach.

But Gary wasn't in the mood for a long, leisurely drive anymore. He wanted to get home as soon as possible and look at the picture.

His car disappeared around the cliff side, his mind awash with questions and suppositions.

Behind him, the lighthouse continued to throw its cone of light out across the dark water, a beacon warning away approaching ships from the submerged rocks lurking just below the surface. Night after night, it protected those who wandered the dark sea.

# Chapter 21

"What else did he say?"

The young black man in front of him was fidgeting again, something Shotgun hated. The boy showed no respect for his elders—if he did, the boy would just get to the point. Of course, the kid was a little nervous, and Shotgun could hardly blame him.

The room was full of angry men sitting in chairs around the table or standing with their arms crossed behind them, leaning on the walls. Alfonse "Shotgun" Pope was sitting at the head of the table, a location he had earned, and the kid was on the other end, looking scared out of his mind.

"Well, he said that they were moving into the area. If I went to work for him, there would be something in it for me. He said things were going to get nasty. If I picked the right side now, things would be better for me."

Mumbling erupted from almost everyone in the room, punctuated with a few low curses. The men didn't seem surprised by what the kid was saying.

Shotgun wasn't surprised, not at all. He'd felt this was coming for a long time—it was a wonder it had taken so long. Thankfully, his intuition had been right—he'd spent the past year and a half consolidating his position, and now it would pay off.

The mumbling continued for a few minutes longer, or, more accurately, Shotgun allowed the mumbling to continue for a few minutes before he slowly raised one hand from the table, silencing the room. Some of the younger kids continued talking. They were elbowed into silence by the people near them.

Respect was all they had anymore. If Shotgun had learned anything from his many dealings with the Italians, it was that an organization based on respect for its elders was the most successful.

Pope's "set," or gang, was the most successful around, but it sounded like that was about to change.

"How did you leave it with him, Tim?" Shotgun asked the scared kid.

The young man looked up at the leader of his set, forming the words in his mind.

"I said I would think about it. They took what stuff I had, though, and gave me a good clock on the head before taking off, so I don't think they believed me."

Shotgun nodded, waving the kid away. Timmy hopped up out of his chair and dashed out of the meeting room, and his chair was quickly taken by one of the older men who had been standing.

The room grew quiet. Shotgun knew what he needed so say, but he let the room stay silent for a long moment before suddenly standing and starting his usual pace around the room. He only talked well when he paced. Of course, no one took his chair at the head of the table.

"This is bad. There is nowhere for this to go except for war, if things go as the Italians plan."

He glanced around and saw that he had everyone's attention. "The Lucianos are getting back into the crime business, so the rumors we have heard are true. They're moving into narcotics, and it sounds like Vincent Luciano is at the head of this. The fastest and most lucrative way to do that would be to muscle us off the nose trade once and for all." It was a vulgar way of labeling the enormous cocaine market in East St. Louis and the big city beyond, but Shotgun knew to use the latest terms—it reminded his underlings that he was still connected to the street in the most intimate ways.

"And if things go as they plan, they will slowly push us out and take over. I assume that they have already managed to locate a source, more than likely one of ours, and they may be negotiating with our other suppliers to cut us completely out of the market. If they can afford to outspend us, it could be dangerous."

There were nods and agreement all around the room—everyone respected Shotgun's leadership, especially when it came to the logistics of running an operation this big. Everyone was aware that he had the most experience of any of them in the dealing and supply side of coke—it was how he had cemented his position at the head of the organization.

He continued walking around the room, thinking about the next steps. He could initiate a gang war, something all of the men in this room probably would endorse, but that would most likely end up as a waste of valuable resources and contacts.

There had to be another way of getting the Luckies' attention.

Shotgun and the East Dogs were the most powerful Blood organization between New York and Chicago. Pope needed to make the Luckies see the reality of the situation.

They could share territories, or divide up the city if they were forced to, but that kind of thing usually only occurred after a summit of some sort—and this time, the Luckies hadn't even contacted him to let him know they were getting back into the business.

The Italians usually shied away from coke—Pope had done his homework and knew that dealing had almost destroyed the New York Mob back in the mid-eighties. But maybe they were ready to get back in. And start making money off his people.

"Okay. It's time to get ready. If they want a war and come looking, we must be ready. Make sure that we are fully prepared, and if there are things we need, get them. Everyone report back your group's status to your captains, and all captains report to Willie B. Reach out to everyone, even the soldiers and associates—we need ears to the ground. Anybody need anything special, tell your captains and they'll talk to Willie."

He stopped for a moment, silencing the low murmuring that had started up when he'd mentioned getting ready for war.

"But if it comes to war, we will have already lost. All the Italians have to do is cap about five or six guys in this room, or arrange for them to be capped by our own people, and this organization will topple—they'll walk right in and take over."

The room grew quiet. Every eye was on him.

Pope nodded. "So I want all the newest boys checked and double-checked, anybody new since...anybody in the past six months. Surely they've been planning this for at least that long. But most importantly, we need options.

"Talk to your people on the streets in O'Fallon and Granite City and Belleville," Pope continued. "Find out what you can about any changes in their organization. I know that old Mike Beneldo and a couple of his guys would never approve of moving into nose candy— they spent too many years making all of the Luckies' business legit. They're probably taking a dirt nap, but if not, we need to talk to them. We need information. Find out where they're getting their stuff and who they've got pushing it. Anybody pushing in this area, we should already know. And if there are any other options, we need to know about them, and soon. This is going to be fast and ugly. Thank you."

This was their cue. The entire group of captains shuffled out of the doors, keeping their conversations low and among themselves. Shotgun headed back over to his chair, where Willie B. and Rugio were still sitting. Willie B. was what the Italians would have considered to be Shotgun's underboss, the man who would take over if anything happened to him. Also following the Italian model, Shotgun had appointed Rugio as his *consigliere*, or counselor. Between the three of them, things had run smoothly in the almost two years since Old Tuan had taken a bullet in his back from an undercover cop.

Rugio spoke first. "Good speech. I think these are just the first moves, and we've got lots of time before we have to worry."

Shotgun nodded. "Yeah, but we have to start getting ready. And if the Luckies want a war, we can use it as an opportunity to grab up some of their business, especially down on the dock."

He was referring to the virtual lock that the Italian family had on the loading and unloading of shipments onto the East St. Louis docks, tucked beneath the Martin Luther King and Eads Bridges. The Italians had never been willing to even discuss sharing the profits from these operations, although by rights of territory, the East Dogs deserved something. If a war came, those operations would be up for grabs. It might even be worth a trade for some of the East Dogs' nose business in the eastern area of the gang's influence.

"Yeah, but war is a bad thing—I know from Compton that there is no way to win," Willie B. said, shaking his head. He was from the big time. He had come into town a few years back to visit family and ended up staying, working up from pushing to running his own crew to working directly under Shotgun, in line for the top job. "You kill each other and grab up some territory, but the cops come down like a wet towel and put everything on hold for months, even years. If we go to war, there would be no way for us to win and win quietly and not have the cops in here every day, driving around in their cars. We pay them now, but they'll need a lot more to look the other way if there are white guys getting offed in Belleville or getting dumped in Lake Carlyle, especially if they track any of it back to us. Lot of difference, two black gangs fighting for space and a black gang fighting some Italians. Could get ugly, and fast."

Shotgun nodded—this man knew what he was talking about. He'd helped them completely reorganize the transport side of their operation, saving them money and headaches by arranging for their own trucks coming up from Florida. It had been a ballsy move at the time, but cutting out that middleman and getting their own truckers had been smart and had saved a load of money.

"Rugio, what do you know about the Luckies?" Shotgun asked.

He shook his head. "Not a lot, Al. The word is out that they're changing direction—it looks like Vincent talked in Tony's ear long enough and they're tired of being legit. No one's seen any of the old *capos* lately, so it's possible Tony had them done, and there's no one left to contradict the change in policy. If that's right, Tony's listening to Vincent about what to do—Tony has no experience in coke, as far as we know. Vincent's run up against us a few times, mostly doing little stuff on the side, and we always pushed back. Maybe too hard, looking back on it. Anyway, they'll start in Belleville and O'Fallon and get a few of our guys to deal for them. Then they'll get their own supplier and undersell our pushers until they run the northern markets. After that, they'll come at us."

Nodding again, Shotgun wondered at the sheer knowledge and talent base in this room. Either one of these guys was good enough and smart enough to run the Dogs, and that made Shotgun feel better. If anything happened to him, the set would be in good hands.

"Willie, check with our suppliers and ask if any of them have heard anything. They might not be talking, so tease them with a big order or offer to bump our price up a little to offset their 'costs.' And see if there are any other pushers getting roughed up—in fact, have a meeting with the crews from the east side and give them a heads-up. Take them something nice—get them some girls. Impress upon them the importance of not leaving the crew. And find out who already has gone, and try and get them back. Use whatever tactics you think are necessary," he said, making eye contact with Willie B.

Willie B. nodded, and he and Rugio got up and left the room, leaving Shotgun alone with his thoughts.

Maybe he should try and contact Tony Luciano directly—or that might just be asking to get killed. If Vincent was running things now, the Luckies were in a lot of trouble. Shotgun had heard plenty of bad things about that guy—he was a loose cannon. Vincent's notoriously short temper might work in the favor of the Dogs.

Or Vincent might go too far, too fast. He might kill a bunch of Shotgun's men, trying to provoke a war. That was the problem with loose cannons—they were, by definition, unpredictable.

# Chapter 22

"Mom?"

His stepmother's voice came back over the phone connection tentatively, as if she was afraid to talk loudly.

"Yes, Gary?"

He jumped right into it, with no preamble.

"What does this picture mean, the picture of the birthday party? I see me in it, but the rest of the people I don't remember. And the name on the cake isn't right. And I don't know who the girl is. Is this all a joke or something? Why did you send this picture with Mike?"

There was silence on the other end, and Gary was about to say something else when she spoke. "Gary, you have to find out for yourself. Your father doesn't want you going back to St. Louis because it's too dangerous, but I think that's the only way you're going to be happy. Now, listen carefully, and I'll tell you what I know. You might want to write it all down."

He listened for a few minutes, interrupting her with questions, and writing down what he could. The story seemed plausible, all except for the part about the phrase....

A sudden pain shot through his head and he dropped the phone, needing both hands to hold onto the kitchen counter without falling. He took several long breaths, in and out, before picking up the phone, his stepmother's voice frantic on the other end.

"Could that be your mind reacting to the news, not wanting it?" she asked after he'd explained what happened.

"I don't know, Mom. The headaches have always come when I have the dream. My head would sometimes hurt when I tried to remember St. Louis or anyone back there, but the picture has made the headaches a hundred times worse."

She was quiet for a moment. "I know, son. I'm sorry. The phrase— your father doesn't remember the words, and he doesn't think there is anyone else alive who would know it. The doctor who hypnotized you was Frank Martin, your uncle, but he died after you and your father moved out here. Murdered, according to your father. You have to be very careful when you get to St. Louis. You can't tell anyone your name. Are you sure you want to do this?"

Gary nodded.

"Yes, I have to. My...real name, my friends, my memories—they're all back there. And I have to go back because...I think that girl in the picture—"

"Judy," his stepmother offered helpfully.

The migraine instantly blinded him. The world swam around him, fuzzy and indistinct, then suddenly went black.

Gary sat up, wondering where he was. The phone was on the kitchen floor next to him. After a moment, he remembered, and the headache came right back with the memory, searing into his mind....

Gary reached over and picked up the phone. "Mom?"

A relieved voice came back. "Oh, thank God! You scared me! I've been yelling into this phone for almost ten minutes, and nothing. What happened?"

"I...I passed out. If what you say is true, then maybe...maybe my mind isn't reacting very well to the news. I need to see a psychiatrist or someone and find out what's going on in my head. And like I was saying, I need to go back."

He paused for a long moment, collecting his thoughts, ignoring the pain. "The...girl in the picture, I think she's the one in my dream, and the dream is the reason for all of this in the first place. If it weren't for the dream, none of this would be happening. The girl in the picture—I think she might be in trouble. That's the feeling I get from the dream. My real name...."

Another sharp spike of pain left him speechless and panting. "My name...and the other stuff, I have to accept and figure out how it's all connected. I have to go back and find out, even if something happens."

The line was quiet for a moment, and then Denise answered.

"I know, son. Things are bad, and I know your father feels horrible about it. He waited...he always thought he would remember the words. He thought he would remember, and bring you up to Sacramento and you two would go see a doctor and finish this whole thing."

She stopped talking, but Gary didn't have the energy to prompt her—he was concentrating on writing everything down. And ignoring the tide of pain in his mind.

"And he's always been worried about you going back there and finding out too much about what happened," Denise said. "Your father's always worried whenever there's a story on the news about something happening in St. Louis—he almost had a coronary during all the flooding there back in 1993. Every night, the lead story on the news was about St. Louis. He was sure that you'd be watching the news and it would trigger something in your head. He worried himself sick about it."

It felt like crabs were digging around in his mind, scratching and clawing and biting and gnawing at the inside of his skull.

"Well," Gary said, "I really don't have any other choice. Should I talk to him about it before I go?"

"I don't think that would be a good idea. This is going to be hard enough when I tell him—I don't think he could take it from you." She was quiet for a moment, and Gary could sense the wariness in her voice. "I'm not looking forward to telling him about the picture—I thought it would trigger the memories, but I guess it only made you more curious. You don't remember anything new?"

The headache surged every time he tried to think about it.

"No, it hurts too much. I looked at the picture and it gave me the worst migraine I've ever had. I think the only solution now is to find the phrase—maybe someone back there knows it, and that will unlock the memories. And the girl...I have to help her."

"Well, at least take Mike with you," she said, agreeing. "I don't want you driving when you have one of those fits and pass out, okay?"

He smiled—she was looking out for him, even when delivering news that would shatter everything he knew about himself. "I will. Mike'll love the idea of a trip, even if he doesn't know what he's getting in for."

"Take care, son. You get better, and I love you."

"Thanks, Mom. I love you too," he said and hung up.

There was no easy way to think about all of this. Twice, near the end of their conversation, his vision had swum in front of him as if he'd just downed a fifth.

He'd noticed that his stepmother hadn't called him "Gary" again. She was just calling him "son," now. She must know that his real name hurt too much to hear.

It was difficult for him to resist grabbing his keys. He wanted so badly to drive to the closest bar and drown himself. He was starting to think that maybe drinking wasn't the problem—maybe his head was just so screwed up inside that he needed the alcohol to think straight.

But that wouldn't solve anything, and he knew that. It would only distract him. What he needed now was the truth, not a detour. He needed to go home—not to Sacramento, but to his real home.

O'Fallon, Illinois, held all the answers, whether the trip was a dangerous one or not.

Gary glanced at his bag, still packed from the trip to Sacramento. There wasn't actually a lot that needed to be done, but he had some arrangements to make, and some planning to do. There were tickets to buy, and people to make excuses to. He'd gotten good at making up excuses during his drinking days, and that skill would serve him well as he planned his trip.

He needed to get started.

# Chapter 23

Shotgun Pope realized that there was going to be a war.

He had become aware of the coordinated efforts the "Lucky" Luciano clan had taken over the weekend to edge into his eastern territories in Belleville and Collinsville, and he was stunned at the significant gains they had made in only three or four days.

Shotgun was reading a disturbing report written by one of his captains, but he was distracted by the horrible grammar. He had spent ten years trying to grow what began as just another East St. Louis Bloods gang into something more powerful and influential than anything that had come before. But too often, poor education—or a complete lack of education—held his soldiers back.

Few of his people took him up on his offer offering to pay for classes—they were much more concerned with scoring chicks or blow, or putting cash away. This 'report' was a classic example—it was barely readable. Reggie was one of his newer captains, overseeing a crew of about twenty soldiers, and they were mostly in charge of coke and a little heroin in East Belleville—there was a good market there, especially with the students at Belleville Community College. But any valuable information contained in the report was masked by the horrible grammar and pitiful spelling—the boy constantly spelled "there" the same way, no matter the usage. It was frustrating.

A buy had gone down in one of the parking lots of the Community College, and one of Rugio's soldiers, a guy named Bennie, was passing along some MJ and a bag of coke to one of the school's dealers. The routine transaction was completed and while they were talking, a dark car had pulled up and two guys had gotten out. At first, Bennie had thought it was a bust and wasn't too concerned—the student was now holding, and all Bennie had was four grand in cash in a paper bag sitting on the front seat of his car. There was a lot more in the trunk to be worried about, but Bennie was pretty sure they wouldn't have a warrant.

It took a moment for Bennie to realize that the men weren't cops. They slowly walked up and stood in front of Bennie and the student. After a moment, the one in front of the student punched him hard in the stomach. The tall guy had moved so fast, Bennie had hardly seen it. The student had dropped his stuff and bent over, holding his stomach, and the tall guy bent over and picked up the dropped coke.

The other guy was wearing glasses, too, but he was a lot shorter and on the chunky side. The chunky one pulled his glasses down and smiled at Bennie. "You're one of Shotgun's boys, huh?"

Bennie didn't know what to say, but the student was still bent over, and the tall guy kicked him again, right in the chest.

Chunky asked again, and this time, Bennie answered. It didn't seem to make sense to deny it, so he didn't.

One of Chunky's arms came out and stopped Tall from kicking the student again, and Bennie got the distinct feeling that Tall was enjoying himself. "You and your boys are done out here. This and the rest of the eastern side of B-ville are going to be part of our territory now—Shotgun should know that. This is too close to our own territory, and we need it just for our own protection. Open your trunk."

Bennie just stood there. Everything he needed to sell for the next week was in his trunk—he'd just picked it up this morning. Did they know that? He was trying to figure out what to do when Chunky suddenly slapped him hard across the ear, stinging it.

"You don't need to think about it, kid. Just open the trunk and give us the stuff," Chunky said, staring at him.

Bennie had slowly reached into his pocket and handed Chunky the car keys, who handed them off to Tall, who headed around to the back of Bennie's car and popped the trunk. The tall guy made three trips back and forth between Bennie's trunk and the trunk of their own car, and the whole time, Chunky just stared at Bennie. Bennie was just holding his breath, waiting for Chunky to pull out a gun and kill him.

Tall closed up Bennie's trunk and tossed the keys back to him.

Chunky smiled at him. "I'm not gonna pop you, kid. Tell Shotgun that this is your free pass, and that if you're out here again selling, or even if you're out here taking a class on how to fix car engines, you're gonna get popped. Got it?"

Bennie nodded, and the two men turned, got into their car, and left.

Shotgun finished the last part of the report quickly, barely able to read Reggie's elementary-school-level spelling. Reggie had had the same thing happen to three other guys, and one other soldier had gone off to make a deal in Collinsville, right near the big ketchup bottle, and hadn't shown up again. That was three days ago, and Shotgun could only assume the dealer was dead. His body would show up in a few days with some clever note on it that read "stay out of our territory" or something else equally witty. Things were starting to get ugly.

The encroachments on his territory were just the beginning—if the Luckies could get established, they'd either cut off his suppliers or undercut his prices. That, combined with a wave of disappearances and deaths among his people, would ruin him.

And he really had no idea what to do.

He pulled out a file on Tony Luciano and began flipping through it. The grandmother, daughter of the original "Lucky," had come west in the years just after the second world war, about the same time Lucky had been deported back to Sicily.

There was an interesting story behind all of that, Shotgun knew. Evidently, in the late 1930s, the Mafia and Lucky had controlled the entire New York waterfront. The U.S. Navy, concerned about possible sabotage and enemy encroachment into the largest American port, began asking questions. Everywhere they asked, they were referred to Lucky Luciano, who was at the time serving a prison sentence in the maximum security prison in Dannemora, New York, for running a prostitution ring. The U.S. Navy, refusing to answer to a mob boss, especially a jailed one, began basing ships in the New York waterfront near the mouth of the Hudson River.

Luciano and his representatives at the waterfront, Tony and Albert Anastasia, hit upon a perfect plan to get Lucky Luciano out of prison—blackmail the federal government.

On the morning of February 9, 1942, just two months after the Japanese bombing at Pearl Harbor, the American ship *Normandie*, once a luxury liner and in the process of being converted into a troop ship by the Navy, mysteriously caught fire. The fire, one of the most spectacular in the harbor's history, burned out of control for several hours before the ship finally turned on its side and capsized in the shallow water.

The Navy supposedly approached the Mafia, seeking a solution to the sabotage problem, but were told that only Lucky had the authority to protect ships at the docks. A month later, the Navy reportedly got their guarantee that there would be no more acts of sabotage and that the Mafia would work with federal officials to ensure the safety and security of the Navy's ships. In exchange for this "assistance," Lucky Luciano was to be released at the end of the war. In addition to their help with the waterfront, the Mafia offered to and eventually assisted the Navy in their invasion of Sicily in June 1943, asking their Sicilian brothers to assist the invading Americans. In the end, Lucky Luciano had been released just after the war and deported back to Italy.

Now, generations later, the Lucianos were still a force to be reckoned with, although a shadow of their former power. After Tony Luciano had taken over, the family had gone "legit," divesting themselves of any illegal activities. They'd allowed all of their political contacts and union officials to drift away, and set themselves up as legitimate businessmen. They leased office space in an expensive building in Belleville.

But in the past three months, that had all changed.

Shotgun set the folder aside and picked up another one, one assembled by Rugio, an excellent investigator and a very intelligent man.

Tony and Vincent Luciano were not close, as far as Rugio could tell. The brothers had drifted apart when Tony, the older brother, was named to head the Luciano family. Vincent had fought Tony's move to legitimacy and begun his own small organization. There was also some mysterious hit that Vincent had reportedly botched—the details on that were sketchy. But Vincent had ended up bartending in a local restaurant and fronting drugs and guns through his old contacts, assembling a small but effective crew of his own.

When Tony had decided to drift back to his mob roots, it was reportedly out of desperation—Rugio reported that the organization had sunk all of its free cash into the gambling ships docked along the Mississippi River.

One of Tony's old *capos* had resisted the change in direction, but Tony had evidently overruled him—the man had been found dead in his home, supposedly a suicide.

Tony and Vincent were taking the family back to where it had begun. They were moving into coke, and there was low-level talk of loan sharking and even some low-rent prostitution.

Shotgun flipped the page, reading about the brothers themselves. Tony lived alone, dating occasionally, a workaholic. Shotgun looked at the man's home address and pictures of the large house, contemplating the home's guards and security systems, then turned the page.

Tony wasn't the dangerous one. Vincent appeared to be influencing his brother to go down this new path, and it was his contacts and suppliers being used to expand their influence. He lived in an old house outside of O'Fallon on Blackwood Lane, a half-mile from the nearest residence. Vincent had a wife, and Rugio had included in his folder some reported instances of abuse, something Shotgun hated to see. Vincent's wife looked like an attractive woman, but her face was covered in each of the pictures they had. The only good photograph showed her face with a nasty patch of bruises covering one cheek and a long laceration along her chin.

Vincent wasn't a man to respect, but evidently he was a man to be feared. Maybe if something were to happen to him, his brother's fervor about the current war would subside.

Maybe if Vincent were out of the way, Tony and Shotgun could come to some kind of agreement. Shotgun set the folder back down on his desk and sat back in his chair, thinking. There might be a way out of this that didn't involve a war, or even much bloodshed.

# Chapter 24

She could hear his Mustang coming up the driveway—he was early today, but then his schedule had been erratic since he'd gotten back into the family business. She was going to have to figure out a way to get more warning.

Judy slipped the palette of paints back into the battered "Mama's Sausage and Pepperoni" pizza box, trying to keep it flat as she walked it out to the laundry and put it back in the big icebox that seemed to take up half of that small room. The paints would keep—they always did, but she was worried about them sliding together and blending. It was so hard for her to buy more paints, and she wanted to be careful with what she had.

Judy ran back into the living room and picked up the painting and easel, carrying them both back into the laundry. This was the one room he almost never went into, and she either kept her paintings in here or up in the attic. Stuff she was working on, like this seascape with a tall palm tree leaning out over the water, went behind the washer.

He came in loudly just as she turned a talk show on and plopped down on the couch. She could hear him move immediately into the kitchen, and she heard the refrigerator open and the sound of a can popping open. She'd bet her last dollar that it was a beer.

Vincent came around the corner and looked at her. "What a lazy bitch! What are you doing, woman?"

She pointed at the screen. "I was watching Springer. Something on adult film stars, the things they go through. Did you know that they have to get tested for HIV infection every three weeks? And they have to bring proof to the set every day before they start filming?"

He just looked at her. She loved moments like this, when he was simply stunned into silence—they were like little diamonds for her to hold onto and treasure against the other times.

Vincent shook his head and turned, heading toward their bedroom. And she smiled to herself. As long as she could keep her sanity, things would be okay.

Thinking about her dreams helped, too—especially the strange dream she'd had the night before.

She'd been sitting in her bed, alone, brushing her hair with her big, silver hairbrush and thinking about Chris O'Toole, wondering what he was doing. Funny how she could remember what she'd been thinking in her dream. Chris's face had been right there. She'd glanced into her hand mirror and for a moment, it had looked like his eyes staring back at her.

That was when the yelling had started, and she'd dropped the brush and pulled the sheets up around her tight. The bedroom door was closed but she could see it outlined in white, like there was some kind of really bright light on the other side, and then it had burst open. Vincent. He came stumbling in, anger written all over his face, and she saw that he was limping and that one of his arms was wrapped in a sling. The other hand was behind his back, and he walked over to her fast—yet at the same time, it seemed like it took an eternity for him to cross that eight feet from the door to the bed. There was a dark sweatshirt tied around his waist, one she didn't recognize.

She was looking up and his eyes were practically glowing with anger—his hair was all messed up and there was spittle around his mouth. He looked absolutely mad.

"You...little...bitch," he'd said, looking down at her, and that was when she had suddenly woken up, sweating and startled.

Judy Luciano glanced around at the white walls of her prison, and shook her head. She didn't understand the dream fully, but she knew it was telling her one thing. She had to get out of here soon—one way or another.

# Chapter 25

"Just up and leaving, huh?" Mike asked. Gary had not been firing on all cylinders the past few months, but now Mike was wondering when his good friend had stepped completely over the brink.

Gary nodded. They were sitting in his apartment, facing each other over the low IKEA coffee table. There was nowhere else to go, and the suitcase was sitting on his bed, visible through the doorway to his bedroom, still packed from their Sacramento trip.

"I'm taking a week off," Gary said. "It's not that big of a deal."

Mike smirked, and started to say something, but Gary interrupted.

"I know Simmons is going to be pissed, so I'm working to finish up those hospital plans. I can have them done by Thursday if I crank. I'll leave Friday and take next week off."

Mike nodded, listening. "And you think this is going to help you...figure things out?"

Gary reached around behind him. "Did you see what was in the envelope my stepmother gave you?"

Mike shook his head. "No, of course not. And I'm sorry about that—she said you shouldn't look at it, whatever it is, alone, but it was so late and I was so tired, I didn't realize it was missing until I got inside. And by then, you were gone." Mike felt horrible —whatever had been in the envelope had had a serious effect on Gary, big enough for him to suddenly take a week off from work and fly back to St. Louis.

"Don't worry about it. It was actually better that I was alone. Here," he said, handing a small color photo over to Mike. "Take a look at this and tell me what you think."

Mike looked at the photograph and was, for a moment, confused. The boy in the center looked like a younger version of Gary, maybe from high school. There was a cute girl on his lap and a birthday cake on the table in front of him.

But the name on the cake was wrong.

Mike glanced up at Gary, suddenly worried. "Why does this say 'Chris' instead of 'Gary'?"

His friend's face tightened at the mention of the name. After a moment, Gary slowly smiled and leaned forward. "Well, evidently my name isn't Gary."

One hand drifted up to his head, and Mike could see the pained expression on his face.

"Wow, these things come on fast," Gary said. "Anyway, my real name's right on the cake."

Mike looked at the picture again.

"And the girl. A girlfriend? She's sitting on your lap and she's getting ready to kiss you."

"That's what my stepmother says. We were...pretty serious there for a while, she says." His eyes were closed when Mike glanced up at him and Gary was pinching the bridge of his nose between his thumb and forefinger.

"You okay?" Mike asked.

"Comes every time I look at the picture, or think about my real name, or think about her. Evidently—you're going to love this one, I promise—I was hypnotized before I left St. Louis. My father had some of my memories forcibly suppressed."

Mike chuckled. "Sounds like a story from a bad soap opera."

"Yeah. I guess when my father testified in that trial, I didn't want to leave St. Louis. I fought and fought, trying to get back to her," he said, nodding at the photo. "The FBI suggested that temporary memory suppression could be helpful to get me to cooperate, so my father agreed. Only the memory suppression wasn't removed as planned, and I've never gotten those memories back."

Mike was stunned. "That sounds like some crazy bullshit to me." If he were hearing the plot of a movie being described to him, he'd keep his six dollars in his pocket. But then, what was with the picture? A prank played on a younger version of Gary? After a moment, Gary hadn't disagreed with him, and Mike continued. "You don't remember the girl at all?"

Gary was quiet for a minute, thinking, and Mike wondered if what he had heard was true. Could someone's memories be suppressed, and for that long? And what kind of psychological damage would result if all of the memories suddenly came back? His friend should be spending the next week in an institution, or getting some therapy, not traipsing around the Midwest, looking for some mystery girl from his past.

"No, Mike, I don't remember the girl at all. After the trial, I disappeared and never contacted her again, so I guess she just went on with her life." He was quiet for another long moment, and Mike looked at him, noticing that his hands were shaking, like he'd just drunk six cups of coffee. "But I've seen her recently."

"What? You've seen her here, in Los Angeles?"

"No," Gary said, looking up at his best friend. "She's the one in the dream."

------

Mike was home, looking at the picture again. Gary had insisted that Mike take it with him, saying the urge to look at it was uncontrollable and always left him reaching for the Advil.

Gary had also asked Mike to go with him to St. Louis. Mike couldn't decide what to do—he wanted to help his friend, but wasn't this whole thing just about ten steps past crazy?

The picture didn't lie—it was clear and focused and apparently genuine, three things that Gary no longer appeared to be. There was no arguing with the image of the girl on the younger Gary's lap, or the cake with the wrong name on it, or the friends around the table that obviously knew Gary. Gary said the faces were vaguely familiar and that one guy's name was Tom or Tim, something like that. Gary said that the headaches didn't come when he thought about the guys in the picture—just the girl and the cake.

Mike had some vacation time at work and could wrap up the Austin airport plans—he'd been dragging them out anyway, trying to do a really good job and spread out the billable hours as much as possible. But the airport concourse and buildings were done; he was left with working on the entrance and approach roads, something he could knock out in a day. So it wasn't the logistics or the vacation time that made Mike nervous.

No, it was the effect all of this was having on his friend.

Gary swore up and down the girl's eyes were the same as the woman's eyes in the dream he'd been having. It was insane. If that were somehow true, then this girlfriend he couldn't remember was in trouble—a fact that Gary couldn't ignore.

Gary had been too busy to think about it, but Mike had been wondering ever since he'd heard about the girl's eyes—what if there were some kind of crazy, tenuous connection between the two of them? Could she be calling out to Gary because she was in trouble?

Mike didn't think it was possible for such a thing to happen. He wasn't the kind of person to believe in all that sappy romance surrounding love—it had never happened to him, and he didn't think it was even possible. Sure, love and dating could have their pleasures, but there was no special "connection" between people. There were no "kindred spirits" or "soulmates" or any of that other happy-crappy spewed out by romance novels and cheap date movies.

There was nothing but physical attraction and mutual affection, and the women in Los Angeles had taught him that. They weren't interested in long romantic walks or shared candlelit baths or quiet evenings at home putting puzzles together. All that concerned them was which model BMW you drove and who you knew in the business that could get them a screen test or a script reading or an agent. It was all so superficial and useless that Mike had long ago stopped thinking about the possibility of deep, truly romantic love.

But Mike was worried about his friend. Worried about these blackouts Gary was having. If looking at the picture made his head hurt so bad that he passed out, what would Gary do when he actually got back to St. Louis?

More than anything, Mike's concern for Gary's welfare made him decide. He got the suitcase back down from the top shelf of his closet where he'd just put it the night before and started packing.

And Mike was curious, curious about the possibilities, about a tenuous and impossible connection. Did that kind of love really exist, the kind that could span the years and the miles between them? Could it somehow be calling Gary back to her? Mike didn't know, but he was open-minded enough to want to find out.

# Chapter 26

"And?" Vincent said, trying to get more out of his brother. It was Wednesday night, three nights after they'd moved in earnest against the East Dogs' territories, and two of the Lucianos' men had turned up dead this morning.

Vincent knew it was only the beginning.

Tony just sat there like a bump on a log, saying nothing. Nothing pissed Vincent off more than when he asked someone a question and didn't get an answer. But he needed to find out how the phone call had gone, and his brother was clammed up tight.

"Look, Tony, I told you things were going to get ugly. This is a big business, and there's a lot of money to make. And the people already in the business want to keep that money, not share it, and certainly not give it up to somebody else, *capiche*?"

"Yeah. The East Dogs are serious about it, and Shotgun wants a 'summit' to discuss our movements into his territory. I think Scott and Gino getting killed was just a sign to us that they're serious."

Vincent was stunned—the resignation in his voice was apparent. His brother had said he wanted to get into more profitable, less "legit" businesses, and now that they were doing it, he was shirking from the duties at hand.

This was disappointing, to say the least. Vincent thought he'd have to step in at some point, but the look on his brother's face, brought on by the reported deaths of a couple of family old timers, told Vincent he'd have to move up his timetable.

"Listen, Tony. Wars are not necessarily a bad thing—we could use one now, if only to clean out some of the dead weight in our organization. And if...I mean when we win, we'll wipe out the East Dogs and take over a very profitable business."

He looked at his brother, but nothing was happening. Vincent wondered if his brother had it in him to run a large and illegal operation—had the guy only been fooling himself? Vincent didn't think so—he thought his brother only needed a little "seasoning," a taste of what this life could be like, and he'd come around. But in the meantime, he'd have to keep an eye on his brother. Somewhere in the space of the past twenty-four hours, after the reported deaths within the organization, Tony had gone soft inside.

Vincent tried another tactic.

"Wars are a glorious thing, too," he told his brother. "Tony, you know the history of our family, the histories of the other families better than anyone I know. Lucky would never have been able to seize power in the '30s and make all of his reforms if he and Frank Costello hadn't started a war and taken out Mangano. Look at what came out of that war—Luciano took Mangano's template for the new *Cosa Nostra* and made it infinitely better. Lucky started the idea of a council made up of each of the *familia*'s bosses, sharing the power across all the families."

Tony was coming around—Vincent could see it in the way he was nodding along, his eyes a little glossed over when anyone talked about the family history. The man was obsessed with it—Vincent knew that his brother could lose himself for hours, watching old gangster movies or reading books on the history of the Mafia.

"You're right," Tony was saying, agreeing with Vincent. "It's going to be like any other territorial dispute, but since there's no council, we have to go to war. Should I meet with Shotgun?"

Vincent thought about that. "If there were a way to meet with him and also cap him, it would be a good thing. But he'll be looking for that, and I know how smart he is. We've had our share of run-ins. Let me work on something, but until then, don't answer. Just work on planning the war and recruiting new soldiers through your *capos*."

Tony nodded. "If we win...well, this is what I've wanted for a long time." He looked up at his brother. "I guess I just wasn't expecting it to be so ferocious."

"Well, Tony, it'll get a lot worse before it gets better." Vincent said, standing and looking down at his big brother. The man wasn't even close to being ready to run this organization properly—Vincent knew that now. And that changed things.

# Chapter 27

Los Angeles International Airport, better known to travelers as LAX, was not a friendly airport.

Getting into and out of there was a nightmare. The airline terminals were all arrayed around a huge central parking garage, or more accurately, a series of about ten massive parking garages. Gary finally found the correct garage across from his airline's terminal and pulled into a spot. The parking was an insane $10 a day—he made a mental note to save some cash to pay for the parking upon returning from St. Louis.

Whoever designed this airport was an idiot, Gary thought. It was as if no planning at all had gone into passenger flow, or the proximity of parking to the gates, or the way the shops and restaurants were grouped. Clearly the airport had been expanded since the original construction, and it looked as if new terminals and garages had simply been tacked onto the original structure. Of course, the airport was a relic from the seventies and sorely in need of an update, but Gary still wondered at the need of some designers to favor form over function. His superiors at MacMillian would never have let him get away with this kind of shoddy planning.

Last night, Gary had dreamed of being in a fire. He'd been surrounded by flames and a strangely billowing smoke colored a thousand different shades of blue. He had absolutely no idea what any of it meant.

Gary climbed from the car and opened the trunk, and Mike pulled Gary's suitcase out for him. For the tenth time since he'd picked Mike up, Gary wanted to thank him for coming along. This was going to be hard enough, and it was great to know that he had someone with him he could count on.

They were leaving from Terminal 3, Gate 32, on the northern side of the airport, and they were early enough to grab a drink at one of the airport bars before heading down the lengthy terminal toward the gates. They checked their bags at the ticket counter and walked to the bar after passing through security. Gary got them a table, and after a minute, Mike settled down at their table with two tall glasses—Mike's was beer, and Gary's was coke.

"Do you have the picture?" Gary asked again.

Mike tapped his shirt pocket. "For the fourth time, yes. Don't worry—it's safe. Any dreams last night?"

Gary looked at him.

"No. The last time was night before last—it seems that since I've decided to go back, the dreams haven't been as bad. Explain that one. It's the same dream, but more manageable, somehow. And I've had a couple of new ones, though I think they're all related."

Mike nodded, keeping his thoughts to himself.

They chatted for a while longer, avoiding the subject. They talked about the Los Angeles Kings and their trading away of Wayne Gretzky. They discussed the layout of the airport and the improvements that could be made, such as improving the flow of passengers through the security area, and talked about the new FAA control tower, which Mike mentioned had just been completed.

For the first time in a long time, Gary didn't feel troubled or particularly nervous—this was all going to be resolved, and soon, and then he would be able to get on with his life.

The plane left on time, and as they banked out over the ocean, Gary's window seat looked down on the Palos Verdes Peninsula. The water crashed against the shore far below, and for just a few moments, he could pick out the small grey shadow of the Point Vincenté lighthouse.

# Chapter 28

Tony assured himself that there was no way anyone could have predicted it would all happen so quickly. He reminded himself that he needed to remain calm, remain in charge. Tony had his guys out, working hard, and so far, things were going well.

Tony glanced down at his notes—he and his captains had just completed their regular Friday morning meeting. Just because some of them were thugs, it didn't mean they couldn't run things in an organized manner, and regular meetings were a part of that.

The Beverage Company business had almost solved itself—as soon as Tony's representative had threatened the president of the drink company, the man had folded. There was no way the company could get its drinks and beverages to area stores unless the trucking company showed up to move them, and Tony controlled the trucking company. For the first time in almost ten years, protection money changed hands in the St. Louis area, and Tony's organization had grown $20,000 richer in a matter of moments.

This was the way the business was supposed to be run, Tony thought as he stood and started pacing around the room. This is the way things had been run back in New York City, back when his grandmother had run her own small crew through the dirty streets of Queens and Brooklyn, scamming and stealing for the Luciano *familia*. There was an honorable history to their family—in fact, back in Sicily the members of the Mafia had been known as "men of honor" or "men of respect." Either one worked fine for Tony.

So far there had only been a couple of casualties, both related to this cocaine business. Looking back, maybe it had been a mistake to get involved with that side of the business so quickly—they should've held off and gotten settled in some of the other new activities before branching out into drugs.

As it was now, Tony was trying to grow the other illegal activities and, at the same time, prepare for a war.

The East Dogs had been making loud noises about their territory. Nothing bad had happened in the past two days, other than the disappearance of one of the new dealers working in the disputed territory. Tony thought the man had probably been taken to inform on his organization. He didn't envy the man, but there wasn't much that remained a secret about the Luciano family—they were making a big move into the cocaine business, and that was that.

And business was picking up—the initial shipment from D.W. was long gone, and Vincent had made two smaller buys from alternate suppliers, moving a fair amount of product in the past week. There was no way to estimate the amount of street demand they would have to satisfy, especially if there were no other strong rival group fronting the stuff in the area. Vincent was preparing to make another large buy tomorrow night, different from the smaller, more cautious purchases they had made in the past. That, combined with what they had been able to steal or intercept from the East Dogs, ensured enough supply for at least another month.

But Tony was more worried about that side of the business than he was letting on. He quietly wondered if going with Vincent's instincts had been the right thing to do.

His thoughts were interrupted by his brother walking into the room and sitting down. The man looked completely calm and relaxed, almost an exact opposite to his fidgeting brother. Tony resented the man's calm—this buy had to go perfectly tomorrow. All the seed money and their profits from the last week were going into this one big buy, securing what would be enough coke to fill the trunk of Vincent's Mustang—over 150 pounds of the stuff.

Even though they had set up an excellent processing center right there on the docks near where the exchange would take place, Vincent insisted on transporting the product himself. The thinking was that D.W. didn't need to know any more about the Lucianos' operations than he had to, and having them deliver the goods right into the processing area would afford him too much information about the Lucianos' setup.

The exchange of goods for cash would be made in the parking lot across from the new boat, and Vincent would then take the drugs and drive away, circling back and returning to the warehouse after D.W. and his people were gone. It seemed the best thing to do, and the safest. No one was sure where D.W.'s loyalties were placed, and trusting anyone in the criminal world was usually a mistake.

But it made Tony nervous, Vincent driving around on the streets of East St. Louis with a million-and-a-half dollars worth of cocaine in the trunk of his car. Vincent was no idiot—he must've been able to see the anxiety written on Tony's face.

"Don't look so glum, brother!"

"I know, Vincent," Tony said, nodding. "Things are going well, but this buy tomorrow night has me very worried. There are so many things that can go wrong, especially with the way you have it set up. I understand that we don't want D.W. knowing where we process the drugs, but...."

Vincent put up his hand and stopped him. "I know, it's a risky move. But doing it at the riverboat is perfect—anything goes really wrong and we dump the product in the water. You give them the money while they load the stuff into my car, nice and easy. I drive around for a little while, then drive my car right into the warehouse and we unload it. No problem."

Tony looked up at him sharply. "A million and a half in coke? There's no way that can go into the water—that money represents all of our capital. If anything goes wrong with this buy or we lose the coke, the *familia* will not recover."

He looked into Vincent's eyes, gauging what he saw there before continuing in a low, quiet voice. "I think we should stop the buy, put it off until we're a little more on our feet."

Vincent leaned away from the table, and Tony wondered what the man was thinking. Tony wasn't naïve enough to assume that Vincent didn't have aspirations of running the family himself, but Tony didn't think he had the courage or the people to make a move anytime soon. And they'd never really gotten along after Tony cut him out of the family business. Tony had made the logical decision, but Vincent had never really let it go.

Vincent steepled his hands and fingers, reminding Tony of their father. He'd always done that when he was about to say something important. Was Vincent even aware of what he was doing?

"Tony, I understand you're worried about this buy. Frankly, I'm worried too. A lot of things could go wrong—D.W. might not show, or the East St. Louis cops might get tipped off, or Shotgun and his crew might show up and make things interesting. But look at it this way—one purchase, like the one we're going to make tomorrow night, and we'll own this entire market for the next twenty years. Tomorrow night's product will go out onto the street at a low price, undercutting Shotgun's prices, effectively putting him out of business. Now, we might get some grief about that from him, but I don't think it'll be anything we can't handle. And with him gone, we'll own a market with a 400% return on investment, minimum, and that's figuring for lost shipments. This is the future, brother. We have to seize the moment. The buy will go smoothly, we'll have secured a major supplier, and Shotgun's crew will disappear."

Tony nodded through the speech, wondering when his brother had gotten so savvy about business. As far as Tony knew, his brother had only run little scams and pulled down money tending bar. But based on what he was saying, the man was a lot more intelligent than Tony had ever given him credit for.

And that last part....

"What do you mean about Shotgun's crew?"

Vincent shook his head and patted the table in front of them with one hand. "Let's just keep you out of that, okay? There are things in the works, things that should happen tonight and tomorrow night to make a lot of our problems go away."

"You mean war? Or something else?" Tony asked, already fearing the answer.

"No, brother. This will not be a war. This will be a preemptive strike against a gang of street punks and junkies. They can't run things nearly as well as we can. Half of their dealers are using the stuff, snorting or shooting up the profits. They don't know how to run a business—Shotgun has been getting along by the skin of his teeth for too long."

Tony wondered about the details, but Vincent didn't elaborate.

"Do you have good guys?" Tony asked.

Vincent nodded. "Yeah, a few from Miko's crew, two made guys with experience in Chicago and Denver. They came over when Miko talked to his contacts in Denver, passing along our new direction. They just got in last night, but Tony Regato out in Denver vouched for them."

Good. They didn't have a lot of experience locally with hits or leaning on people. But that was all changing, and quickly.

"Okay. Let me know how the hits go, and I'll decide tomorrow whether or not we make the buy."

Vincent looked up at him sharply.

"No, brother. We make the buy either way—it took a long time for me to set this whole thing up. They've gotten it into the country already, a big deal for them, and we have to take it or they'll never sell to us again. We'll come out looking like idiots and have no product to sell when Shotgun's crew goes away."

Tony looked at his brother carefully, gathering himself. "I guess you didn't hear me, brother. I know you want this sale to go through, and you've worked hard to set it up, but this whole new side of our business makes me uncomfortable, and I need a little while to think—"

"Uncomfortable?" his brother practically shouted, leaning in to the table. "This makes you uncomfortable? This buy makes great business sense and will turn us a bigger profit than all of your little pissant money laundering and loan sharking schemes could pull down in a year! We have to make this deal!"

Tony didn't like the way this was going. He sensed something in Vincent's eyes. "Vince, this isn't a debate. I run this family, and you need to remember that."

Vincent grew quiet.

"Okay, now here's what we're going to do," Tony spoke slowly, looking at his brother. "Make this Shotgun thing happen tonight and call me tomorrow morning. If things go well, we'll move forward with the buy, okay? But this shipment will be our last for a while—I need some time to figure out if this is a business I want the family involved in. I know that it's a good money maker—Lucky knew that too when he tried to corner the coke and heroin markets from Sicily after he got deported. I know it's good business, but it still makes me uncomfortable. I think we need to concentrate on the other activities, establish our base a little more, before we branch out in this direction. The cops won't look too kindly on us if we get really dirty, and we're not ready to withstand a lot of close scrutiny. We'll need more of them on the payroll."

After a few moments, Vincent nodded.

"Okay," Vincent said. "I can live with that. As for tomorrow night's buy, do you want to be there? That is, if it happens."

"Yeah. We need a solid front for D.W. to see, and if we decide to buy anything else from them, they'll negotiate better if they see us both. The dock and parking lot are secure?"

Vincent nodded and stood, smiling. "Yeah, we're doing it in the main parking lot—off the boats and with easy access to the roads if something goes wrong. But nothing will, brother, and after tomorrow night, things will look a lot different to you. I promise."

# Chapter 29

The plane from LAX landed three hours later at Lambert International Airport, just north of St. Louis, Missouri, right on schedule. After Mike and Gary collected their bags, they headed for one of the dozen car rental counters near the exits to the parking lots.

Gary took care of the car and in only a few minutes they were on their way, heading east.

St. Louis, Missouri, was a sprawling city, completely nondescript except for the downtown area and the stunning Gateway Arch near the riverfront. The rest of the city was as generic as any other decaying urban center. As Mike and Gary passed the red brick buildings and strip malls of the northern suburbs, they could have been driving through the outskirts of any of a dozen other Midwestern cities—Akron or Indianapolis or Kansas City or Oklahoma City—they all looked the same.

Gary vaguely remembered this area of town, but he'd only been to the airport a couple of times to pick up relatives, and he really hadn't paid attention. His mind was elsewhere—he was wondering about the girl in his dream; even in his mind, he had trouble saying her name.

More out of habit than anything else, his hand reached into his coat pocket and pulled out his tarot deck. He shuffled it mindlessly with one hand as he drove. If it made Mike nervous, he didn't say anything—he was watching out the windows at the blighted buildings flashing by, one after the other.

After a couple of passes through the deck, he set it in his lap and flipped the top one over, glancing down at it as he drove. It was a reversed Three of Swords, which could mean any number of things, none of which were particularly good. Mostly it symbolized distraction and confusion, mental anxiety, loss, and alienation—accurate, considering his current state of mind. After a moment, he tucked the deck away in his pocket and watched as the road curled southward.

The Gateway Arch suddenly loomed ahead from behind a group of low brick buildings, the graceful arc of stainless steel bright against the blue, cloudless sky behind it.

Gary remembered that monument so well—seeing it every day growing up, looming on the horizon or curling up into the sky above him on his many visits to its foot. He remembered riding up to the top in those strange round elevator cars. Visitors could walk around the top gallery, looking out the slit-like windows on either side of the metallic arch. He remembered once staring out the windows, looking down at Busch Stadium; a day game was in progress, and he could see the little baseball players on the grassy field. He remembered watching for a few minutes before her hands alighted on his shoulders, urging him to leave so they could move on to the next destination on their date—

The pain engulfed him, with no warning. It was an instant migraine, worse than anything he'd felt before.

He let go of the wheel.

Gary bent over in pain, holding his head in his hands.

The pain was there, and nothing else. His head throbbed with his pulse. He pushed in with both hands on either temple.

The car drifted over into the next lane, toward the center median and the concrete dividers.

"You okay, man?" Mike asked, glancing over at him for the first time—he must've been staring at the Arch, too, and hadn't noticed Gary's response—and gasped, grabbing for the wheel. The car jerked back into its lane, and Mike shouted at Gary to pull over.

For a long moment, Gary didn't respond, but finally he nodded, sitting back up. He could feel the migraine back off a fraction, and he concentrated, lifting his foot up off the accelerator. He watched as the world swam around him, alternating fuzzy and sharp. His heart was racing, pounding in his chest. A part of his mind told him that Mike was directing the car onto the shoulder, and his foot began applying the brakes, ignoring the harsh honks and squealing of tires behind him.

Seeing the Arch—there was a memory, about her and him.

The car came to a stop, and Gary came back into the moment, realizing that Mike was shouting at him.

"Gary! What the hell was that? I couldn't get you to take your damn foot off the gas, and we were racing along like a bat out of hell! You pass out? Are you okay?"

Gary nodded slowly, his hands still gripping his seatbelt. "Yeah, I'm okay. More...memories coming back. I have a feeling that it'll just get worse. Thanks . . .thanks for grabbing the wheel."

Mike didn't say anything.

Gary smiled weakly. "Maybe we should switch seats."

Mike smirked and climbed out of the car as Gary slid over. "You scared the hell out of me, man," Mike said as he got back in the car. "Now I'm glad I came along—somebody's got to keep you from killing yourself."

Gary nodded, watching Mike as he started down the highway.

It was crazy, the idea that he was really someone else with a different name. How much else of his life had been sublimated by the hypnosis? If he'd been thinking straight, he would've gone and seen his father first, talked to him and found out what the hell had happened, but the dream seemed to be calling to him to come back here, and fast. Maybe the dream was just his mental wall finally breaking down.

There was no way for him to understand all of it yet, but something inside him said his father's information, though immensely helpful, would have delayed something crucial, something to do with the girl in the picture, the girl in his dream. There was some reason he had been drawn eastward. He hoped these debilitating headaches wouldn't hamper him—how would his mind react when he saw her, if he did manage to find her? He was practically knocked out just from seeing a stupid landmark. Seeing her would probably drop him to the ground, rolling around in the mud and drooling like a maniac. That would be impressive, certainly.

Memorable.

Mike followed Gary's curt directions, angling the car through the confusing maze of roads that was downtown St. Louis, heading over the Poplar Street Bridge and the Mississippi River.

Gary turned around when they were on the massive bridge that spanned the wide river and looked back at the city. There was Busch Stadium, where the Cardinals played, and Union Station, and he could see gambling steamboats on the eastern side of the river, tied up to new docks—evidently the legalized riverboat gambling business was paying off.

And he saw the Adam's Mark Hotel, where the O'Fallon Township High School had its prom in 1987.

A complete memory of his high school years popped into his head, unbidden, and this time, he had no adverse reaction. Gary could remember renting a tux and getting a corsage, and he could remember the dancing and the bad food and the large ballroom the prom committee had rented out for the senior class. And his date had been...a blank. Nothing. He had a memory of the prom and of dancing with someone—his clothes had been tight and itchy, he remembered. But who was he holding? He felt the beginnings of a headache again, flirting with him, and he wondered if he'd taken the girl in the picture to his prom.

But remembering his prom was a good sign, he thought. There were memories back here, plenty of them, and he turned around again, facing east, facing the place where he had spent so many years. He wondered what would happen when he remembered it all.

# Chapter 30

Vincent pounded his hands on the dashboard of his Mustang, hitting the dash so hard he left impressions in the leather.

This wasn't the way things were supposed to be going. Things were moving smoothly, and his brother had been cool about letting him set up the buys and work on reducing their competition.

So what had happened?

Vincent started the car and drove away from the little complex of buildings that had served as the offices of the legitimate Luciano family businesses for ten years.

That first meeting, several months ago—that had been good. His brother had listened to him talk about the way things had been long ago, and Vincent had been surprised to hear that his brother had already come to many of the same conclusions.

Vincent and Tony had talked for a long time, and it was in the course of that conversation that they had come to a real understanding, something that had not happened in the intervening years since their father had died. They agreed to work together toward a common goal. And their goal, to resurrect the memory of their noble past, could only be accomplished by one thing—taking the family back to its roots.

Now it sounded like his brother was getting cold feet. Hell, he would've cancelled the whole buy tomorrow night if Vincent hadn't talked him out of it.

Vincent drove the car out toward The Hole. Everyone there knew him, of course, but no one really liked him too much—he'd never been a nice guy. He didn't care what these people thought of him, or thought about what he did—he was making a new name for himself. And leaving The Hole had been a move in a positive direction. But he liked the place, liked the food, and needed a place to meet with the guys.

Vincent had, a few years back, begun his own little criminal enterprise, back when the dingy restaurant had been called The Watering Hole. It had started in those dark booths off the bar, and although his organization had never grown to rival his brother's in size or profit, it had afforded him a good income and a nice home. There had been money from the schemes, little things like running booze or guns or cigarettes up from Tennessee or over to Missouri, or setting up a small bookmaking operation run completely out of one of his guys' houses.

He trusted his guys completely because he'd known them for years. They were excited that he was moving back into the Luciano family, knowing what that would mean for them and for Vincent. Lots of money, and lots of opportunities to make even more money.

Vincent took the Centerville exit off of I-64, pulling up in front of The Hole and getting out, heading inside.

Doris was working behind the counter. She was the older sister of a girl named Doreen, a girl he'd dated a few years back. Doreen—she'd had the strange nickname of "Bird"—had been fun for a while, but of course, it didn't last very long. Unfortunately, the girl had gotten way too interested in him, and after he'd dumped her, she'd taken it personally. One night she'd taken some pills and killed herself.

Every time she saw Vincent, Doris looked like she wanted to kill him—he understood why she hated him, but it hadn't been his fault. Her sister had been a crazy, clingy bitch.

But Vincent tried to remember to smile at the older sister, which drove her even more crazy. Today was no different, and after he smiled at her, she turned and stormed away, making him smile even more. He'd only wanted to bang her sister, not marry her—he'd already made that mistake. It wasn't his fault the girl had fallen for him, and it wasn't his fault she'd taken one too many pills and ended up taking a dirt nap. He had never figured out why the old woman held such a grudge.

Only one of his guys was in the bar, sitting in a booth along the far wall, nursing a beer and flipping through the paper.

"Hey, Steve," Vincent said, sitting down and waving at the new bartender, a guy Vincent had trained before he'd left.

Steve folded the paper closed. "Hey, Vince. How'd it go?"

"Well, the guy's getting cold feet. He's 'uncomfortable,' and I had to do some fast talking to keep him from canceling the buy."

"Serious?"

Vincent nodded. "I think he wants to concentrate on some of the other things, get those going good, and then move into what we want. Anyway, the buy's still on schedule, for now."

Steve sipped from his glass. "So, what next?"

"Well, Tony's still thinking about the coke business. If tomorrow night's stuff moves fast and turns a good profit, he'll be fine."

His beer came, delivered by a new girl he didn't know, a cute waitress who scooted away from his table without even making eye contact. That bitch Doris had probably been filling the girl's head full of lies about him.

Vincent sipped down the head a little and set his glass back down. "That's the only way to go. If he gets cold feet, I'll make sure tomorrow night's buy goes through—it's either that, or the family goes broke. How's the other stuff going?"

"Good. The guys are out and running around, getting ready. We already hit two guys, and the other nine are happening tonight. Shotgun will go under as soon as he hears about his guys getting dropped. You knew that going into this, though, didn't you?"

Vincent smiled. "I don't want to hit him—we don't need to. We hit the ten captains and his underboss and he'll run so fast we won't see him leaving. If we're hitting his men he'll assume we're hitting him, and he'll run."

Vincent, sipping from his beer, eyed the new waitress, imagining what she would say when he told her he was a millionaire.

# Chapter 31

Rugio wasn't a cautious man, usually. East St. Louis was a dangerous place to live, to grow up, and he'd learned a long time ago how to take care of himself.

He was in his car, heading west up I-64 toward Fairview Heights. One of his dealers at the mall—he usually had at least three working the mall and its surrounding parking lots—was having some trouble, and he had called Rugio and asked if they could bump the prices down to offset the sudden, low-priced competition.

The Lucianos were making life difficult for his dealers on the eastern side of the East Dogs' territory, and sales in Fairview and Belleville, especially the eastern side out by the community college, were way down. Rugio didn't want to bump down prices, but Shotgun had reminded him that, first and foremost, the stuff had to be moved. And, as strange as it sounded, they needed to reinforce customer loyalty and make sure they lost as few regular customers as possible.

Shotgun seemed to think a war was coming soon, but Rugio doubted it—there hadn't been a turf war for drugs in a long time, and he figured the rival groups would find a way to share the profits of this business. God knew, there was plenty of money to go around.

He was busy thinking about the future of his business and didn't see the car come up on his left side, passing him in the fast lane. The passenger window was down, and the person in that seat pulled something up from the floor, something long and metallic, and pointed it out the window.

Rugio looked over at the car pacing his and suddenly realized there was a man leaning out the passenger window, pointing a shotgun at his car. Rugio's first reaction was to swerve away from the car, and as he jerked the wheel, he heard a loud "boom" and knew he had been too slow.

The car's window exploded inwards and the car careened off the road, hitting the soft shoulder before leaping into the air and flying almost thirty feet, crashing into one of the trees that lined either side of the freeway. There had been no other cars on the highway in either direction, and the car with the two men in it slowed down and changed lanes, calmly taking the Fairview Heights exit before disappearing into the local traffic.

# Chapter 32

They got into O'Fallon late on Friday night—there was nothing they could do except drive around and look for a motel. It had been an early flight out of LAX, but with the three-hour trip, the time change, and jet lag, all they really wanted to do was find a hotel and crash for the evening. Gary wanted to drive around to see if the town would bring back more memories, but Mike reminded him that they didn't have a place to stay. They could start their search for answers on Saturday morning, after a good sleep.

It turned out that both of the motels in O'Fallon were booked for the night, so they stayed at a small motel near the Interstate. It was a nice motel about halfway between O'Fallon and Centerville and just off the Centerville exit, and the rates were reasonable. It also had a cool glass hallway that connected the lobby of the motel with a restaurant and bar complex next door named The Hole. Mike and Gary had a nice dinner there before turning in, and they were served by a friendly woman named Doris.

Mike watched TV in bed while Gary tried to rest—it had been a long and interesting day. He wanted a drink badly, and he tried not to think about the bar next to the restaurant.

Before falling asleep, Gary followed his normal routine, even in the strange surroundings, and shuffled and pulled a card from his tarot deck, a ritual that seemed to be more and more important to him with each passing day. It was a card marked "The Tower." It showed a tall tower against a dark sky—the top of the tower was glowing with light, a crown atop the tower, and there were two figures falling from it. A plant grew around the base.

He didn't know the meaning of this card and couldn't remember seeing it before. He reached into the box and pulled out the little instruction booklet, which contained short interpretations of each card.

"The Tower: A tall tower with a crowned roof has been struck violently by a blast of lightning and fire. Only the top, the crown, is severed, signifying a clean break from the past. The flame is a symbol of a strong and dominant occurrence. The structure is made of roughly hewn stone and has three windows. Two persons, a man and a woman, are falling to the ground. Meanings: complete and sudden change, breaking down of old beliefs, abandonment of past relationships, changing of one's opinion, unexpected events, or loss of stability. The falling figures may represent head-first escape from the past and sudden immersion into new events. Reverse meanings: continued oppression, following of old ways, or inability to effect any worthwhile change."

None of those sounded very good to him—did the break from the past mean he was about to learn all about his missing memories, or that he would never learn about them, causing a permanent break from his past? The abandonment of past relationships—that sounded like he wasn't ever going to meet the girl in the picture or find out what truly happened between the two of them. Then there were a lot of things going on around him—maybe it just meant he was working toward a solution and wasn't as close to reaching it as he hoped.

Gary put the cards and the instruction book back in their box on the nightstand and turned over to try and get some sleep. Tomorrow was going to be a long day. He'd glanced at the phone book before hitting the sack and found a short list of the psychiatrists in O'Fallon. He might need to talk to all of them if he was going to track down someone who might remember the late Dr. Frank Martin.

And then Gary could take care of this whole crazy memory business and get on with his life.

# Chapter 33

It was Friday night, and Judy was home alone, just the way she liked it.

She had every light in the house on, and the TV was cranked up loud. She wasn't worried about Vincent coming home anytime soon—since he rarely came home before 2 or 3 a.m. on Friday nights, Judy knew she had several hours of quiet, uninterrupted time alone before she really needed to pack up her stuff and go to bed.

Judy had set up her easel in the living room and was busy painting.

It was an ocean scene, tall waves and angry cliffs overlooking a rough sea. On one side of the painting stood a tall white lighthouse perched on a jagged outcropping of rock. The light of a subtle crescent moon illuminated the beach and surf, picking out beach grass and rocks and reflecting in the pools of tidewater. She thought it was probably her best painting in the last three or four years—she had been working on it off and on for about three weeks, and tonight it would be finished.

Judy stood back and looked at it and was suddenly intensely proud. A part of her realized that for the first time in a long time, she was happy.

Even if things were horrible in the rest of her life, she had her painting. At some point, Vincent would die in a wreck or get knocked off by one of his criminal buddies and she would be free. Until then, she would just have to console herself with her paintings. She had the letter from Texas upstairs, taped to the back of one of her dresser drawers, where Vincent would never find it. With that letter and Vincent dead or gone, she could make a new life for herself.

She'd move to California, rent a little house by the beach, and paint all day.

And look for Chris.

There was something wrong with the sea grass in the bottom left-hand corner of the painting—the way it stood against the distant cliff made the sea grass look too tall. She leaned in to touch it up. Her paint palette, resting in the crook of her left elbow, was covered with all the appropriate colors, the sea greens and the deep blues and the blacks she'd used to paint the sky. She dabbed up a little of the blue and mixed it with a touch of brown and a deep red to retouch the dark stone cliffs, covering the tops of the sea grass. Her light, practiced brushstrokes brought the cliff out a little more and made the grass seem shorter.

She leaned back and smiled.

The beam of the lighthouse was the last thing she needed to correct—it was too dark. On her palette, Judy mixed some bright white and with a little of the yellow—it needed to look bright against the darkened sky, but if it looked too bright it would seem out of place. Using a knife tool instead of a brush, she scraped the white into a growing cone of light coming out of the lighthouse, pulling a thin layer of paint across the canvas.

Judy was completely lost in the painting. She was wondering how far the light would travel into the darkness, wondering how much moonlight the clouds would reflect, and she didn't see the flash of headlights pass quickly through the room.

She liked the way the lighthouse light looked. She dropped the knife and picked up another small brush. Getting a little of the white and yellow mix on her brush, she softly touched the tops of the waves below the cliff, making the water reflect the bright beam of light. Judy studied the painting for a long moment and then began dabbing the brush at the tops of the waves on the other side, bringing out the highlighted reflection of the moon's light on the water.

"What the hell is this shit?"

She jumped, spilling some of the paint from her brush as it brushed against her arm. Her heart flipped from complete serenity to an insane pounding as she turned and saw her husband standing there, staring at her. A strange woman stood in the open door behind him, her shape outlined in the light from the front porch.

Judy had no idea what to say.

This had always been her secret—it was what kept her sane and centered, through all the beatings.

Vincent was looking at the painting, his bleary eyes traveling across the spray of stars and the roaring silence of the crashing waves. There was no way for her to know what he was thinking, but some naïve part of her hoped that he might be pleased—maybe so pleased with what she had done that he would allow her to continue, or even let her hang some of the paintings in the house.

He turned and looked deep into her eyes. She must have been smiling a little because she could see his eyes do that narrowing thing, coming together like he wasn't really understanding what he was looking at. Slowly, he smiled.

Judy suddenly realized that all the beatings and torture that had come before were only a precursor to what would come now, things that she could not even imagine. She saw the look of someone who really wanted her dead. There was no appreciation for her talent—only anger at her presumption there could be anything in her life that did not involve him.

All of this passed between them in the space of a heartbeat.

She glanced at the woman behind Vincent, relieved that there was someone else here with them—maybe it would be the only thing that could save her.

"Gina! Go upstairs, into the bedroom, and wait for me!"

Vincent pointed up the stairs without taking his eyes off his wife. He had that look on his face again, the one that had always accompanied the worst beatings, but there was something else now, something more.

The girl hesitated, and for one long moment, Judy thought the young woman might turn and bolt for Blackwood Lane and get away. In her mind, Judy was torn—the woman was an interloper, but her presence might keep Vincent from killing Judy with his bare hands.

Slowly, the girl walked across the living room, glancing at the painting. She silently climbed the stairs and stepped into the bedroom, closing the door quietly behind her.

Vincent turned and looked at Judy and the painting.

"So, you've been busy, huh? Is this what you do with your time when I'm not around?"

Judy nodded, unable to speak. Nothing she could say would matter anyway.

"Instead of cleaning this house?" Vincent said, his voice growing louder with each word. "Instead of making food for me, or taking care of all the other things you're supposed to?"

Silence. She couldn't think of what to say, but she couldn't imagine her life without her paintings. She would fight him if she had to, but if she didn't have….

He turned and picked up the painting.

"No!" she shouted.

Vincent Luciano turned and looked at her and smiled.

"No? You're going to tell me 'No'?"

The room was quiet. Judy stood still, but it felt like every nerve in her body was vibrating like a guitar string.

"You say 'No,' and then what—I'm going to listen?" Vincent asked. "You're my wife! You're supposed to be taking care of things around here!"

One of his fingers brushed against the lighthouse, streaking and marring the wet paint, blurring the colors together. He looked down at the painting.

"I guess you're pretty proud of this, aren't you?" Vincent asked. "Well, I'm no art critic, but I can tell you that I've seen kindergarten kids who paint better than this. You're wasting your time if you think you're any good."

Judy stayed quiet. There was no point in arguing. Maybe, if he got it out of his system….

He looked up at her, waiting for a response. He was waiting for the fight, she could tell, but she wouldn't give him the satisfaction. After a long moment, Vincent shrugged his shoulders.

"I don't know how many of these you've done, but gather them all up and throw this crap out. All the paints and brushes and shit, too. Next week I'll search the whole house, top to bottom, and if there's any of this crap here, I'll beat you senseless with it."

He glanced up the stairs, then back to her. Judy looked at him for a long time, meeting his eyes. Usually she looked away, not wanting to provoke him, but this time it was too important.

After a long moment of staring into his eyes, she said one simple word. She had never said it to him in quite the same way before.

"No," she said quietly.

It sounded strange to her ears. She sounded confident, angry. Her paintings were all she had left.

Vincent seemed to sense a sea change in her, and he stepped back involuntarily. His eyes searched hers, and then he laughed, loudly, breaking the tension.

And then he stepped over and punched her in the face.

She felt the teeth in her mouth rattle as she hit the ground. The paintbrush flew from her hand and painted a long blue streak of ocean and night sky down one wall before falling to the carpet.

"You don't ever say 'No' to me!" Vincent shouted over her. "You don't even know the meaning of the word!"

He threw the painting of the lighthouse to the carpet, face up, and grabbed her head, bunching up her short hair into a rough ball behind her head.

"You don't talk back to me, ever! You don't defy me, ever! And you never give me that look again. Never!"

Vincent dragged her over to the painting. "Look at it—stupid! What is it even supposed to be? You've never even seen the ocean, so how would you know how to paint it? It's like some kind of kid painted it!"

Judy Luciano was staring down at the streaked colors of her marred painting and her husband had her by the hair on the back of her head and he was yelling at her and screaming at her and telling her she was good for nothing and something inside of her snapped.

She felt a wall collapse—as though something previously contained had suddenly spilled free of its enclosure.

A small part of her mind recognized this moment as when she finally, inextricably crossed over the hazy line into madness.

She planted her arms and legs and kicked, hard, catching him waiting for her answer. She bucked him off her and stood up straight, looking at him, her eyes blazing with a fire she could feel coursing all the way up from her feet.

Judy yelled and came around the coffee table and shoved him, knocking him backwards. He stumbled and fell over the table and onto the couch.

Judy felt ten feet tall. She felt she could pick him up and body slam him to the carpet like she'd seen the guys on television do.

"That's where I want to be—anywhere but with you!"

She felt something new in her mind. There was a strange, high-pitched whining in the air, like she was standing too close to a power transformer. She felt herself clenching and re-clenching her fists, waiting. Perhaps this would be the moment when she could figure out a way to kill him—she needed something heavy, like a frying pan, or maybe the axe from the woodpile outside—

He leapt over the table at her, screaming.

She was angry and full of fire, but he outweighed her by at least a hundred and fifty pounds. He tackled her to the ground, then rolled off and punched her hard, three times. He stood and kicked her like it was a real fight, not a man beating his wife. No pulled punches, no open-faced slaps—these were the kind of blows designed to hurt or maim. They came and came and she fought back as best as she could, scratching at his arms and face, but he was bigger and stronger. The new fire roared within her, giving more strength than she had ever known, and twice she kicked out her leg to catch him in the balls, but he deflected her. She swung her arms and tried to claw at his eyes, but his punches came faster—too many and too fast and they hurt too much.

Judy rolled away, trying to get up, but he pounded her again. She felt her arm grow suddenly heavy, numb. He kicked and punched and screamed at her, and after a while the words and the blows all blended together into a haze. He was shouting something at her, over and over, but she didn't hear the words—a fog had taken over and she was having trouble opening one of her eyes and her arm hurt like hell.

After a while, Vincent must have grown tired because the beating stopped. She couldn't see him—she was balled up on the floor next to the couch, bleeding from her nose and mouth. Judy tried not to moan—each time she did, the beating would start again—but the pain was something that could not be contained. She felt herself bleeding from a dozen wounds, and wondered at the beautiful release death would afford her. The madness that had lurked within her before had abandoned her, leaving only pain and emptiness.

"This is where you want to be, huh?" Vincent yelled again, and some part of her realized that these had been the words he'd been shouting over and over.

She opened one eye—he was standing over her, panting and pointing at the painting of the lighthouse on the ground near her. He leaned over and grabbed the back of her head and dragged her over to the picture.

"You want to be here?" he asked, and then shoved her face down into the painting.

She felt the paint ooze around her skin and into her open mouth and nose. He pushed hard, not letting up. He ground her face into the rough canvas before lifting her head and flinging her head to one side with enough force to spray the extra paint from her face onto the opposite wall.

Vincent stood and stormed away from her, heading off into the kitchen.

What would he kill her with? It would be the screwdriver, or the hammer. What would he choose?

The paint was stinging her eyes, but she couldn't brush it away—it hurt too much to move anything. The tears came, and she blinked and watched in the direction of the kitchen—she heard cabinets being opened and slammed shut, then heard him move into the laundry room.

She prayed he wouldn't find them, but her prayers fled with a loud shout of joy from the laundry room.

Vincent came back into the living room carrying two more paintings, the last two she had finished. She hadn't had a chance to move them up to the attic—they had been hidden behind the washing machine.

One was a beach scene with a family splashing in the water, and the other showed a crescent moon reflecting on a dark bay. Both were good. If she had had any energy left in her body, she would've gotten up and beaten him for them.

But she couldn't feel one arm and the rest of her was going numb and her eyes refused to stay open. All she could do was will him to suddenly drop dead of a heart attack.

"These too?" Vincent asked. "Wow, you've been a busy little beaver. Well, I think these suck, too! Look at these stupid kids!"

Vincent threw the paintings to the floor beside her. She reached numbly for the one with the family and he kicked her in the ribs.

"Don't you get it, woman—nothing you do amounts to anything! You've spent all this time sneaking around and for what? A bunch of crappy looking paintings—paint-by-numbers shit."

He glanced around and held up the first picture, her picture of the lighthouse, for her to see.

"This is the only one you've done around here that looks halfway real—and that's 'cause I made it better. What do you think?"

She looked up and saw her painting—or what was left of it. Right in the middle of her painting was the image of a face, of cheeks and a jaw and a forehead, everything outlined in smeared paint and blood. It was disconcerting to see the reverse image of her own face pressed rudely into her painting—it was a good enough impression to be recognizable. The face was smeared in a dozen colors and surrounded by the undisturbed painting of the beach and the lighthouse and the stars above.

Vincent stooped and picked up the other two paintings and walked out the still-open front door, heading out onto the front lawn. After a long moment, he came back inside and dragged her painfully out onto the front porch.

She opened one eye to see what was happening. Her paintings were in the small fire pit on the front lawn, sitting on some sticks and small logs from the woodpile. As she watched, he hefted the gasoline can they usually kept on the front porch, sprinkling gasoline onto the paintings.

He walked over and dragged her to the fire, handing her a book of matches. "Okay, strike a match. We're going to get rid of all of this crap, now."

Judy looked at the book of matches, then down at her paintings on the dark grass of their front lawn.

Beyond them, she saw the sodium-yellow runway lights of Scott Air Force Base, highlighting the horizon. Beyond was the rest of the world. But nobody in that world cared about this little drama on the lawn. Or about her.

But she cared.

Judy struck a match. As he leaned in to take it from her, she burned his arm.

He yelped and punched her in her bad arm—it felt broken. She saw stars and crumpled to the ground. He pulled her up and slapped her again and again until she came around.

"Now light me a match, you stupid bitch, or I swear to God you'll be burning right along with your stupid paintings. And I don't think anybody would miss you."

She struck a second match and handed it to him.

He took it, smiling at her for long moment her, and dropped the flame onto the small pile. The paintings caught instantly. The flames were multicolored and gave off an odd smoke that twirled and danced in a thousand different shades of blue before drifting up and disappearing into the dark sky.

She envied the smoke.

The dancing fires mesmerized her, and in the minutes it took for the paintings to char and burn, all she could think about was the fire, dancing crazily up from her proudest work.

Vincent watched her staring helplessly at the fire and must've thought it hadn't been humiliating enough, because he stepped up next to the smoldering fire and unzipped his pants. He laughed as he pissed on her paintings, putting out the fire.

But it all really didn't matter—something else had let go inside her. It had started with the fight inside and had ended with the fire. Now something angry roamed her mind, and any notion of trying to control it had drifted away with the smoke.

And for the first time in her life, Judy didn't have the slightest care in the world.

Vincent went inside and closed the door behind him. Judy wondered if he was trying to teach her a lesson or if he was just insane.

Slowly, she stretched out her arms and crawled over to the fire. Picking through the remains of her paintings, she found that most of the lighthouse painting was still recognizable but that the other two were charred and lost. She left them in the ashes and crawled back to the porch, her arm throbbing.

Judy heard the sounds from her bedroom window, the one that opened out onto the roof of the garage. They were the shouts and groans of a man and woman in the throes of passion. Or maybe all the noise was just for her benefit. Either way, she didn't really care.

She was going to get better, and then she was going to kill him. And that pleasant thought accompanied her mind down into the darkness.

# Chapter 34

Mike relaxed, waited until his friend was fully asleep before turning up Letterman a little louder. Just before Gary had gone to bed, he'd been fiddling with that deck of cards again, something he'd done during most of the flight from LA, flipping the cards expertly. It looked like a nervous habit to Mike.

Mike watched through the reading of the Top Ten list before thinking about the cards again. He glanced over at Gary and saw that he was sleeping soundly. Mike quietly stood and picked up the box of cards. Sitting back down on his bed, he pulled the cards from the box and began looking through them.

They were a large stack of color, illustrated cards, larger than playing cards. There were four "suits," except these suits were called Cups, Rods, Swords, and Pentacles, and each had numbered cards from ace through ten, a page, a knight, a queen, and a king. There were twenty or so other cards with interesting pictures—the moon, the sun, the devil, stars, and a dozen other symbols. Other cards showed pictures of ominous figures labeled "Justice" or "Death."

Mike flipped through the little instruction book and began reading, shuffling the cards as he went. He took cards out of the stack at random and found them in the booklet, reading about what it was supposed to mean, and he began to understand what Gary had been doing. Each of these little cards was like a personal horoscope, and just like those blurbs printed in every newspaper in the country, the "meanings" of each of these cards was open to speculation. Any event could be interpreted in many ways. Flipping through the cards and finding something "important" and "insightful" all depended on how willing the viewer was to make the card's predictions fit with reality.

Mike shuffled the cards and pulled one out.

The card was an upside-down Six of Rods, a picture of a rider on horseback carrying five wooden rods while another man next to him on foot carried the sixth. Atop the highest wooden rod was a wreath.

Mike found the description in the booklet.

"Six of Rods—a horseman carries a flowering rod decked with a wreath while a companion walks nearby. Meanings: conquest, triumph, good news, gain, advancement, expectation, desires realized as a result of efforts. Reversed meaning: indefinite delay, fear, apprehension, disloyalty, superficial benefits, inconclusive gain."

That didn't sound very good, but then the "inconclusive gain" part just about summed up this entire crazy trip for him—he was here because his best friend in the world was taking a walk on the "losing it side."

That, and the fact that Mike was more than a little curious about the girl in the picture—was she truly the old girlfriend Gary could never remember? And what if there were some kind of crazy explanation about the dreams?

He glanced back down at the card again, shaking his head. It was like a horoscope or one of those crazy psychic readings Gary was always getting—someone reaching at straws would grasp for the first thing that looked reasonable. These cards were interesting, but you didn't have to be a psychic plying the dark mysteries of the occult to know that this trip would be interesting.

Mike put the cards away, turned off Letterman in the middle of his interview with some Hollywood director, and went to sleep. Tomorrow would be a long day.

# Chapter 35

Shotgun got the word early on Saturday morning, and he knew immediately what it meant.

His three top men had died on Friday: two in car wrecks and another gunned down in his own living room. Two other men had gone missing—he could only assume they were dead or dying.

The Lucianos were making their move. It was only a matter of time before someone came for him.

Shotgun didn't even take the time to pack—he grabbed a few important things from one of his houses and threw them into a bag along with several dozen thick stacks of cash, all hundreds banded together with rubber bands. The money would get him pretty far.

The Lucianos were serious. The best course of action would be to take as much of the profit he had gained over the past few years as he could and start again somewhere else. He hated to give up like that, but people he trusted and liked were getting killed, and there was no way he could mount an offensive quickly.

Shotgun looked up to see Willie B, his number two man, come into the room, carrying his own suitcase and pulling on a jacket.

"How much you got there?" Shotgun asked him.

Willie B. hefted a big suitcase with one hand, and Shotgun saw the muscle stand out on the man's arm. "About $320,000—mostly cash, but some diamonds from that deal last year. I have more in the car, but that's all I had stashed at my house and the club. There's more at some of my men's places, but I don't think we have time."

"Nah, we gotta go now," Shotgun said, shaking his head. "I've got about a million four, I think. Between the two of us, we'll be fine. LA, you think?"

"Yeah, I like that." Willie B. agreed. "I've got friends out there, and with this kind of money we could get set up fast. Or regroup, and come back at the Lucianos. But...well, I heard something, boss. Something you should hear."

Shotgun stopped packing wads of cash into the second duffel bag and looked at him. "What?"

Willie B. set his bag down on the bed. "One of my guys said he heard about a huge Luciano buy tonight. Supposedly they're buying from D.W. at the dock, by the riverboats."

"Here?"

Willie nodded. "Yeah, right under our noses. I guess they figure we'll all be gone or dead by tonight, so they'll have nothing to worry about."

Shotgun sat down. This could be an opportunity, or it could be a trap. "How well do we know him—whoever you heard this from? Is he one of ours, or a new guy?"

Willie shook his head. "No, I've known Jackie a while—he helped out with that Collinsville stuff last year." When some local kids in Collinsville had decided to get into the pot growing and selling business, some of Shotgun's men had had to talk with them. Two broken legs had convinced them. "Jackie said he heard it from a good source—all of the Lucianos' money is riding on the deal. They're making one big buy that's supposed to last them three or four months."

Shotgun did the calculations in his head. "At least a hundred pounds. More like a hundred and twenty."

"More like one fifty—they're still undercutting our prices, so they need more product. Of course they'll raise the prices after we're gone, but until then, they'll need more from their source."

"Yup, you're right," Shotgun said, wondering how to exploit this. The Lucianos were either going to hit him soon or assume he left town—either way, if he dropped out of sight they would assume he was gone. If he could get a few good people together and plan something…

"Well, boss," Willie B. said, smiling. "It's good to see you planning instead of packing. Makes me feel better about things."

Shotgun stood and walked over, slapping his friend of more than ten years on the back. "No problem, man. We just might come out of this thing looking good."

# Chapter 36

Gary and Mike were sitting at a booth next to the windows, enjoying breakfast on Saturday morning. They were in the small restaurant that was attached to their motel by a glassed-in walkway, and Gary was staring out the window, wondering what to do next.

He distracted himself by studying the walkway that connected the two buildings. Gary had always been fascinated with architecture, and he loved to see surprising buildings or interesting features in otherwise-normal structures. Whoever planned this motel/restaurant/bar had put some thought into it, the first sign of good architecture—they had tried to consider the wants and needs of the people who would be staying in the motel or eating at the restaurant. Careful planning showed through into good design—the connecting corridor made it easier for motel guests to grab a meal during a snowstorm or rainstorm.

And he remembered the weather here—it was always changing. In Los Angeles, it was always 72 and hazy—he'd heard that being a meteorologist in LA was something of a running joke. Did they ever even change the map on the nightly weather report?

Here it was different—the weather was a changeable entity with a mind of its own. People actually checked the weather before heading out on a cold winter's day, or glanced at the dark sky to determine if they could reach their destination before a rainstorm hit. The winters were mild, but occasionally brutal—he vaguely remembered getting snowed in on one occasion. He and his father had climbed out of a second-story window, sliding down a snowdrift to dig out the front door of his parents' home.

Gary wished he could relax in this restaurant and enjoy a meal with snow coming down outside in winter, knowing that you could enjoy the weather and still take the connecting glass hallway back to the motel.

But he felt exposed—his father had said over and over not to return to St. Louis, though he'd never clued Gary in on the true reasons for the warnings. "There are people back there that will remember you, Gary," his stepmother had said only a few nights ago on the phone, after he'd seen the picture for the first time. "They'll remember you and your father and the trial. It's dangerous—very dangerous—for you to go back there. But if you do, keep a low profile."

Gary remembered that she was quiet for a long moment, and then she'd added, "Your father would never forgive me if anything happened to you."

"Seriously!" Mike exclaimed, pulling Gary from his thoughts. Mike was pointing his fork at the half-eaten stack of huge pancakes in front of him. "What do they put in these to make them so good?"

"Butter," Gary answered, smiling. "Lots of it."

Mike nodded and went back to eating. Gary had to admit that the pancakes and eggs were excellent. Mike had commented several times on how much better the food was "back here," and how nice everyone was. Somehow, it all made Gary strangely happy—this was where he was from, where he had learned his moral code, learned how to treat people. He felt a strange pride to be back in his element, even if he'd forgotten most of it.

And Mike had probably never really enjoyed home-cooked meals—he and his family were all from LA. Dinnertime was for being seen at a fancy restaurant or waiting for the personal chef to finish braising his rabbit, not for meals with friends and family around a rowdy table covered with homemade dishes and mismatched silverware.

After the meal, Gary headed back to the room to get ready—he didn't really need to do anything else to prep, but he was simply delaying the inevitable. Mike went to the motel's front counter to book the room for another night—they were using his credit cards to pay for everything, just to be safe.

As Gary brushed his teeth, he wondered at what they should do first—he'd really only thought things out to this point. He had no plan going forward. He needed to look into his past, but in a way that didn't alert any of the wrong people or send his mind off into a pain coma.

And Gary had to find her.

Was she okay? Was she even living in the area, or had she moved on long ago, forgetting all about him? His mind slid away from remembering her too intently—every thought of her was accompanied by the beginnings of a headache. But he'd been working around the memory, trying to picture them together or thinking about the prom or trying to remember the birthday party depicted in the photograph.

But Gary was here now, in O'Fallon, and he needed to get out there—he just wasn't sure where to go first. He felt like Frodo at the Council of Elrond. "*I will take the ring to Mordor. But I do not know the way.*"

When Mike returned, keys in hand, Gary asked if they could start out slow by driving around O'Fallon. He wanted to remember more about the town and his years here before he started talking to people.

They climbed into the rental and headed up U.S. Highway 50, away from the Interstate and into O'Fallon.

Everything looked familiar—the intervening years had not changed the complexion of the town much, but there were new things along with the old. Near the highway and the motel was a smattering of new stores and restaurants, including a Sam's Club, a Jack in the Box, and a giant Wal-Mart. He had worked for several years at a Western Sizzlin' Steak House that had been located near the highway, but now it was a Chinese buffet. There was a new Quality Inn located behind the restaurant in what had been a field where his coworkers had taken their smoke breaks. The large open field next door had been suddenly replaced by a new strip mall and a Taco Bell.

He felt like Marty McFly from *Back to the Future*—it seemed as though had somehow traveled into the future of his long-forgotten hometown, and all the familiar landmarks, although still there, had been joined by flying car dealerships and new stores and new everything. It was a little dizzying.

As Mike drove away from the congestion of the highway overpass and closer to O'Fallon, things began to look more familiar. There were differences, surely, that he was not recognizing, but the overall look and feel of the small town was the same as what he saw in his emerging memories. He saw a new Sonic Drive-in, and another new strip mall with a CVS.

As they approached the intersection of State Street and Lincoln Avenue, he saw the Bank of O'Fallon and remembered getting a savings account there—he couldn't have been more than eight or nine, but he remembered how his father had stressed the importance of keeping track of his money. Gary smiled at the memory of his father, ever the accountant, trying to explain the concept of interest to an eight-year-old.

Across the street from the bank were a BP gas station, another large strip mall that he easily remembered, and other shops and buildings that flanked the busiest intersection in town.

"Where to?" Mike asked as they stopped at the red light.

Gary had a sudden thought. "Turn right."

The main portions of O'Fallon were to the north and east, but Gary had asked Mike to turn south, into a residential area.

As Mike drove the car and Gary directed him, Gary started to grow more and more nervous. Soon, they reached their destination on Dartmouth Street.

The house was still there.

"Just stop here for a minute," Gary said, pointing at the curb in front of a squat suburban house. Gary stared at another house, two doors down and on the opposite side of the street.

"What are we looking at?" Mike asked after a long couple of minutes.

Gary pointed at the two-story home on Dartmouth Drive.

"That's where I grew up," he said quietly. "My father told me it had burned down."

Mike nodded, not saying anything.

Gary looked at the home—it had seemed so large when he was growing up, one of the few two-story homes on the southern side of the street. On the outside, it looked exactly as it had the day his mother had died, the last day he'd seen it.

Gary pointed at the street in front of the house.

"That's where my mother died. She was parked at the curb and I walked down the driveway and dropped my hat. I remember stopping and picking it up, and then I looked at her and was shrugging—I thought she might be mad because I was delaying her. And then the car just exploded."

Gary looked for burn or scorch marks on the road—there was nothing. Even if they had ever been there, they had been paved over a long time ago.

Mike didn't say anything, and Gary was glad for that, glad for the long moments of silence that his good friend was giving him—time to process, time to grieve.

Gary glanced back at the house—there was a new family living there, and he had a sudden urge to knock on their door and ask for a tour.

"You okay?" Mike asked.

Gary glanced at him, nodding.

"Yeah, it's just weird. I've thought about that day a lot lately, and about my mom. It's strange—thinking about her doesn't cause any headaches. So it seems that my memories have been selectively altered. But I wonder why those were left in there and other stuff was taken out. I mean, if you could prevent a teenager from having to relive watching his mother die, wouldn't you?"

Mike shrugged. "I don't know. It's strange to hypnotize you to change your name—to make you think you have a new name, to be more precise—and then leave such a painful memory."

After a few more minutes, Gary was ready to go, and he gave Mike directions back to the main intersection where they had turned.

When they got to the Bank of O'Fallon, he had Mike turn right. "Straight up Main to the high school, then left. I'll tell you where."

He tried to put the memories of his mother out of his mind and concentrate on the drive. This was the part of O'Fallon he remembered—Southview Plaza, with the Dollar General and the Ace Hardware. There was Ice Cream Haven, an outdoor ice cream stand where he remembered getting treats and ice cream with his mother.

Gary saw that the McDonalds, which had been on the corner behind the BP, had moved down and across the street. He saw the squat Hardees restaurant and suddenly remembered that he'd worked there and been fired from there—that had not been pleasant. There was a strange smattering of old and new—old shops he remembered, and new names on old places, and completely new buildings—he smiled when he saw that O'Fallon had even managed to get its own Starbucks.

As they continued east on U.S. 50, there was an a large open area up on the left—O'Fallon Community Park, where he'd spent many summer days at Little League games or playing on the equipment.

"Something going on?" Mike asked.

Gary followed his eyes and saw that a good portion of the park was taken up with some type of carnival—inflatable rides and cotton candy booths were set up in the center of the park, along with a Ferris wheel and other rides.

"Oh, it must be Mayfest weekend—it's the big fair they have here, once a year. Rides and greasy food and 4-H displays. That's cool that it's this weekend—I could use a funnel cake and some fun."

"What's 4-H? Is that like a car show?" Mike asked.

Gary just looked at him and laughed.

They continued on to the east and turned on Smiley Drive, the road that ran in front of the high school.

The high school sat on the east side of town, almost on the edge of the township's city limits, and as Mike drove the car slowly past, the faces of old friends and teachers drifted back into his mind like specters from his past. Their names came more slowly, but seeing the outside of the school, the parking lot, the baseball and football fields that separated the school itself from the main road, all reminded him of events long past. There was a line of Bradford pear trees that grew along the road in front of the school, and he noticed how much they had grown in the years since he had been here.

He remembered once wearing a silly apron and walking down the streets near the school, throwing candy to people lining the streets on both sides. It was a parade of some type, probably homecoming, and he had been walking with other students, keeping pace with a float in front of them. It wasn't really a float, but more like a small town's impression of a float—a big, vaguely clam-shaped lump of wood and chicken wire that had been covered with bright blue and gold crepe paper and bunting. On the back of the trailer had been a large banner that read "Crush the Clams," the mascot of the team they'd be playing in the homecoming game. The memories edged the borders of his mind like forgotten friends. He gave directions quietly, guiding Mike on a tour through the town, but in his mind he was experiencing a tour of a long-hazy past.

Mike drove the car up Smiley and through the old section of O'Fallon, and Gary remembered the shops and the restaurants and the smaller branch of the city library. It occupied a small corner site that looked onto the narrow central intersection of the old town, and he remembered that the clock, mounted on the corner of the building and sticking out two feet from the bricks, was often the victim of damage from turning trucks as they tried to negotiate the tight corner.

It was funny to see the clock still there, although it looked like it needed repairs, but it was still keeping time, still ticking along as if the idea of replacing it or taking it down had never even occurred to anyone. As they approached the library, he saw that it had become the O'Fallon Historical Society—he might have to come back here if he couldn't track down anything about his past. Maybe going back through the old newspapers would help. But what had happened to the library? They probably had built a new location somewhere in the intervening ten years.

Gary had a sudden inspiration.

"Turn left here, then go over the train tracks and make a right on First Street," he told Mike.

Mike followed his directions and turned into a strip of shops that faced the train tracks and the back of the Historical Society. On one side of the parking lot was a large red train caboose—Gary had never really understood what the point of it was, other than to perhaps celebrate the town's rail heritage. But they weren't coming to look at the train—he was crossing his fingers, hoping that one of his childhood memories would somehow remain intact.

Wood Bakery, a small shop located in the strip mall, was still there, the red sign and the brick exterior and the big, inviting windows. The memories of warm cookies, pastries, and amazing chocolate-iced brownies flooded his mind. The smells came to him the moment he saw the sign. He directed Mike to park in front and sat back and looked at the place, remembering.

"A bakery?" Mike asked. "We just had breakfast."

Gary remembered locking his bike up at a bike rack in front of the place, but the rack was gone now, evaporated into the past.

"No, I used to come here as a kid," Gary said, and climbed from the car. He looked around for a moment, taking in the quiet downtown streets and the caboose and the sunny sky, and then turned and pulled the door open. A small bell attached to the door jingled as he headed inside.

It was just as he remembered it.

On the left was the bakery, with a huge case of cookies and cakes and brownies that his mom had loved.

But there was something else here, too. Something he shouldn't be trying to remember—

The headache came, unbidden.

An old woman stepped from behind the glass case of cookies and pies and walked over to him—the headache had come on so suddenly that he was bent over in pain, leaning against the windows just inside the door.

"Are you okay, son?"

Gary looked up—her face was a little older, but he remembered her. And with that memory the headache grew tighter across his forehead, like heavy bands of rubber squeezing together, trying to crush his head. He put his hands up to his temples and massaged them, willing himself not to pass out—not when he was making progress.

The little bell on the door jingled as Mike stepped into the bakery.

"You okay, buddy?"

Gary shook his head, massaging his temples as he lowered himself into one of the small chairs near the door. He was trying to not think about the smells or the memories locked inside this pleasant place.

Mike looked over to the old woman.

"He's...he's not feeling well. Do you have some water?"

She smiled.

"Of course—he scared the tar out of me, though, coming in here and then acting like he was having a heart attack. Let me get that water, son," the woman said, disappearing behind the counter. She reappeared only moments later with a plastic glass of water, handing it to Gary, who took it without looking up.

He thanked her and sipped from it slowly. After a minute, he felt better.

"Sorry about that," he said to Mike and the woman. "My mother and I used to come in here, and I guess the memory was a little too much for me."

Mike nodded, glancing at the woman as she stared at Gary.

"You say you and your mother used to come in here, boy?" she asked.

Gary nodded and handed her back the half-empty glass of water. "Yeah, ten years ago. There was a travel store next door, where that hardware store is now. My mom used to love the chocolate-iced brownies. Coming here was always a big treat—she would buy me a dozen of those chocolate chip cookies," he said, pointing in the direction of the glass case. "They were great."

Gary looked up at her and saw Mike behind her, his eyes wide. He knew what his friend was thinking—they were supposed to be keeping a low profile, checking things out. But Gary could see the old woman trying to remember. What if she suddenly shouted out his name, and it wasn't Gary? Would that prove anything? Gary thought it was worth the risk.

"Gary, let's go," Mike said suddenly, taking Gary's arm to help him from the store. Clearly he didn't agree with Gary spilling the beans. "I think we've taken up enough of this nice lady's time, don't you?"

If Gary was going to go through with it, he needed to do it now.

No matter what the cost.

"Yes, ma'am, I used to come in here a lot. My mother's name was Gloria O'Toole. My father worked for the Lucianos as an accountant."

The woman stepped back and gave a little gasp. Mike had a completely different reaction—he let go of Gary's arm and backed away, rolling his eyes.

"You...are you the young man whose mother was killed in that car bomb?" the old woman asked, her hand on her throat. "Your father, was he the accountant that testified against the Luciano family, got the old man sent to jail?"

Gary stood and slowly nodded, looking around the store and trying to push back the edges of the headache.

"Yes, that was my father. After the trial, my father and I were moved to California by the FBI. Witness Protection Program." Gary stopped for a long moment and tried not to look at Mike, who was shooting him daggers.

"Maybe we shouldn't be talking about this," Mike said.

Gary turned and looked directly at the old woman.

"Do you remember me?"

The old woman tapped her chest absentmindedly, looking from Gary to Mike and then back.

"Of course I remember your name, son," she said. "Everyone in this town knew your name, you and your family. After you disappeared, everyone thought you were dead or the FBI had packed you off—guess that's what happened. That was a bad time in this town, but it got better after the trial. Your father was good to stand up to them, even if it cost him his wife and—"

Gary interrupted her. "What...what is my name?"

The old lady looked at Gary, then back at Mike.

"What is this foolishness?" she asked, shaking her head. "What do you mean? I've got a store to run here, and I don't have time to fool with you, boy," she said, turning to leave.

One of Gary's hands shot out and clamped on her arm, hard, keeping her in place and spinning her halfway around.

"What's my name?"

The lady shrieked and tried to pull away, but his grip was too tight. Mike grabbed at Gary's hand, but the woman shouted first.

"O'Toole, for God's sake, let go of me!" she shouted, clawing at his hand. "Your name is Chris O'Toole, you stupid boy!"

Gary let go instantly, both hands going to his temples. It was bad, worse than he'd thought it would be. He bent over suddenly, as if someone had kicked him violently in the chest. The deck of tarot cards fell from his jacket pocket, spilling all over the tile floor of the bakery. He'd been preparing for it, but when she'd said it and—

Out of the corner of his eye, Gary saw the old woman turn and walk behind the counter, grabbing the phone. Mike walked over to her.

"You get away from me, son," she said to Mike. "I'm calling the police."

Gary saw Mike walk up to her—even though he was in pain, his mind was still keeping track of what was going on around him. But he knew he needed to leave this place, to clear his head.

"Look, my friend and I aren't going to hurt you, ma'am." he said, smiling. "Please, hang up the phone. I promise, we're on our way out the door. Let me check on my friend, and then we'll leave."

She looked at him for a long moment and then put the phone back up on its hook.

"I'm sorry I grabbed your arm, ma'am," Gary said, standing up slowly and putting one hand on the door. "Mike, I'm going to get some air. Can you get my cards?"

Mike nodded, and Gary turned and fled the bakery, the little bell jingling as he stepped out into the sun.

# Chapter 37

"Wake up." Someone was whispering in her ear.

Judy sat up slowly, her back killing her.

She realized that she'd slept the whole night on the front porch. There was a moment of confusion and then she felt the pain in her side and along her face and remembered what had happened last night—the burning of her paintings. The last thing she could remember was that strange and colorful smoke drifting away into the night sky.

Vincent was standing over her.

"Clean up the house—the place is a wreck. I'll be home around 9 p.m., and I want this place looking nice—we may be having guests. And clean up that mess on the front lawn," he said, smiling at her.

She nodded, her jaw feeling like it weighed a hundred pounds.

Behind Vincent was the girl from last night, looking nervous. Vincent turned to see what Judy was looking at and told the girl to go outside and wait by the car.

"Now, listen. When I get home with my friends, I want to see this place spotless. As for that other crap last night, we'll have a long and interesting discussion about that soon," he said, smiling in that way that made her stomach turn.

He walked away, stepping on her broken easel as he left. Vincent was wearing his favorite boots, the ones with alternating strips of leather and rattlesnake skin. They had short metal chains that looped beneath the arch of the boot, and she listened to the sound of those little chains jingling as Vincent walked away.

# Chapter 38

Gary was gone, and Mike needed to calm this woman down before she got the cops involved.

"Okay, I know what you just saw was strange," Mike began, "but there's an explanation for it."

She looked from Mike to Gary, who was standing outside the bakery, then slowly nodded.

"You see, he's been away from this place for a long time," Mike continued. "Since he's been gone...well, let's just say that he has a different opinion of himself. Most of what happened to him here, he can't remember. He's remembering it now, but some of it isn't coming easily, and his mind is fighting it."

"What are you talking about?" she asked. "You mean he doesn't remember anything that happened to him here in O'Fallon?"

"Something like that," Mike said, nodding. "It's all coming back to him, but there are parts of it he can't remember. Like his name."

"Oh, you're kidding. Is this some kind of joke?"

Mike stared back at her. "No, I'm completely serious. He almost wrecked the car yesterday—he'd seen the Arch for the first time in ten years, and it brought back memories. I think parts of his mind are blocked off, and it doesn't want to recover these old memories. He gets terrible headaches—see how he's hurting?"

She looked at Gary outside for a long moment, and then nodded. "Sounds crazy, but I don't remember the last time I saw a boy that shade of white. He looks like he needs to see the inside of a hospital, and the sooner the better."

She looked at Mike, continuing.

"That was a nasty business, when old man Luciano went to jail. Chris's father put him away," nodding at Gary. "The old man died in prison a couple years after that."

Mike nodded. "There are parts of the story we know, and others we're trying to find out. It's been a long time, but he's back to visit and get some answers. Seeing the places where he grew up is putting a lot of strain on him—try not to think too badly of him, okay?"

The woman slowly smiled and patted him on the arm.

"That's just fine, son. Mike, right? I had a brother named Mike, but he passed on couple of years ago. You just see to your friend there, okay?"

She turned to walk away, then stopped and looked at him.

"One more question. When you were trying to get him to leave, you called him 'Gary.'"

Mike nodded. "He thinks his name is Gary. Gary Foreman. Somewhere along the line he was hypnotized to forget his old name. Evidently there was a girl back here he thought he was in love with, and his father had Gary's memory of her suppressed to keep him from destroying the case and getting more people killed."

She looked at him curiously. "Wow, now that does sound like a load of bunk."

Mike nodded. "I know. I'm still trying to believe it all myself."

The woman smiled. "It is a stretch. But she was broken up when he went away."

"Who?" Mike asked.

"Judy, Judy Nelson," she said. "Chris's girlfriend when he disappeared. Actually, they were engaged, I think."

"You know her?" Mike looked at the woman.

"Of course I know her," the woman said. "She used to work here. I think this is where they met."

------

Judy moved slowly around the house—now that she was up and moving around, her arm didn't hurt as much.

She wanted to go upstairs and change clothes, but the idea of going into that bedroom, where her husband and that girl...no, she could get along for a few more hours in the paint-streaked white shirt and blue jeans she was still wearing from yesterday.

Judy gathered up the bits and pieces of her art equipment that had been strewn around the living room during last night's fight and spent a few futile minutes trying to scrape off the blue streak of pain that ran down one wall. He had hit her so hard that the paintbrush had just flown through the air.

She tried not to remember that feeling in the pit of her stomach of complete and utter surprise, when she had been painting and blissfully unaware of his presence.

A part of her mind offered up excuses for him, his surprise at walking in on her engaged in an activity that had nothing to do with him, his overreaction to this new sign of her independence, something he had never tolerated on any level. She knew that he had been surprised, but why couldn't he have been pleasantly surprised? The years had changed him—if she'd shown an interest in painting when they were first dating, maybe he would've been supportive.

But he'd changed, sometime around his trip to Sacramento—he'd returned different, and angry, and getting kicked from the family had been the nail in his coffin. Maybe he was incapable of empathy now.

Either way, she would not excuse him. And she knew now, without her paintings or even the prospect of painting in the future, she had nothing to live for. Sometime over the next week he would search the entire house and find the other twenty or so paintings in the attic, along with all of the art supplies that she'd surreptitiously bought in town. And he would be watching her like a hawk, trying to catch her painting.

But without her paintings, she was nothing.

------

"And she quit just a few days later," the woman said, finishing up.

Wow. It was crazy.

Judy Nelson, the girl from the picture, had worked in the bakery for several years—in fact, it had been here that Gary and Judy had met. Gary had been buying brownies with his mother, and it had been Judy's first day and she'd screwed up the order. He'd said a few kind words to her and that was how it had all started.

Judy and Gary had been dating for almost a year when the trial started, and Judy had talked daily about the progress of the trial and the danger to the O'Tooles. When Gary's mother had been killed, Judy had come into the bakery hysterical. Evidently, all Judy could talk about was the end of the trial, when things would get back to normal.

Then, one day Judy had come in, seemingly stunned. She had seen Gary at the courthouse and shouted hello, but he had looked right at her and not recognized her. Then he'd turned and walked away, climbing into a waiting car.

But his father had looked at her—she'd seen him getting into the other side of the government car, and he'd looked right at her with a pained expression before being pushed into the car by a burly FBI agent.

What happened next had become a part of the town's scant mythology. After the trial, no one had heard from the O'Tooles—they were gone. There had been discussion about what had happened to them—the theories revolved around two major options. The most popular theory was that the FBI had whisked them away to some secret location, protecting them from the vengeful Luciano family. Of course, the other rumor was that the Luciano family had somehow found them and had them killed.

Mike had listened as she told the story, occasionally glancing outside at Gary, who was leaning on their rental car and rubbing his head. The fact that the girl had worked here might explain Gary's reaction to coming into the bakery. But it also might explain why he'd wanted to stop here in the first place, which might mean that some of the memories were coming back.

The woman finished up by telling Mike about the girl's marriage to Vincent Luciano.

"They got married a couple years out of high school, and he pretty much locked her up in that house out west of town. He's not very nice to her, if you know what I mean. She's always got bruises when she stops by."

Mike got the hint. He couldn't understand how any man could treat a woman that way—it took a person with no self-esteem, but that didn't help the victim.

He excused himself for a moment and went outside to check on Gary, stopping on the way out to collect the fallen tarot cards that littered the floor by the door.

"You doing okay?" Mike asked Gary.

Gary was sitting on the rear bumper of the car, still rubbing his temples. "I've felt better. It's like this place, just being in there, was giving me a headache."

"I know," Mike said, handing him the deck of tarot cards. "This is not a good place for you to be. I need to talk to this lady a little more, and then we'll leave."

Gary looked up. "Why? Does she know something? Does she know the girl?"

"I'm not sure," he lied. "Can I have the picture? And what was that doctor's name we're looking for?"

Gary handed him the picture. "Martin. Dr. Frank Martin. He had an office near the post office."

"Okay. I'll be right back."

Mike walked back inside and over to the counter, where the woman was transferring donuts from a baking rack onto a display tray.

"Is this her?" Mike asked her, showing her the photograph.

The old woman put on her glasses and looked at the picture, nodding. "Yes, that's her. The picture looks like it's from when she was working here."

Mike nodded and put the picture away.

"Do you know where she is now?" Mike asked. "Or do you remember a doctor in this town named Martin? Dr. Frank Martin?"

The woman looked at him, her face suddenly serious.

"Listen carefully, son," she said, her voice low. "You don't want to mess with this—you need to leave that girl alone. You need to leave all of this alone—tell your friend that she moved away or something. Don't get involved."

Mike looked at her, trying to understand the sudden shift in the conversation. "If this husband of hers is treating her bad, maybe she needs some help," Mike said, putting the picture away.

The woman shook her head.

If you and your friend show up at Vincent Luciano's house and try to talk to the girl, he will probably kill you. And that doctor you were asking about? He's dead. Died right after the trial and right after the old man went to jail."

Mike was unsure of what to say.

"No one was really sure of his connection to the case, but he was Chris's uncle," the woman continued. "The doctor's sister was Chris's mother," she said, glancing out at the boy leaning against the rental car. "Knowing about that crazy hypnosis, now it makes some kind of sense. He was about the only person in town back then with enough schooling to do something like that. If he helped the case happen by doing what he did, it's probably what got him killed."

She grabbed his arm and pulled to get his attention.

"Now listen, boy, and take this to heart. Leave this alone. Vincent and his brother Tony are dangerous. You and your friend could go bumbling around and end up dead. As for the girl, if you can get your friend to just forget about this whole thing, it would be best. She's made her choices in life, and now she has to live with them. There's nothing you or your friend can do."

Mike nodded.

"I understand," he said slowly. "And thanks for all of your help. If anything happens, we'll come by and see you again before we leave. Can I get a dozen of those chocolate chip cookies for Gary? He said they were good."

She smiled and moved around the counter, bagging up more than a dozen and handing them to Mike. "Take them, no charge. And take care of your friend out there. He looks like he needs somebody to lean on."

Mike thanked her again and left, heading out to the car.

Gary was just leaning against it, staring off into space, and seemed to wake from some dream when Mike tapped him on the elbow.

"Mike. There you are. I can remember this place. There's something here that I can't remember, but there's a lot that I can—I can remember being parked out here, in front of the bakery, waiting for someone."

"It was her, Gary, from the picture," Mike said, handing back the picture. "She worked here—this is where you met."

Gary turned suddenly and looked at him, his face wrinkling up—from surprise or from more pain, Mike didn't know.

"She worked here?"

"Yeah," Mike said, nodding. "That woman in there knew a lot about you, stuff I need to tell you. But we need to get you someplace safe, someplace where you can think about the things I'm telling you instead of constantly remembering new stuff. We're going back to the room."

Mike unlocked the doors and got in, and Gary climbed in the passenger side.

"She really knows the girl in the picture? What did she say about her? Was what my stepmother said true, about me and her?"

"Gary, I'll tell you, okay? I'll tell you everything, or at least everything I think you can handle," he said as he pulled out into the street and headed back to their motel.

# Chapter 39

Judy rolled over, finally getting up off the couch. She didn't want to go upstairs, but desperately wanted to shower. It was only a matter of time before she'd have to go in their bedroom and clean up. Or at least pull the sheets off the bed and wash them.

For now, she didn't have the energy to do much of anything. And at this point, she just didn't care.

Last night, she had felt a rage building up inside of her she had never known before. But this morning the rage had evaporated, leaving only a residue of failure and humiliation.

She felt like a robot, slowly tidying the living room, trying not to think about going upstairs. That was what Vincent needed, and wanted—a robot to follow him around and clean up after him.

Judy Luciano went into the kitchen and started to make herself something to eat but gave up halfway through, leaving the food sitting on the counter.

She wanted to go, to leave everything behind—it was too bad that her ill-fated trip to the lake hadn't been better planned. Now he would be watching her more closely. Now, he'd be checking on her, making her life harder and harder. If she had just planned it better, taking her time, maybe she could've gotten away.

Or maybe that was the wrong approach. Maybe she should have spent less time planning. Maybe she should have just left and started walking. Avoiding all the roads, sleeping in the woods, eating scraps. Anything would be better than sitting around here, waiting for Vincent to come home and torture her.

But a walk sounded like a good idea, so she left. The only conscious thing she did before she walked out the door was to put on her shoes.

She thought for a moment about going upstairs and getting the letter taped to the back of her dresser drawer, but she didn't have the energy to climb the stairs. She didn't want to see that bed, either.

Judy had no idea how long she would be gone—she left the door unlocked behind her. A large part of her wanted to just keep on walking, forever.

# Chapter 40

"And he's not someone to be messed with, supposedly."

Mike finished telling the story—they were still sitting in the parking lot of the motel. Mike had started telling the story on the drive back to the motel, but Gary had continued asking questions, so they'd stayed in the car, staring at the ugly door of their room.

At least they were out of O'Fallon.

But as Mike told the story, Gary couldn't help thinking that this was all too strange to believe. It didn't take a brain surgeon to make the connection—Gary had been dreaming about this abused woman, and now they had independent confirmation that the woman was in fact involved in a very abusive relationship.

It was so much to take in all at once. Suddenly Gary was very glad that Mike had come along—he was looking out for Gary, getting him out of that bakery and passing along the information somewhere else. It wouldn't have been good if he'd come here by himself—he would've been passing out every time someone gave him a new piece of information. How would he have ever held a conversation with anyone?

But his...his old girlfriend had worked at that bakery, and the old woman had filled in a few of the holes with new information.

The doctor, the girl—and the hypnosis, it now appeared—had all really existed. They were real things, people that he had known, or things that had really happened to him. He'd even been engaged to her.

The doctor was Gary's uncle, someone his father would've trusted. Gary didn't remember the man, but he did recall that his mother's brother had been a doctor of some sort. That the man had died soon after the trial could be explained by a connection between him and Gary and his father. And it helped to explain why the mental wall had not been removed in a later therapy session—the man who had created the wall had died.

The weirdest thing, so far, was his lack of surprise when Mike had told him that Judy...that the girl in the picture was in an abusive relationship. He'd seen the proof a hundred times in the dream. It had been like watching a movie over and over and then having someone explain the plot to you, but to find out that on some level, it might actually be true—that was too much. Gary had known a woman was in trouble—he just hadn't known who she was.

And Vincent Luciano sounded exactly like the guy in the dream. Gary remembered Vincent and Tony Luciano—they had grown up together, hung out. His father had worked for their father. Why hadn't Gary remembered Vincent before?

There had to be some kind of connection between Gary and the girl. But how could he be living through her, seeing through her eyes?

"Pretty crazy, huh?" Mike said, looking at him after a long period of silence in the car. It was starting to sprinkle outside. "I don't understand it at all," Mike said. "I don't see how it's possible."

Gary nodded. He wanted to go to her, to see her, but he didn't know if he could take that chance. He couldn't even say her name without the headache edging in—what would happen if he actually saw her?

"Yeah," Gary answered, getting out the cards and shuffling them. "This is seriously screwed up. I don't even know who to talk to next."

"Well," Mike answered. "I do. We talk to that other doctor, the one the old lady mentioned. He took over Dr. Martin's practice ten years ago, and she's heard he's the best psychologist around. We're lucky he's located here in O'Fallon."

Gary nodded, feeling a little better. At least Mike had a plan.

"But I think we should be careful," Mike continued, serious. "This Vincent has two reasons to hate you: he knows your father and what he did, and he's married to your ex and beats the crap out of her. Sounds like she'd bail if she could, but the old woman said that will never happen. Vincent is a powerful guy, and he's got powerful friends. Your ex-girlfriend is trapped, and there's no getting her out of there."

Gary looked at his friend, trying to get a read on him. Was he trying to motivate him or caution him? "Well, if this was a Rambo movie, we'd go in there and rescue her."

Mike smiled, getting excited. "Yeah, we could fly a helicopter and rappel down those rope lines onto the roof of her house. I could throw one of those flash-bang grenades and then you could rescue her."

Gary smiled.

"But we'd have to have a helicopter, or at least some really big muscles," Mike said. "I can't help you out there. Now if you need an old lady in a bakery charmed, I'm your man, but I don't think we're riding in to save her like a couple of cowboys. But we could go out there and talk to her, if we can find the house. How do you think you'll react? And what do we do if he shows up? Did you remember your .357 magnum?"

Gary shrugged his shoulders, appreciating Mike's attempts at humor. "My brain—well, you could end up doing most of the talking. It would be good, though, to see her face, to know that she really exists. Since the bakery, it's been easier to think about my mom and what happened. Easier to remember the town and to think about...Judy. I know this might sound crazy, but I think being back here is really helping."

"That might be the first thing I've heard today that didn't sound crazy," Mike said, smiling and starting the car.

"So, where to, chief?" Mike asked.

"Well, let's go see the doctor first. Then maybe drive out to where she lives—I know Blackwood Lane, and it's pretty famous around here. The road is supposed to be haunted. Anyway, I'm sure we can find the house," he said, his voice tight with anticipation.

Gary didn't look at Mike—he flipped a card out of the tarot deck and studied it intently. He didn't want his friend to see just how nervous he really was.

------

"Can I help you?" the man said from behind his half-opened door.

Gary smiled through the crack.

"Yes, Doctor. My name is...Gary Foreman. I have a bit of an emergency and need to speak to you immediately, if you have the time. The receptionist said you had a noon lunch that cancelled, and you might be able to see me."

Dr. Myers looked over at Nadine, his receptionist, and saw that she was shrugging her shoulders and giving him one of those "sorry, Doctor, I couldn't help myself" smiles that she used on him whenever she wanted her way. She was chatting with a man standing next to her desk, a tanned guy that looked like he could be a model.

"A mental emergency? This I have to hear."

He held the door open for Gary and asked him to sit, then walked around his large wooden desk.

"How can I help you?" Dr. Myers asked, getting out his pad and pen.

"First question—what do you charge an hour?"

Dr. Myers smiled. "I usually get between $75 and $100 an hour, but I'm on my lunch now, so let's hear what you want to talk about. After I figure out how long I think it will take, I'll quote you a price, okay?"

The young man on his couch nodded, adjusting the cushions. Dr. Myers could tell he was nervous—the body language said it all. Nervous and stressed.

"Just be forewarned," Dr. Myers continued, trying to put the boy at ease. "If you talk all the way through my lunch and I don't get a chance to eat, I'll have to charge you at least $50. Okay?"

Gary nodded and sighed, heavily.

"That sounds great, Doc. Is it okay if I call you Doc?"

Dr. Myers nodded, not saying anything. The easiest way to get someone talking was to leave a comfortable silence for them to fill.

"It's a complicated story," the boy began, "but I'll give you the condensed version. You seem to be about the only doctor in O'Fallon qualified to speak on the subject of suppressed memories. Is that correct?"

The doctor was surprised, leaning forward in his chair. He figured the guy was here to talk about a bad relationship or a sudden loss of a job. The young man didn't look familiar, but Dr. Myers had dealt with enough unstable people to know that they could see any change in their routine as a threat to their very existence.

But this sounded like something different.

"Well, yes, I guess you could say that," Dr. Myers answered. "I've published several papers in the journals, and two of those were related to the suppression of memories."

Gary sat back. "Well, I just learned a few days ago that I had some memories suppressed about ten years ago, and against my will. The procedure was performed by a doctor here in O'Fallon, Dr. Frank Martin, my uncle. He's dead, now, or I would be talking to him, I guess. The memories that he suppressed were of my true name and of a girlfriend I had at the time. Fiancé, actually."

Dr. Myers held it in for a moment, then gave up trying and laughed out loud. Laughing at your patients wasn't the best clinical technique, but he couldn't help it.

"Ah, well, that doesn't sound very likely, son," Dr. Myers said. "You wouldn't be taping a segment for the Jerry Springer show, would you?"

"Why do you say that?" Gary said calmly.

Dr. Myers's smile faded—now he was more than a little curious. Most patients reacted differently when you laughed at them. This boy seemed completely calm or was at least working very hard to control his emotions.

"No mental blockage technique can keep a memory suppressed for that long," Dr. Myers said slowly. "It's not clinically possible. If it were that easy, I could just tell people to stop smoking and they would never smoke again. Any mental wall, even one constructed using the best hypnotic techniques by the world's most experienced psychiatrist, would have broken down a long time ago."

The young man nodded thoughtfully and reached into his back pocket. "But what if it didn't?" Gary asked. He pulled something from his wallet, handing it over to Myers along with an old photograph he'd been holding.

Dr. Myers took them both and looked at them.

One was a driver's license—it looked completely normal, listing the young man's name as "Gary Foreman" and showing his address in California. For a moment, Dr. Myers wondered what this boy was doing so far away from home.

The other item was more interesting—it was a picture of the man, younger and surrounded with friends. There was an attractive woman on his lap, a woman who seemed vaguely familiar to the doctor. In the picture there was a cake, obviously for the young man. But instead of saying "Gary" like it said on the driver's license, the cake read "Happy 17th Birthday, Chris."

Dr. Myers glanced up at the young man—it was the same face in both pictures.

"I don't understand," Dr. Myers said.

The young man on his couch smiled.

"Neither did I, when I first received that photograph a few nights ago from my stepmother. Anytime I try to remember what that girl's name is or anything about her, I get these horrible migraines, right across the front of my head," he said, indicating with his hands and messaging his temples. "The headaches are the worst whenever I try to remember that my real name is Chri—"

The young man suddenly stopped talking, his face tightening in obvious pain. The young man's hand drifted up and touched his jacket pocket.

This was strange—Dr. Myers had never seen anything like this.

Real physical pain brought on by a mental instability was rare, and it was even more rare for someone to try and fake it. But headaches were a logical manifestation of an unresolved mental blockage. Of course, it couldn't have lasted this long….

"Do you need some water?" Dr. Myers asked.

The young man shook his head slowly. "No, thanks."

Dr. Myers was quiet for a moment, then continued. "You say that you get these headaches whenever you try to remember?"

Gary nodded. "Yeah. I flew back to the area yesterday to find out what's happening. My father and I moved away from the area in 1987, and the only clues I have brought me back here to learn more. Do you know Wood Bakery?"

Dr. Myers nodded—anyone who spent more than twenty minutes in O'Fallon knew about Wood Bakery.

"I was there this morning," the young man said. "After a couple of minutes, I could remember it quite clearly—my mother and I used to go there when I was growing up. But then I got this horrible pain, like a vice closing on my head, trying to crush it. There was nothing else in the world except for the pain." Gary paused for a moment, rubbing his forehead. "The woman there recognized me."

------

Judy was walking, her feet trudging through a field behind her home, but she wasn't paying attention.

She was thinking about her death.

The idea wasn't a bad one, as far as she could tell. She enjoyed the very idea of an end to all the pain and humiliation.

It would all be over, and maybe by some freak occurrence Vincent would be caught and tried for killing her, if he ended up being her executioner. If she killed herself, no one would have to go to jail, but if she could somehow arrange for him to kill her….

Of course, if left to his own devices, he might kill her soon enough—she had never seen him as angry as he was last night.

She tried not to think about the pile of burned paintings she'd seen this morning on the front lawn as she'd left to go walking—somehow, they looked even more pitiful in daylight.

Her parents were gone now, and all she had left of them was that envelope from Texas. There was money waiting there for her, but it might as well be on the moon—or in California.

And Chris was long gone—he'd surely forgotten all about her after so many years. He was probably happy and healthy out there in Sacramento, with a cute wife and two or three kids.

She had his ring and nothing else. She doubted he would even remember her—if they were to somehow bump into each other in downtown O'Fallon, he'd probably not even recognize her.

No one would miss her, and she took some comfort in that. There was nothing else to think about except the method. As she strolled through the fields and valleys near her husband's home, she pondered on the best method to afford her sweet release.

# Chapter 41

Dr. Myers caught himself leaning forward and reminded himself to control his body language.

"The woman at Wood Bakery, she told my friend that I used to shop there with my mother," the young man continued, staring at the ceiling. "The woman also told my friend Mike that Judy—"

He broke off at the mention of a girl's name, and then continued.

"—that the girl in the picture used to work there. It was where we met. That and other details seem to be confirming each other."

Dr. Myers looked at the young man. There were a lot of facts coming out very quickly. It looked like he wasn't going to be getting lunch any time soon.

Not that it really mattered. This was a fascinating story, if it was true.

He grabbed his notepad and scribbled down what he could remember and asked Gary to repeat what he could not remember, which he did without hesitation. Playing dumb, Myers also asked him to repeat more, and the young man obliged. So far, there were no cracks in the story.

As he asked the questions, the young man reached into his jacket pocket and took out what looked like a large deck of cards. While Dr. Myers wrote, the young man took the cards out of the deck and shuffled through them, taking one at a time out and looking at it, then shuffling it back in. Dr. Myers ignored it for now.

"Okay, just a couple of quick questions," Dr. Myers continued. "Why would your stepmother send you the picture when she must've known it would upset you? If she knew about your suppressed memories, she could guess that seeing that picture would be traumatic. Why would she do that?"

The boy looked away for a moment, glancing out the window. Dr. Myers felt his reluctance to answer.

"Well, this is the crazy part of the whole story," Gary began.

"Crazy piled on top of more crazy. For the past few months, I've been having a series of nightmares about a woman. In each of the dreams, I see this woman being abused. The dreams have started to affect me, even when I'm awake—I can't stop thinking about them."

Dr. Myers scribbled on his pad and nodded, keeping quiet.

"About a week ago," Gary continued. "I thought I remembered the man in the dream, but I couldn't put a name to the face. I thought he might be someone I remembered from back here, so I drove to Sacramento to see my father and ask him about the man. He didn't have any idea who I was talking about. My stepmother, who suspected the dreams might be of this girl, sent me the picture to jog my memory. It turns out that I've been dreaming about her," he said, nodding at the picture on Myers' desk.

Dr. Myers nodded, understanding. "Well, that could be the memories starting to come through the blockage—it could be breaking down on its own, or Dr. Martin may have programmed the memory wall to break down after a given amount of time. Either way, if your memories are starting to seep back into your conscious mind, the dreams are a good place for them to show up first."

Gary nodded, thoughtful.

"My father said that Dr. Martin gave him a set of words that would remove the blockage, but my father forgot them a long time ago. You say that the dreams might be my mind's way of slowly reminding me of this woman?"

"Certainly," Dr. Myers agreed. "The mind is a strange construct, something we don't understand well, even on the most basic level. There are reported cases of suppressed memories coming back spontaneously after a long time, but most of those are related to some kind of trauma or abuse. But those are things that the mind itself has suppressed to keep the person sane by literally 'forgetting' the horrible event. I've never heard of an intentional block lasting this long, or breaking down on its own."

"Is it possible?" Gary asked.

Dr. Myers chuckled. "Who knows? We can send a little rover to drive around on the surface of Mars, but we still don't know how language is stored in our own minds. We don't know how you and I access our stored memories from all those little synapses in our head. Who's to say what is or isn't possible?"

Gary nodded. "What's causing the headaches?"

"Well, assuming this is all true and you're not just pulling my chain, the headaches would be your mind trying to keep you from remembering too much at once. The memories and the blockage are both parts of the same mind, making the whole thing very tricky. The memories want to come out, and the blockage is trying to hold them back. Your organic memory knows that if you remember everything all at once, it would probably shatter your mind and drive you insane."

Gary laughed. "Is that the clinical term? 'Insane?'"

Dr. Myers smiled at him. "People step over the line into insanity all the time—you've read about seemingly 'normal' people who kill their families and commit suicide. You hear the neighbors on TV saying something like 'he was such a nice guy, so quiet.' There are a thousand reasons for someone to break from sanity, and there are a thousand ways that insane people deal with their own psychotic tendencies. But the mind is a powerful construct, and it adapts to serve the body, to preserve the entity it is commanding."

Dr. Myers watched the young man closely, gauging his reaction to Myers's standard 'everyone is a little crazy' speech, which he used often to gauge the mental state of many people that came through his door. Some people got defensive, some got angry or belligerent—this young man simply accepted the explanation, moving on to his next question without hesitation.

It was the first real sign that the young man truly believed these things were occurring to him. Dr. Myers made a note of it.

Myers decided to press the issue and continue down the same path. Sometimes the only way to force a breakthrough was through confrontation—it wasn't the best clinical method, but this boy looked like he could bolt out the door at any moment, and Myers wanted a couple of answers.

"Ted Bundy was famously normal," Dr. Myers continued. "Sometimes it's difficult to tell the difference. Bundy masked his insanity very well, and blended in. In one case, a group of people were searching for him after he'd escaped from a Colorado jail, and he managed to convince one of his pursuers that he was not Ted Bundy."

The young man was quiet.

"Do you remember that story last year," Dr. Myers continued, "about that man who travelled the country in a white van, killing people from coast to coast? It was a disturbing story. He was a true serial killer, not like those you see in the movies; he was a sociopath, but the man was so successful because he could suppress his anger and his emotions and act normally whenever he wanted to. He was a chameleon, changing into whatever the situation required. "

Gary smiled. "I hope you're not comparing me to Ted Bundy."

Dr. Myers shook his head. "Of course not.

"Do you think you're crazy?" Dr. Myers asked, another standard diagnostic question.

Gary looked at the ceiling, quiet. "I don't know, Dr. Myers. I don't think so, but when the headaches come, I lose control of myself. And I smell cigarette smoke, whatever that means. Does that mean I'm crazy?"

Dr. Myers shook his head. "Of course not.

"Then why can't I say her name?" Gary continued. "Or mine? Even in my head?"

"That's your mind trying to protect itself. You'll need some time before you can start thinking of yourself in a different way, or start remembering this girl—don't forget it was a deliberate act, suppressing those memories. Do you know why they did that?"

"Yes, my father used to work for the Luciano family, and he testified against him in Federal Court ten years ago. I didn't care, and I didn't want to enter the witness protection program or leave my fiancé, the girl in the picture, so I fought it."

Dr. Myers nodded—he had heard snippets of this story in his years in O'Fallon.

"Supposedly," Gary continued, "I jeopardized the case to the point where it was either hypnotize me temporarily or physically remove me from the state. My mother had been killed in a car bombing, and that convinced my father that he had to testify and then get us away. The hypnosis was supposed to be temporary, but he told my stepmother later that there never seemed to be a good and safe time to reveal to me my true name or allow me to remember...the girl. There was still a contract out on my father's life, a contract I'm pretty sure still exists. The memories stayed suppressed until I started having these dreams."

It was all too much for the doctor to write down, but he scribbled as fast as he could. His secretary Nadine would have a fun time trying to follow his chicken-scratching.

The young man waited patiently, going back to flipping through his cards until Myers was finished scribbling.

"What are those?" Myers asked.

The young man looked down at the cards and then smiled, as if realizing what he was doing. "Oh, these are tarot cards—lately I've been very interested in palm reading and crystals. The tarot cards supposedly predict the future," Gary said sheepishly.

Dr. Myers nodded. "That makes sense—your mind is looking for answers. It's like a talisman for you."

"What's that?" Gary asked.

"A talisman is an object of supernatural or mystical power. In this context, your talisman is some object that gives you comfort, allowing your mind to relax. The fact that the cards hold an almost supernatural power for you is even better—do they give you comfort?"

Gary looked at the cards. Dr. Myers could tell he was thinking about it for the first time.

"Yes," the young man said. "I guess they do."

"Then I see nothing wrong with them."

Gary nodded, putting the cards away. "So what do I do now? I found out where the girl and her new husband live, and I want to see her. Something in me tells me she's in trouble. I know it's not the smart thing to do, but…."

Dr. Myers shook his head.

"If you see her, the first thing your mind will do is shut down. You'll pass out, or worse. For now, I think you need to rest, here in my office or back at your hotel. We need to explore the entire story, from beginning to end, and then you and I will deal with how to best handle the future."

Gary looked at him, and the doctor finally understood what was happening here—the boy wasn't looking for a cure.

He was looking for a direction.

The boy was obviously worried. Did he think his dreams of the girl's abuse were somehow true? Did he believe that the dreams could be some type of precognitive cry for help from the girl? That would explain his restless….

"I can't do that, Doctor," Gary said quietly.

Dr. Myers nodded. "You believe that the dreams are true, don't you? Are you thinking you're somehow connected to her mind, seeing through her eyes?"

"I don't know, Doc," the young man said. "But I have to find her and make sure she's okay. As long as I know that, I can spend the next ten years in therapy, trying to get my head on straight. But first, I need to know she's okay. Everything else is secondary. What can I do to mitigate the headaches?"

He was determined, Dr. Myers saw. Of course, if he truly thought the girl was in jeopardy, he would want to go to her.

"Gary, you need to listen to me," Dr. Myers cautioned. "The headaches are going to get worse as long as your mind fights the memories. You need to calm down and relax and try to handle your pain. And you need to slowly repeat to yourself, your true name and the name of the girl. If you start doing that, you'll find the headaches may decrease in intensity. You just need to get used to the idea before your mind will completely accept it."

Gary nodded, getting up. "Thank you for all your help, Doc. If this turns out for the better, I promise to come back and see you before I leave for Los Angeles." He turned toward the door, but Myers stood and pushed it shut.

"Gary, you can't go to her," Dr. Myers said. "If you see her, you'll collapse or pass out. It could seriously damage your mind. That isn't going to help her. Is that what you want?"

Gary's eyes came up, and he stared at Myers intently.

"I have to know she's okay."

Myers nodded and his hand came slowly off the door.

"Good luck. And come see me before you leave town." Dr. Myers pulled the door open for Gary and, at the same time, fished a business card out of his shirt pocket.

"Call me, anytime, day or night, if you need help."

Gary smiled and took the card, thanking him again. As Myers watched, Gary collected his friend, who nodded curtly at the doctor and smiled warmly at Nadine, and they walked out together. They climbed into a rental car with Missouri tags and drove away.

Dr. Myers had no idea what to think about all of this.

He went back into his office, closed the door, and spent the next half hour rewriting all of his notes. It was a fascinating tale—he tried to remember all the details, filling in a few of the places with speculation on the boy's mental condition.

Dr. Myers was so engrossed in the story that he forgot all about lunch.

# Chapter 42

Blackwood Lane wound through the hills and fields north and east of O'Fallon, but Gary and Mike found the Luciano home with no trouble. There was a mailbox marking the house from the road, and Mike turned the car into the long driveway and slowly approached the house.

The two-story farmhouse with an attached garage sat by itself, both surrounded by a large, well-kept yard. To one side, a hundred yards from the house, stood a barn-like structure, an outbuilding between the house and the field that fronted Blackwood Lane. Two broken-down cars rested in the sun in front of the barn like tired dogs.

Mike parked in front of the house and they climbed out—it didn't look like anybody was home.

They walked up to the front door and Gary rang the doorbell, but there was no answer. Mike knocked on the door and leaned over, peeking into the windows, but he saw no one inside. He could see the living room and a kitchen beyond, but there wasn't anyone here.

Mike tried the door and found it was unlocked. After a glance at Gary, he eased the door open.

The interior looked like any other home—a living room filled with furniture and pictures. There were stairs leading up to the second floor. Gary peeked inside as well, but they both seemed unsure of whether or not they should enter.

"Hello?" Mike called loudly, making Gary start. "Is anyone here?"

There was no response. After a long moment, Gary punched Mike hard on the shoulder and stepped off the porch.

"Ow, what was that for?" Mike asked as he continued to look around the living room from the threshold.

"You scared me, yelling like that," he heard Gary say from behind him.

Mike called again but heard nothing—everything looked perfectly normal, with nothing out of place. He pulled the front door shut again.

"Wow," he heard Gary say from behind him.

Mike turned around and looked at Gary, who was holding up what looked like a burned piece of newspaper.

"What is it?" Mike asked.

Gary turned it around for Mike to see.

"I found this in the yard," Gary said. "Couldn't you smell it? Something burnt—it's a painting."

It looked like a mess—Mike could make out something along the bottom that looked like water, and along one side was a tall blob of white and black. The rest was unrecognizable.

"Who burns a painting?" Mike asked.

"It's an ocean scene," Gary said, pointing. "There are waves, and a beach, and up here on the right, there's a...."

Gary looked at him, his face white.

"It's a lighthouse. Like Point Vincenté, where I looked at the photograph for the first time."

Mike looked, but he didn't see it—there was something there that might be a lighthouse, but the paint was smeared badly. "I don't know, Gary. It could be anything."

"No, no. That's a lighthouse. Jud—she must've painted this."

Mike looked at his friend. "Now, don't go there. You don't know...."

Gary shook his head. "I know, Mike. Sorry. It's just that...it feels right. It feels like she painted this. I can tell, just like I could tell when we pulled up here that she wasn't here. I don't know how I know, but I do."

Gary looked around, looking back out at Blackwood Lane and the trees on either side of the road.

Mike shook his head.

"Well, you're right about her not being here. What else should we do?"

After a long minute of silence, Gary shrugged. "There's nothing we can do," he said, and walked back to the car.

# Chapter 43

Tony walked into the room where Vincent and the other men were working. He stood for a moment and then spoke up.

"How are we doing?" Tony asked Vincent, smiling nervously as he eyed the men arrayed around the room.

Vincent looked up at him from the table—they were in one of the larger rooms of the warehouse at the casino boat dock, using the secure location as a temporary processing room where they would prepare the cocaine for distribution. There were seven other men in the room setting up tables and packaging materials and stacking bags and baggies at several stations. Two men were in charge of setting up twenty scales, zeroing them out and getting them ready to measure the coke for bagging.

Next to each station were two large bags of dextrose powder, a white sugar substance made from cornstarch that would be carefully measured into the coke to cut the intensity and increase the yield. It was an old-school ingredient—most modern operations used baking soda because it was cheaper. Some used amphetamine sulfate or talcum powder or even powdered vitamin B-12, which lent the coke a faint pink color.

"Good," Vincent said, pointing at the tables. "We're set up, and the car is ready." There was a large open area in the middle of the room next to the garage doors where they would unload Vincent's car.

Tony nodded, looking around. "Do you want to count the money again?"

Vincent shook his head. "No, brother. You've counted it twice, right?" He could see the sweat on Tony's brow. "You nervous?"

Tony nodded again. "Incredibly," he said quietly, looking around to see if any of the other men were within earshot. "This has to go well." It was 3 p.m., less than two hours from the buy.

"I know," Vincent said. "Go for a walk or something, okay?

Work out the kinks. Things will go fine, and we'll have the stuff in here in no time, processing it. And then you'll have a lot more money to count."

Tony nodded, taking the hint and heading outside.

He came out of Warehouse Two, which sat next to the large parking lot that would service the new riverboat. The boat was nearly finished. Visiting the *Princess Margaret* always made him feel better, more relaxed, and he strolled in that direction.

Tony was proud of the Pier 32 dock and its facilities—he'd grown them from a stretch of broken-down industrial buildings that had sat abandoned for decades on the waterfront into what it was today. It had been a lot of work, negotiating with the locals and bringing in his own contractors and keeping the security level high enough to permanently discourage petty criminals and the like from trying to steal from the facility. He'd lost a few cars and some equipment before the large fence, topped with barbed wire, had been completed. That fence, along with the massive lights, kept the criminals away. Or the other criminals, Tony thought, smiling.

Directly across the wide expanse of the Mississippi River stood the glittering buildings of the St. Louis skyline. Tony loved the view from here.

Tony Luciano's first gambling riverboat, the *Princess Anne*, was just shutting down business for the day—Saturdays were very lucrative, and he hated to be closing early on a Saturday evening, but having the buy at the warehouses made sense—it was the most secure location they controlled. It was announced that the *Anne* was closing early tonight to hold a large private party and boat cruise—Tony had decided that if he were going to have to close the ship, he'd make it a publicity opportunity.

He watched as the last of the paying customers left the parking lots and headed home. Tony had given the staff of the *Anne* the evening off, even the cleaning staff. They all thought he had staffed the private party with an outside catering service. What they didn't know wouldn't hurt them.

The second riverboat, the *Princess Margaret*, was docked a hundred feet downriver next to the new gangplank building, which would provide easy access and funnel guests onto the ship. The *Anne* used a simple walkway up and onto the boat, and they'd had to fish a few drunken customers out of the shallow river after they had stumbled off and fallen between the boat and the loading dock.

The simulated smokestacks for the *Princess Margaret* stood at the dock, right next to the boat—they were to be lifted into place by large cranes next week, capping off the last of the exterior construction. Tony strolled over to the temporary gangway that led over the shallow river and onto the *Margaret*.

The interiors were not nearly as close to completion as the exterior—there were bare studs where the last walls needed to be installed. In the finished areas, poker tables and roulette tables were in place, and most of the carpet was down, but some of the areas, like the restaurant and upstairs lounge, were still several weeks from completion.

He walked through the boat, checking the facilities, liking what he saw. Tony was sure the *Margaret* would be a huge moneymaker, but it was also simply beautiful. Tony hoped the *Princess Margaret* would turn things around for them—his family would be able to get away from the cocaine business. It was distasteful, something that he'd hoped to avoid, but Vincent had told him over and over about the vast amounts of money they would be able to make.

If this worked, Tony would have all the money he needed to finish the *Margaret*, and then he'd talk to Vincent, give him the good news. After a lot of thought, Tony had decided to allow Vincent to run that side of the *familia*, separating the drug side from the areas Tony was more interested in—the gambling boats, the clubs, and the other entertainment-related businesses. It was smart to compartmentalize the business anyway, and Vincent seemed born to do what he was doing right now—setting up drug buys and pressuring existing distributors out of business.

He headed up the stairs to the top deck of the *Margaret*. This would eventually be an outside dining and dancing area, and on one end of the top deck was a small bandstand. When he'd worked with a designer to lay out the boat, Tony had immediately seen the possibilities of a rooftop dance area—his customers would drink and dance their nights away while enjoying a stunning view of downtown St. Louis across the river.

That was the kind of business he enjoyed doing—making money while bringing people something they liked.

He walked to one end of the boat and looked over the edge, where it was tied up with two large ropes. The boat would have operating engines and be able to move up and down the river—Tony planned to offer daily cruises down to Louisville or up the river to Hannibal, Missouri. But for now, the ropes and a series of large underwater supports kept the riverboat in place. When the dock area was complete, the underwater supports would be adjusted to hold the boat more tightly, reducing the boat's movement, and then released when it was time to take the boat out onto the open water.

Near the back of the *Margaret*, secured to the top deck, was a small emergency motorboat that could be lowered into the water by a winch. A small emergency craft was required by law on any ship as large as the *Margaret* for passenger evacuation, in the unlikely event the riverboat would founder.

Tony had it stowed up here on the back of the top deck, behind the bridge and out of the way. The motorboat could also be used for quick jaunts to and from shore without docking the *Margaret*, or to visit areas on shore that didn't have a riverboat dock.

He headed back down into the riverboat, weaving back and forth inside the main casino areas and walking down the gangplank to the dock.

Directly in front of him was the brand-new large parking lot that would serve the *Margaret*—in some places, the paint and concrete were barely dry. On his left was the smaller current parking structure. On his right were Warehouses One and Two—One was the staging area for all the interior construction on the *Margaret*, and Warehouse Two held the riverboat offices and the new processing area for the drugs.

Tony's walk had made him feel better—if they could pull this off, he could use the money to finish construction of the *Margaret* and begin the process of distancing himself from the new and very lucrative illegal activities Vincent had planned for the *familia*.

A glance at his watch told him that D.W. would arrive in less than an hour. Tony walked back toward the entrance to Warehouse Two, hoping that all the preparations were finished.

# Chapter 44

Gary was depressed.

He looked over at Mike sitting on the other bed, watching TV. It was getting later and later in the day and he didn't have a clue where to go from here.

They'd gone out this morning with such high hopes, but nothing had come of it—the incident at Wood Bakery had sent Gary on his way to discovering more about his past, and the visit to the psychiatrist had helped. The drive to her home had been the ultimate anticlimax—he'd been all keyed up to see her, preparing his mind for the shock of it, and there had been no one home. The headaches had come and gone and come again, all day long.

They'd left and driven around for a while, directionless, and then come back to the motel for a late lunch.

Gary had no idea what to do next. All he wanted to do was sleep and try to forget everything. Even though he was sitting perfectly still in the chair, looking out the window, his mind was racing—he was still thinking about that odd burnt fragment of what, to him, looked like a painting of Point Vincenté.

After they'd left her house, he'd had Mike drive around for the past couple of hours, looking for anything that triggered a memory, but nothing had come. There were new memories, and places he'd remembered, but nothing gave any clue what to do next.

"Well?" Mike asked, shutting off the TV and looking over at Gary.

Gary set the tarot cards down—he'd been endlessly shuffling and shuffling them, laying them out on the small table by the window. They had afforded no insight, either.

He looked over at Mike.

"I don't know," Gary said. "This isn't...I'm not getting answers, and it's getting more and more frustrating. I don't know what to do next, or where to go."

Mike nodded. "I know you're frustrated. Maybe you need to relax for a few hours and stop trying so hard to remember."

Gary nodded. That sounded good to him.

"You want to go to that 'Mayfest' thing?" Mike asked, suddenly inspired. "I've seen posters for it all over town—it's going on all weekend. It sounds like fun."

"It is fun—it's O'Fallon's claim to fame. Every year it's a big deal, and just about the only time you can ride a carnival ride. Actually, you might be right," Gary said, relaxing already. "That might be fun."

# Chapter 45

D.W. pulled up in his car at precisely 6:00 p.m.

Tony loved punctuality. He walked over with Vincent and greeted D.W. warmly—he might find the whole business distasteful, but Tony was smart enough to see a money-making venture through. A quick glance around told him they were alone, except for the Lucianos' eight security guards patrolling the perimeter of the parking area. D.W. had, evidently, trusted the Lucianos enough to not bring along his own security, only one associate, who climbed from the car and followed D.W. at a respectful distance.

"Thank you for seeing us."

D.W., nodded, smiling. "You are good for business, my friends. This is one of the largest purchases anyone has ever made from us— it was very exciting, getting this order from you. I have to say that we are surprised things are going so well for you, and so quickly. I hope we will be able to do this type of business in the future."

Tony nodded and glanced at Vincent, seeing the smile on his face. Vincent's part of the family business was booming—Tony could see he was practically drooling at the idea of how much money would be made from tonight's shipment.

"We're glad you could provide us with such a valuable service," Tony answered. "Do you want to begin?"

D.W. smiled and nodded. "Yes. The product is in the trunk."

They walked over together and D.W. nodded at his associate, who popped open the trunk of the shiny Volvo as the two brothers and D.W. walked up.

The trunk was stuffed full of cocaine.

Every corner of the Volvo's trunk had been stuffed with bags of the white powder, stacked on top of each other like small sandbags.

Tony shook his head—it was almost impossible to believe.

Vincent took one long, admiring look at the piles of bags in the trunk of the Volvo and left to go get his car. So far, no one had men-

tioned that all of the buildings and parking lots around were part
of the Luciano complex, and Tony thought it better not to mention
that fact. D.W. surely knew some aspects of their operation, but they
didn't want him to know any more than necessary. Too much information could become a valuable commodity for D.W.

Vincent's Mustang rumbled up next to D.W.'s Volvo, and Vincent
climbed out and walked over carrying a large duffel bag from the
Mustang's front seat.

He handed it to D.W.

"One and a half million dollars," Vincent said quietly.

D.W. smiled and handed the bag to his associate, who knelt down
to the asphalt, opened the bag, and began confirming the contents.

D.W. looked at Tony. "Do I need to be worried about what's in
that bag?" he asked, carefully studying Tony's face. Tony knew that
this could still all go very badly, and surely D.W. knew that it paid to
be cautious.

"No. There's nothing in there except for your money. I counted
it myself, twice." Tony shared, and then, seeing the look on D.W.'s
face, continued. "But if you prefer, I can have my brother ride with
you until you're out of the city. If that makes you feel more comfortable."

Vincent eyed Tony strangely, and Tony knew why—this had not
been part of what they had discussed.

D.W. shook his head. "No, that won't be necessary. Just your
offer assures me there will be no trouble." D.W. nodded at his associate, and he and Vincent began transferring the bags of coke from the
Volvo to the Mustang. When the job was finally done, Vincent joined
Tony, nodding.

Tony smiled. He'd been worried that something might go wrong,
but now the deal was done. He turned to D.W. and put out his hand to
shake. That was when the first shot rang out.

Vincent dove behind his Mustang, pulling out a handgun. Tony
and D.W.'s reflexes were a little slower—Tony dove behind the Volvo, but the coke distributor spun and fell hard to the ground next to
him. A gaping, bloody hole took up what had been, only a moment
before, the entire right side of his head.

"Who is it?" Tony shouted at his brother as full automatic fire
plowed into the passenger sides of both cars.

"Must be Shotgun's boys," Vincent shouted. "I thought we got
all of them!"

Tony looked around, trying to assess the situation. Logical, calm
action—that was what he needed, not panic.

"They're on top of the parking structure," Vincent shouted. "We've got to get to cover—come on!" Vincent stood suddenly, slamming the trunk of the Mustang. He ran past the Volvo, and as Vincent went by he bent and grabbed the duffel bag of money, then raced toward the warehouse, shouting at Tony to follow him.

D.W.'s associate yelped and took off after Vincent, leaving Tony unarmed and alone in a hail of gunfire.

Tony peeked over the edge of the Volvo when the gunfire ceased for a moment. On the top level he could see several men with automatic weapons, and he knew Vincent was right. It made sense for Shotgun or whatever was left of his crew to hit them now, right in the middle of the buy. If they played it right and killed everyone, Shotgun and his guys could get away with over three million dollars in cash and high-quality cocaine.

Hindsight is always twenty-twenty, as they said, but Tony could have kicked himself for not increasing security more—he thought eight would be enough, but he hadn't thought to station people on the roofs of nearby buildings. He saw several of his security guards running toward the four-story parking structure.

As Tony watched his brother try to make it to the warehouse, a hail of automatic gunfire sparked off the parking lot around Vincent and D.W.'s associate. Vincent and the other man dove behind a car. The associate tried to return fire, but Vincent suddenly changed tactics, bolting away from the warehouses, running to the unfinished *Princess Margaret*, docked at the waterfront fifty feet away.

Tony heard the strange bark of a completely different type of gun and saw D.W.'s associate crumple to the ground. The gun didn't sound like any of the other automatic weapons, and the range and accuracy were too precise. It had to be a long-range rifle with a scope.

Which meant Tony and his brother were next.

# Chapter 46

Mike was starting to really like this place.

Gary was moping around like a zombie, and Mike couldn't figure out what to do to get him out of his funk except to set an example. Maybe if Mike had a good time, he could distract Gary from his memories.

A loud, buzzing fair should be able to get anyone out of a funk.

The O'Fallon Mayfest was like something out of a movie—it was exactly what Mike would have described if he'd been asked to imagine a small-town fair in a Midwestern town. There were cotton candy vendors and bumper cars and a Ferris wheel.

Gary was sitting on a bench nearby, absently eating a snow cone and watching the crowds—Mike got the impression Gary was worried that someone at the Mayfest might recognize him. Of course, it was so dark and busy that Mike didn't think anyone would notice him, but he kept his opinion to himself. At this point, Mike just wanted Gary to relax a little bit and let his hair down. Arguing with him wouldn't help.

"Crazy, huh?" a voice asked Mike—he'd been staring up at the Pirate Boat, a ride he'd heard about but never actually seen in real life.

He turned to look at her—she was young woman with long brown hair and even longer legs. Mike smiled.

"Yeah, I've never seen one in real life," he said.

She looked up at the Pirate Boat and he noticed the curve of her neck—she was amazing. "The Pirate Boat?"

He nodded. "Yeah. I've seen them in movies. And I've had a funnel cake before, but what is that thing?" he said, pointing at her plate. She was holding something that looked like a folded-up pancake with powdered sugar.

She looked down. "Oh, it's an elephant ear," she said, pointing over her shoulder at a stand that sold them, along with a dozen other fried treats. "It's good. Want some?"

Mike smiled. "Sure. I'm Mike, by the way. Want to ride the Pirate Boat? I'm a little nervous," he said, winking. "Is it dangerous?"

She smiled, and then unexpectedly punched him in the shoulder. "No, silly. You're just saying that to get me on there, and you know it." she said. She smiled and turned and started for the Pirate Boat.

Mike glanced over at Gary, who had been watching Mike talking to the girl. Gary smiled for the first time since the bakery, and then Gary waved Mike in the direction of the girl.

When Mike looked back at the girl, he saw that she'd stopped a few feet away and was looking at him. "I'm Tina, by the way. You coming?" she asked in a no-nonsense tone that Mike liked very much.

After a second, he nodded and followed her.

# Chapter 47

Vincent was running. He'd recovered the money and it was safe, but he couldn't get to the warehouse or his car. The buildings would have afforded him the most cover, but he couldn't get there. What were they using, Uzis? And there was at least one sniper—he'd recognized the sound of the gun.

Vincent saw three men in the doorway of the large warehouse, firing back at the men on top of the garage, but they didn't seem to be making any progress.

A gun battle erupted in the lower levels of the parking garage, and Vincent knew that parts of the security detail were trying to clear the parking garage and take out the shooters on top. All Vincent had for protection was his little Beretta handgun and the twenty rounds in the magazine.

Vincent reevaluated his situation—trying to get to the warehouse was pointless. He'd be cut down in an instant, running toward the gunfire.

Out of the corner of his eye he saw the *Princess Margaret*—he was halfway between the warehouses and the riverboat, but he'd have much better luck getting to the riverboat. And there were several cars between him and the gangplank that lead up onto the *Margaret*.

And there were guns on the riverboat.

A week before, Tony had taken Vincent on a tour of the soon-to-be-completed riverboat, and one of the things he'd pointed out was a secured locker, fully stocked with weapons and ammunition. Tony had said he'd put it in just in case there was trouble on the riverboat, but Vincent thought that there might be another reason—Tony might be planning on using the boat as a base of operations wherever he went up and down the Mississippi.

He waited for the sound of gunfire to slack off, and ran for the *Margaret*, lugging the heavy duffle bag. He wove between the cars and up the gangplank, and just as he cleared the main entrance, a large chunk of the doorway next to him exploded, showering him with wood and paint and plaster.

Someone had been aiming for the back of his head.

------

A pitched battle was raging between the first and second levels of the parking garage—the casino security detail was attempting to make progress, but Shotgun's men were laying down suppressing fire that kept them back. There was no way the detail could get onto the upper level of the garage and stop the hail of automatic fire falling on the parking lot outside—they were simply outmanned and outgunned. In the time it took two of the Lucianos' men to reach the second level, the other three had been cut down in the crossfire or taken out by the sniper. The security detail, now down to two men with a limited amount of firepower, fell back and secured the bottom level of the garage, hoping to at least trap the gunmen in the parking structure.

------

Tony watched as his brother made it up the gangplank and onto the *Margaret*. A chunk of the entrance exploded just as Vincent made it inside and that told Tony the rifleman, presumably Shotgun, was gunning for them personally. Tony had heard that Shotgun had been in the military once—he was known for his organizational ability—but evidently he or someone on his crew was a crack sniper as well.

Tony glanced around the Volvo and saw that Vincent's Mustang was okay—the trunk lid was down and the car appeared drivable. The passenger side windows had been shattered. Tony couldn't see the condition of the other side of the car, but the coke was secure, for now, and he made a split-second decision to run for the warehouses. His men were in there, returning fire, and one of them had been waving at him to run.

Tony saw a few reinforcements arriving from the security detail always on board the *Princess Anne*. It looked like the lead security guard on the ground level of the parking structure was explaining what was happening. One of the *Anne* guards was using his walkie-talkie, and Tony hoped he was communicating with the men in the warehouse and the remaining guards on the *Anne*, requesting assistance. They also had a few special materials hidden away—Tony hoped they remembered to use them. If there was ever a time to break out the big guns, it was now.

Tony waited for a break in the gunfire and ran for Warehouse One, the larger one. Several of his men were in the doorway, and when they saw him making a break for it, they all opened fire on the parking structure, trying to keep the gunmen pinned down and protecting their boss.

He ran, diving from side to side and running between his men and into the warehouse. Tony stopped a little way inside the door, his hands on his knees as he bent over, panting, trying to get his breath. He could hear the gunfire outside, and one of his men in the doorway was hit, groaning as he fell to the pavement.

This was all too crazy.

Tony looked around the warehouse, wondering what he could do. There were rows of stolen items and inventory he'd acquired at very good prices—it was all destined to be sold at a profit. There were boxes of clothing, rows of televisions and VCRs, still in their original boxes. One corner of the warehouse held ten pallets of tires, the result of leaning on his associates at a tire manufacturer up in Granite City. There were scores of boxes of various items: crates of mustard and ketchup, boxes of cheap reproductions of fine paintings, two dozen dishwashers and washing machines, and a half dozen stolen cars.

In the back of the warehouse was an airplane. It was a small two-seat biplane normally used to dust crops. The engine didn't work, but he'd acquired it for a song and had thought it amusing at the time. He'd always wanted to take his business to the air, and Tony had played with the idea of working air delivery into his stable of businesses.

But he didn't see anything that would be useful. He could hop into one of the cars and try to get away, but that wouldn't end the gunfire or save his brother, now holed up on the *Margaret*.

What Tony needed was a plan.

------

The last security guard finally showed up at the parking garage with three boxes of the stuff, and the remaining members of the security detail got ready. There were at least five more gunmen remaining on the top and second levels of the parking structure.

The lead guard lit the first stick of dynamite and stood, flinging it around the corner and up onto the second level of the garage. A moment later, a huge thud shook the structure, and he and the other guards stormed up the ramp, turning onto the second level and opening fire on the stunned men.

------

Tony heard the gunfire outside die down. Only one of his defenders in the warehouse was still on his feet.

Tony ran back over to the doorway and picked up one of the detail's Uzis and walked over, checking on his last defender.

"You okay?" Tony asked.

"Yeah, boss. Got nicked here in the leg, but I'm okay," the guard said, gesturing at a hideous wound in his thigh. "It looks worse than it is."

Tony didn't believe him. "Here, get inside. It might start up again anytime." He helped his man back into the warehouse and leaned him against a table well inside the door. "Here, tie that up," he said, looping a piece of fabric around the man's thigh. "All you need to do is guard the door, okay? Anybody comes in who doesn't look familiar, you shoot them. *Capiche*?"

The guard nodded, wincing as he tied off the tourniquet. "That's better. Where's Vincent?"

Tony glanced toward the doors, wondering why the gunfire now sounded contained within the parking structure. Maybe his guards were making progress, fighting it out with Shotgun and his boys.

"He grabbed the money and made it onto the *Margaret*," Tony said. "It was too dangerous coming this way—the guy with the rifle is a good shot."

"Yeah," the guard answered. "He was taking potshots at us, too. Got Steve and Neil."

Tony nodded. "I'm gonna take a look."

He walked over to the door, cradling his weapon. He'd only fired an automatic weapon a few times. There hadn't been much call for it in all the years the Lucianos had been a legitimate enterprise, but he knew which end was dangerous. He skirted the door opening and looked out onto the parking lot.

------

Willie B. and Shotgun returned fire, spitting up chunks of concrete as they fired at the approaching guards. Shotgun had brought ten guys, but the guards had been using dynamite and that had evened the numbers. Now only Shotgun and Willie B. and three other guys remained.

"Go up the ramp and shoot back down!" Shotgun shouted at one of his men. "Flank them!" He'd worked hard, teaching some of the crew a few basic infantry commands, and it was paying off.

There was at least one of them in the hidden concrete areas between the ramps, and he'd pinned in Willie B. and one other guy, backing them into a far corner with weapon fire.

Another blast of dynamite rocked the garage, sending up a pall of smoke.

Shotgun had traded his rifle and scope in for one of their Uzis, but now he picked up the rifle again and trained it on the darkened area between the ramps. He looked through the thermal scope, watching for movement, any kind of fluctuation in coloration against the darkened background. Shotgun was rewarded a few moments later and squeezed off a round.

He heard the shot hit someone in the darkness. The security guard spun out of the dark notch, holding his chest and collapsing to the pavement. Shotgun's men, now facing only one more gunman and not a deadly crossfire, stormed down the ramp and dispatched the last man in a few moments.

Willie B. and the remaining men came back up the ramp, smiling. "That's all of them, boss. Now what?"

Shotgun glanced over the edge. He could see Tony Luciano below in the doorway of the larger warehouse, peeking out and holding an Uzi.

"We get the brothers," Shotgun said carefully. "One's on the larger boat with the money, the other is in the big warehouse. The coke is in the Mustang, so avoid any more gunfire on that target. We don't want it to burn."

He looked at the men, all sweaty and keyed up. "And we do not split up—we take the one in the warehouse first, then the one on the boat. And I kill them both unless absolutely necessary—is that clear?"

All of his men nodded in unison, and for the first time in a long time, Shotgun felt like he was in the military again. This group of men was a good one, and he'd be proud to go into combat with any of them. But wasn't that what they were in now?

Shotgun slung his long sniper's rifle over his shoulder and picked up his Uzi, checking the clip. "Let's go."

# Chapter 48

"This is my friend, Gary," Mike said, introducing the young woman to him. Gary could see why his friend was smitten—she was cute, with that charming Midwestern demeanor and a friendly, open face. Nothing like the girls in LA.

"Hi, I'm Tina," she said, smiling. "Mike says you guys are back here on a little vacation?"

Gary nodded. "Yes, I grew up around here, and I've been bending Mike's ear for years about how great it is," he said, glancing at Mike. "I told him he'd love it."

"You guys are from Los Angeles?" she asked.

"Well, Mike is," Gary said. "I went to school out there and then ended up staying. But Mike here, he's never been around real people before. Go easy on him, okay?"

Mike smiled at him. "Thanks, Gary."

"No, seriously," Gary said to Tina. "You should have seen him this morning, eating real pancakes. It was like he'd discovered a whole new food group."

Mike shot him another look, and Tina glanced up at Mike, then back to Gary. "We're getting ready to ride the Ferris wheel—do you want to join us?"

"No, that's okay," he said, looking around. After a moment, they excused themselves and headed away to the far side of the fair.

Gary watched the other folks at the Mayfest, but no one seemed to realize who he was. The longer he strolled around the carnival, the more relaxed he became. It had been a long time, and it was good to let his defenses down and just enjoy something. The whole business with the dream and the woman in trouble and Vincent—it could wait until another evening. Tomorrow, he'd drive back out there and see her, or at least figure out what to do next; tonight, he was going to relax.

Impulsively, he got in line at one of the food booths for a funnel cake, a rare treat that he hadn't had in years. He wondered if it would be as good as he remembered.

"One, please," he said to the woman when he got to the front of the line. He fished out his wallet to pay.

"You want strawberry topping on that?" the woman asked, not looking up.

"No thanks."

The woman slid a funnel cake in front of him.

"That'll be four dollars."

He pulled out a twenty and handed it to her. She looked at him for a long moment.

"Chris? Chris O'Toole?" she asked, still holding his money.

The headache was like a punch to the face. He leaned hard on the counter and tried not to put his head down in the funnel cake.

"You're Chris O'Toole, right?" she said again, bringing on another way of pain. "You graduated with me, class of 1987. Christine, Christine Pryor."

He looked up at her and nodded, one eye closed.

"Hi," he said weakly.

"Wow, how have you been?" she said, handing back his change. "You moved away..." she started to say, then stopped.

"You okay?"

Gary nodded. "Yes, I just have a headache. Nice seeing you again," he said pathetically, turning away.

"Hey, wait!" the woman said from behind him, but he didn't turn around. He stumbled off with his funnel cake, looking for a dark alley to duck into or an empty bench to sit on. He finally found one and sat down heavily.

The headache washed over him like the tide, and he just sat back, accepting the pain. He'd been worried that someone might recognize him, putting him and Mike in danger. Gary hadn't even thought about his mind's reaction to hearing the only name for him these people knew.

He felt like an idiot. Why put himself in this situation? Of course there would be people back here that would recognize him, and the longer he hung around, the more likely it was that one of them would see him. And the one person he wanted to talk to, he couldn't find.

But others knew who he was, and now the headache was back.

Gary tried to do what Dr. Myers had suggested and repeated his real name over and over. It didn't hurt as much as it had that night at the Point Vincenté lighthouse, but it still hurt.

"There you are," the woman's voice said, and he turned. It was

Christine. "You forgot your change."

He looked up at her, and her smile faded.

"Are you okay?" she asked again, sitting down next to him on the bench.

Gary had no idea what to say, so he just said the first thing that came to mind. "Hi, Christine. Don't say my name, okay? It gives me horrible headaches."

She looked at him strangely.

"I know," Gary said. "It doesn't make any sense. How have you been?" he asked, desperate to change the subject.

Christine sat up, her face still showing concern for him. "Good, good. It's good to see you. I'm head of the high school boosters—that was our booth. I got married to Tommy, Tommy Weber. Do you remember him?"

Gary shook his head. At this point, it was hard to remember anything with his head pounding. He took out four Advil and dry swallowed them.

She watched him but didn't comment.

"Tommy and I have two kids, now, and he's an accountant over in Belleville. And you?" she asked warily.

"Oh," he replied, not expecting the conversation to swing back to him so quickly. "Uh, I moved to California and got my degree. Architecture. Now I work at a firm in Los Angeles." He rubbed one of his temples.

Christine leaned forward again.

"Do you need a doctor?" she asked.

Gary laughed out loud—he couldn't help it. The situation was just too bizarre. "Actually, I saw one today. No, it's nothing—I just need that Advil to kick in."

She nodded and handed him the change. He could tell by the look on her face that she had about a hundred questions she wanted to ask. Finally, she picked one.

"Do you ever see Judy anymore? Weren't you guys engaged?" she asked.

He doubled over in pain, letting out a shriek. If he'd had the capacity to be embarrassed, he would have felt bad about the girlish squeal, but he didn't care. The funnel cake slid from his lap and plopped to the ground. Gary pushed on either side of his head with his hands, willing everything to stay inside his skull. The pulsating rush of blood made it feel like his eyes were bulging from their sockets.

After a long moment, he sat up a little and looked at Christine, who looked like she was trying to decide whether to comfort him or rush off to the medical tent for help. The spinning lights of the midway and the screaming carnival music of the fair didn't help.

"I'm okay. I'm okay," Gary repeated. "Just don't say her...actually, I haven't seen her in a long time. Not since I was back here."

Christine bit her lip. "She's married now, but you probably knew that. To Vincent Luciano—do you remember him?"

Gary nodded. He'd been spending a lot of time thinking about Vincent lately.

"Well," Christine began, "he's not very nice to her, if you know what I mean. I know there's probably nothing you can do, but if you ever cared about her...."

"I did care. I still do. I tried to go out and see her today but no one was home."

Christine sat back. "Well, don't let Vincent catch you—he almost killed a man last year for looking at her. I think they were at the grocery or something. Anyway, you know his family better than anyone," she said, nodding. Clearly she remembered the trial and everything that had happened.

After a long moment of Gary not responding, she bit her lip again and continued. "But she's trapped out there in that big house," Christine said. "If you can help her at all, it would be good. Just be careful."

Christine stood and walked away, leaving Gary sitting on the bench, confused.

# Chapter 49

Tony saw them coming. It didn't look good—they were walking calmly down the ramp of the parking structure, five of them, and they weren't being opposed. That meant all the members of his security detail were dead.

Tony realized they would come for him first—surely they knew where Vincent had gone with the money, and he was trapped on the boat. Tony had the best chance of escape, so they would eliminate him first.

Tony slid the doors closed and looked around, not sure what to do.

This wasn't really his specialty—if someone in the *familia* needed a favor, Tony was the right man for the job. He could organize anything, or work out a problem, or arrange for financing of a new business venture. He looked good in a suit, and he could hold his own in a boardroom. But a gunfight was not something he had any experience with.

He could hide, but he didn't think Lucky Luciano would have hid. And Vincent wasn't hiding—he was probably figuring out a way off the *Margaret*, or calling in his crew to help him, or trying to hole up in a defensive place on the boat for when the gunmen came aboard.

Vincent wasn't panicking, Tony was sure, or hiding. But Tony had come up with a plan, and after that he had two Uzis with full clips and he would be going out the back of the warehouse, heading for the *Margaret*.

But before that happened, he was going to try and eliminate a few of Shotgun's men.

Tony finished rigging the Oldsmobile. He'd put a heavy brick on the gas pedal and now the car engine was idling loudly, the car pointed at the double doors that led out into the parking lot. Tony assumed Shotgun and his men would come through there, and he wanted to be ready. The barrel of gasoline took up most of the trunk, and the lid of trunk stood open.

Inside the enclosed warehouse the smoke and carbon monoxide from the roaring engine was starting to make him lightheaded, but Tony waited, watching the door.

------

"It's a trap," Willie B. said quietly.

Shotgun nodded at Willie B.

"I know," Shotgun agreed. "But it's the only way in on this side, and we don't have the manpower to go around—we have to keep an eye on the boat. When I signal, you guys approach the doors from either side and try to pull them open. Watch out for more dynamite." Shotgun and his men now had some dynamite of their own, but Shotgun had a better idea than just blowing out the doors.

He directed his men to either side of the door, and when they were in position, he opened fire. Some of the shots ricocheted off the metal, but many pierced the heavy doors, taking out anyone right inside.

------

Tony could hear gunfire from outside, and holes appeared in the closed doors. He reached in and pulled down on the gearshift on the steering column, throwing the car in drive.

The Oldsmobile lurched forward and sped toward the doors. It actually picked up speed as it raced forward, and just as the car neared them, Tony opened fire, aiming for the barrel of gasoline sticking half out of the car's trunk. He walked the line of bullets up the concrete floor of the warehouse, trying to stay between the rubber streaks left by the car's tires, and finally, just as the car hit the closed doors, one of his bullets found its mark.

------

Shotgun heard the car engine and the gunfire from inside the warehouse and immediately knew what it meant, but his recognition of the threat wasn't quick enough. He stopped firing and waved his men back, but they were already reaching for the handles of the closed metal doors.

It was too late. The large metal doors exploded outward, and Shotgun dove for cover.

The car smashed through the doors, plowing into Shotgun's men and exploding with the force of a small bomb. Men flew through the air, thrown by the power of the explosion or the impact of the car. Shotgun watched for a horrible moment that seemed to go on forever as the upper half of Willie B.'s body flew through the air and landed near the Mustang.

The explosion threw Shotgun ten feet into the side of parked car. Heat and flames licked toward him, and he crawled behind the car, pulling his rifle and Uzi with him. His left leg had gone numb.

Shotgun's men were decimated—only one of them even appeared to be moving, and he was rolling around on the pavement, legs on fire.

If this had been a war, Shotgun would be losing, badly.

------

Tony couldn't believe how well his plan had worked—he peeked out into the parking lot and saw the bodies of several men scattered around the opening he had blown in the doors. He didn't see anyone else—surely anyone within fifty feet of the blast would be dead.

The flaming hulk of the Oldsmobile had continued across the parking lot and crashed into another car, and both were on fire.

The plan had worked, except that the doors of his warehouse were on fire as well. He grabbed the guard with the leg wound and dragged him out through the burning hole in the warehouse doors and leaned him up against a car.

The fire was spreading. There was valuable inventory in the massive warehouse, and he'd answer to the authorities to keep the contents from burning. Tony pulled out his cell phone and made a quick, anonymous call to the East St. Louis Fire Department, giving the location of the warehouse, and then started toward the *Princess Margaret*.

------

Shotgun crawled out from behind the car and looked over the hood at the warehouse.

The doors were burning, and fire was running up the sides to the roof—it looked like the whole place was going to go. Good. Hopefully, Tony Luciano was still in there and would burn up himself.

He glanced at the gangplank leading up onto the larger riverboat and saw the older Luciano brother running aboard.

Damn!

Shotgun shouldered his guns and stood painfully—his leg was broken. But Shotgun ignored the pain and started toward the riverboat, getting out his dynamite.

# Chapter 50

"I'm heading back to the motel," Gary said when Mike returned from the Ferris wheel. He noticed that Tina kept a respectful distance—she probably thought he was crazy. He'd been yelling Mike's name, over and over, and people around him were looking at him strangely.

Gary was smoking, hoping to calm his nerves.

"What happened, Gary? Did someone recognize you?" Mike asked, joking, but then the serious look on Gary's face must've made Mike realize that he wasn't joking.

Gary looked around at the rest of the people enjoying the fair, but he couldn't share their buoyant attitude—after talking to Christine, he just wanted to leave.

"No, I just want to get out of here. You stay—I don't want to spoil things for you," Gary said, nodding at Tina.

Mike turned and looked at her for a second, then shook his head.

"No, man, this is more important. Let's head back to the room."

Mike started to walk over to Tina but Gary grabbed his arm.

"No, it's okay," Gary said. "I ran into a girl I graduated with, and she said my name a couple of times. And...and her name, too. Now I've got a splitting headache and just want to lie down. You stay and have a good time," Gary said, nodding at Tina again. "There's nothing here that I haven't done a dozen times before," he said, glancing around at the booths and rides that came to O'Fallon every May.

"This place is fun," Mike agreed. "And everyone just seems so... nice here. Are you sure you'll be okay?"

Gary smiled. "That's the Midwest, Mike. I told you people in LA are rude, but you never listened. People are just nicer here. And I'll be fine. I'll head back to the motel, maybe grab a beer."

Mike stopped and looked him, serious. "Now, don't do that."

"Don't worry—I think I can handle it." Gary nodded, taking the keys as Mike handed them over. "I'll probably be asleep when you get back, anyway. And I think we can get out of here tomorrow and get back to LA—it was probably a mistake to come here at all. We'll go talk to her tomorrow and then head out of town. I think I know enough about my past to know that I should just leave it there. There's no way I can go back, and coming to this Fair tonight just proves that—I remember having so much fun here once, and now all I want to do is leave."

Mike nodded, and Gary could tell he was working out whether or not to agree.

"Okay, one beer, and then off to bed," Mike said. "And don't do anything stupid. I'll see if I can catch a ride with Tina, or else I'll grab a cab. Do they have cabs here?" he asked, serious.

Gary shook his head and walked away, giving Tina a little wave.

He hoped she didn't think he was crazy—maybe he was. Dr. Myers had used the word "insane" in their discussion, which felt like it had taken place hours ago. Myers said that if too much happened too quickly, it might push Gary over the brink.

If I can't talk to her tomorrow, he thought, then this trip will have been pointless. The place was full of people that remembered him—how long until he ran into someone in this town who hated his dad, and hated him because of what his dad had done? Would the anger still run deep enough to cause trouble, or get him or Mike hurt? Gary wasn't sure one way or another, but it didn't seem wise to risk it.

It would be better this way, anyway. He could let Mike have a good time and not worry about running into any new 'old' people that might trigger more memories—at this point, all he wanted to do was just forget the past.

He walked slowly through O'Fallon Park, enjoying another cigarette, and found the rental car parked on U.S. 50, the main east–west road through O'Fallon. Across the street he saw the Animal Hospital of O'Fallon, where he vaguely remembered taking a pet—a little dog, he thought. It had been a long time ago, and the dog had been a stray. He remembered that his mom had made him take the stray to this vet and get him checked out before she would allow him to stay overnight inside the house. Gary remembered that he had paid for the examination out of his own pocket rather than kick the dog out.

Next to the animal hospital was a Pizza Hut, and he remembered dozens of visits there—pleasant times with friends and family.

This place held too many memories, all wanting to get to him and force him to acknowledge their presence. It was just too much. Ignoring them was like trying to ignore the roar of the ocean when you were standing on the beach—it was always there, no matter how hard you tried to shut it out. The lapping of cold water against your feet only served to remind you that trying to forget was pointless.

No matter what you did or how strong you were, the memories would come, like the tide. You couldn't hold them back—no one could.

Gary Foreman climbed into the car and left, heading back to the motel.

# Chapter 51

Tony knew the drug buy was a bust, but the brothers still would be able to come out of this on top. They had the drugs in Vincent's trunk and all the money they were supposed to give to D.W., now dead in the parking lot.

"Vincent?" he yelled, walking into the main casino area. Someone had tipped over a number of the roulette and poker tables, facing them all toward the door. Thousands of black and red poker chips littered the floor around Tony's feet.

"Vincent? I got them all," Tony called. "You can come out."

There was no response.

"You here?" Tony called again.

A moment later, he heard his brother's voice come back to him. It sounded strange, metallic and amplified. "I'm here, brother. Can't you see me?"

Tony wasn't in the mood for games.

"No, I can't," he answered. "Come on out of the security room— the warehouse is on fire and the cops are going to be here soon. Shotgun and his men are dead, but we need to get the cash and the coke out of here, now." Why was his brother acting so strangely?

"I can see you on the cameras," Vincent's voice carried through the ship. "This is a pretty cool setup—I can see almost every room."

Over the speakers, Tony heard a small chuckle from Vincent that raised the hair on the back of his neck.

And then Vincent asked another question. "Are you worried people are going to cheat on you?"

Tony knew that Vincent was in the security office on the second deck, the middle deck of the ship that held the offices. The bridge and outdoor restaurant were on the third, or top, deck. Tony turned and headed for the stairs.

"Don't, brother," Vincent said.

Tony stopped. "What's wrong, Vincent? Why are you acting like this? We need to get out of here, and now!"

The chuckle, again.

"Don't bark at me, Tony," Vincent said slowly. "I don't know if I can trust you anymore, brother. Would you have really asked me to ride along with D.W. as proof that the money was good?"

So, that's what this was about.

"Yes, Vincent, I would have," Tony answered, standing his ground. "D.W. needed to trust us to complete the deal. It was a spur-of-the-moment decision, but it doesn't really matter now, anyway, does it? They're all dead. I couldn't have volunteered to go myself —I'm in charge of the *familia*."

There was a long silence and then Vincent replied.

"Ah, but there's the rub, isn't it?"

------

Shotgun cautiously approached the gangplank, dragging his broken left leg. He wasn't really worried about that—they'd taught him in the military how to ignore pain, how to sublimate it beneath the needs of the task at hand.

Whatever the mission was, it had to be more important than the blood or the pain or the loss.

And now, Shotgun was on a mission.

The *Princess Margaret* was a good defensive position—the Luciano boys obviously had the advantage. If he could get up the gangplank and on board, he'd be lucky. Shotgun needed an advantage of some sort, something to even the odds a little.

------

Tony made his way through the casino floor, stepping on poker chips strewn on the carpet, and found the stairs up to the second floor. He passed the signs that said "Employees Only," still talking to Vincent, but his brother wasn't answering anymore. Tony made his way toward the security office—he'd shown it to Vincent on a tour just a week before. There had been a lock on the door, but Tony guessed that Vincent had shot it off.

Tony rounded a corner and saw his brother, standing in the hallway. He had a large machine gun out, pointed down the hallway at him.

"Whoa, Vincent," Tony shouted. "Don't shoot, okay?"

Vincent looked at him coldly.

"You would have sacrificed me to make the deal, right?" Vincent asked. The gun moved slowly in his hands. "You offered me up as a bargaining chip. Your own family."

Tony put his hands up slowly. "Now, just calm down, Vincent. You didn't say anything after, when we were counting the money or loading—"

"I loaded the coke, Tony," Vincent yelled. "You and D.W. stood and watched me and that lackey load the coke. You didn't help or lift a finger."

Tony wasn't sure what to say.

"And I couldn't say anything," Vincent yelled. "I wanted the deal to go through as much as you. Maybe more. But I would never have offered you up to make the deal, Tony. Never."

Tony nodded, understanding.

"Okay, Vincent, I understand why you're angry," Tony said. "Put the gun down—we can talk through this."

Vincent shook his head. "No, brother, I don't think so. I know where you're going with this whole drug business—this is our last buy, and then you'll end it. You're much more interested in your casino boats and your less 'distasteful' businesses than you are in making real money. And when you get the *familia* out of the coke business, you won't need me anymore, right? Or was that the whole plan tonight—get the coke and get rid of me at the same time?"

Tony shook his head.

"No, that's not what I'm planning," Tony said. "But you're right—I do find this whole business distasteful. Just look at all the problems tonight—we've got at least a dozen dead men out there, and the big warehouse is probably already half gone. But you were right about the money. We can do this right, and believe me, we can do this together."

Vincent was looking at him. "What do you mean?"

"I was going to tell you after the buy," Tony answered. "I think the best thing to do is let you run this side of the business, make the buys and sell the product. You can run it however you want—I don't even want to know about it. And I'll worry about the other businesses."

Vincent seemed to think about that for a moment. "Humph. How can I trust you?"

"Trust me? Trust me? I'm *familia*, Vincent. There's no one else you can trust more than me—I want this to work. And I want the *familia* to be successful."

A long silence, and then Vincent shook his head.

"Sorry, brother. I just can't believe you," Vincent said, his voice sad.

Tony was speechless. After a second, Vincent shrugged and lifted the gun, aiming it at Tony's chest and pulling the trigger.

# Chapter 52

Judy was still out—it was getting dark, and she knew she should be heading home, but she couldn't face that house anymore. The place was a jail to her, and the woods and fields behind their house were a vast and open jail yard. She had spent the last six hours just walking around, but eventually, she would have to return. So many conflicting emotions crowded inside her mind that it seemed that if she gave in to any of them, she would have to give in to all of them. Suicide, murder, loss, death, anger, regret, pain, and loss—these ideas were her only friends.

There were the feelings of anger: anger at Vincent for hurting her and anger at herself for getting herself into this situation. There was anger at her parents for leaving her so completely on her own, leaving nothing for her but a letter from their attorney and a promise of money—neither of which she could pursue without Vincent finding out.

There was anger at Chris, for proposing and then disappearing, leaving her in Illinois. She tried to blame him...she wanted to blame him for everything that had happened to her, but it was difficult. She had made her own decisions all along the way. His actions had only started her down this very dark and lonely road.

No, she had no one but herself to blame.

She sat in the middle of the large field that separated their house from Blackwood Lane, ignoring the cold and the wetness of the ground. She was looking up at the sky, waiting for the stars and the moon to come out.

Her life had taken a long and painful series of bad turns, and last night had simply been the latest. There was nothing left for her, nothing she was interested in, nothing to look forward to. She felt as though she had fallen down a long well and would never be able to climb out.

Maybe she should just end it all.

The idea sounded so good that, for the first time all day, she smiled. There was no other way out, as far as she could tell. If she stuck around, Vincent would continue beating her and beating her until one day he beat her to death.

And even then, he might not go to jail—he had so many powerful friends now, since he was back in good with his family. Not only could he hurt her badly or kill her whenever he wanted, he could also get away with it. He could push her down the stairs and then just explain it all away.

She thought he might burn down their house, or run her over with his new car, but then neither one of those things were likely to happen. He loved his things, his house full of possessions, and Vincent loved his new car even more. Hitting her with the Mustang might scratch it up or dent the front of the car, or some of her blood might get into the engine or stain the leather seats or the convertible top.

And if he swerved to avoid her, there might be an accident.

The beginning of an idea began to form in Judy's mind, and for the next few minutes, she followed it through to its multiple logical endings.

# Chapter 53

The first three pieces of dynamite detonated along the pier, severing the strong metal supports that held the riverboat in place.

The second group of explosions was stronger, causing the massive riverboat to lurch a foot into the air before it settled back down into the river. As Shotgun sprinted though the smoke and up the gangplank, the boat rocked in the water, moving away from the dock.

The second explosion had freed the boat completely from the dock but had also opened a large hole in the side of the riverboat at the waterline. As the boat settled, it began to take on water. Shotgun saw the gangplank slide along the dock before falling away into the water. The *Princess Margaret* floated free, moving away from the docks and toward the speedy current of the Mississippi River.

Shotgun readjusted his guns, deciding to drop the rifle and scope—it wouldn't do any good in the close quarters the boat. He checked his Uzi and the magazines in his pocket, securing the other sticks of dynamite, and then cautiously made his way inside.

------

The massive riverboat lurched beneath both of them, throwing Tony into a wall and Vincent to the ground. The gunshot meant for Tony went wide, and he rolled behind one of the desks in the security office and scurried toward the door.

The *Margaret* lurched around him, and Tony saw desks and plants and light fixtures shudder and fall. Nothing inside the boat had been secured for movement—they hadn't planned to take the boat out onto the river until long after it had opened for business. The lurching motion clearly indicated the boat had come free of its moorings. Tony had heard the explosions outside—one of Shotgun's men had somehow survived the warehouse explosion and used the dynamite or something else to blow the moorings.

Tony stood and staggered toward the bridge.

The rudder should be operational, giving some steering control, but the engines hadn't been put in yet, so he'd have no way to slow the ship down enough to dock. The only way to get the riverboat stopped would be to run her aground on a sandbar.

He didn't see Vincent, but Tony kept an eye out as he made his way to the bridge. There were at least two other people on this floating casino, and both of them wanted him dead.

------

It had been a good plan.

Vincent had known Tony would come looking for him, and somewhere during the waiting, with the gunfire raging outside, he'd decided. This wasn't the kind of business Tony could run—he'd bankrupt them somewhere along the line, probably over something stupid. He'd lose his nerve or decide that the business made him too "uncomfortable" and unilaterally decide that the Luciano *familia* would have to get out of the drug business.

But Tony wasn't the only Luciano, and Vincent didn't agree with him. Vincent didn't think they had much in common any more except for their mutual desire to see the *familia* wealthy and prosperous. But if Vincent and Tony couldn't agree on the best course of action for the *familia*, then Tony, as the head of the organization, would have the final say. And Vincent didn't think he could live with that.

He would eliminate Tony tonight.

Doing it during the gunfight, Vincent could blame it on one of Shotgun's men, and with that one small move, Vincent would be in charge of everything. In charge of making the decisions, in charge of deciding who they would do business with and which businesses they would be involved in.

In charge of the *familia.*

That prospect far outweighed any respect or emotion he felt toward his brother. The man had kicked him out of the *familia* years ago, only coming back to him when he desperately needed Vincent's help. And now that Vincent had finally gotten back into the *familia*, Tony was going to kick him out again? No, that wasn't going to happen.

Tony's precious riverboat was floating down the river, somehow broken free of the dock, and Vincent was stumbling around in the main casino, looking for his brother.

Suddenly, someone was firing at him. He ducked behind an upended roulette table—he'd tipped all the tables over to afford more cover. Someone else was firing at him! He'd only gotten a glimpse of the guy, but he knew immediately that it was Shotgun. Tony had said he was dead—had that been a ruse, a trick to get Vincent to surrender? Or was Tony just so incompetent that he didn't even make sure that Shotgun and all his men were dead? Either way, it was just more evidence that Tony wasn't cut out for running a criminal organization.

The boat lurched to one side, tilting the deck. Vincent leaned from behind the roulette table and sprayed the far end of the room with bullets, then ran for the stairs up to the second and third decks.

He wasn't sure, but Vincent thought he saw a figure moving to follow him.

------

Tony was on the bridge, looking out the front windows of the riverboat, desperately trying to steer, but things were not going well.

They were already in the middle of the river, and the current was picking up fast. The boat's speedometer read seven knots—he was surprised the gauge was even operational—and Tony was trying to steer the boat out of the fast current. The heavy riverboat was turning sharply to one side, tilting in the water.

A hundred yards in front of the riverboat, a massive barge floated in front of them, taking up a third of the river channel.

Gunfire roared behind Tony, from the back of the top deck. He jumped as bullets shattered the windows behind and in front of him. Bullets punched into the rudder controls and the gauges. From the ground, Tony grabbed at the wheel, trying to steer the boat, but it was pointless. As he crawled into a corner and prepared for the impact, a sudden wind buffeted him with spray from the river below.

------

Shotgun topped the stairs and fired again as he stepped up onto the top deck. There was a small motorboat and a large deck strewn with tables and chairs. At the back of the boat was a small bandstand, and for a moment, he noticed the dazzling city lights reflecting on the dark water. There was an open central area that looked like a dance floor.

He walked slowly to the wheelhouse. There was no one in the small room—just a central control panel that was smoking, and a large wheel. The room was surrounded with shattered windows.

Shotgun glanced out the windows. He saw the barge a moment too late.

------

The *Princess Margaret* smashed into the back corner of the massive barge, and the superstructure of the riverboat bent in half as the boat began to wrap itself around the barge. Laden with almost four thousand tons of wheat destined for processing in New Orleans, the barge didn't move. After a few moments, the riverboat slowly detached itself from the massive barge and spun dizzily back into the river.

The entire middle of the riverboat was punched in, as if some god had picked up the long, floating casino and bent it in half. The two halves, still connected, bent around the straining middle, tearing out walls and wires and pipes, spilling tables and chairs from the open wound into the churning water.

As the *Margaret* floated slowly away from the wheat barge, she began to twist slowly in the water and founder.

------

Tony grasped the side of the railing, making his way along the outside of the second deck. He'd dropped down when the boats had collided, catching himself on the second deck railing. There was only a small ledge here. Below him were the windows and railings of the first deck, and, below that, only dark churning water.

He'd been thrown out the bridge window but was trying to find a way to climb back up onto the third deck. The entertainment deck, full of tables and chairs, would be the last place to sink. If he could get to the motorboat....

Tony lifted himself up onto the top deck, cursing with the effort. His beautiful ship was sinking, and there was nothing he could do but abandon her.

Tony was running for the bandstand when he saw that someone was already there, working on the motorboat.

It was Vincent.

------

Shotgun peeked up from the bridge, looking out onto the top deck. It was railed on all sides and most of the tables and chairs he'd seen earlier had toppled over. Someone had climbed over the railing and was running across the dance floor. Shotgun didn't hesitate—he opened fire.

------

Vincent almost had the boat hooked up to the winch ropes. It was only a small motorboat—could probably hold only four people, but he didn't care. It only needed to hold one person and one exceedingly large bag of money for about ten minutes.

The *Margaret* lurched around him, and he cursed again. Vincent glanced up to see where she was going—the deck was lurching and he could see the stars over his head spinning lazily. He went back to the winch—Vincent needed to hook it to the motorboat before he could lower it into the pounding froth of the Mississippi.

The deck wasn't even flat anymore—hitting the barge had thrown Vincent to the ground, and he'd almost lost the bag of money over the side. It had also buckled up the flooring. It didn't take a genius to realize that the *Margaret* was going down, and fast.

When Vincent looked over the edge of the bandstand to see where the boat was going, he suddenly saw that the *Margaret* wouldn't have time to sink.

The Poplar Street Bridge loomed in front of the boat, arching across the Mississippi River. One of its massive supports, a hundred thousand tons of metal and stone, loomed in front of the *Margaret*.

Gunfire erupted on the deck, and Vincent ducked, turning to wrestle with the winch controls one more time.

------

Tony ducked behind tables and chairs and moved quickly from one place to another, working his way past the bridge toward the back of the boat. Shotgun was in the bridge, and—

The *Margaret* lurched again. Tony fell onto the deck, rolling into the open.

Shotgun saw the man roll into view—it was Tony Luciano, and he looked unarmed. The man was just kneeling there, and Shotgun followed with his eyes, looking for whatever the cowering man was staring at.

Vincent Luciano stepped from behind the bandstand. Shotgun

saw the gun come around as Vincent pointed it at him. Shotgun froze, expecting to be dead in the next moment.

Shotgun watched as Vincent stepped around the edge of the bandstand, his gun trained on Shotgun. Out of the corner of his eye, Shotgun saw Tony climb to his feet, brushing himself off.

"Good, Vincent," Tony said. "Kill him, and then we can talk."

Shotgun looked over at Tony, then back to Vincent, who wasn't looking at Shotgun. He was staring at Tony.

Slowly, Vincent turned, aiming the gun at his brother.

"No, brother. I don't take orders from you. And I don't want to talk anymore." Vincent sneered and pulled the trigger.

Tony collapsed to the deck, his eyes still on Vincent, the shock turning into pain and confusion. Tony held his shoulder weakly—there was blood coming from it in pulsing waves, staining the white deck red beneath him.

------

He just shot down his own brother, Shotgun thought.

Vincent Luciano had been pointing the gun at Shotgun and could've killed him at any moment. The two brothers could have gotten away with everything: the money, the coke...everything. But when the barrel of the gun had spun toward the older Luciano brother, Shotgun couldn't believe it. Who could do something that cold?

But in that moment, Shotgun finally understood. Vincent Luciano had only ever wanted one thing—power.

Vincent glanced up at Shotgun and smiled and brought the gun back up, casually squeezing the trigger several times. Shotgun tried to get his gun up in time to return fire as he saw the bullets peppering the deck around him. He felt the impact and then he felt nothing.

------

Vincent emptied the clip in Shotgun's direction—the man was finally down, but Vincent suddenly felt like he could control the world.

The *Margaret* was nearing the massive bridge support—the Poplar Street Bridge loomed above the foundering riverboat, blocking out a large strip of the night sky.

He walked over to his brother.

The man was dead. Too bad. He had a few more things he would have liked to say to his brother.

Screw it. The man had been weak. To run the *familia* in the way it needed to be run would take a man of courage and vision, someone who knew what they were doing.

Someone like him.

The boat lurched again, more violently this time, and Vincent watched without emotion as his brother's body rolled toward the railing along the edge of the deck. The bridge support loomed larger in the corner of his eye. Vincent didn't move at all as his brother's body slipped over the side and splashed into the water below.

------

The front of the *Margaret* bore down on the massive bridge support. Eddies and currents tried to move the foundering riverboat around the bridge's footing, but the bulk and momentum of the boat carried it into the large concrete island surrounding the base of the support structure.

Crumpling like a huge tin can, the *Margaret* split in two. The naked decks opened to the roaring might of the river, flooding the interior spaces and washing the roulette tables and light fixtures and desks and a thousand other items into the water. The bandstand crumpled and crashed to the deck. Chairs and tables crashed through the railing, twisting in the air and falling into the black water.

The giant paddlewheel at the back of the *Margaret* reared up into the air as the back half of the riverboat began to sink. The water around the footing of the bridge frothed as large pieces of the riverboat floated and bobbed and finally sank beneath the dark water.

Twenty thousand gambling chips spun away from the wreckage, a small part of the flotsam carried by the river's current toward the Gulf of Mexico.

------

Vincent directed the small boat back toward the docks along Pier 32. It wasn't hard to find—the fire was lighting up the horizon. As he approached, he could see at least four or fire engines and two dozen firemen working to contain the massive blaze.

He slowed the engine and passed the first dock, moving beyond the *Princess Anne,* pulling the launch up behind it. He smiled. He guessed the boat was his now.

Vincent tied off the motorboat, grabbed the duffle bag, and climbed up onto the dock.

The entire parking lot was full of firemen and police cars and fire trucks. He circled around the parking structure and moved toward his Mustang—thank God the trunk had been closed when Shotgun and his men had opened fire.

Vincent tried to walk as nonchalantly as possible. He avoided the looks from the cops and strolled up to his car, fishing out his keys.

A cop walked up to him. "You need to get out of here, buddy."

Vincent nodded. "Yes, officer. That's my car. Can I move it? I'm afraid it might be in the way of the firefighters."

"Yeah, it is. Can you tell me something, though..." the cop said, walking Vincent around to the side of the Mustang away from the fire.

There were at least twenty large-caliber bullet holes punched into the side of the automobile.

Vincent smiled and shook his head. "What the hell happened here? I park my car here to do some gambling, then come out and find this?" He looked at the cop and shook his head again. "I don't know what to tell you, sir."

The cop smiled, leaning a little closer. "I don't think you've been gambling, Mr. Luciano. I ran your plate a minute after I got here. This looks like gunfire, and there are a lot of curious people around, wondering what happened here."

"Fortunately," the cop said quietly, "I'm the only one who knows about this car of yours. I've been hanging around, hoping you'd show."

The cop smiled.

Vincent looked at the man, gauging him, and he suddenly understood. He unzipped the bag a little and reached in, pulling out a small wad of cash. The cop was looking around, making sure no one was watching.

Vincent set the money on the Mustang, and the cop quickly pocketed it. Vincent had learned a long time ago never to hand money directly to someone—it gave them a chance to honestly say they found it if they were ever questioned or subjected to a polygraph.

"Can I go now?" Vincent asked.

The cop nodded, backing away. "Sure, Mr. Luciano. And I hope you remember that I helped you out."

Vincent nodded and climbed into the Mustang, tossing the duffle bag onto the passenger seat. The cop cleared a path for him through the fire trucks and police cars to the road leading away from the dock. The cop also waved him though the police line set up to keep spectators back.

As the Mustang passed him, the cop gave Vincent a jaunty little salute, and smiled.

Vincent couldn't help but smile back.

# Chapter 54

The room was cleaned and someone had turned the beds down for them. Gary flipped on the TV, but there was nothing that caught his interest. He had told Mike he was tired and wanted to get some rest, but in truth he had just wanted to get away from the Mayfest.

He sat for a few minutes at the table by the window, repeatedly shuffling and laying out the tarot cards, doing a few readings, but it didn't calm him down. The same cards seemed to be coming up, over and over, and none of them made any sense. The "Fire" cards kept coming up, over and over, but he didn't understand what they could mean. Dr. Myers had called the deck of cards his "talisman," but it didn't feel like the cards had any magical powers tonight.

After an hour in the room, he left and went to the restaurant. It was busy, with all the booths taken, but he found a seat at the counter. Doris, the nice lady who had served him and Mike dinner the night before, came over, smiling at him.

"Can I get you something, son?" she asked, opening her notepad in a way that instantly reminded Gary of Captain Kirk flipping open his communicator—strange how the smallest things can seem funny, he thought.

"Yeah, can I get a beer?"

Just one drink. He didn't think one beer would kill him, and a beer would really hit the spot right now.

She shook her head. "Sorry, son." She nodded at the arched door-way that led into The Hole. "Can't serve alcohol except in the lounge. You'll have to head in there."

He thanked her and stood, walking into The Hole. The place was packed. He waited in the crowd near the bar until he was able to order a bottle, paid for it, and headed for a quiet corner. All the tables and every seat at the bar were filled, and the crowded area near the bar was starting to spill out into the seating area. Gary saw that part of the dance floor had been cleared and that someone was setting up a drum set.

Suddenly, he was glad he'd come. The place was bustling and full of activity, and he needed the distraction. But he didn't get the feeling anyone was recognizing him. And there was going to be a band, hopefully something loud to get his mind off his troubles.

He sipped his beer and tried to put it all into perspective.

Gary was pretty sure the whole dream had just been a way for his mind to get him to come back here and remember his past. He doubted that Judy was in any kind of serious trouble. The girl probably wouldn't remember him anyway—the old woman had told Mike that she had made her choices. Gary thought she probably didn't need him showing up after so long.

Finishing with the drum set, the guy working on the band's instruments propped a couple of guitars up against their stands and plugged them in. He tested them by strumming a couple of chords and tapping the foot pedals on the floor, making different sounds come out of the speakers on either side of the dance floor. Gary was watching the guy work as people jostled past him on their way to the restrooms.

The last thing the guy set up was a microphone stand. He tested it by speaking into it over and over until the sound guy at the back of the room waved at him. Gary thought that if the band had a sound guy and roadies to set up their equipment, they must be pretty good.

"You bitch!" Gary heard from somewhere in the bar.

He felt the skin crawl up the back of his neck. He knew that voice.

Gary glanced around but didn't see anyone. After a minute, he went back to watching the roadie setting up.

"I told you to shut up, didn't I?" someone shouted, and Gary instantly knew.

Gary watched as a man stood up from one of the booths—he'd been sitting, and Gary hadn't been able to see him.

It was him. It was the guy from the dream—Vincent Luciano. Gary knew that voice anywhere—he'd been listening to it every night for months.

Vincent was a big guy, smiling and laughing with a group of guys huddled around one of the bar tables. As he watched, the man picked up a large duffel bag that had been sitting on the floor beside his feet under the booth. He reached into it, taking out small bundles and tossing them to each of the guys at the table. They were stacks of money.

Vincent turned and looked at Gary.

Gary's stomach leapt into his chest and he looked away, hoping the guy had not seen him. Out of the corner of his eye, Gary watched as Vincent stood and approached.

Slinking down into the chair with his beer up to his face, Gary closed his eyes and willed the man to ignore him. Vincent pushed through the crowd past Gary and into the bathroom in the back.

Gary relaxed slightly, but didn't know what to do.

There was obviously a feeling around here about the guy—the crowd had parted like the Red Sea when he passed through, and it didn't seem out of the ordinary for him to pass out large stacks of cash at the table. No one questioned or confronted him. He looked like a thug, wide across the shoulders and with an angular and intelligent face, like a weasel or a vulture.

Suddenly he felt sorry for Judy. If this was her husband, she was in more danger than anyone knew. This guy looked like a killer.

Vincent didn't stay in the bathroom long, and Gary watched warily as the man passed him—he was wearing snakeskin boots with short chains that jingled when he walked. Vincent returned to his table, but he didn't sit back down. He said something to his friends, grabbed the large duffel bag, and headed for the door.

Impulsively, Gary followed.

He didn't really know why he was doing it, but it seemed like the right thing to do.

Vincent walked through the restaurant and out the door, only stopping long enough to flip a small wad of bills to Doris, the waitress. Vincent smiled as the woman caught the bills, looked at them for a moment, and then threw them back at him. Vincent caught the bills as Gary watched from the archway that led into The Hole. Vincent kicked the restaurant doors open and headed outside, laughing heartily.

Gary waited a couple of moments and followed Vincent outside.

Vincent was climbing into a shiny Mustang. There were strange holes along the passenger side, and the passenger window and the back window were both broken out. The guy tossed the bag into the passenger seat and started the car.

Gary began walking toward his rental car when two large hands grabbed him roughly, spinning him around.

"Who are you, man?" a rough-looking punk asked him, holding onto his jacket. "What do you want with Vince?"

He was one of the guys from Vincent's table. The guy's breath smelled like beer and he looked like he'd been smoking for several hours straight—his eyes were so red that for a moment Gary thought the guy might have pinkeye.

Gary shrugged, his eyes wide.

"Nothing! I just thought that was Vincent Luciano," Gary said, trying to sound giddy and a little star struck. "I've always wanted to meet him—he's famous!"

Gary didn't know if it sounded convincing or not, but he was trying. The guy backed off and let go of Gary's jacket. Behind him, Gary heard the Mustang drive off.

"Oh," the big guy answered, a little confused. "Uh, yeah, well, that was him, all right."

Gary turned to look at the road as the lights of the Mustang headed off to the west. "Wow, do you know him? He's like a rock star!"

The man stood a little taller. "Yeah, he's a friend of mine, so I guess that makes me famous, too, right?"

"Really? I was going to ask him for his autograph, but I guess I could get yours too—you know, I think he'll be really famous someday. Maybe you will be, too! Do you work for him?"

This was making Gary's stomach turn, but the guy seemed to be buying it.

The man nodded. "You think he'll be famous? Yeah, I guess so. Sure, you can have my autograph if you want it." The guy reached into his pocket and pulled out a wadded-up napkin. "You got a pen I can borrow? And what's your name?"

Gary nodded, handing him a pen. He said the first name that popped into his head.

"Chris. My name's Chris."

The guy signed his napkin with a flourish, smiling, and handed it and the pen over. "I can ask him for an autograph for you, the next time I see him, if you want."

"Wow, that would be great," Gary smiled like an idiot. "I better get going. Thanks again!"

Nodding, the guy turned and went back inside, and Gary looked down at the napkin. It was signed "To Chris." Why had that name popped out first? Gary stuffed the napkin in his pocket and hurried off to the car. He wasn't really sure what he was doing, but it felt right.

Backing out of the parking lot, he sped off to the west, looking for the Mustang.

------

The decision was made, and she had made it for herself, something of a rarity. It was probably the last decision she would ever make.

Judy was going to kill herself.

But she wanted someone else to know what had happened, someone to know the pain she had gone through. The only person she could think of was Vincent, but he would certainly never empathize with her. She'd tried too many times to get him to think about her as a person instead of something to be used, but he never had paid attention.

Vincent loved his new car, though.

She needed to figure out when he would be coming home and step out into the road in the path of his speeding car.

Blackwood Lane was dark and twisty for much of its length, but the forest was particularly dark near the turn into their driveway. Streetlights were rare along the country road, and there were none on the stretch by their driveway, and tall, ominous trees closely lined each side of the road. The road was only two lanes wide and the trees and deep ditches along the sides left little in the way of a shoulder. She would walk across this field, wait in the trees for his sound of his car, and then step out in front of it.

When the car slammed into her, the impact should kill her instantly, painlessly. It was certainly a better fate than the next twenty years of her life, if she managed to live that long. She didn't think she would make it another year or two, the way the beatings had been lately. And without her paintings....

No, he would kill her instantly. Or he would swerve and wreck his car, killing himself. Either way she would be free. It was a win–win situation.

Not that she dreaded dying. The thought actually pleased her. She was tired of life, tired of the beatings and the pain. She was tired of thinking about the way things might have been, tired of wondering what happened to all her dreams.

Judy Luciano was tired of everything.

She got up, leaving a rounded impression in the moist earth where she'd been sitting. Pulling her loose white shirt around her, she glanced across the muddy field at the house, but there was nothing in there that could help her now. There was nothing there that she needed, not where she was going.

She glanced at her watch. It would be nine o'clock soon, and Vincent said he'd be home at nine. She didn't believe him, but she had nothing else to do but wait.

Turning, she started for the trees that lined each side of Blackwood Lane. Her white shirt flapped around her in the quickening breeze.

------

Vincent Luciano was on top of the world.

In the past six hours, he had seized control of the Luciano crime family, while at the same time singlehandedly wiping out the entire East Dogs drug organization. And he would see to it that the Lucianos were a real crime family, now that he was in charge. The Lucianos would be taken seriously, even feared.

Vincent had the finances now to really kick things off—the duffle bag in the passenger seat contained almost one and a half million dollars, and the 150 pounds of cocaine in the trunk was worth even more. Cut correctly with inert substances, the coke would yield more than 200 pounds of finished, saleable product, with a street value of almost four million bucks.

Of course, Vincent had killed his own brother. He wasn't sure how he felt about that yet—on some level he would miss his brother, but the man had been weak and didn't know the first thing about respect.

Vincent would have the respect of the *familia* now—he'd taken down his own brother and wiped out the only major competition in the area through a series of targeted, aggressive assassinations. No one would second-guess Vincent now.

He could run things exactly as he wanted. There was no one to stand in his way.

Vincent turned the Mustang onto Blackwood Lane, roaring up the road toward his home. Vincent remembered that this stretch of road was supposed to be haunted by the ghost of a young woman. Whoever heard of a road being haunted, like a house? He'd heard about the horrible wrecks that seemed to happen with frightening regularity—bad wrecks, with people getting killed, but Vincent didn't think the road was haunted—all the twists and turns just made the road a challenge.

He didn't care about superstition or rumors. He didn't care that the public works guys had trouble keeping the few streetlights working—did that mean it was haunted? Please.

Vincent remembered the warehouse—it had still been burning when that dirty cop had waved him away from the scene. Of course, now he'd need a new processing location, he thought with a smile. His brother had spent a lot of time and money building up that casino operation, but now with the one boat destroyed and the warehouse burned, Vincent didn't think that part of the Luciano business would survive.

But Vincent would be fine. He glanced over at the duffle bag on the passenger seat, smiling.

It was a long, dark road, but he always took it fast, and tonight would be no different. He sped up, driving even faster than usual, feeling energized by tonight's turn of events. If Shotgun and his men hadn't shown up, guns blazing, things would have turned out so differently....

Vincent also remembered that there were a few things he needed to take care of at home.

He needed to have a little talk with his wife, teach her who was boss, once and for all. But after that, he could move out and leave her in this house—it was cute, but Tony's house, the official Luciano residence in downtown O'Fallon, was now vacant. He could move in and make himself at home—Vincent had always wanted to be a real gangster, a good example of what his grandmother and great-grandfather had stood for.

He took another corner fast, swerving around the sharp turn. Beyond, the road was dark—there were no streetlights for miles.

And Vincent couldn't wait to start spending his money. He would get set up in the new house and start having parties, big parties, with lots of women, hot women in skimpy clothes....

Out of the corner of his eye, Vincent saw sudden movement along the narrow shoulder. His foot came up slightly off the gas pedal.

It was probably that small reaction that saved his life.

A ghostly figure appeared from the trees, stepping into the cones of light projected by the twin headlights on the front of his car.

His first reaction was to swerve.

The ghost woman spread her arms out, as if to grab him, a robe or a white flowing shirt spreading out around her like a ghostly halo. Her short blonde hair caught the light.

Vincent pulled hard on the wheel and swerved around the ghost, braking hard and curving around it into the other lane.

The shrieks of the wrenched tires and metal echoed loudly on the silent, darkened road.

The car swerved, but Vincent overcompensated while trying to get back into his lane and lost control of the car, swerving on the pavement. The car spun wildly and, racing backwards at over fifty miles an hour, plowed into a massive elm tree, trunk first. The car crumpled against the tree, the back half of the car folding up into sheet metal.

# Chapter 55

Judy was still standing in the middle of the road, her heart paused between beats. She had made up her mind and quickly stepped out in front of the Mustang—no other car in town sounded like his.

She only had time to notice her white shirt billowing out around her like a veil before the car was upon her. She raised her arms, welcoming the release of death, and tried not to think about how much it would hurt.

For a moment, Judy was completely calm. There was nothing else to do now but wait. This was the right thing to do, and it was all going to be over in one moment.

She held her arms up to greet the car...and it swerved.

Judy heard the tires and brakes working as the driver tried to avoid her, and she opened her eyes. The car roared at her and then, lurching to her right, missed her by inches. She felt heat and wind as the car rushed past her, and the side mirror grazed her hip, knocking her aside sharply with a sudden stab of pain.

Judy listened as the car swerved behind her and crashed loudly into the trees, but her mind was still numbed by what had just happened to her. One moment she was welcoming death with open arms, and the next, the hot metal of the car had rushed past her, sparing her life.

She had hoped against hope that this would happen—Judy could admit it to herself. Now it had happened, and she was okay, and her hands drifted down to touch her arms, her body, her legs, almost unbelieving. Her side hurt from the mirror, and that was it. She was okay, and Vincent—

Judy turned and saw the car. His new Mustang was wrecked, looking like a crushed-up tin can. He had spun out and hit a tree off to the right side of Blackwood Lane back-first—from the condition of the car, it looked as if he'd backed off the road going sixty miles an hour. A white cloud of smoke drifted around the car—it was probably catching fire.

The back half of the car was splayed out in all directions from the scarred blackness of the unforgiving tree trunk. A thin line of fire was running up the tree as well as flickering around the base of the car and the tires.

She moved slowly to the car. Vincent was in the driver's seat, and for a moment she thought he was dead—there was blood everywhere. The fire would come soon, and in the coming of that fire she would be freed....

Vincent moved, coughing and spitting up blood, and she saw that one of his arms was bent in an odd direction. His head came up and he looked in her direction. A long moment of recognition passed between them.

He began to laugh.

After a moment, Vincent started coughing again. Judy was overcome by an almost uncontrollable urge to help him, to pry the door open and pull him out. But after a moment, the coughing stopped, and then nothing. She saw his eyes close, slowly, and she waited another long moment, but he didn't move.

He would die now—either from his wounds, or the fire. It would only be another minute or two, and then she would be free.

Judy smiled and turned, walking slowly to the house.

# Chapter 56

Gary wasn't following closely enough to see the crash—in fact, he'd lost track of the Mustang twice and was five minutes late in arriving to the scene. He slowed the rental car—strange lights were flickered in the trees on the road in front of him.

There was a moment of disbelief as Gary came around the corner and saw the smoking wreck of the Mustang—he'd just been following it minutes before, and here it was, wrecked and about to catch fire.

Gary stopped the car and backed up, parking the car on the road. Hopefully, anyone coming around that blind corner would be able to stop in time, or his rental car was toast.

He hopped out and approached the car—a wall of smoke already hung over the entire wreck, making Gary cough. He covered his mouth with his shirt and saw the flames flickering beneath the Mustang. If there was anything to do for Vincent, Gary would have to do it fast.

The car had crashed into the trees back-first; the guy had probably swerved to miss an animal or lost control. Maybe he'd had too many beers back there at The Hole—it was a Saturday night, and Gary had no way of knowing how long Vincent had been at the bar.

Gary glanced at the road—it seemed like they weren't far from Vincent's home, if Gary remembered right, but he didn't see any lights.

He approached the car and peered into the front seat. Vincent didn't look good at all.

Gary tried the door and managed to pry it open, grabbing the guy by one arm and pulling. The man screamed and Gary let go, using the other arm to pull Vincent free from the car.

The flames were licking around the bottom of the car, and Gary thought the gas tank would explode soon. There was a strange, gritty smoke in the air, and he thought that it might be from something burning in the wreckage, insulation or something.

He dragged Vincent away from the car and dropped him onto the road at a safe distance.

Gary knew that he needed to find a phone. Gary thought about going to Vincent's house, but he wasn't sure he could find it in the dark. Vincent was in pretty bad shape, and Gary decided he would backtrack to a gas station he'd seen a mile back, on the outskirts of O'Fallon. Vincent needed an ambulance.

Gary bent over and pulled off his sweatshirt. He balled the sweatshirt up and tied the arms around the guy's waist, using it to slow the bleeding from a major wound in the guy's side. After the man was more stable, Gary climbed back into his rental and, turning the car around, left for the gas station.

# Chapter 57

Judy kicked off her muddy shoes once she was inside and closed the door behind her. She was cold and wet, and she instinctively flicked on the wall switch that ignited the gas fireplace she loved.

Judy was moving like a robot, her mind flooded with so many thoughts and wishes and regrets, her body moving on autopilot. Her eyes were glazed over, trying to understand the strange turn of events, and wondering what to do about them.

Only minutes ago, she had wanted nothing more than to die, quickly and painlessly.

Now, more than anything, she wanted to live. Now that he was dead, she could do anything she wanted.

But first, she needed a shower. Yes, a hot shower, and then she needed to put on pajamas.

The police would be here soon, coming to the house with their hats in their hands to tell her about the accident on Blackwood Lane and her dead husband. He'd wrecked his car, they would say. And she would be surprised.

And saddened—she needed to remember to act sad. Couldn't forget that part.

The police would nod their heads and say how sorry they were for her loss. And she would agree with them—there was no point in arguing the finer parts of that discussion. And after the cops were gone, she could finally settle in and get a good night's sleep.

Tomorrow, she would start her life over.

Pulling her shirt and jeans off, she climbed into the shower. The water had never felt so good, one of a thousand little delights she had never expected to experience again.

Now everything would be even that much better.

# Chapter 58

Vincent was shuffling along the muddy field, dragging D.W.'s leather duffle bag and trying to ignore the pain. Like him, that bag had seen a lot of action tonight, but it was holding up better than he was.

His hip was killing him, and he was dragging one of his legs. He was carrying the bag with his left hand because his right arm felt broken, strangely angled. There was a nub of white bone sticking out of his elbow, and his arm and shoulder roared with dull pain.

The walking, with the arm moving and hitting his chest and stomach as he walked, wasn't helping.

When Vincent had awakened, he was lying on the shoulder of the road. It had taken a couple of moments for him to remember what had happened, but as he sat up to look at the burning car, it had all came back to him. The drug buy and the riverboat and the shootout. The money in the duffel bag. Driving home after a quick beer with his crew to celebrate.

Vincent had been driving fast and he'd rounded a corner and seen a ghost step out onto the road. Vincent had swerved and missed it, and in that moment he could remember wondering if it was a real ghost.

Then the car had gone completely out of control, spinning around and crashing, and then sudden horrible pain all up and down his right side. His arm was broken, and the emergency brake handle had broken off and stabbed him in the hip.

After the wreck, the smell of smoke and fire had brought him around. He'd glanced up and seen the ghost again, staring at him, looking in through the broken windshield, and....

No, it hadn't been a ghost at all.

It had been Judy, wearing something white and loose that billowed out around her like a ghost's veil.

It was his wife who had stepped out onto the road and tried to kill him.

But that was not the last thing he could remember before waking up on the road. No, the last thing he remembered was the face of his wife, ghost-like and sallow in the flicking light of one failing headlight. Vincent remembered the slight smile on her face.

He should've killed her when he had the chance.

He stopped walking and readjusted his tentative grip on the heavy bag, then continued toward his house.

After Judy had left, he must've passed out again, because he woke up on the side of the road, well away from the car. Vincent chalked it up to his own strength—he must've unconsciously crawled from the wreckage. Judy certainly hadn't helped him, and he didn't remember anyone else.

After he'd come to, he had gone back to the Mustang and gotten the duffel bag out of the passenger seat. He stopped at the trunk of the car, scooping up and snorting several large pinches of coke, enjoying the cocaine before it was lost to the fire. It was a shame, seeing all that beautiful coke wasted. He hated to think about how much money had been lost, all because of his stupid wife. The bitch was going to pay.

Painfully, slowly, he'd climbed the tree-covered embankment that separated the road from his house.

It was slow going, but the fire that burned in his heart drove him on. The coke made him feel giddy and powerful. He was sure that, if not for the cocaine, the pain in his shoulder and hip would now be completely unbearable.

He could see the house now. Vincent trudged slowly up to the front door and realized that his keys were in his ruined car. He started around the side of the house, looking for an open window.

# Chapter 59

"No, he was here," Gary said again, talking to the shorter cop. "I swear it. See, there are blood stains on the asphalt." He pointed at the pavement. The two cops had gotten to the accident scene before Gary had even returned from the gas station.

One of the cops, the taller one, was spraying the burning Mustang with a fire extinguisher he had pulled from the trunk of the police cruiser. The shorter trooper was standing next to Gary, looking down at the bloodstain.

"So, you pulled him from the car, then went up the gas station and called it in?" he asked, repeating what Gary had already told him twice.

"Yes," Gary nodded. "I think he lives near here, so maybe he tried to get home. But he didn't look like he was in much shape to move."

The shorter cop nodded.

"Yeah, he lives right around the corner. You climb that embankment of trees and there's just a field between here and his house." He turned and watched as his partner put out the last of the fire, spraying under the car at the little flames that refused to die. "Follow me," he said to Gary, starting toward the car.

Gary followed, not knowing what else to do. Where had Vincent gone? He didn't think that the guy could've gotten up and walked away—he'd had a broken arm and that nasty, bloody hip wound.

The taller cop waved them over and pointed at the broken remains of the trunk lid.

Gary stepped around and stared.

There were at least a hundred or more good-sized packages in the trunk, and the wreck had broken many of them open, spilling a thick white powder out onto the trunk of the tree and the ground around the point where the car had impacted the tree. The cloud of white smoke was worse here, and Gary realized that the smoke around the crash site wasn't in fact smoke at all.

"That's a lot of coke," the tall cop said, matter-of-factly.

"That's all...cocaine?" Gary asked, unsure of what else to say.

The shorter cop brushed a finger against the trunk lid, streaking a patch of the white stuff, and gingerly tasted a tiny portion then spit it out.

"Oh, yeah. Very pure." He glanced up at his partner, shaking his head, then turned to Gary.

"Okay, sir," the short cop said. "Thank you for calling this in. We can take care of it from here," he said, nodding and motioning for Gary to leave.

"But what about the guy—are you going to check on him?" Gary asked, not wanting to leave. "Will you make sure he's okay?"

The short cop walked Gary over to his rental car. "Yes, we're going there next to check on him. Thanks for calling it in." The tone was clear—he was being dismissed.

Gary nodded and climbed into his car. Why were the cops chasing him off? Did it have something to do with all that coke, or was it something else?

Gary didn't know what to do. There was more to this. Vincent had cracked up his car, a car with a whole hell of a lot of cocaine in the trunk. The woman at the bakery had told Mike that the Lucianos were involved in a lot of bad stuff. Maybe this was just more of it, and maybe the cops were in on it. That might explain why no one had ever helped Judy—everyone around town knew she was in trouble, but no one seemed able to help. Why couldn't the cops?

Gary realized that he'd just had his first coherent thought about the woman in his dream without the stabbing headaches that normally accompanied thoughts of her.

Why did the cops want him to leave? Why wouldn't they want Gary to see the guy and make sure he would be okay?

Gary started the car and pulled away from the scene, passing the crash site and driving on down Blackwood Lane. The turn for the Luciano house was not far down, if he remembered correctly, and there was just too much going on for him to drive away now.

He crested a small hill and saw the driveway coming up on his right. Gary glanced in the rearview mirror and couldn't see the wreck anymore, so that meant the cops couldn't see his car either.

Gary slowed and turned into the drive.

Going on what he remembered from this afternoon, when it had been sunny and clear, he directed the car up the long, winding drive that led to the house.

The old two-story farmhouse was lit up—someone was home this time, at least. To one side, about a hundred yards from the house, stood an outbuilding that sat between the house and the field that fronted Blackwood Lane. Gary parked his rental on the other side, shutting off the lights and turning off the engine. He remembered to take his foot off the brakes, extinguishing the twin lights in the back that would've surely given him away. And then he sat and waited for the cops to come.

From here, he had a view of the front door.

# Chapter 60

Judy went into the bedroom, locking the door, and climbed into bed, tired.

She'd been wasting time, doing her hair and tidying up the bedroom, waiting impatiently for the police to hurry up and come and give her the bad news so she could cry. Judy was saving it up, waiting for them to get here, but they weren't tears of sadness or loss. They would be tears of joy for the sudden, unexpected change in her life. The policemen wouldn't know the difference—to men, all tears looked the same.

It had been a horribly long day, and all she wanted to do was go to bed, but she needed to stay up for the cops.

Judy got out her brush and started brushing her hair again to pass the time. It was matted and tangled from the full day outside and the shower, and she worked the brush through her hair, missing the length of it that was now gone.

She had always been proud of her hair, of the way it had looked hanging down to her shoulders and catching the light. Vincent had known that—he had been good at taking away things that mattered to her.

There was a sound from downstairs, and Judy stopped.

It didn't sound like a knock at the door—it was probably the cops, pulling up outside. Surely someone had seen the wreck by now and called the cops, who would immediately recognize the vehicle. They were coming, she was sure, and when those cops knocked on that door downstairs, her life would change forever.

Judy would sell this house—it would be the first thing to go. Between that money and the envelope upstairs, she would be able to escape. The Luciano family wouldn't care, now that Vincent was gone.

And she would move to California.

She could get a little house near the beach, and she could paint all day long. She could paint the beach as it really looked, not like she imagined it to be. Judy could walk on the sand and stand in the water and feel the gentle crash of the waves against her legs. She could take her new easel out onto the porch and paint the setting sun as it high-lighted the crests of the waves marching in to shore.

And she could look for Chris. He was out there somewhere, and if she was lucky, he would remember her. For some reason she felt closer to him than ever before—maybe it was just the fact that she had plans to go west. It felt almost as if he was in the same room with her, right now.

Judy glanced at the reflection of her eyes in the shiny brush han-dle, and wondered if the dark circles underneath them would ever fade away. Her hair was different and she looked years older, but hopefully he would remember her.

There was a crash just outside her bedroom door, a sudden loud crinkle of breaking glass.

Startled, she looked up. The bedroom door was outlined in harsh light. Why would the cops bust in instead of knocking on the front door? Who else would it be?

Something hit the door. The doorknob turned slowly, but the door did not open. She heard something solid rest against the door, and then someone kicked it, hard. Another kick, and another, and then the door burst open, spraying shards of wood through the air.

The door slid slowly open.

It was Vincent.

He looked bad—like someone had finally gotten the better of him. His right arm was tied up in a makeshift support. It was broken, she thought, and he'd used a dish towel from downstairs to support it. There was a maroon sweatshirt tied around his waist, one she didn't recognize. It looked like it said "California State University." How... what did that mean? Where had that come from?

She screamed. She couldn't help it—everything was going wrong—

Vincent shuffled forward, coming toward her. She had no idea what to do. It was too much to understand. He was dead. He'd been dying in the car and it...there had been fire, and it wasn't possible that he was here. Who would have saved him?

His face was twisted up into a strange leer, and Judy suddenly realized that she was going to die.

It wasn't going to take long, and there wouldn't be time for for-giveness or excuses or lame attempts to convince him otherwise.

There was nothing else in the world except her in the bed and Vincent coming slowly toward her, his left hand behind his back.

Like he was bringing her a surprise.

"You...little...bitch!" he said, walking slowly to the side of the bed. There was thick runner of blood coming from one side of his face, running down his cheek and dripping slowly from his chin. "No...nobody..." he started, then seemed to resign himself.

"Please," she pleaded, and some part of her was disgusted. *Why are you begging?* it asked. *He's going to kill you anyway.* "Please, don't hurt me, again, please," Judy begged. "I'm sorry about the accident! It wasn't supposed to be like that...."

She realized that she was calling out to Chris in her mind, calling to the only person who had ever really meant anything to her. The screams were incredibly loud and at the same time silent. All she could think of to cry was "Help!" over and over again, screaming for a boy who had long since forgotten her.

There was nothing else to do.

Vincent's arm came around, and she saw the knife. It was the largest, sharpest knife they had in the house. It had a serrated edge that could probably cut down a tree.

The breaking glass she had heard earlier was the glass covering of the hall light, because now, as he held up the knife, its wicked edges caught the reflection of the suddenly bright light in the hallway.

The light made the knife look even bigger.

"Shut up...you don't know who you're messing with, but you're going to find out, I guarantee it. Things were going so good..." her husband said, stepping closer to her.

He wasn't moving very fast, but the very notion of trying to get away had not even occurred to her—she was in shock. Too many things were happening too quickly, all crowding together, and now she wondered somewhere in her mind if she really did want to just die.

"You don't even know what you did, you stupid whore. I had it all set it up..." he said, starting to cough hard. He spat blood onto the white carpet. "That's okay. It's okay. I'll be okay," he said to himself, and for a moment, it looked as though he'd completely forgotten about her. The knife wavered in the air, and she began to slowly slide backwards on the bed.

Then his eyes cleared. He looked down at her and smiled. "But you won't be."

The knife went higher into the air.

Vincent hesitated a moment at the top of the arc.

Did he still have something in him, something good? Judy didn't think so. Maybe he was just trying to think of something clever to say before he killed her.

No. He'd stopped. He was listening to something.

Judy strained to pull her thoughts away from how sharp the edge of that knife looked. She realized someone was pounding on the front door, beating on the door with something that sounded like a pipe.

How had she not heard that before—had she been unable to hear or see anything else except for Vincent and the knife?

His face twitched and he stepped back, lowering the knife. "Don't think about going anywhere, bitch. This isn't done, not by a long shot."

Vincent turned and slowly left the room, taking the knife with him.

The crying came instantly, and she couldn't stop it. The tears of sorrow and joy and fear all crammed together, trying to get out of her. For a long moment, her body shook with the tears of a pardoned man moments from the electric chair.

She could hear voices downstairs, and it was the sound of other voices besides Vincent's and her own that brought her out of the tears, brought her around to think about her situation.

Judy hadn't been pardoned—her execution had only been stayed temporarily. This place was truly her prison, and the warden had only momentarily stepped away from the switch. In a few minutes, he'd be back to finish the job.

If she was ever going to do something about it, it had to be now. Right now.

She stood up.

There were no other doors out of this room except for the main door, which led out onto the landing and looked down onto the foyer and the front door. If Vincent was down there, talking to cops or whoever had come, he'd be able to see her. If there were cops down there and she asked for help, she didn't think they would act. The Lucianos were just too powerful.

The window. It was the only option, and she went to it, pulling the window open. She was wearing only her pajamas, but she didn't care.

Outside the window was the slanted roof of the garage—she had never been able to figure out why they needed a garage plus another building near the house to park cars, but now she wasn't asking. She could see the barn and the broken cars parked around it, and beyond that was the muddy field and the road.

If she could get to the road, she could get away. He was hurt, and, for once in her life, she could outrun him. It wasn't much of an idea, but it was better than sitting here, waiting for her husband to come back.

She slipped out the window and down onto the cold roof of the garage, looking for a way down. Judy didn't want to climb down on the front side of the house—she could see the police cruiser there, and surely she'd be spotted by Vincent and the cops. She needed to find another way down, and then she'd run.

------

Gary could see fine, but in the silence, he could hear even better. It didn't look like the cops were planning to arrest Vincent—from the snatches of conversation he could pick up, it sounded like they were trying to get him to go to the hospital. The conversation also seemed good-natured. It looked like Vincent Luciano was in good with the cops.

After a couple of minutes, Vincent disappeared back into the house and then reappeared, handing something small to each cop. Gary didn't know what it was, but it didn't take a lot of imagination to guess.

He began to understand why the cops had told him to get lost.

The old woman at the bakery might've even underestimated the amount of influence the Lucianos exerted in this town.

Something caught his eye.

Gary glanced away from the cops and saw someone on the roof of the garage. As he watched, he saw the person drop down onto one of the junk cars on the opposite side of the garage from the cops. They scrambled off the car and disappeared.

Gary looked back at the cops and their chummy conversation with a drug dealer and made a split-second decision. He took out his keys and reached up, turning off the car's dome light. Slowly, he opened his door, climbing out quietly and closing the door before ducking down behind one of the other cars. He walked toward the back of the house.

As he came around the corner, he saw that the person was already well across the muddy field that separated the house and barn from the road beyond. It was a slight figure. It looked like a woman in her nightclothes.

Gary started to run. After a minute, he caught up with the woman and grabbed her arm, turning her around.

Gary saw her face and even though he'd been preparing himself for this moment, seeing Judy's face was like being struck by lightning. The intensity of the massive, skull-piercing headache knocked him to the ground, his knees buckling. He fell to the ground, landing with a thud in the muddy field, and passed out.

------

She had climbed down from the garage and was running as hard as she could across the muddy field when she heard someone chasing her. Someone's feet pounded the mud behind her, and when she felt the hand on her shoulder, tugging her around roughly, she'd known it would be Vincent, though she knew he was hurt.

Him or one of the cops. Either way, she was dead.

She spun around and saw a young man that she didn't immediately recognize. In the next moment, the man threw his hands up to his head, crumpling over as if she had shot him, falling into the mud.

Judy wasn't sure if she could take many more surprises.

She dropped and rolled the man over, looking at his face.

It was Chris.

Somehow, beyond all logic or wishing or hope, it was Chris O'Toole. Chris laying there in the muddy field next to her house, his eyes closed to the stars above them.

She screamed.

It was out of her before there was anything she could do about it. Her hands flew up and clapped over her mouth.

What...what was he doing here?

What strange fate had brought him to this field? After so many years of wondering what had happened to him, how had he ended up here, tonight?

There was nothing else for her to do. Judy leaned over and kissed him.

"Chris? Chris, can you hear me?" she asked him, gently tapping his face.

His eyes came open and he jerked away from her, sliding away on the mud. He sat up slowly, looking look at her; Chris was squinting, like he was looking at the sun.

She didn't understand, but she tried to move toward him.

He put up his hand, stopping her.

"Just give me a moment. Don't move...don't move, okay?" He was rubbing his temples roughly. And he was crying.

She didn't understand what was happening.

"Are you okay, Chris?" she asked. At the mention of his name he jerked again, as if he had been stung by a bee. He bent over, looking like he might pass out again. She put a hand on him to steady him, amazed that he was real. Solid, not a figment of her troubled, racing mind. The phantom that was Chris O'Toole wavered for a moment in the mud and then sat back up again.

Chris looked at her again, squinting.

"Please, don't say my name anymore," he said. "It hurts too much."

He looked down at her clothes and the tears on her face, and she could see the concern in his eyes. It was a look she hadn't seen in anyone else's eyes in a very long time.

"Are you okay?" he asked.

Judy nodded, smiling at him, and then shook her head. There were too many emotions running around in her mind.

"I have to leave, and now," Judy said quickly. "Vincent...he's my husband. He's...very upset with me, and I think he's had enough. I was leaving, going to the road to see if...what are you doing here? It's been so long, and you never called or wrote or anything. What's going on?"

Chris looked over his shoulder at the house, then back to her.

"I've been having some dreams...no, we don't have time. Vincent might come looking for you. I've got my car over by the barn—if we can get there without your husband or the cops seeing us, we can leave once the cop car leaves. And then we can go somewhere, and talk."

That sounded like heaven to her. To be away from Vincent would be enough, but now that Chris was here....

She saw the police car pulling away.

"They're going," Judy said. "Vincent probably paid them off to not report the accident." She suddenly hated the man more, if that was even possible. Not only would he kill her if he could, he probably would get away with it. It only took a few handfuls of cash, pressed into the right palms.

"Let's go," she said, moving to help him up from the ground.

"I'm okay," he said, waving her off.

Chris didn't want her touching him, or calling him by his name— what did that mean?

They headed for the car, and she saw that he wouldn't look at her—he kept his eyes focused on the muddy field, glancing up at the house every few seconds. She wanted to ask him a thousand questions, but when she tried, he asked her to be quiet.

------

Gary's head felt like it was filled with a thousand marching bands, all competing for the "who could be the loudest" prize. It felt like his mind was threatening to ooze out of his ears.

The connections and organizations in his mind had collapsed like a rickety house of cards. He concentrated on getting to the car, but his hand went unconsciously to the deck of tarot cards in his jacket pocket, holding it like a lifeline. Dr. Myers had said the cards were like his talisman. Gary knew it was all crazy hocus pocus crap, but it still made him feel better, especially now, when his mind felt like it was going on strike.

It felt like someone was using a spatula in his head, flipping pieces of his mind over on some kind of hot mental stove.

Thinking about anything else, or even glancing at Judy, made his head hurt even more. He smelled cigarette smoke, even though there were no cigarettes in this muddy field. Maybe the cops had been smoking, or Vincent, but it smelled so strong, and reminded him of alternating lines of white and dark. He had no idea what any of it meant.

Gary saw the rental car. He got out the keys, letting her in the passenger side before going around the car and climbing in behind the wheel. He hoped the field wasn't too muddy to get the car through. It took three tries to get the key in the ignition—he was having trouble doing the simplest of tasks. He couldn't see through the red tide of pain that had taken over his mind. He glanced over at her again and instantly wished he hadn't; more waves of pain crashed over him every time he looked at her.

Gary wondered what had been going on inside that house to make her climb out of the second-story bedroom in her pajamas and run away. He smelled cigarette smoke again. None of it made any sense.

He finally got the key into the ignition and was about to start the car when he glanced up.

Someone was standing in front of the car.

Judy screamed. It reverberated loudly inside the car. If he hadn't already had the worst headache of his life, the noise would've given him one.

It was Vincent, holding an axe. He lifted the axe high, up over his head with one arm, and then brought it down. The axe planted itself firmly in the middle of the rental car's red hood, burying itself up to the head in the sheet metal.

Judy screamed again.

Gary's mind offered up another useless piece of information: it had been a good idea to get the rental insurance.

Gary saw Vincent working the axe handle back and forth, freeing it from the metal car hood. The man, his face covered in blood, stepped away from Gary and around to the passenger side of the car, looking at Judy. After a moment, he swung the axe wildly at the passenger window. Judy ducked down and away from the passenger window as it shattered, the axe head swinging through the car and decapitating the headrest off of the passenger seat.

Gary started the car and floored it. He kicked the gas pedal so hard, he heard it smack against the floor of the car. He spun the wheel, reversing away from the man and his axe. The car fishtailed in the muddy field as Gary tried to back away and turn at the same time, and he crashed into one of the junk cars.

Vincent jogged up as Gary's rental car came to a stop. He didn't pause—to Gary, the man looked like he was on autopilot, running on adrenaline and anger. Vincent reached into the passenger window and grabbed Judy around her neck, pulling her up. He was trying to drag her out of the window. Gary grabbed at Vincent's hand, but it was slippery with blood and Gary couldn't free her. Judy was cut in a dozen places by the shards of broken glass around the passenger window, and now she was bleeding too. Vincent pulled, lifting Judy's head and shoulders through the car window.

Gary knew that if he floored the accelerator again, with her hanging halfway out the window, she'd get hurt or killed.

He jumped out of the car and raced around to the passenger side. "Let her go!" Gary yelled, coming at Vincent.

Vincent glanced around and clearly dismissed him; he was a little busy, trying to drag his wife out of the car window. Vincent was working from an awkward angle, using just his left arm to pull Judy out by her neck, but he was turned around and couldn't get any leverage.

Gary punched him as hard as he could in the right elbow, where the arm appeared to be broken.

Vincent screamed and dropped Judy, stepping back.

She collapsed against the passenger door, the bottom half of her still in the car. Her hands went to her throat.

Gary turned to Vincent and the punch caught him straight in the face, knocking him to the ground. Vincent leaned over him, shouting.

"Who are you, boy?" Vincent screamed, his eyes wild. "People around here know not to get involved. You think you're gonna take my wife from me? Do you have any idea who I am?" Vincent leaned into the rental car, reaching over his wife to pull the keys out of the ignition. He stood, throwing them away into a field.

"You're not going anywhere!" Vincent shouted. Gary stood, wondered how they would get away now, without the keys. He didn't have long to think about it.

Vincent came at him, and Gary flailed out, catching him again in the arm. Vincent bellowed—it sounded like an injured bear—and punched Gary in the face again. Gary felt blood spray from his nose as he staggered back from the punch. Then, a big wet hand tightened around his throat, and suddenly there was no air. None at all, nothing for him to breathe.

Gary swung and hit the broken arm again but the grip did not lessen. Vincent was looking at him and smiling.

Gary started to lose feeling in his legs, and his hands scrabbled at Vincent's dirty hand as it gripped his throat, and then suddenly the pressure was off and Gary could breathe. He fell to the ground, sucking at the air, taking in so much that he coughed.

After a second, he looked up and saw Judy drop the tire iron. She'd hit Vincent in the back of the head with it. Gary looked over and saw Vincent lying face down in the mud.

She came over to Gary and checked his throat, then looked up at his eyes.

"I need to get some things from the house, and I need clothes. He'll be out for a couple of minutes. Can you find the keys? Pull the car up in front and just stay in the car. I'll just be a second—I can't forget to get the ring. I kept it, all these years."

Gary looked at her, not understanding. She was looking at him strangely, excited and happy even though her neck was bruised and there was blood in her hair.

"The ring," she said again. "The one you gave me."

Clearly she was trying to tell him something he couldn't remember, so he smiled and nodded.

Gary glanced back at Vincent—he hadn't moved—and nodded at her, holding his throat. He pointed at the house—he couldn't talk yet, but she understood and ran off toward the house.

A ring—had he proposed to her? How could he not remember something like that? Maybe some part of his mind had known all along that he was engaged and that was why he'd never been able to stay in a serious relationship.

Stranger things were possible.

Gary also realized that he could look at her now without so much pain—maybe the shock and surprise were wearing off, or maybe the pain in his throat was muting the effect she had on him. He smiled and turned toward the field, where he thought Vincent had thrown the keys to the rental car.

# Chapter 61

Judy couldn't believe it—she was back in the bedroom. In just the past few minutes, everything had changed. Vincent was badly hurt, and now Chris was here. Chris! How was that even possible? Her mind raced as she changed clothes as fast as she could—she pulled on jeans and a clean shirt.

She was doing it—she was getting out of here, breaking free. She grabbed some jewelry and a little bit of money she'd managed to squirrel away, shoving it all into her front pocket.

The envelope. She had to get the letter and the engagement ring.

He had looked at her funny when she'd mentioned the ring. Had he forgotten about proposing to her? She guessed it was possible—it had been a long time ago.

She yanked the top drawer of the dresser out and jumped away as it crashed to the floor. Taped to the back of the drawer was the envelope. She ripped it free of the tape and folded the letter in half and stuffed it into her back pocket, feeling the thick part of the envelope where the ring was.

From downstairs, she heard the front door creak open.

------

"Chris, is that you?" Gary heard her calling from upstairs, but he was too busy to answer. The name wasn't affecting him as badly as it had been before, but it still hurt to hear it.

No, he was more worried about the guy with the axe.

Gary slammed the door behind him, grabbed a loveseat, and dragged it over in front of the door.

"He's coming, Judy," Gary yelled up the stairs. "He's coming, and he's pissed! We need to go!" Gary finished pushing the loveseat over just as the door burst open, and he cursed himself for not locking it. The door only opened a few inches before catching on the loveseat.

Gary had found the keys and gotten the car stopped in front of the house when he'd turned and seen Vincent, fully recovered, coming after him with the axe. There are few sights to compare with the image of a bloody man walking toward you with an axe. Gary hoped that if he made it through this, he'd never have to see anything like that ever again.

He'd raced inside and tried to block the door, but now the crazy man was banging the door against the back of the loveseat, trying to get in.

Gary looked around for a weapon.

There was a fire going in the fireplace, and he grabbed one of the fireplace tools, the long pointy one used to move logs around. He didn't know what it was called, and at the moment, he didn't really care.

The door slammed against the loveseat again. One more hit and Vincent pushed leaned inside, looking at Gary holding the fireplace poker.

"What'cha got there, man?" Vincent asked, shoving the loveseat aside and stepping around it. "You gonna put out my eye or something?"

"Just stay back, Vincent." Gary gulped, holding the poker with both hands.

Vincent stopped and looked at him, his eyes focusing for a moment.

"Chris? Chris O'Toole?" Vincent asked.

The world swam, but Gary tried not to fall.

"What are you doing here?" Vincent asked. "You and your dad got my father killed," the man said quietly, ominously.

Gary nodded.

"That's all water under the bridge, Vincent," Gary said, trying to reason with the man. He knew it was useless, but maybe he could buy Judy more time to escape. Hopefully, she'd already climbed out the window for the second time tonight and was sprinting away from this madhouse.

Vincent looked at him for a long moment, squinting as if he was trying to focus. "You're the reason I got kicked out of the *familia*," Vincent continued.

"I don't know what you're talking about, Vincent," Gary said, shaking his head. "You're not making any sense."

Vincent nodded, remembering. The axe drifted down and the head tapped against the floor with a thump. "You. I was supposed to go out to Sacramento and kill you and your dad. It was the mission they sent me on. It took years for my family to get over it. And it's taken me years to get back in. Now, I guess I'll finish the job. I'm not letting you or that bitch screw it up for me."

Gary didn't understand how the man could be standing there, reminiscing, with his arm broken and his hip dripping blood onto the carpet.

"Just stay back, Vincent," Gary said quietly. "I don't want any trouble."

Vincent's eyes went wide. "You don't want any trouble? *You* don't want any *trouble*? What do you think this is, coming into my house, trying to take my wife away?" he shouted, his voice climbing higher and higher in pitch until he was screaming. "Well, you've got trouble now," Vincent bellowed, hefting the axe again.

Gary began backing away.

Vincent darted at Gary, swinging the axe with one hand like he was swinging a baseball bat.

Gary ducked and the axe buried itself in the mantle of the fireplace, knocking several pictures of Vincent onto the floor. Gary noticed that there weren't any pictures of Judy or of them together— only pictures of Vincent by himself or with friends.

Vincent turned and almost slipped on one of the framed pictures that had fallen. He pulled at the axe, trying to get it out of the thick wooden mantle.

Gary ran around the back of the couch, leaned into it, and shoved it across the carpeted floor of the living room. He pushed it toward Vincent and toward the fireplace.

Vincent was still tugging at the axe, but it was lodged deeply— how could he have buried it that far only using one hand? Gary thought he must be running on pure coke and adrenaline—the broken arm and the massive hip wound, covered with his CSU sweatshirt, didn't seem to be affecting him at all.

Giving one good shove, Gary knocked Vincent over, pinning him to the stones of the fireplace.

Vincent let go of the axe and shoved, climbing up onto the couch. He dislodged one of the thick white pillows, which fell through the open grate and onto the fire.

The axe finally came loose with one last tug and Vincent swung it again, wildly, in a huge arc, missing Gary by inches.

Gary struck back with the poker, hitting Vincent on the hand that held the axe.

Vincent screamed. The axe fell to the carpet.

Growling like an animal, Vincent bent over and charged, hitting Gary in the stomach and bucking him backwards. The deck of tarot cards flew from his pocket and broke open, the cards spilling onto the floor. Gary flew through the air, passing the heavy bookcase next to the stairs and hitting the edge of the dining room table.

Gary rolled over, groaning.

That had hurt—his back felt weird, out of whack. Gary saw that, amazingly, he was still holding the fireplace poker.

Gary slowly stood and turned, looking for Vincent.

Vincent picked up the axe. Behind him, the couch was just beginning to catch fire, a runner of flame snaking up the left arm of the couch. The curtains of the window next to the fireplace caught, the flames running upward like burning smoke, flashing up the curtain and licking at the ceiling.

"You pissant little prick! Look what you did!" The axe jerked toward Gary as Vincent came toward him, punctuating each word. "You set my house on fire, boy!"

Gary waited a split second too long.

That was his mistake. He thought Vincent would come at him with the axe, as he'd done before.

Instead, Vincent's arm whipped around his body. Vincent let go of the axe handle.

The axe flew through the air and hit Gary squarely in the shoulder.

The sharp edge of the axe missed him, but the heavy metal head slammed right into his shoulder. The momentum of the axe handle carried it up and over him, crashing into the dining room table behind him.

The pain was like fire, far worse than any of the headaches.

The bone along the front of his shoulder snapped in half, and a huge gash suddenly bloomed on his left shoulder. Gary could see the bone. The blood welled and filled the wound in the half-second he looked at it, and then it poured over and out of the wound, running down his shirt.

Screaming, Gary dropped the poker and put his hands to the wound, trying to hold his blood in. Gary could feel with terrifying accuracy his heartbeat as the blood surged between his fingers. Somehow, he was still standing.

Gary heard laughter and slowly looked up to see Vincent standing, looking at him.

"You got yourself a little boo-boo there?" Vincent asked, smiling.

Gary lashed out, not knowing where the energy or the anger was coming from. He stepped and swung his left leg, kicking for the sweatshirt and the hip beneath it.

Gary's foot connected—he felt something broken grind under his foot. Vincent stumbled backwards and slipped on the tarot cards that littered the floor, dropping to the ground.

Half of the living room was in flames. The banister and stairs leading up to the second floor were catching. The couch and loveseat and other furniture in the living room were on fire, and it looked as though the carpet running back into another room—probably the kitchen—was going up fast. There was already a thick black smoke in the air, making it hard to see even the open door leading outside.

Judy. He had to make sure she had gotten out.

Before he could move, he heard a strange whistling sound as the fireplace poker spun around and caught him in the back of the knees, knocking him onto the carpet.

His legs screamed in pain. They hurt, but then everything hurt. Gary wondered if all the pain would ever end.

Vincent, holding the poker, slowly climbed to his feet.

Gary crawled for the stairs. They were smoldering, smoke rising up out of the parts of the carpet that were already burning. Maybe he could get up there and find Judy and get her out. Even if he didn't make it, maybe he could warn her.

There was another surge of pain as Vincent hit the back of one of his legs again with the poker. Over the crackling of the fire, he could hear the man laughing.

Gary crawled faster, past the bookcase next to the stairs, and he grabbed the banister, the one that hadn't caught fire yet. He pulled himself up onto the first carpeted step, trying to avoid the burning patches.

"Where you going?" Vincent screamed.

Gary ignored him, pulling himself up.

"You think she's up there?" Vincent shouted, his voice going hoarse from the smoke. "Don't worry—I haven't forgotten about her. I'll take care of her in a minute, so you don't have to worry, *capiche*? I'll take care of her good, just as soon as I'm done with you."

Vincent stood only a couple of feet from him, holding the poker over his head. Vincent was looking down at Gary on the second step of the stairs, and he was smiling.

"Guess you just picked the wrong place to visit, huh?" Vincent asked.

Gary started to say something to delay the inevitable, something, anything to keep Vincent from killing him, but as he started to speak, something in his peripheral vision moved.

For a second, he thought his eyes were playing a trick on him.

The heavy bookcase next to the stairwell looked like it was moving. Slowly, agonizingly, he saw the bookcase tip over and crash onto Vincent, knocking him down. The heavy case fell onto Vincent's hips and legs, pinning him to the smoldering carpet.

Gary looked up to the top of the stairs and saw her standing there. Judy had been behind the case. She had been waiting for Vincent to be in the right position before she pushed it.

------

"Thanks," Chris said weakly, looking up at her at the top of the stairs. The bookcase had fallen on Vincent—she had been worried that he would hit Chris again before he'd stepped forward, but he'd moved at just the right time.

She smiled at Chris and glanced around the room. "This place is going up fast. Are you...oh crap, you're bleeding like crazy!"

She ran to him, avoiding the burning patches of carpet on the stairs, helping him to his feet and pulling him to the door.

Vincent suddenly moved and kicked. He screamed and shoved at the bookcase, but it didn't budge.

"We have to get you to a hospital," Judy said. "And fast."

The room was fully ablaze now. Flames ran up the walls, and the wallpaper was peeling in the heat. The couch was a pyre, shooting flames to the ceiling. Judy wondered how long the ceiling would burn before the second story collapsed.

On the floor next to the open door was a big leather duffle bag and, as Judy struggled to half push, half carry Chris to the door, he leaned over and scooped up the bag up with his bloody right hand.

Judy shoved the loveseat aside with her hip and pulled the door open far enough for both of them to squeeze through and out into the mercifully cool night air.

Smoke poured out the door with them as they escaped the house.

They shuffled down the steps and she helped him to the car, leaning him against the passenger door. Chris looked up at the house and shook his head.

From inside the house, they could hear Vincent screaming for help.

"Keys?" she asked the man she never thought she would see again. His eyes were bleary, and smoke and ash smudged his face, but he nodded and dropped the leather bag and fished them out of his pocket with his left hand.

He handed her the keys, smiling weakly. She felt him shiver.

Judy took them and opened the door. "Get in."

Chris sat down heavily in the passenger seat and grabbed the bag from the ground.

She went around and climbed in and sat down, starting the car but not putting it into gear. Chris had one hand resting on the duffle bag in his lap possessively.

Through the broken window of the rental car, she watched for a few moments as the house burned. Chris turned and looked at the house, then back to her.

"Are we waiting for something?" Chris asked.

Judy nodded, her eyes still on the house. She watched for the door to move, or for any sign of Vincent, and then she glanced at Chris. "When I'm sure, we'll go."

He nodded and shut his eyes. "When we get to the hospital, I need to call my friend, Mike. He's probably wondering where I am."

She pulled her eyes away from the burning house. "Who's Mike?" she asked, looking at Chris for a long moment.

"He's my friend," Chris answered, his eyes closed. He was absently touching his empty shirt pocket. Judy wondered how long it would be before he passed out. "He came out with me from LA."

She looked back at the fire—the second floor was burning now, and still no one had stumbled from the front door. Fire ran up the outside of the house, and the roof was beginning to catch.

It was finally her concern for Chris that made her leave. Judy started the car and drove away.

She needed to get Chris O'Toole to a hospital, and as she drove down the long dirt driveway toward the road, she heard the first of the sirens. It was okay that they were coming—it had been long enough, to be sure. Her prison and her warden were both gone now, and the spinning lights and pressure hoses could not change that.

She was going to be okay.

"You live in Los Angeles?" she asked him. She needed to keep him talking, keep him conscious. "I thought you were in Sacramento."

He opened his eyes and looked at her. She listened to him begin to talk about his life as they drove, and it was wonderful. She passed the first fire truck as she turned out of the driveway. When she got to Blackwood Lane, she turned left, heading for O'Fallon and the hospital.

# Epilogue

"You don't need to do this," he said, smiling. "We've got plenty of money."

Judy smiled back, but he could tell she wasn't listening. She had her plane ticket in hand and was ready to go. Her new suitcase sat at her feet, and the open door of the cab waited behind her.

"I know, Gary," she answered. "It's just something I have to do. My parents...I need to make that connection again, even if they're gone. I need to see the places they lived, and talk to the lawyers. It's not about the money they left me—I want to remember them."

Gary nodded.

"As soon as I'm done, I'll fly to California," she said. "I'll call, and you can meet me at the airport."

"Just be careful," he said, nodding. "I worry about you."

He shifted his left arm, but the cast didn't let him move much; there was a risk that he could further injure the shoulder. The doctors at the O'Fallon Hospital said he had at least another week of recovery before he and Mike would be able to fly back to California.

One of the doctors had spoken to Simmons, his boss at MacMillan, explaining the injury and why he couldn't fly immediately after surgery. Gary was sure he'd be famous in the office when he and Mike returned—their weekend vacation had turned into three weeks. At least part of their trip back here, about the riverboat crash, had made the national papers.

Judy leaned over his wheelchair and kissed him. "Don't worry, Chr...Gary. I'll be fine, and I'll call you. But I don't know if I'll ever get used to that name," she said, smiling.

"It's okay," Gary said. "I'm getting more used to the other one, too. Look, we'll be here another week or so before flying back. If I can get Mike to leave," he said, rolling his eyes.

Judy nodded. "Well, she is very cute."

Gary smiled. Mike was smitten with Tina, the woman he'd met

at the Mayfest. They'd been inseparable since that evening. When Mike couldn't track down Gary at the hotel or in the bar, he'd gotten worried. Tina had volunteered to drive him around to look for Gary, and by the time they had arrived at the hospital, they already seemed like a couple.

"I'll be done soon," she said. "And then we can get on with our lives."

He smiled up at her, touching her elbow. "Together."

Judy nodded. "Yes."

She kissed him again and climbed into the cab that would take her to the airport.

Gary smiled, thinking for the first time in a long time how happy he was. He was in pain, but the pain was freeing. It was as though he'd paid whatever price it had required. He could live however, wherever he wanted.

And with whomever he wanted.

As the cab pulled away, Gary tried his best to wave until the car disappeared out of sight.